The Return
of
Private Fischer
A Love Story

Robert Fischer

Martin Pearl Publishing
www.martinpearl.com

Published by
Martin Pearl Publishing
P.O. Box 1441 Dixon, CA 95620

ISBN:9780981482279
Library of Congress Control Number: 2011929902

PRINTED IN THE UNITED STATES OF AMERICA

10 9 8 7 6 5 4 3 2 1

Respectfully Dedicated

To my wife Helga and to all those Allied POWs still suffering in Siberia and China.

Cover designed by:
Mark Deamer Designs

Cast of Characters

San Francisco

Jack Fischer, Private, USMC - *San Francisco teen captured at the beginning of Korean War*
Nella 'Babe' Barsi - *Jack's teen love in San Francisco*
Mary Alioto - *San Francisco friend of Babe*
Tara Carr - *San Francisco teen friend*
Paco 'Nick' Mateo - *San Francisco teen, refugee from Nicaragua*
Bruno Fischer - *Jack's father*
Rosemary Fischer - *Jack's mother, union organizer*
John Maldonado - *San Francisco teen and fellow U.S. Marine in Korea*
Dorin Stafford, USMC - *Medic and Korean War POW*
Quido Barsi - *Babe Barsi's father*
Martha Barsi - *Babe Barsi's mother*
Peter Mattioli - *Mafia-connected San Francisco Italian in trash business and politics*
Claudette Mattioli - *Daughter of Peter and Babe Mattioli*
Joy Jaing - *San Francisco television reporter and daughter of Qi Jaing*
Jenna Mattioli - *Daughter of Babe and Peter Mattioli*

Korea-China-Soviet Union/Russia-Taiwan

King Poo Koo - *Chinese soldier in Korean War*
Officer Lee Wu - *Sadistic Chinese Army junior officer*
Zo Wu - *Ruthless brother of Lee Wu*
Alexander Ivanov, Colonel, Soviet Army - *Gulag commander*
Jin Jaing - *Korean war survivor and electronics' industry titan in Taiwan*
Qi Jaing - *Jin Jaing's brother*
Rudolph Rauer - *Jin and Qi Jaing's father-in-law, Taiwanese businessman*
Song Koo - *King Poo Koo's mother*
Leroy Robinson, Sergeant, USMC - *Imprisoned America POW defected to the Soviet Union*
Captain Wiley - *American POW*

Doctor Paul Schwarz, Major - *German Army POW imprisoned in the Soviet Gulag*

Cognac - *Soviet POW, originally a gypsy, captured by the German Army in WWII*

Attica Niarcos - *Female Soviet POW and companion to Jack*

Yuri Senya - *Soothsayer, conjurer, and phony physic and healer*

Yakir Petrov - *Prison camp commander in POW compound near Chita*

Desu Ursala - *Out-of-favor Moscow film maker banished to Siberia*

Chin Xion, Captain, Chinese Army - *Friend of both King Poo Koo and Jack Fischer*

Tom Obuchowski, Corporal - *American POW*

John Fischer - *Son of Jack Fischer and Attica Niarcos*

Vladimir Kruchlov, Russian President

<u>Back in the United States</u>

Joel Conklin, President, United States

Allen Hurst, Vice-President, United States

Greig Rivers - *Political aide to Vice President Hurst*

George McBain, United States Senator

Bob Smith, United States Senator - *Outspoken advocate for missing POW's in Korea*

Bob Dornan, United States Congressman - *Outspoken advocate for missing POW's in Korea*

Prologue

San Francisco
1978

THE uniformed man in the tattered and faded black and white photo was seventeen years old when a borrowed box-camera captured his image. How many times had Babe pulled this picture from her wallet? How many times had she run her fingers over the young, somber face? She'd lost count long ago.

Babe had been fifteen and Jack seventeen when she first met him. That was thirty years ago. Even then, Babe Barsi had known that Jack Fischer would be her one true love. She reflected on the life that might have been, as she had done almost daily during all of that time.

Babe picked up the telephone and dialed.

"Mary, it's Babe. I'm not calling about anything special, just feel like talking with someone. How're you doing in the real estate business anyway?" Babe asked her friend, trying to sound casual.

Mary hadn't heard from Babe for some time and assumed the call might be business related. "Babe? Don't tell me you've finally decided to list that Broadway Street house with me—or is your divorce from Peter still on your mind?"

Babe laughed. "Cut the drama, Mary, and meet me for a drink, say in about an hour?"

Feigning shock, Mary Alioto, Babe's friend for most of their lives, replied. "Hey! Good Catholic girls don't go to bars to have drinks unless they've lost all hope. You want to confess some sordid secret to me that you're too embarrassed to tell a priest?"

"Just a drink," Babe replied. "Meet me at The Shadows."

"Okay, but if you try to depress me with your long lost love life or you bring up Jack Fischer's name, I'm outta there! On the other hand, though, considering the prices they charge just to look through a window at the bay, if you're buying, I might let you bring up Peter's name."

Babe's news was much more dramatic than talking about her divorce and her ex-husband Peter's girlfriends. She had just learned that Jack was alive in some hellish Soviet prisoner-of-war camp and she needed to tell someone.

The Shadows on top of Telegraph Hill sits in the shadow of San Francisco's Coit Tower. Parking costs more than a meal itself, and tourists gawking from inside the cocktail bar windows often distract from an otherwise romantic atmosphere. It is private and very secluded. The booth, upholstered in gray-silver velvet, framed Babe's forest-green business suit; like an emerald on a pillow. Gray streaks in her hair and all, men still looked her way.

Mary, wearing oversized jewelry and upswept dyed-black hair, plopped herself down next to Babe. She looked, and then looked again at Babe's outfit. "Okay Babe, what's up? You're dressed like a fashion queen." She grabbed the back pocket of a passing waiter and bellowed. "Two martinis, straight up and hurry."

After a half-hour of catching up failed to reveal the purpose of the meeting, Mary could not wait any longer. "Okay kid, it's Mary Time. Come tell Sister Mary all your sins. Tell me about the delicious and ruthless men you shou'da introduced me to, the scandals you've gotten yourself into and why the hell you brought me all the way across town to a place that's holding my car for ransom. And worse, you're plying me with liquor. What gives?"

Even though Babe had been told not to talk about it, she had to tell Mary; *it's what you do with lifelong friends, you tell.*

Babe looked at her old friend for a long moment. "Mary, what I am about to tell you is a secret. I don't mean like a social secret, I mean like—like a life and death kind of secret—although there are some things I can't tell you. I have to trust you never to breathe a word to anyone, ever."

"Babe, you know you can depend upon me for life itself—so shoot, dammit."

"I can't tell you how I know," Babe began, "but I am here to tell you that Jack Fischer is alive and held captive in a Soviet prisoner-of-war camp somewhere in Siberia."

Mary tried not to appear shocked, particularly because Babe

had been under a lot of stress lately and had recently been rushed to San Francisco General Hospital with an angina attack. Mary sat still. Looking at Babe, she wanted to hold her, hug her and tell her everything would be okay. She wanted to protect her best friend from any hurt that might result from her most outrageous delusion—Jack Fischer, alive! *Poor Babe,* she thought. *And look at her hair, her makeup, beautiful. She could be with any man in the world. Poor Babe.*

"Look," Mary finally said. "You've been under a lot of stress. Maybe you should take some time off. I'll go with you to any place that we can legally wear our bikinis and not get arrested."

Babe slowly passed a plastic-covered four-leaf clover across the white linen tablecloth. Mary watched the small object approach her side of the table and wondered. *What the hell is going on?*

"Mary, I gave this pendant to Jack just before he left for Korea, the day the troop train pulled out. There is someone who was in a prison camp with him in Manchuria. He brought it out; along with a letter written to me. I can't tell you who he is or who these people are or how the whole story came to me, but I am telling you that as God is my maker, my Jack is still alive." Her eyes moistened as she spoke and tears ran down her cheeks.

Mary slowly realized that her friend's belief was not an illusion or wishful thinking. It was real. Babe carefully unfolded Jack's letter and gave it to her friend. Tears streamed down both faces as Mary read. Babe's hands shook so hard that Mary reached over and held them tightly in her own.

Mary took a deep breath. "The Jack that you knew might be different now. Christ, that letter could be twenty or thirty years old. What do you think you're doing nurturing a teenage fling all these years? You're both nuts! You're an adult now; besides, nobody's love affair lasts that long. People forget. Hell, you've told me about Jack so many times I often wondered if you were just harboring a love fantasy. I didn't mind you having a fantasy, but think, girl, in the real world people don't stay in love over all those years without ever seeing each other."

"I know," Babe said. "You and I have talked about this a lot and you always arrive at the same conclusion. Jack was my first love, a woman never forgets her first, and so he becomes more significant. Isn't that your standard line?"

"Exactly!" Mary said emphatically. "I remember my first love and I'll bet damn few women ever forget, but it's not like I still want him. You're just a little screwed up mentally is all. You've romanticized too long. Give it up. Besides, what do you know about him today? He's still in Siberia, for Christ's sake! And not getting out anytime soon!"

Babe had heard Mary's opinion on Jack Fischer a hundred times.

Sensing that Babe was about to make a speech, Mary, pretending to hold a pen in her hand replied, "I can tell—oh!—don't stop. It's time for me to take notes, isn't it?"

"If you shut up for a minute I'll tell you why I fell in love with Jack and why I'm still in love with him. When I was fifteen Mom married Dan, a really nice guy. They moved to Hawaii and left me here with my father, Quido. Well, you remember him, when we were young, he was always drunk. He'd bring one-night stands home to our flat while I was in the other bedroom. I could hear everything and he didn't care. When he went to Italy that time with that rich woman, he told me he wouldn't be back and that the rent was paid. It wasn't and I was scared. I moved around like a gypsy living first with Tianna and then with other friends. The boys in the neighborhood, sensing a wounded bird in their midst, harassed me with as much bullshit as they thought it would take to grab a feel of my tits, and when I wouldn't cooperate, they tried making me feel like an outcast. 'Everyone's doing it,' they would say. It was miserable. I couldn't finish high school because I had no money and no steady place to live."

Mary sipped her martini and raised one eyebrow. She knew most of the story; she'd heard it countless times before. But she hadn't heard the last part. "Oh, Babe, I always wondered why you dropped out of St. Bridges. We were in different schools later and I guess that got past me. Why didn't you tell me?"

Babe rolled her eyes, sipped her drink and went on with her story.

"You introduced me to Jack and loaned me your cashmere sweater for our first date because I had nothing else to wear except my school uniform. Off we went and it didn't take me long to see he was something new. He wasn't all over me trying to get laid. Despite how bad the Italian neighborhood Catholic School boys would have me believe this Galileo High School red-haired, part-German, outsider was, we became friends before becoming lovers."

"I remember everyone being after you back then," Mary sighed. "Your tits still look pretty good if you ask me."

Babe ignored Mary's comment. "Jack was interested in me. He loved to hear my voice. I found that I could talk up a blue streak when he was around, and when I talked about someday becoming rich or a famous cook, he believed me. I told him I wanted to be a bride in a flowing white gown, and he neither ran away nor made fun of me. Instead, he promised to be my husband just as soon as his job became full-time, and I promised to marry him. We belonged to each other at a time when no one else wanted us. Mary, I never belonged to anyone. It was a new experience for me, to be wanted by someone, to be loved. He gave me flowers. He bought me hot chocolate. It was the first time these things were part of my life. Did you know that he gave me most of his salary every week to help me out?"

"No, I thought your mom sent you money I guess. I can't believe you didn't tell me that before."

Babe shrugged. "We walked all over North Beach and he showed me things I'd never seen or noticed; a wonderful clock on Columbus Avenue, the produce center below Montgomery, nets of cargo being unloaded from freighters along the docks, Chinatown's back alleys and lots of rich people's houses. I learned about Jack, my friend and my dreamer. We talked about things important to him and important to me. I wanted to understand things about Jack that were of no consequence, like finding a fountain pen that made him feel proud or buying a microscope. Remind me to tell you about those things sometime. The point being that those discussions about insignificant things had deep meaning to Jack, and I understood. He wanted to become an artist, maybe a commercial artist, and that's what I wanted for him as well."

"Yeah, I remember the art thing."

"Jack had it rough at home, too. His father beat the hell out of him for no reason that either of us could understand, and his mother was absent. She was too busy starting a union where she worked, and the daily assurances that Jack needed from her as a mother came from me instead. He needed me, I was important to him, and I was filled with the promise of our future together. I never once doubted that we were soulmates destined to spend the rest of our lives together. Remember when Jack's mother stopped us from going to Reno to get married?"

Mary answered, "Sure I remember that, what a disaster."

"Well, I was devastated. I think back from time to time and still feel sick to my stomach. The people around us never seemed to have had that kind of love and never understood they were witnesses to the real thing. Jack and I understood what had happened to us, and all we ever wanted was to be alone together."

Breaking in, Mary waved to the waiter for a round of martinis. "What you just told me could have been almost everyone's love experience, to some degree, and after time people become indifferent, get divorced, have arguments and move on with their lives. Any reasonable person would come to realize that a teen love affair is hardly the foundation for a lifelong belief, or that theirs is that one-in-a-million relationship that makes it through to the end."

"It's not that complicated, Mary. Jack and I trusted each other. We were friends from the beginning, and each of us wanted the other to be happy and fulfilled. Look back at our own marriages or for that matter most everyone else's. How often do you see absolute trust and selflessness? It's rare, like you just said. But for me to believe in Jack Fischer and in our love together is not far-fetched. It's the benchmark that I've used all of my life to measure my relationships. Even Peter came to resent not being as perfect as the mysterious Jack Fischer. Not because I ever brought Jack's name up, but because he knew who Jack was and he could tell."

"Okay, okay, Babe, I give up. So you're not neurotic, just an average woman who has been waiting for her lover for almost thirty years to show up and whisk her away. I can buy that, though I hope you haven't sold the movie rights to that story. The big question is; what are you going to do now?"

Babe gripped her friend's hand and with eyes blazing with determination replied, "Mary, I'm going to Siberia to find him. I'm leaving San Francisco at the end of the month."

PART ONE

Chapter One

Jack
1931

JACK'S father, Bruno, was as good a violin player as the famous 1930's Fritz Kreisler. He worked during the day as a scientific instrument maker: surveyor's equipment, weight calibrators and that sort of thing. Basically, he was a machinist with a great musical talent who was afraid to try his dream at an audition. Bruno practiced in his living room overlooking Union Street from the second floor. He would open all the windows and play his philharmonic best accompanied by a blasting Zenith record player. People heard Viennese waltzes, gypsy music, songs like "Jealousy" and other haunting melodies. People passing by would be surprised by the sound. They often stood on the sidewalk for long periods listening and applauding. Periodically, Bruno would peek surreptitiously through the lace curtains to see who was listening and to bask in their adulation. In his living room he was famous.

He was a visitor to San Francisco when he married Rosemary Cahill. Rosemary was only sixteen years old when they moved to Milwaukee. There they suffered the 1930's Great Depression. Jack was born in 1931, followed by Bob and then Carla. Bruno played the fiddle in taverns on weekends for extra money, but he had not worked a day job in seven years and it had a demoralizing effect on him.

Bruno began to blame his firstborn for his arrested career as a concert violinist. Without family responsibilities interrupting his career, he imagined, he could have had an adventure-filled, romantic life playing the violin in Argentina, Brazil and on elegant ocean liners. As the firstborn, Jack interrupted those grand plans, which resulted in his being beaten for the slightest infraction. Later, when the family returned to San Francisco, just before the big war started, Jack became a regular punching bag, and the constant fear caused him to stutter.

They returned to San Francisco because Rosemary won a chess tournament there and refused to return to Milwaukee. Worse, she arranged for Bruno to work as a machinist at the Leitz Company on Commercial Street in San Francisco, starting in one month. Imagine! He could not even get a job without his wife's help! Poor Bruno packed the rest of the family onto a Greyhound and headed west.

After the family arrived, Rosemary went to work for the Garfield branch of the Telephone Company, where she eventually became a key organizer of the Communications Workers of America. She was mostly absent from the house, and all of the duties that went with being at home fell to Bruno and the kids. Soon, the only symphonies Bruno became part of were shrill and vicious arguments and the steady reminders by Rosemary of his endless failures. She often used innuendo in its sincerest and deadliest form: "Armando is just a stupid immigrant living next door and *he's* going to radio school at night—*to make something of himself!*" she'd hiss. "Dan O'Glove never had a high school education and *he owns a bowling alley!*" "You played music with Liberace in Milwaukee. Why don't you write to him and ask him for a job on his show?" "*Jesus*, if I had just a fraction of your talent, I'd be on one of those radio talent contests! Who would ever use that contraption of yours? Imagine anyone cutting anything with an electric knife! Completely *useless.*"

Bruno's electric knife invention went the way of his unpublished songs. Bruno's rear action defense was to explain to all who would listen that big business controlled everything. International manufacturers and the Jewish bankers were in league together and the little guy didn't have a chance to make it big. Besides that, you needed connections, you needed to know rich people. How was he going to meet rich people in that dead end job his complaining wife stuck him with?

Bruno, in turn, criticized Jack's school performance, which was abysmal. Helping him with his homework consisted of demanding to know what 12 times 16 was at the dinner table. If Jack could not instantly answer, he was hit hard on the face. Sometimes Jack quietly picked himself up, returned to his chair at the table and continued to eat, but this lack of reaction further enraged Bruno and invited still more pummeling, often with split lips or a nosebleed. Jack learned to lie still on the linoleum floor until the rush of anger passed. Sometimes it did. Other times, Bruno would put Jack's plate on the floor suggesting he eat from it there. The slightest imagined failing or forgetfulness brought a rain of blows with balled fists, and many came at the end of deliberate taunting. Bruno needed to punish someone for his own failures and Jack never fought back.

Several times, Jack asked his brother Bob why Bruno hated him so much. His brother didn't know either. At age fifteen, disgusted with his father's rages against Jack, Bob grabbed an ancient cavalry sword hanging on the dining room wall in honor of some ancestor. It was too long to swing without hitting a wall and Bob could not afford to miss. He chased his father through the house, cutting skin and drawing blood while using the sword-guard as a battering ram. Bruno rushed forward with a chair held high and on the downswing, one leg crashed into a wall just above Bob's head. Bob countered with a smashing blow to the chest with the sword handle and Bruno fell backward. The fighting stopped when Bruno developed an understanding. He knew that Bob would strike in earnest and Bruno became afraid of him, enough so that the beatings stopped. But, by that time Jack was eighteen and the damage had been done. Bruno's hatred for his son Jack now transferred to Bob.

Jack could not solve his lack of understanding the punishment and convinced himself that he must have done something wrong. He found ways to change the subject and stay clear of Bruno and that meant Jack was away from home most of the time. He also discovered there were other boys and girls in the neighborhood who were alienated from their parents so he hung out with them. Jack was comfortable with these friends, and for that reason it was easy for him to develop creative ideas and do something about them. He learned that having the right people around amplified individual personalities and together they became more productive. He liked having a voice and that people listened to him.

It amused Jack when he and five other boys removed a 1933 Ford chassis and a rusted eight-cylinder engine from a nearby scrap collection depot. They hand-carried it to Peter Alioto's place because it had a garage, but no car. Alive with the dream of someday owning and driving a real car, they worked hard at finding parts they could not afford to buy. They managed to install springs, wheels and a rear bumper section. Unfortunately, the Korean War swept through the neighborhood and as the boys left, the old Ford chassis again became scrap. But Jack never forgot the thrill of working together, accomplishing something each could be proud of and making a dream come true. Years later this experience would save his life.

Jack's mother, Rosemary, was rarely home. When she was, her time was singularly devoted to union work, which either put her on the telephone or stuffing envelopes. Her second job was arguing with Bruno. Jack longed for her love; instead he received insincere shows of affection as thanks for being a good boy.

"If you do the laundry for me, Mommy will be so happy!" Or, "Be a good boy and get Mommy her cigarettes!" were words that sounded okay, but felt terrible.

No one hugged. No one visited school to see their children's work firsthand. No one attended a track meet or an art competition. Nor did anyone pay much mind to who their kids were hanging around with.

Rosemary would often say, "I'm working to make life better for you kids, and someday we are going to have a real home." Happiness, Jack presumed, was something you got when enough money was put together to buy a house.

"If I left everything to your father, we would have nothing. Who do *you* think paid for that washing machine?" A Maytag tub-washer with rollers was certainly better than using the washboard and wringing by hand to squeeze water out of the laundry, but Rosemary never used it; that task was for the kids and Bruno. She would often bring that up because it was a state-of-the-art tub. Home became a place she sometimes visited.

Jack's brother lived mostly at his best friend George's house on Sacramento Street, where a real mother and a super woman named Aunt Flo, who looked like a football player, worshipped everything the boys did together. Aunt Flo always sat up until the wee hours in the morning waiting for her boys to come home so she could fix them tea and treats and pick up on the latest gossip.

Jack's sister Carla divorced the family by training seven days a week for the Olympics. She actually won a springboard diving berth to go to Helsinki, although she ultimately did not go there to compete. She opted instead for an early marriage. Anything was better than home.

Jack didn't have anyone regular at home. He found solace with friends who took him for what he was rather than harassing him to be somebody else. Besides, he learned, the less time he spent at home the less was his risk of being beaten. He spent some of the time with two neighbors, one a Mexican boy named John Maldonado, and the other a refugee from dictator Samoza's Nicaragua named Paco Mateo; everyone called him Nick. Those households had real people at home, and there were always tortillas, cookies and hot chocolate or refried bean sandwiches at the ready when the boys got home from school. Both families accepted Jack as being one of their own whenever he was around.

Jack loved being in these houses and he dreaded going home. His search to be loved was partially filled by friends and neighbors; his experience with them and their open goodness to him sponsored a budding belief that there was truly such a thing as love. Jack knew, by comparison to his own home life, that life in these homes was different. Jack knew that the lack of love in his home was probably the cause of his shyness with girls. So it had been a damn good thing, in his mind, that the girls found him attractive, especially Babe.

Chapter Two

North Beach
1945

BY the age of fourteen, Jack had walked the entire Italian neighborhood of North Beach, as well as China Town, Telegraph Hill and all of the Wharf area. These were his exploring trips, and when he explored, he dreamed. Twice he bumped into telephone poles by not paying attention. One such pole blessed him with a chipped front tooth. While walking up Columbus Avenue one August afternoon he became aware of a beautiful clock mounted on the sidewalk in front of a shop that looked like a jewelry store. Although it once had been a jeweler named R. Matteucci & Company, it was now a pawnshop, which Jack really did not understand. He looked through the clock's thick glass that covered the mechanical workings and noted that it had stopped at 4:08.

Jack wondered why such a magnificent clock was on the sidewalk in front of only one shop. It was the clock, he thought, that made that shop stand out so elegantly. He rubbed his fingers on the bronze lettering that spelled "Seth Thomas Clock Co. 1908" and wondered if they knew their clock had stopped. The more he thought about it, the more curious he became. He peered into the pawnshop window and saw lots of jewelry in glass cases. Tennis gear, skis and tools sat around in heaps and it all looked like it had belonged to somebody because it was scuffed and beat up. Then he noticed a small microscope with a mirror for reflecting light. Unable to help himself, he ventured inside.

The proprietor, with nothing better to do, indulged Jack's interest by explaining how tiny things could be seen through the scope. He demonstrated by putting a drop of water on a glass slide and focused the mirror to the daylight. Jack peered and saw water bugs wiggle around, and he knew he had to have that microscope. He offered to buy it, but the price, $5.50, was equal to twenty two weeks of allowance at twenty-five cents.

The proprietor explained that he wasn't supposed to sell to minors but in this case he would. The only way was to put the item on hold, and if Jack never missed a payment, the microscope would be Jack's. The microscope would stay in the window until paid. If Jack defaulted, then all payments made would be lost, along with the microscope. Jack agreed. He made a lot of payments and told no one about his secret purchase. Several times he shook his brother down for money and as a consequence had to tell him why he needed it.

Despite his passion, Jack missed an installment and one day when he passed the pawnshop, he saw that the microscope was no longer in the window. He rushed inside, but the proprietor reminded him about the missed payment and told Jack the microscope had been sold. Jack felt ashamed and left the store wanting to cry. Instead, he vowed that he would someday have another microscope. Months passed and the Christmas ritual played itself out with the opening of presents; each one accompanied with pauses for the suitable thank-you. The usual things were there, an erector set for Bob and clothes for Jack and Carla—nothing eventful. After all the presents had been opened it was time to go into the kitchen for something to eat.

When everyone rose to leave the living room Jack spotted the microscope on the fireplace mantle. He was stunned. No one thought to say anything to him; they had forgotten. To Jack, it was just magically there. He clutched it and held it close to his body for the longest time, and then wept and shook uncontrollably. Nobody in the family could stop him or understand why he was crying and neither could he.

Bob had spilled the beans to Bruno, and the microscope made its way to the mantle for Christmas. That was the short of it, but it *was* there, and *surely*, he thought, it must have meant someone loved him enough to participate in his secret and make his dream come true. The microscope was proof.

Jack never forgot that day and how such a simple thing could be the object of such intense emotion. He promised himself that if he ever gave anything special to someone, he would remember how he felt about that microscope.

Three years later, on the same block near the pawn shop, Jack looked down, as was his habit when avoiding sidewalk divider lines, and saw a silvery glint just under the front wheel of a parked car. He reached down and picked up a Waterman fountain pen made of pure silver with gold touches on the cap rim and pocket clip. The ink bladder was full and the pen was not marked or scratched. Jack looked to see if anyone was watching and put the pen into his leather jacket pocket. Later, he studied the pen, used it and marveled at its obvious value and his lucky find.

Jack had never owned anything so priceless. He walked everywhere with it in his shirt pocket for everyone to see, knowing that people would attach worth to the wearer of such a valuable thing. The first time he wore the pen, a man looked at him and Jack blushed, imagining that the man must be thinking, *I wonder where the kid stole that.*

Jack knew that people his age were off to college, working good jobs, making good grades at school, had career prospects, dressed better than him and that some even had cars. He also knew that they could see right through his unworthy self, and he unconsciously walked softly, gliding past their attentions. Still, the pen transformed Jack from being a hopeless teenager with a meaningless part-time job delivering supplies for Crocker Stationery, into a man of obvious means. Like the prow of a mighty ship, that pen parted the ways, and he knew that everyone who saw him with it would readily deduce that Jack was somehow worthy. It made him stand taller, walk firmer and think about taking night classes.

Chapter Three

Babe Barsi
1948

THE Crystal Plunge was an indoor public swimming pool on Lombard Street where Carla, Jack's sister, originally trained for the Olympics. Babe Barsi swam there three times a week and loved it. Today though, she cut her swim short. She had to get ready to meet some red headed-guy that her friend Mary kept raving about. Babe was living off and on in North Beach with her father, Quido Barsi, an Ellis Island original who was proud to have made it all the way to California, where he pretended to be a successful immigrant. He was one of those oily, flamboyant types who usually had the loudest voice at the tavern, boasting about things he knew little about. He had an opinion about everything and never stopped talking. If anyone wanted to know the real story about Mussolini, Joe Lewis or Roosevelt, he expounded whether or not anyone wanted to hear.

While married to his wife, Martha, he acted like a tenant waiting for his lease to expire. If he stayed home silently and miserably long enough, he thought, Martha might just drift away and hopefully take Babe with her. He needed a break from the Great Depression, the war, the rat race and especially from them. Besides, he had plenty of pretty opportunities that promised greater rewards and appreciation for his latent abilities. Sooner or later, he figured, something had to happen that would give him the opportunity to blame everything on Martha, and he would be gone with a good dose of righteous indignation. Quido, after all, had dreams and he loved sharing them with the wives of other men. But, until then, he could pretend to be a good husband and go through the motions of being a doting father. Everything takes time.

One day, his wife looked at her husband sitting on a wooden bench at a favorite outdoor bocce ball court, a place where his fellow countrymen surrounded him with a mixture of adoration and contempt. Quido was supposed to be at work, but instead he sat there like a retired well-to-do paisano without a care in the world. He wore his good church clothes, too. *Like everyone else there, they were all losers.* Most wore the Sicilian uniform, church clothes that implied status. There he sat with his collarless shirt, an open black suit vest with a gold watch attached and a fedora with the brim pushed up at the front. All he needed was a shotgun at his side and he would be the very personification of a Palermo Don.

Quido also slobbered on those horrible little wine-soaked cigars and he drank endless amounts of red wine out of thick-bottomed glasses. He was drunk again and Martha finally understood that her dreams of Quido amounting to something were never going to happen. Quido Barsi was where he belonged and, in 1941, they divorced. Martha remarried in 1948; Babe, for a short time, stayed with her father.

She wondered if her father really loved her. He acted like it, he gave her things and he would take her to restaurants where everyone knew him. She had convinced herself that he must love her. Except when they hugged, it was artificial, a kind of compulsory bit of Italian theater with outstretched arms embracing. The touch was distant and Quido always seemed to be in a hurry to get it over with.

Babe often dreamed that she was a Hollywood film heroine separated from her father by tragedy, only to be reunited by fate in a beautiful summer field, both rushing toward each other's embrace as music played in the background. She cried when watching tear-jerking movies like "My Son, My Son." When she was with her father, she believed that his drinking was the result of something broken inside him, and that life somehow wounded him, leaving him in need of some kind of help—hers. She felt certain that her own feelings of love could fix problems that her mother had given up on a long time ago. When he was better, she thought, the distance between them would fall away; they would become family.

Although her real name was Nella, most people called her "Babe," the name she preferred. Although it had an Italian connotation as in "she's a little baby or bambino," in fact, she was a true "babe" with a sultry dark look, a big full-lipped smile, a stunning figure and a rolling, generous and affectionate personality. In short, Babe was irresistible. People felt they were the center of her interest. A touch of her hand on new acquaintances' cheeks or whispering, "thank you so much for coming," subtly promised a genuine friendship. She brought them into her world comfortably and people liked belonging. Men, of course, took particular note. People never forgot her. They sought her company and she never forgot a name.

***

When Babe arrived home, Quido was in the neighbor's backyard drinking with his friends who had all been together for the last three days pressing grapes they had chipped in to buy and make wine. Their consensus was that Petri Brothers had the best grapes. They talked about that and about how much wine they would each have to share and how long the batch would last through the year.

Their voices carried over the fence and Babe listened. Someone was playing an accordion and she could hear the snap of Pinochle cards hitting the table. Italians, she reflected, always grunted *"Dio Cane,"* a dog's day, after drawing unwanted cards. The din of familiar noises had hummed her into a dreamy state and she decided to sit in the yard for a while before getting dressed for her date.

The olive tree, which was the only one in the neighborhood, was full of big green olives, as it was every year, and the tree gave just enough shade to make the yard comfortable to sit in. The tree was exceptionally tall and when the wind wafted, it swayed like wheat in a field—like the fields in her dreams. She looked up into the warm haze of the afternoon and imagined herself as one of the brides that she saw every Saturday at Saints Peter and Paul church on Washington Square. She loved weddings and could visualize herself walking slowly up the aisle in a white flowing dress.

She had figured out why queens and brides all had such long dress-trains and veils; the shape and long flow of the dress was a way of outlining the bride's obviously successful essence. The bride's aura was then a scent for the unwed to follow, she reasoned, and that it was the transferring of this essence that made the throwing of the bridal bouquet such an important catch by the still unmarried. *Nobody ever fought over the flowers at a funeral, did they?*

Babe swayed to the music playing next door and thought how rich and important she would be as a bride. A playing card slapped a table, an olive fell in the breeze and it was time she left the house for her date.

Chapter Four

The Palace Theatre
1948

HOGAN'S Soda Fountain and Hot Dog Emporium was in an older part of North Beach on a hill leading to Coit Tower. Three schools were nearby and many students found their way to Hogan's for a cherry Coke or root beer float after school. Jack enjoyed the envious looks he got as he strolled into Hogan's with Babe. Jack and the local Galileo High School teens hung out at Hogan's. Catholic schoolgirls went there, too, even though the nuns frowned on good Italian girls consorting with boys in such establishments. Babe, who attended Presentation High, and her best friend, Mary, who now went to St. Mary's, lived in the neighborhood near Lombard and Taylor Streets. Jack lived three blocks away on Union Street. Mary knew a school friend of Jack's, and so it came to be—a double date—hot dogs at Hogan's.

Jack was awkward at first. He shook hands with Babe as if he were on a job interview and then became appalled and embarrassed with himself and turned red. Even after the foursome were seated in a booth with root beer floats in front of them, Jack felt that he had narrowly dodged a disaster.

He was saved when Babe, sensing his discomfort, said, "I hear you're quite the artist; can you draw me on this napkin?"

"Sure, look straight at me and don't move," Jack directed.

Grinning, Jack scribbled for ten minutes and produced a stylized characterization of Babe that looked very sexy with exaggerated, languid eyelashes, pouting lips and large dark eyes. She was impressed with the drawing, and that gave Jack the opportunity to look at her without glancing away and Babe an opportunity to watch him. He learned later that she was impressed with how confident he was when he was drawing. Afterward, they studied each other and both liked what they saw.

After enjoying Hogan's, the four of them walked to Washington Park where they sprawled on the grass and talked about their commonly shared pains of youth suffered at the hands of teachers they liked or hated. They talked about the boring routine of school and their dreams of leaving home and getting away from their parents. Mary talked a lot and brought up the subject of the Chinese.

"What do you guys think about the students from Chinatown infiltrating the Italian neighborhood schools?"

Mary's date, Bill Partucci, looked skyward while exhaling cigarette smoke and saying, "no problem. Anyway, they mostly go to Francisco Junior High and we're in high school. So we don't have to see 'em much."

"Yeah, I know what you mean," Mary said. "Do you know that all their students go to another school in Chinatown for classes in Chinese and math? Pretty scary when you think about it. I wouldn't want to be in the same classroom with them when it came time to getting grades. Hell, I'm lucky to pull a 'C' average as it is." She looked over at Babe who'd barely said a word.

"Hey Babe! You part of this conversation or have you fallen off the earth?"

"Oh! My mind was somewhere else," Babe responded. "Were you talking about that movie across the street?"

"No, for Christ's sake, we're talking about Chinamen!"

Babe seemed puzzled. "I don't know any Chinese men. Should I?"

"Forget about it, lover girl."

Jack came to her rescue. "It really doesn't matter. People are people. I don't have any problem being around Chinamen." *She's just great,* Jack thought to himself. *Beautiful too!*

"You like the movies, Babe?" Jack asked.

"Yeah. Why?"

"Oh, I just thought that if something good was playing someday, you know, maybe we could meet there with the gang or something."

"Maybe," Babe replied, looking at Jack.

"I just got a record with Nat King Cole's song '*Unforgettable*' on it," Bill said, "I must'a played it a hundred times already. You hear it yet?"

Babe started singing, *"Unforgettable—that's what you are,"* and for a few minutes they sang together, half humming the words they didn't know.

Jack had just fallen in love.

They smoked their cigarettes in an affected manner that mimicked the haughty and tough movie images of Bette Davis and Humphrey Bogart. With their middle fingers they casually flicked butts onto the grass around them. They practiced blowing smoke-rings, but when Mary tried to French-inhale, she choked on the smoke, and Bill slapped her on the back until she slapped him back. It was fun being together, doing goofy things, being at ease with each other and laughing. Babe and Jack promised to meet at the Palace Theater on Friday night.

Babe wouldn't let Jack come to her place. She was too embarrassed, but agreed to meet him at the Palace. Jack wore a leather bomber-jacket with the collar pulled up, a white rayon scarf wrapped around his neck. He splashed on some Old Spice after-shave, hoping it would make a good impression. It scared him to think she might not show, but Babe arrived wearing a baby blue cashmere sweater with a heavy chained cross riding provocatively between her breasts. Relieved that she came, he led her inside and stopped for a bag of popcorn. Sitting together in the balcony gave Jack the opportunity to lean toward her when talking, but in truth he could not take his eyes off Babe's beautiful, full breasts.

Pathê News ended and a Bugs Bunny clip popped onto the screen. Jack felt uneasy about reaching for Babe's hand during an unromantic cartoon, but he didn't want to wait. *What if she decides she doesn't like me?* Babe, just as uncomfortable, perched herself high on her seat, like a proper Catholic girl.

Jack and Babe shared popcorn. Their arms and shoulders touched. Jack brushed the front of her cashmere sweater accidentally. They looked at each other, oblivious to the movie. Their hands came together and no more needed to be said.

Chapter Five

Jack and Babe

JACK was of German and Irish stock, fair skinned, topped with orange-red hair; he had good looks and a great smile, although what made him so appealing to Babe was his chipped upper front tooth. With his unassuming personality, he was often overlooked in a crowd of young people, which was okay with him. Jeans and a shirt were all that Jack ever wore and he liked to say that he was a lover and not a fighter, which was true. If there were fights at school, no one looked for Jack to be part of them. His easy demeanor did sometimes invite the local toughs to abuse him, especially when it became known that he was dating a highly sought after Italian neighborhood girl. It was shortly after World War II, when the subject of Italy joining the German Axis became a neighborhood controversy and gave some people reasons to question the Fischer family loyalties. Twice, swastikas were painted on his home mailbox and his school locker, long after the war was over.

Jack was not a good student and he had no mechanical skills, but he could draw anything and could give it personality. He dreamed of being an artist, but he also read youthful books on subjects ranging from rocket trips to the moon to how-to books on hypnotism. He loved the notion of being able to hypnotize people and half believed he could do it, even when all attempts with his brother or friends ended in laughter.

After the Palace Theater date, he and Babe began meeting and going for long walks. They often went to friends' houses, where they could be alone. One afternoon they were at Bob and Josie's, who were not expected back for at least three hours. One thing led to another and Jack told Babe about his interest in hypnosis. They talked seriously about it, even though he felt foolish at first. Babe encouraged him to be her hypnotist. She watched Jack's swinging pendulum and listened to him talk softly to her while she pretended to be mesmerized.

"Your eyes feel heavy," he said in a monotone voice, several times. "They are closed and you are imagining yourself floating, sailing freely in the air."

Babe was tempted and did almost peek. She held down a chuckling spasm by muffling the urge with deep, deep breathing. Jack watched her breast heave up and down, up and down and finally he took her cue. "You are breathing deeply now," he said, not knowing what else to say while watching her breasts.

"Is that you, Jack?" Babe said in a faint, distant voice, searching for him, out there somewhere.

Jack moved his mouth to her ear and whispered, "yes, Babe, I'm here." He paused, and then added, "I'll always be here for you."

With her hands folded beneath her breasts she replied. "Yes, Jack, I know it's you. Where am I? Hold my hands."

His hand reached for hers, they touched. She cupped her hand over his and guided him to her breast. "Oh, Jack, I can feel you now, so soft, so soft. Do you love me?"

"I'll always love you, Babe, always."

"It's so warm, so warm. Jack, take off my sweater. Please, it's so warm."

She rose to help and the sweater came off easily. As the trance deepened, he began taking the rest of her clothes off, ever so gently while silently praying that he would not wake her. The closer to naked they both became, the more intense were the breathing and hypnotic incantations. With the lights out, except one window half-shaded to the afternoon sun, the magic moment arrived. Jack told Babe he loved her, he was gentle and persistent. Babe, still supposedly hypnotized, also uttered loving and soothing words. It was their first time and he smiled when remembering how much both healer and patient enjoyed it. Later, Babe whispered, "Jack—you shouldn't have taken advantage of me while I was in a trance." They could always make each other laugh.

Chapter Six

Before the War
1949

AFTER working late at Crocker Stationery, Jack waited for the cable car at Powell and Market Streets and noticed that the flower cart, established there for generations, was closing for the day. He looked on with curiosity and saw the vendor was about to throw away a batch of gardenias. Jack asked why they were being tossed out. The vendor explained they would be no good the next day, so there was no point in saving them. Jack asked if he could have some and was told to help himself. He picked six of the best ones, and before leaving, the vendor smiled knowingly and gave him fern leaves and wire. When he got home, he made the most beautiful corsage he had ever seen. Jack had a date with Babe that night and she had no idea where they would go. When Jack called, he told her to dress up because he had a big surprise for her.

Jack had not told his father, mother, brother or Babe that he had joined the Marine Corps Reserve. In 1949, he was eighteen years old and felt he did not need anyone's permission. His brother, their friend John Maldonado, and others who were younger, had joined because they got to wear a uniform. It was peacetime and all the boys had to do was show up at the Marine base on Treasure Island once a month and listen to lectures. Mostly, they skipped those meetings. Regardless, every three months the Marine Corps would send $32.50. That was the deal; you were not supposed to wear your uniform at any time other than at meetings. But Jack decided to take a chance.

It was Friday night, Jack had the gardenia corsage, his uniform on, and $14.27 in his pocket when he rang Babe's doorbell. When she answered, Babe nearly fainted.

"What the hell got into you? Why didn't you tell me? *What* is this supposed to mean? Is this some kind of game? *No!* I'm not letting you in until you tell me everything!"

Jack was dumbfounded at Babe's anger and passion and felt humiliated, embarrassed and a bit confused. Standing there on the doorstep being yelled at was a far cry from what he'd expected. Finally, inside the flat, Jack explained everything and emphasized the money he would get for doing practically nothing, and the fact that there was no war going on made it all right. Besides, everyone in the neighborhood had joined. Babe listened, but Jack could tell she did not like it.

Anyway, the gardenias were a big hit. Babe had never worn a corsage before. She had never attended a school prom where these were part of the evening wear. So this was something special, and when Jack told her where the flowers came from and how he made up the corsage, it touched her. The flowers softened the atmosphere and Babe looked thoughtfully at Jack squirming through his explanations.

"Jack, you're an idiot, but no one ever gave me anything like this before, and I love you with all my heart."

Relieved, Jack said, "me too." They kissed.

They left the house all dressed up like a World War II couple with little time on their hands. They felt a heightened sense of importance—the uniform, the corsage, nylon stockings. People noticed them, but a middle aged couple spit on Jack because the uniform reminded them of the last war.

A commercial district known as the Barbary Coast ran along Pacific Avenue. It was named during the days of sailing ships when Pacific Avenue was a wharf, before it was filled in for office building developments. The Gold Rush had created a shortage of sailors. Drunk and unsuspecting men were often "Shanghaied" by dropping them through trap doors into waiting rowboats that stood ready to take them away to ships desperate for crews. During World War II, military men arrived at the Barbary Coast eager to explore the mysteries of its bawdy reputation. Four years after the war the only establishments that still featured live music and bouncers were the House of Pisco, the House of Blue Lights and The Barbary. The Ink Spots were featured at the House of Blue Lights and Jack and Babe, pretending to be old enough to drink, walked in. There were maybe a dozen patrons, a flower and cigarette girl, a photographer, a hatcheck girl sashaying around, and a drink waitress who treated them like regulars.

"Champagne?" they were asked.

Jack spoke casually. "Two rum and cokes." *Bogart should see me now,* he thought.

They nursed those drinks all night, listened to the Ink Spots and danced. There was something magical about acting like adults, doing grown-up things, feeling protected by each other and admired by strangers. But when the bill came they were informed there was a two-drink minimum, plus a surcharge of $3.00 per person, for a total of $18.25. Jack put down his $14.27 and pleaded that they only had one drink. Finally the manager said they could go. As they left Jack could hear the Ink Spot's singing the words from a World War II song *"He's just the boogie-woogie bugler boy from Company B."*

***

After World War II, Communist North Korea had been separated at the 38th parallel from the American-supported South Korea. Now both China and Russia wanted them out of the southern portion. Korea, being near the Japanese mainland, was in an ideal location to threaten American interests there. In June 1950, Chinese soldiers, dressed in North Korean uniforms and supported by Russian military hardware, blended with North Korean regulars and began the invasion of South Korea. Most people in America did not know where Korea was; let alone what the fighting was about. Another boogie-woogie bugler from Company B was about to change all that.

***

A month after his date with Babe at the House of Blue Lights, Jack left work, as usual around six in the evening. It was the middle of a hot summer, but the fog had come in early that day and, in typical San Francisco style, it was so chilly he nearly froze. He couldn't wait to get home and boarded a Powell Street cable car. While hanging on an outside step in front of a seated passenger reading the *Call Bulletin* newspaper, he glanced at the headline facing him. It was about an invasion going on in Korea. It didn't mean much to Jack. He hadn't been to a Marine Corps meeting since his first one. In his mind he wouldn't be part of the war anyway because, he thought, if he didn't show up for meetings they would undoubtedly drop him from the rolls. That was what other clubs did.

When he got home, he opened his mail. One letter was from

Heald College accepting him as an art student for night classes. His heart leaped. At last! He would be getting on with his dreams. The other was a notice from the Marine Corps demanding he report to Treasure Island immediately. He was stunned. What did this mean? He felt sick and a bit panicky and called around to his friends. Two others had received the same notice, but they all decided it had nothing to do with them and that they would just ignore the letter. Maybe, they thought, they would do something about it if a second letter arrived.

But Jack's brother had received his own notice early that day and had gone to Treasure Island. He was lucky he wasn't held there. He told Jack that the Korea thing was real and that if he didn't go right away, the Military Police would be looking for him.

Jack felt the panic rise again. He didn't know what to tell Babe or what to do about work. Jobs were hard to find and he was well liked at Crocker Stationery. If he told them he had to go, he feared his job would go too. Friends called, worrying about the same kind of problems and collectively the reality of going to war began to sink in. Jack realized he had to go, but rationalized that maybe it was only for training. Anyway, the neighbor next door said he was going and Jack reluctantly decided he would as well.

Jack couldn't tell Babe the news on the telephone and he worried all the way to her place about what he would say to her. He walked slowly, mentally rehearsing. *I'm probably going to be assigned guard duty someplace, maybe Hawaii,* he would tell her, which was partially true because Jack's brother told him that the Corps deliberately spread that rumor hoping to limit the number of no-shows. *They're going to send the older guys, you know, vets, guys with experience. Hell, they can't send me anywhere. I've never fired a shot and they'd have to give me at least a year's training before I went anywhere and by that time it will be over.* He liked that story best because it was so logical.

He stood at her front door trying to get up the courage to ring the bell. He was scared. Jack was afraid of what might come next, of losing Babe, and of being yelled at for being such an idiot. *Who is going to look after her when I'm gone?* His throat tightened as he reached for the doorbell. His promise to provide for and protect the only person he ever loved ripped at his heart. They would be separated. It was something he never considered. *I'll tell her I want to get married tomorrow, before I give her the bad news.* He barely heard the bell ringing. Babe answered and looked puzzled at Jack who had burst into tears. Shuddering with remorse and guilt he grabbed her and cried. He shook while telling her he had to report to Treasure Island and that he would be leaving from a rail depot in Oakland to a base, Camp Pendleton, north of San Diego. She was calm. Not once did she berate him for being an idiot. She hugged him, caressed him and made him half-believe that things might not be so bad. After all, she kept saying, it would only be for a short time.

***

Generally, only girls were taught to type at school. In fact, Jack's brother Bob was the only male student in typing class. When Bob showed up at Treasure Island, officers yelled out for anyone who could type. Bob raised his hand and was assigned to a Headquarters company. In that capacity, he knew when the trains were leaving. Bob had called his mom to tell her.

The next morning, the only girls on the station platform embracing their boyfriends were Babe and Bob's girlfriend Theresa Joyce. Many men on the train wept at that site and cheered the girls as the train's whistles threatened the final call. Earlier, Jack had bought a Ronson cigarette case and lighter for Babe. Although she had quit smoking, there was nothing left at the PX to buy. He gave it with a promise to someday have it engraved. Babe gave Jack a tiny, plastic-covered, four-leaf clover pendant without the chain. It was all she had. There was so little time to get him anything meaningful, to even know what to do.

She said, out of instinct, "Jack, you better come back here and bring this four-leaf clover with you! You understand?" Their eyes searched each other while their hearts raced. Whistles began blowing and officers started yelling. Babe smiled bravely, forcing herself not to cry and make things worse. Jack climbed aboard to a thunderous applause by the troops who had no one to see them off.

***

At Camp Pendleton, Jack stood in line to use one of the few outside pay phones. He called his mother collect and said he would be leaving San Diego in four days time and that he could not reach Babe by phone. Rosemary wrote down the details and called Babe urging her to get down to San Diego before it was too late.

"How?" cried Babe.

"Leave it to me," Rosemary said.

Rosemary used her union influence at the telephone company. She employed a little trickery to get a flight arranged for Babe and for someone to escort her by car to a very scarce hotel room once she arrived. It was a simple strategy. She had one of her overseas operators call through to the airline saying: "This is Senator Bigalow's office calling to make an urgent request for a seat on Flight 301 leaving from San Francisco for San Diego tonight at eight o'clock."

After a few moments the airline manager came on the line, "I can give you one seat, but I have to bump someone to do it. I hope it's important."

"Our office is calling on behalf of General Barsi, whose daughter is stranded in San Francisco. She is to join him, and both are flying out of San Diego to join the war effort in Japan."

"That's good enough for me lady. What's the passenger's name?"

"Babe Barsi."

"Okay, you're booked. Mention my name to the Senator, will you?"

***

The long-distance telephone operators, who were Rosemary's friends, coordinated every detail and even organized a personal telephone call from President Truman to Jack in San Diego.

"Hello Mr. President. I am glad you took my call. My name is Rosemary Fischer. I represent the eighteen thousand Communication Workers of America on the West Coast who are coming out to demonstrate on behalf of you and the war effort. We have some of our publicity people in San Diego right now, and we thought it would be very patriotic and newsworthy if you could place a telephone call to one of the Marines who is about to leave for Korea. Can we connect you, Mr. President?"

The president responded in a strained voice. "It would be an honor. What is his name?"

"Private Jack Fischer," she answered, and made the connection.

Rosemary wanted Babe's trip to be a success, because the war and its uncertainties had convinced her that she made a mistake preventing Jack and Babe from eloping to Reno three months earlier.

On the way to Nevada to get married, Jack had telephoned home from The Nut Tree a popular roadside stopping point in Vacaville, California to tell his mother he was going to marry Babe. Rosemary was immediately upset because she felt they were not old enough. She threatened to call the police and stop them, claiming Babe was not legally old enough. Actually she was, but at the time, mentioning it was enough to cause a delay. They hesitated and came home unmarried.

What made Rosemary's guilt worse was the belief that Jack could have been deferred from immediate active duty if he had been married. While that was just an unfounded rumor, she never put the thought out of her mind. For the rest of her life she blamed herself for being the cause of never seeing her son again.

***

The little four-story hotel in San Diego was their dream come true. Neither Jack nor Babe had ever stayed overnight in a hotel, and those two days together, when remembered, seemed to stretch into weeks.

It was awkward at first. Jack stood shuffling his feet from side to side. Babe, having just arrived after being treated like a celebrity on the airplane and in the chauffeured ride to the hotel, felt it was anti-climatic. Now, it was just she and Jack, with President Truman and "General Barsi" fading to black. A few hours ago she had been just a kid and now she stood in a hotel room where she was supposed to act like a grown woman. Everything was moving too fast. She had no idea how a war bride was supposed to act.

Finally, Jack spoke. "Babe, I promise never to forget you and to write every day."

"Don't make any promises you can't keep, Jack. Just hold me. Don't talk."

Jack moved next to her with his hands at his side. "Put your hands on me Jack. Love me. This may be our only time together." *God, didn't I hear those lines in an Ingrid Bergman movie?,* Babe thought to herself.

Jack put his hands on her hips. "I fell in love with you at the park when you sang 'Unforgettable.' Something struck me that day. I felt so helpless with the urge to be close to you. I was afraid to move. Remember when I touched your hand?"

"Yeah! I nearly fainted." Babe laughed as she answered.

"Mary kept rattling on about a Chinese man in North Beach, but I couldn't concentrate on what she was saying. I wanted to hold your hand to my breast—so bad—I think I blushed thinking you knew what I was thinking. You know what I mean?"

"I think so, but it's a good thing you didn't do that in the park." They both laughed and were themselves again.

In the semi-dark, he stood behind her kissing her neck, inhaling her essence and tasting her skin. He pulled the blouse loose from her skirt and slowly moved his hands onto her stomach and up onto her breasts. Softly, he pushed her brassier over her nipples and held her firmly. Gasping, she whispered, "take off my bra Jack." He did and then heard her skirt fall to the floor. It made the loudest noise his heart ever heard. He turned her around, removed her panties and lifted her onto him, falling slowly backward onto the bed.

"You're beautiful," Jack said.

"Put your hands around me. Pull me to you. I want to watch you do it." Jack did. Her hips rose over him. Slowly she slid down, burying his manhood, locking them together.

In the background, they could hear the snick of tires on the damp pavement below, foghorns in the distance and the noises coming from other rooms. The crappy little radio at their bedside itched away at scratchy unmemorable tunes. They moved into each other over and over again, each time more consuming and more exhausting. Life's little pieces flowed between them. Closed eyes saw stars scattering in the heavens. They floated down ancient rivers and, with the wet moistening their baptism into the kingdom of love, they would always be one.

"I love you with all my heart, Babe. I know I would die without you."

"Don't talk about dying. Lie still. I just want to hold you."

"Well, I could be stuck over there for a long time."

"Jack, I have waited to love someone all of my life and when you came along I felt like a princess in a fairy tale. I would never have believed that this would ever happen to me and I'm never going to let you go. And if you do get stuck over there somehow, I am giving you my solemn oath that I will find you and bring you back."

"Geez Babe, nothing is going to happen to me." He knew that what he had just said was forced bravado and so did she, but he wanted to reassure her. Both knew enough to be scared, and they were afraid of losing everything they had in each other.

"I used to go to church every Sunday. Mostly to watch weddings," Babe said as they lay in each other's arms. "I always dreamed of being a bride in a long white dress." She rose up and hung the bed sheet across her shoulders and posed like a proper bride.

"When I get back we will be married the minute the ship docks," Jack said.

"I don't mean like that, Jack. You know a romantic wedding."

"Babe, we don't have the little piece of paper that says we're married, but people have been pledging oaths to each other for centuries. I want to give you my oath that I take you as my bride."

"I accept. Is that for better or worse?"

"It will never get better than this," Jack answered. "I will protect you with my last breath."

"Me too," Babe said, embracing him with all of her might.

They promised to love each other forever, to live eternally for each other, to write letters every day and to make a wish on each evening star as it winked into life. And they promised to look up every day at the sun at exactly noon to transmit their love messages, knowing that the same sun would shine over the other within twenty-four hours. That first night Babe cried as she walked up and down the little room with a bed sheet in tow over her shoulders pretending to be a bride with a veil, and Jack said "I do," over and over and over, and he too cried. They never left the room until it was time for Jack to go.

She watched him board the ship and stayed until it faded over the horizon. With tears in her eyes and a clenched jaw she stood alone, a solitary figure on a broken down dock thinking wild thoughts. They took her Jack away from her and she was heartbroken and angry. Like a bad omen, a cold wind blew through. She glanced at the horizon one last time. "They damn well better bring him back here."

PART TWO

Chapter Seven

Korea Invasion
1950

JACK and hundreds of other new recruits sailed for Japan on the World War II Liberty ship, the USS Noble. Many had been told that they had been assigned to guard duty in Hawaii. If the troops had thought they were going to Korea, many would have gone AWOL, and the officers weren't taking any chances.

The late realization that the ship was going straight to Kobe, Japan, came as a shock to the reservists from World War II. Many of them had stayed in the service to earn time toward their pensions, never expecting another war to break out. It was an even bigger shock to the young boys who had joined the Reserves at age 15 and 16—for the uniform and for the girls. Korea? Where the hell was Korea? War was meant for real men, those larger-than-life John Waynes in the movies. The only Reserve meeting Jack attended was the very first one, and like most of the others he was jammed in with, he had never held a weapon in his hands. He had no idea what a mortar or a Browning Automatic Rifle was. Knowing this, officers began small arms training on board ship; men learned to clean their rifles and judge their aim by shooting from the ship's gunnels at ocean waves or sea birds. Jack tried his best to lower and raise the rear gun sight on a beat-up M-1 rifle that he was allowed to use. He gave up and tried pulling the trigger, but nothing happened. A Marine sergeant screamed at Jack and pointed toward the ocean.

"You fucking idiot—don't point that damn thing up. You're gonna kill someone on the upper deck, asshole."

"I think the rifle's jammed sir; I was just looking inside the barrel to see if the bullet got stuck," Jack replied.

Outraged, the Marine bellowed, "you fuckers aren't Marines, you're dog shit and that's what I gotta put up with. Gimme that thing."

Not knowing procedure, Jack passed the rifle with the barrel pointing directly at the sergeant.

"You, you stupid sombitch," the sergeant yelled, yanking the rifle away and turning its muzzle toward the sea. But, before he could finish his tirade, the rifle discharged twice, blowing a hole through a signal lamp. Jack hadn't fired a single shot, but holding that misfired rifle somehow qualified as training.

The ship had bunk beds welded onto the bulkheads below decks; duffel bags, weapons and Marines were piled everywhere. There was no room to breathe down below, and the air was foul with cigarette smoke and sweat. Men wandered aimlessly and took turns topside, desperate for fresh air and to ward off seasickness.

Men from the 1st Platoon of B Company formed on the fantail of the ship where Jack met Sergeant Don Gill, Sergeant Anthony "Tony" Marcantante, Lieutenant George Belli, Captain Wesley Noran, Sergeant Clayton Roberts and Private Chuck Kuzenga, men he would soon be going through hell with.

Tony had enlisted before the Korean War and had just come out of boot camp at Paris Island as a Drill Sergeant. Trained as a machine gunner, he was a very tough looking New Yorker who had joined the Marines for the adventure and to put distance between himself and some legal problems. Prior to boarding the Noble he was one of the few issued a semi-automatic Browning Automatic Rifle (BAR), a much slower weapon than a machine gun. Without warning to his comrades, he fired ten rounds off the rear end of the ship.

"Knock it off, Tony!" Captain Noran shouted. "You're wasting ammo."

Noran approached Tony and directed him to form a three-man fire-team with Don and Jack. "Those guys probably never fired a shot before and there might not be an opportunity in Japan. Show them the ropes and report back to me in two days," Captain Noran said.

Not everyone had a uniform. Mindful of that, and knowing uniforms had been loaded on ship prior to leaving San Diego, Noran turned to Jack and said, "Before you start, run down to the blanket storage room below decks and have them fit you with a uniform if they have any." Noran looked at the others. "Lieutenant Belli, you do the same with Sergeant Roberts and Private Kuzenga. Find, borrow or steal the weapons you need and be back here in an hour. I want to see some shooting."

"Sir," replied Kuzenga, "I've been trying to find weapons all morning. I think C Company has some. I heard them shooting. Maybe I can borrow a few rifles."

"God help us," Captain Noran said in a lowered voice. "Lieutenant, if we run into the enemy, these kids will be slaughtered."

Jack overheard and tried to imagine a pending war. *It's so near, Babe. I don't like what I'm thinking,* he thought.

***

At Kobe, Japan, the USS Noble was quickly provisioned for the invasion of Korea: landing craft were slung onto the ship and cargo nets were made ready to throw over the side when it came time to climb down and into the boats. The USS Noble joined other ships. When the convoy was at sea they were told their destination, the invasion of the harbor city of Inchon in North Korea. They were also told that the tide would recede three hours after the landing attempt and that the Navy could not stand off shore to support the troops if the assault failed.

The night before zero hour the men were silent. Some slept, but most, like Jack, wondered if they would see a sunset again. He unconsciously rubbed Babe's four-leaf clover.

I'm not going to be the first guy off the boat, that's for damn sure, Jack thought. Unconsciously, he looked around for the largest man he could find and wondered if he could run behind him when the enemy began firing. Others were silently thinking similar thoughts. Some looked hard at their feet, speculating on shooting one so they could be returned to the ship. Jack didn't realize it, but he dozed off in a sitting position with his precious rifle in one hand. He was issued it in Kobe and learned how to clean it, but shooting practice off the ship was no longer allowed.

Whistles blew and a voice blared over loudspeakers ordering all landing craft lowered and the cargo netting tossed over the side. Officers barked and men began crawling up gangways toward the main deck.

"Stay close," Tony yelled at Sergeant Gill and Private Fischer.

Marines climbed over the ship's railings and crabbed their way down to the tossing boats. Some lost their weapons; others fell into the surging sea. Officers screamed desperately to be heard and landing craft bumped dangerously against the ship. Chaos, amplified by the still dark sky, kept men from focusing on what they imagined was next or worrying about being discovered by North Korean aircraft.

Finally, the time had come. The landing boats, in formation, cast off and began plowing through a heaving sea. The Navy and air bombardment blasted a fortified complex on Wolmi-Do Island south of Blue Beach where the 1st Marines intended to land. The Marine Division's landing crafts moved through Flying Fish Channel without being fired upon, and when they reached the beach, a man-made sea wall rose ten feet above their bouncing boats. It had to be crossed. Anticipating this obstacle, primitive ten-foot-long wood ladders had been nailed together on board ship for use by the men when they got there. They succeeded in climbing the wall without being hit by small arms fire. Two hundred yards in front of them, Navy shells pounded every possible defensive position. The Marines moved forward and, as smoke cleared from the bombardment, North Korean bullets and mortar rounds began finding targets and men screamed. Jack had not been hit and most of the First Battalion was in good order.

Inchon was taken without much resistance. The North Korean Army, having been caught by surprise, reacted by withdrawing from their positions surrounding Pusan at the southern tip of Korea where previously they were close to victory over a battered U.S. Army. Enemy divisions raced north, but before they could arrive to help defend Inchon, the enemy threw every soldier available within the vicinity of Seoul against the American bridgehead. The North Korean soldiers fought well, but there were not enough of them and they had no air cover.

Once Inchon had been secured, the 1st Marine division rushed toward the Sorth Korean capital of Seoul, but the city of Yong Dong Po on the Han River lay before it and had to be taken. Bridge approaches on the enemy side of the river had been blown by American Navy shells to prevent reinforcements coming into Inchon, and now the Marines had to use what was left of those bridges.

By then, the enemy had established a strong defensive position overlooking the bank. Jack and the rest of B company attempted to cross a bridge spanning the Han River at Kalchon Creek. The men moving in single file between twisted and shattered bridge girders encountered machine gun fire that lashed the entire length, stopping the advance.

The bridge effort failed with six men wounded and two dead. Later, using armored amphibious vehicles brought up from the rear and an artillery bombardment, the men made the crossing.

On the opposite side of the river, B Company, very exposed, ran crouched over an open field toward a warehouse. The Marines entered from the rear, but the enemy was seen approaching between the rail line and the front of the building. The Marines fired frantically at them. Jack and everyone understood immediately that they could not retreat. The open field they'd just crossed would lead to slaughter if they ran; survival meant holding the warehouse until help came. But one hundred seventeen men could not defend four sides of a structure that ran three hundred feet along the loading tracks and one hundred fifty feet deep. It was obvious to Jack that the building had been a train repair facility. Its sixty-foot-high ceilings echoed boomingly. He looked around and figured it was now a cement factory that the enemy had decided could not be permitted to fall.

Corporal Jesus Martinez studied the overhead crane sixty feet above them. He also saw a thick flat metal plate about ten feet square dangling below. It was obvious that this was used to load bags of cement from the warehouse onto the rail cars outside. Jesus lowered the hook and screamed, "Get these fucking bags onto that plate—put the bags in a circle, stack'em high—move it, move it!"

He motioned frantically to his buddy, John Maldonado, to help load grenades and a machine gun onto the metal plate inside the bagged cement wall, which was to be hoisted to the ceiling. With the rest of B Company giving covering fire, Jesus speculated, they could traverse the crane toward the outside of the building and over the rail line itself. From there they could fire down onto the enemy. If they killed enough of them maybe there was a chance at getting out of the building alive.

The iron plate was stacked eight bags high on four sides and was loaded with one machine gun, two rifles and two crates of hand grenades. Martinez and Maldonado boarded and were hoisted electrically up to the ceiling where they dangled and rotated in view of the enemy rushing the building. Preceding their attack, twenty or more mortar rounds flew through the roof, missing the dangling gondola, but exploding among the thousands of hundred-pound cement bags stacked ten-feet high in rows. Bags whirled through the air and cascaded down, collapsing corridors and burying several Marines.

Jack rode down from the top of two separate cement avalanches and scrambled back up again to meet yet more tumbling sacks. Coming to rest at the top of a container of empty bags, Jack spotted the electric controls for the crane and fumbled with them, but nothing happened. He looked around and could see that cement powder from broken bags had plumed into the air, obscuring vision and covering everything with a thick layer of gray dust. He and other Marines shot at every dust shape that moved or at cement clouds that billowed when struck by bullets. Panicked shouts echoed off the walls.

"They're coming through—on the left—left—left.—Look out! Gooks—right—right—!"

Ghostlike, the enemy crawled over the cement-bagged landscape, advancing in several directions, tossing grenades, firing burp guns and trapping the Marines into isolated pockets. Inside the building, explosions vibrated the sheet metal walls, causing an echo like the inside of a metal drum. Shouting for ammunition or help was useless. Jack burrowed under bundles of bags and tuned himself to the slightest movements around him; any sound that seemed close drew instant fire from friend and foe alike.

The nearest Marines, rock-like figures covered thick with dust, were motionless, and Jack feared these men might believe they could hide from discovery and somehow save themselves. Out of desperation, Jack exposed himself and reached again for the crane controls. This time they connected and he began to roll the gondola along the length of the building. Jack screamed at Jesus to drop grenades and fire his machine gun, but Jesus could hear nothing above the gunfire and exploding grenades.

Jesus hadn't fired from the gondola for fear of his own discovery and couldn't hear Jack, but he could see more than anyone else. When the gondola-like gun pit suddenly began moving, Jesus nearly jumped out of his skin. He fired his machine gun blindly down at enemy groups, while John furiously lobbed grenades. The ceiling attack drew enemy fire immediately, bullets hit the bottom of the gondola causing it to wobble and turn slowly in swinging circles like an enormous Mexican piñata. Each time the pit turned toward the daylight breaking through the blasted front doors, Jesus would let loose gun bursts at the enemy outside the building. This confused them into thinking the Marines were counterattacking from outside the warehouse, and they hesitated.

Silence fell, nothing moved. Jack peered out and he could see the fuzzy sun pouring from ceiling holes. The gondola looked like it was on its way to heaven. Light shafts pierced the dust-filled air around it and Jack sensed that the next attack, when it came, would be the end one way or another. Some of the men could have risked escape during the pause, but Jack Fischer, and all of the able men, shouted pledges to each other not to leave the wounded and dead behind if the enemy did continue their assault. They would all come out together or not at all. The attack finally came in waves of unending explosions, and Jack desperately piloted the crane controls. The piñata tilted wildly each time Jack changed its direction, giving the enemy opportunities to shoot slantwise into it. It received so many rounds on one side of it that cement bags began falling away, exposing Jesus. With renewed fury he stood at its center, hoping to prevent more tilting, and this gave him an even better view of the enemy below. He was enraged, howling like an animal. His desire to kill was so great; he nearly dove off the platform to plunge into the carnage. Dead bodies piled up. The enemy attack fizzled, then they broke and ran. As they did, Jesus slaughtered them viciously, even the ones that raised hands to surrender. Other Marines joined in the carnage. And then there was silence.

Sergeant Gill emerged from beneath a dozen cement bags, shook himself into a dust cloud and said flatly, "are they gone?"

"Yeah," said a voice somewhere near a pile of dead enemy.

"Jesus, you did great," Jack choked. "We would have been goners."

"Captain, look over here!" a private yelled. "Bastards were shooting at us with U.S. made stuff. Must'a got'em from 8th Army at Pusan."

Marines, wounded and dead, lay everywhere, some still buried under cement bags. Captain Noran blinked his dust-encrusted eyes and thought, *what a catastrophe*. Part of him felt it might have been his fault and that maybe it was bad leadership, but Marine artillery rounds, whooshing overhead toward targets three hundred yards beyond, reminded him that it was time to go.

"Okay," he yelled, "Chuck, you take six guys out front and form a defense perimeter. Stay only long enough to cover our withdrawal. Move it!"

Noran turned to Private Maldonado. "One of your eardrums

is bleeding, so watch me when I talk. Take twenty guys, find our wounded and carry them back to the river. I don't care how you do it. Jack, you and Tony strip enemy dead of weapons. We were lucky, goddamn lucky, our ammo lasted. If you find anything that looks like maps or other intelligence, get it to me right away."

Jack, surprised at his indifference to the dead he searched, discarded personal photos and other memorabilia with abandon. A near-dead enemy moaned and obviously deserved to die, so Jack shot him. *I wonder how many there are,* was all he seemed to care about, but when it was his turn to leave the warehouse he felt uncomfortable, maybe even guilty.

Bloodlust still throbbing in their veins, the men began withdrawing from the warehouse. Heavy, sporadic weeping was heard, but no one spoke. With weapons pointed high, and eyes wild and wary, the soldiers looked everywhere.

After rejoining their unit, Jack wrote to his aunt saying that he was really scared and that he "got eleven of them." When he wrote to Babe, Jack made no mention of the incident, only that he was okay and that he looked up at the sun that day to say how much he loved her and that he hoped she got the message that he was leaving Seoul by ship to go somewhere and that the food was lousy. He also told her the four-leaf clover helped.

The men retold the warehouse story often. With each telling, the piñata swung more wildly, the cement in the air got thicker and sometimes, John boasted, it even hardened their private parts.

Private John Maldonado, drawing heavily on a cigarette, boasted, "we were throwing candy at the peasants, wishing them their last birthday."

Jesus chimed sarcastically. "Awh, we were just hanging around. Remember, you Yankee assholes, it was the fucking Mexican Air Force that saved your worthless butts!"

Jack and his friend Don Gill cracked that the action made them prematurely gray and that the event helped to 'cement' relationships. Suggestions were made for Jesus and B Company to patent their flying gun pit, but messages arrived with orders to board ships waiting in the harbor.

Chapter Eight

Kojo

B company boarded a small ship and sailed from Inchon, around the Korean peninsula and then north to anchor outside the port city of Wonson. The idea was for U.S. forces to create a giant pincer with one prong heading east from Inchon and the other west from Wonson, trapping the enemy in the middle. The maneuver was grand, but it did not work quite as planned. Instead, troops of the Republic of South Korea or the "ROKs," who fought alongside Allied forces, had pushed up the coast on the heels of the retreating enemy and overran an area south of Wonson and occupied the city before the Marines arrived.

Inside Wonson harbor, the division felt frustrated sitting on ships with their mission aborted. Officers protested to Marine General "Chesty" Puller about the conspicuous lack of intelligence. Worse, the men later discovered that they could not have landed anyway because the bay had been mined, a clean-up task assigned to the Navy that it failed to execute. Colonel Buckley screamed into a microphone connected by radio to headquarters.

"Don't give me that shit. There could have been a half dozen enemy divisions waiting for us to land and you assholes wouldn't have known it." He held his earphones tight to better hear the reply. "Are you telling me you don't know what our orders are now? Don't know if we should land or take a cruise?" A radioman overheard a static-filled voice drifting from the Colonel's head phones.

"MacArthur wants you to land. He wants it on film. We'll call you." Abruptly, transmission ceased and Colonel Buckley's neck bulged red.

"What the fuck!" he growled, hurrying out of the radio shack.

Clearing the harbor took days and during that time men talked.

"Whaddya think of 'Mona Lisa', Nat King Cole's latest record?" a voice said.

"Reminds me of my girlfriend," Sergeant Gill lamented. "If I still have one."

"Smooth," Private Maldonado joined. "Personally, I like 'Cry' by Johnny Ray. Now, that guy can sing."

Music talk led to rumors that the war would be over by Christmas and to speculation about China officially coming in to support North Korea. Several wondered why the atom bomb wasn't being used. "What's the point of having it if we don't use it?" Talk of home and the afterlife got too sentimental. Jack casually brought up hypnosis and hinted at having used it successfully.

"Bullshit!" John Maldonado bawled. "You telling me you hypnotize chicks and they fuck you?"

Surprised and angry, Jack said, "it worked on my girl friend—I swear. And it wasn't fucking, you asshole, it was making love." Sarcastic laughs and overly polite applause rippled among the men.

Jesus joined the conversation enthusiastically. "Hey, man, the next time we go to a bar we're going to send Svengali in ahead and he's going to get everyone naked for us. What do you say, huh?"

"Fuck you guys," Jack said.

Landing craft were lowered into the water. Boarding nets hung over the sides of ships, men filled the boats and in formation, the 1st Marine Division rushed to the beaches of Wonson where film crews recorded the grand triumph. It was embarrassing, but according to some, it was good for the home front. Company B, already formed up near a single-line track, was ordered to board a train heading south. Its engine puffed, whistles blew and men, exhaling vapor plumes, pulled ship-board blankets around their bodies, shuffled forward and piled themselves into straw-matted rail cars without seats or glass in the windows. They placed their duffel bags on the floor to maximize space, to provide some comfort and to make sure their weapons weren't obstructed for firing.

The trip from Wonson took the Company fifty miles south to the coastal village of Kojo. The train—a narrow-gage, steam-driven antique—pumped black smoke through the open-windowed rail cars. Outraged men howled, coughed, put cloth over their mouths and tried blocking the openings with ponchos. Nothing worked, there was no room and few found enough space to squat. Huddling for warmth was all they could do.

"I'm freezing," Jack complained. It was his turn to point his rifle out a window and watch for enemy. "How long before we get there?"

"How come we don't have winter gear?" someone said in a shaking voice.

"Maybe another hour," Lieutenant Belli barked. "And quit complaining. You don't see me wearing an overcoat do you?"

"Shit, I thought you'd have pull. This icebox you ordered up is going to kill us before we get there."

The Marines were sent to Kojo to guard a large ammunition dump captured by the South Korean army, but the entire dump had been carted away and it was too late in the day for a return to Wonson. There were also signs that scattered remnants of the enemy were around. It was decided to divide the force into three groups and occupy the three highest slopes that ringed the eastern side of the village in a crescent.

The climb up those hills was difficult and tiring and the men knew they would be leaving in the morning, so they decided not to go all the way to the top. Besides, the sun was getting low on the horizon and the men still had to dig foxholes in hard ground. Fortunately, nearby villagers who acted as guides volunteered to dig holes for many of the men willing to trade can rations or cigarettes.

Jack and Tony were ordered to dig at the lowest point of the hill, which would be the first position to be attacked if there was such an unlikely event. Both were angry being stuck with digging their own hole.

That night, the North Korean Fifth Division, Black Diamond Regiment, numbering almost five thousand men, passed through the village outskirts. They were told by the villagers about the Marines in the hills and where the foxholes had been dug. They offered to guide the soldiers to those positions. The opportunity to wipe out their American enemy was handed to them. They moved quickly in the dim light, climbing the rear of the three hills until they were above and behind the Marine positions from which an attack would not be expected.

Jack and Tony were half-expecting an attack from below, but felt comfortable that they would hear movement before any danger arose. They were awake and talking in low voices.

"Tony, do you think there is any truth to the rumor that North Korean guerrillas in mountain areas are being rewarded fifty American dollars for every Marine head they collect?" Jack asked.

"It's probably bullshit, but I don't really want to find out," Tony replied. "If you know what I mean."

"You ever think about your girlfriend when we're in the shit like this?"

"Yeah," Tony half-whispered. Something bothered him and he began peering hard down the hill into total blackness.

"It's almost a full moon. I usually think of Babe at times like this. She's my girlfriend."

"Shush," Tony whispered, pointing a finger over his lips.

Jack noticed the sound that loosened rocks make by moving feet and the noises scratched at his paranoia. He searched upslope, elbowed Tony sharply and pointed.

"Holy shit!" Tony yelled, with just enough time to point his machine gun up the hill and begin firing at the sounds of the enemy running down onto their positions with grenades and burp guns.

A grenade exploded below the lip of their foxhole, blowing Jack clear of the hole. Uninjured, he rolled left and began firing his rifle at shapes illuminated by battle fires and ammunition blasts.

"Tony, I'm okay. Look left, must be a dozen," he yelled, beyond fear and confusion.

"Don't throw grenades," Tony screamed. "They'll roll back."

Jack discharged an empty bullet clip and quickly reloaded and fired. Less than twenty feet away five figures fell. Enemy burp guns angrily shredded the ground nearby.

Tony's quick reaction caught the enemy by surprise and killed many outright, slowing the assault. Above their position, the remaining Marines panicked, bolted out of their holes and plunged down the hillside, streaming past Jack and Tony, who kept up a withering fire, not realizing they were being abandoned. Tony was wounded, but kept shooting. Jack yelled for a medic. Quietly, from the down-slope, a medic, Corpsman Dorin Stafford from Oregon, who also did not realize the hill was being abandoned, crept to their foxhole. Soon all three understood they were alone and surrounded. Exploding ammunition and moldering fires cast shadows of the dead.

Silence swept the scene. Minutes passed and nothing happened, then they heard and saw the enemy yelling and waving at them.

Tony was hurting and he pleaded with Jack and Dorin.

"Please, guys don't leave me here. I'm not sure they'll just want to interrogate us."

Jack, nearly frozen from the cold and paralyzed with fear, whispered,

"Shit Tony. What am I supposed to do, ask them if they know Marilyn Monroe? What do you think we should do?"

Dorin removed his Medic armband and handed it to Jack to wave on top of his bayoneted rifle. Slowly Corpsman Stafford emerged from the foxhole with his hands up. Minutes later the three of them were prisoners.

Chapter Nine

Prisoner Fischer

AT five o'clock that morning, the North Korean soldiers had crawled quietly toward the Marines in hopes of catching them asleep in their foxholes. They were in luck and heard men snoring and saw huddled shapes in ponchos. Unattended rifles, pointing uselessly at the sky, advertised each target. The battle was fierce but the element of surprise gave the North Koreans victory quickly. The Marines abandoned the hill in chaos, leaving their injured and a few healthy ones that never realized their Company was retreating.

The victorious soldiers stripped the dead Marines of everything that could be carried. Combat boots were the most prized, followed by heavy wool coats, weapons, ammunition, food, medical supplies, watches, Zippo lighters, ponchos and eyeglasses. North Korean dead were left where they fell.

The handful of Americans that survived the raid were taken prisoner. Tony, Dorin and Jack huddled together. They shook with cold and fear.

Oddly, the three prisoners were not tied. Jack and Dorin moved to help Tony, whose neck and shoulder were pebbled with grenade shrapnel thrown when his machine gun broke enemy silence. A bullet lodged in his calf seeped blood.

"Most of us are dead," Jack whispered. "They've been shooting the wounded, even their own."

"You're right," Dorin said. "If they think you're too bad off they'll shoot you, maybe shoot all of us."

"I don't know why they haven't," Jack added. "They must want something from us."

Dorin scanned the area. "There's no stretcher, Tony. We can't carry you without one, but we'll help you down the hill. Can you handle that?"

"I'll try."

The men were herded downhill toward the railroad tracks that had brought them there. Thinking quickly, Dorin placed his Corpsman's band on Jack's arm and passed him his aid handbook. Dorin's helmet was marked with a Corpsman's insignia. He hoped that the enemy would believe he and Jack were medics and that the charade would keep them alive. Jack wrapped one arm around Tony's waist and, together with Dorin, half-carried him across the rugged terrain.

Jack's group marched into a long valley toward a small village thirty miles distant called Tonam-ni, but Tony fell behind when their captors ordered the prisoners to stop carrying their wounded. The column did not stop there but hurried through. Curious villagers assembled, staring in awe. The American prisoner with the orange-red hair was something they had never seen before; some were afraid, but others boldly stepped forward to touch it.

Jack carried the aid manual in his leg pocket and looked at it as often as possible as he bandaged enemy casualties whose wounds were not severe enough to be a burden to the regiment; only the salvageable were not killed by their officers. He innovated as best he could remember from his own brief combat observations. As primitive as his work was, the enemy wounded appeared grateful. Jack sought Dorin's medical advice, but guessing that they might be separated, Dorin had Jack draw pictures of various bandages, slings and wound closure methods to provide a means of referencing for some of the more complicated procedures. Jack sketched duplicates of the bandaging procedures on old maps or shirts torn into sections and used these to demonstrate the art of patching to his captors. This helped lighten an impossible workload and it actually created a little camaraderie.

It was another hundred miles to North Korea's capital, Pyongyang, their rumored destination. The enemy and Allied soldiers collected along the way inched through a frozen, mountainous terrain for twenty days. It was torturous and many died. Along the way Jack crafted bandages from blankets, shirts and belts. Tree branches made adequate splints. Threads from truck seat covers were a workable suture material and metal seat springs salvaged from destroyed trucks were sharpened into crude stitching needles. Salt and disinfectant were not available, and few fires were allowed to boil water for fear of attracting American aircraft patrolling roads leading north. Winter temperatures plummeted to thirty-eight-degrees below zero. Prisoners' gloves, shoes and stockings were confiscated by the enemy, and prisoners' blood from torn feet smeared the snow. More men died. Some begged to be killed. Blackened by frost, unfeeling fingers and toes were pulled or cut away by Jack without protest from the men.

A new POW camp, forty miles east of Pyongyang, intended to hold only United Nations soldiers, was under construction in late December 1950. Named Kadong by the guards, but Camp Nine by the prisoners, it was this camp that ended their journey. Hillside caves, barbed wire and punishment holes were everywhere and an appalling stench filled the air. The prisoner of war confinement was run ostensibly by the North Koreans but managed by Chinese troops who had reoccupied most of Korea north of the 38th parallel. Tony never made it to camp; he disappeared after he had fallen behind. Neither Jack nor Dorin knew exactly what had happened to him. The two of them were assigned to Kadong and spent the first week being questioned by Chinese interrogators, then by Russian officers wearing Chinese uniforms. Initially, Jack thought the Russians were captured Americans because all prisoners had been issued Mao-style uniforms and the Russians looked exactly like him.

Allied POWs arrived at an appalling rate and were in such horrible condition that many pleaded for a merciful death at the hand of anyone willing. Meanwhile, makeshift medical facilities occupied Jack and Dorin's time, and as things settled down, the duo were sent under guard to other POW camps northeast of Pyongyang to establish medical facilities.

Prisoners heard rumors that American and Allied POWs were being transferred to China and Russia via Manchuria. Jack wondered why; because the war was with North Korea, not the Soviet Union. They had no answers, and there was no one to ask.

Soon, columns of frightened men marched north, away from Kodong. Everyone understood that no one in America would know where they were or that they even existed. North was not the direction to go if they ever wanted to see home again.

Chapter Ten

The Home Front

JACK'S mother, Rosemary, received a telegram in November 1950 notifying her that Private Fischer was missing in action. It also stated that he was to be awarded both the Silver Star for bravery and a Purple Heart for having been wounded. Rosemary called Babe with the news and both cried convulsively on the telephone. Between sobs they talked.

"How could they know he was wounded if Jack is missing, Babe?" Rosemary asked suspiciously. "How can that be?"

"He has to be a prisoner. I'd be willing to bet on it," Babe broke in and with a raised voice said, "How can we find out?"

"We could call the Marine Corps, maybe."

"Geez, Rose that could get us into trouble with the government. You know how things were in North Beach during the war." Sobbing hysterically, Rosemary couldn't speak. Babe waited. "It's okay, Rose. They'll find him."

***

When Bruno got home from work, Rosemary, waiting inside the hallway behind the front door with hatred in her eyes, slowly and deliberately read him the telegram and with deep, deep loathing, added, "Well, if he *is* a prisoner he will have a *much* better chance of surviving the brutality. He had *plenty* of experience with beatings under *this* roof." Scolding angrily, venom poisoning every word, she hovered over Bruno like a predator. Helpless, he staggered down the hallway. Rosemary couldn't stop herself. He couldn't escape, couldn't think and couldn't speak. He wanted to run, to disappear, to deny and to defend, but the verbal torrent was overwhelming.

"This is *your* fault," she screamed. "You treated him like an *animal*--that's *why* he left home, to get away from *you*. You son of a bitch, *you* killed him." A silent wail screamed through Bruno, but he could hear no more. He felt himself floating through the flat without touching the floor or walls. Those things that Jack had touched; his bed, his clothes, the kitchen table, his letters home, glowed iridescently, staring back at him, magnifying his guilt. He could not bear looking at those things without wishing for his own death. Bruno the violinist, the dreamer, the beater, was nothing, and like a defeated boxer he stumbled on his feet. He protested soundlessly as the snarled words he could no longer hear pounded through his body. Tears welled in his eyes. Distance spun white and he tried to yell, but in his thoughts he only heard, "*Mama, mama.*" Bruno grasped his chest, but ice had already gripped his heart. Bruno was dead, still standing with his eyes open. Clawing at the air in outrage, Rosemary followed after him and did not stop hissing until he fell to the floor, where she kicked him repeatedly yelling. "You *bastard*! You *bastard*! You *filthy bastard*!"

Babe arrived just as the ambulance was taking Bruno to the hospital. Neighbors told her what had happened and she rushed up the stairs to embrace Rosemary's grief. A son and now a husband, both gone. Rosemary sat motionless in the living room and Babe tried her best to say uplifting words, but it did no good. Rosemary stayed silent for days and Babe called in Rose's absence at work. She did the shopping and the cleaning, fielded the telephone calls and in general took charge. It was during this time when Rosemary and Babe attached themselves to each other, creating a bond that would last over fifty years. Babe knew that Rosemary felt a sick guilt for having prevented Jack from marrying her and for not being a very good mother. Each felt the loss of what might have been had there been a newborn, and both fantasized about how different life might have been if they had done something different. Babe became Rosemary's daughter, her confidant and her friend, and Rosemary could no longer remember why she had ever thought Babe as an under-aged bimbo trying to trap her son into being a husband. Now, Jack would always be alive because Babe was part of him.

Chapter Eleven

Manchuria

JACK thought often of Babe. He would write and re-write long letters in his mind, promising himself that he would compose them on paper when the Red Cross post became available. At first the paragraphs complained about starvation, beatings and his fears. Later, these mental paragraphs began to focus on details of his old life: a root beer float at Hogan's Creamery, sitting next to Babe and just holding hands, making sandwiches, touching her, helping Babe whiten her saddle shoes while she got herself ready for the Friday night dance at Fugazi Hall. Thoughts drifted through his dreams for days as Jack's train headed north, sometimes stopping to avoid fighter planes but usually because the train needed water for its steam engine.

Using a finger, Jack sketched Babe's likeness on a cracked and dirty window, and wondered *how many days and stops will this thing make before getting somewhere?*

"Girlfriend?" A voice behind him spoke, just before being drowned by the roar of tunnel noise.

Coming out of the tunnel, Jack didn't answer. Few had talked since boarding, everyone knew this would turn out badly and they were too preoccupied. Some thought about loved ones, others thought of suicide.

Late that night, the train wiggled and shook its way over a snowfield on warped bomb-damaged rails before slowing to a hissing stop. Low in the sky, a half moon dimly cast faint shadows. Curious, Jack elbowed a companion. "Let's get out and stretch." Bored guards weren't bothered if a few prisoners got off the train. Jack's small group, passing around the few cigarettes left, milled beneath the light pools between railcars.

"Christ, its cold. Must be below zero," Corpsman Stafford said, exhaling a frosted breath.

"What's here?" someone asked.

"Must'a stopped here before. You guys see anything?" a youngish voice replied.

"No," Jack said, shuffling to keep warm. "Nothing but those snow mounds. Almost looks like they were put there for effect."

"It's too cold, let's go back inside."

Before anyone moved, a man wearing a triangular sheepskin hat, probably an officer, shouted orders. Prisoners, including Jack, were herded together to form a work party. Hand tools were tossed from the train, and it became obvious from the guard's body language that work had to be done in a hurry.

Jack hadn't paid attention before, but now, waiting alongside the track, he saw that most of the railcars were enclosed. Tanks, some with battle damage, and artillery, were chained onto flatcars and covered, ghost-like, with ice. Roofless metal railcars carried coal, but at eye level some cars appeared to be empty. Directed toward the empty coal cars, the men were ordered to board. Jack, the second man to climb a metal ladder, reached the top and reeled backwards at the sight of dead prisoners clumped together and frozen solid. The men were ordered to pry the bodies loose, scrape them from the frozen metal floor and toss them on top of the mounds beside the trains. The men now knew they weren't just snow mounds but mounds of bodies covered with snow. This wasn't the first POW train to have passed this way.

A guard climbed into the boxcar with a long-handled crowbar and demonstrated separating the bodies. A protesting Marine refused and began climbing out of the coal car. He was riddled with a burp gun. Seeing the man tumble backward, men quickly grabbed axes, saws, shovels and pry bars. Jack almost fainted the first time he swung his axe at a body, an American body. Sometimes his axe bounced when he hacked arms and legs off. He used a pry bar and got pretty good at it. Soon, body parts piled alongside the tracks, but with time short and two box cars still holding more than fifty dead, smiling guards used grenades to loosen the piles, making it easier for men to shovel the debris over the side. Switching to a sharper axe, Jack growled angrily under his breath to no one in particular.

Those poor guys held each other to keep warm and froze to death, what kind of people dreamed this shit up? Communist efficiency, he learned, required a fully used train.

The piercing shrill of whistles ripped through the air, hurrying prisoners back to the train. Smeared with blood and body fragments the frightened men stiffened and began to sense they were near their destination and likely separation. The grisly account of what Jack and his group had just experienced raced through the train. It was bad for moral. Jack realized he should have prevented that from happening, because it pushed buttons in men inclined to premonitions of death, who then began beseeching others to remember their names or to carry letters for them to loved ones.

"Cool it, guys," Jack said with a loud voice, to a handful of men. "Don't let them get to you."

"Easy for you, Doc," someone bawled in the background, mistaking Jack for a medic.

"Look, it happened. Okay?" Jack said. "Maybe they were unlucky. Maybe we should start working together instead of complaining."

The train, darkened to avoid fighter planes, chugged through the night without stopping. Some slept, others wept.

While he was doing his ghastly work, Jack speculated that he could fall over the side of the railcar, pretending to be one of the dead, and make his escape. But he had discarded the notion because he didn't know where he was, he had no food and he couldn't speak Korean or Chinese. Besides, his red hair would stand out in a sea of Orientals. What he needed was an interpreter, money in his pocket and food, all quite impossible. Prisoners who had stayed on the train listened to Jack describe chopping up the dead Americans and his escape idea of hiding among a batch of frozen bodies the next time the train stopped. But everyone realized that just thinking about desperate escapes meant hopes of a Red Cross rescue or a prisoner exchange were sinking.

When the train pulled into the next station, Jack looked out the window. Four naked white men were roped together. They bled from being whipped like cattle. Trying desperately to pull a wagon of laughing Chinese soldiers along a rutted, snow-filled road, the men fell again and again. Jack and his fellow POWs watched silently and prayed the train would pull out. It didn't.

Officers with pistols in hand blew whistles and began sorting prisoners by skills, as Jack would later learn. Groups were marched under guard in two directions. Jack and four other POWs were taken by truck to a group of tents in a field near the Manchurian town of Huadian. The arrival scene stuck in everyone's mind. On ground blanketed with snow lay a mass of still-living bodies; a few on stretchers. As they approached, a foul haze of rotting limbs, urine and excrement hung in the air. Jack and his small group were ordered, in Chinese, to sort out supplies, erect more tents and generally go through the motions of improving what would later pass as a field hospital.

It was harsh cold work. In the beginning, Jack didn't realize that he was in charge, but after being prodded, he assigned prisoners and some enemy soldiers to digging trenches, damming creeks, buildings, mud walls and making wood walkways. Prisoners talked quietly about when the spring waters came and how they would have first pickings of the frogs, snails, snakes, moss and roots. But they had to live to find out, and for the time being they would do well enough with the rats they could catch, smoke, eat or barter—and there were plenty of dead bodies to attract the rats. The death rate among the Allied prisoners was so high, Jack began to wonder when the Chinese would realize that he too was no longer any use to them.

"Babe," Jack mumbled in a dream, "I love you." He turned over knowing she had heard him.

Chapter Twelve

King Poo Koo

ON a hot Shanghai day in late 1938, three Chinese schoolboys walked lazily across one of the main city bridges spanning the Wampo River. A Japanese soldier guarding the far end waited until the boys were at the middle before he brought his rifle up and killed two. The guards laughed. The third boy, Poo Koo, stood frozen. Then for no explainable reason he marched, military style toward the guards, saluted and walked past them. As the distance between the boy and the guards grew, the Japanese shouted and aimed their rifles, but they did not shoot. Poo Koo never forgot the sheer terror of that day, of the shots, of that walk or the feeling in his spine and neck. No shots came, and the boys on the other side came to call Poo Koo, "King." They had never seen a braver act. Later, his name became King Poo Koo.

King was eleven years old at the time, but he knew that the shit in his pants did not make him a hero. Although he did enjoy his newfound status, he was reluctant to join any group, in part because he had work to do, but also because his skin was darker, and many Chinese considered that to be inferior. King wouldn't join a group that made him the butt of jokes.

King's mother, Song, was from Cambodia, where she taught English part-time at a missionary school. Song met her soldier husband-to-be in the late 1920s after her arrival in Shanghai. She had witnessed Chaing Kai-shek's American-supported army slaughter more than a hundred thousand Communists who had once been allied with him. Song's husband was killed by Chinese warlord troops looking for hashish among their herb collection. The Japanese push into China was stopped at Shanghai. Chaing Kai-shek's and Mao Zedong's armies joined to drive the Japanese out of the capital and out of China. It was a dangerous and confusing time when Song went to work at the still-open American Embassy on the Bund, a Shanghai waterfront boulevard. King was her only child, and as an interpreter, she feared for their safety if Mao's anti-American army became the victor.

Mao conquered China and "Yankee Running Dogs" became a slogan describing those who ran with westerners. Citizens continuing to adhere to the Chinese Confucian traditions of learning and respect became suspect and were sent to re-education camps. Doctors, schoolteachers and other professionals went into hiding, and some raised calluses on their hands to avoid suspicion of being a capitalist. Property was confiscated. Millions of people were organized into labor battalions, millions more were slaughtered. In central China, even more millions were deliberately starved to death to avoid starvation in the rest of the country. Mao knew famine was at hand and that it would be widely headlined in western newspapers. He achieved power promising to end the annual cycles of famine. World headlines would discredit him and his promise of a bountiful Communism. The reformer, the hero of the revolution, would not permit China's peasants or the world to learn of his failure. Desperately needed food was also exported to Russia to buy weapons. Chinese who spoke a foreign language quickly moved away from neighborhoods where they were known. Those who did not die at the hands of Communist mobs were transported to labor camps where they were worked to death or executed.

Song resigned from the American Embassy and accepted a job with an herbal shop in a remote multi-ethnic neighborhood on the Whangpoo River because her English was now a political liability and she feared harassment or worse. The herbalist was in his late seventies and welcomed the help of anyone who knew something about the selecting, drying, grinding and general processing of herbs. Song had learned these chores from her late husband Lei.

King's father, Lei Koo, an herbalist, met Song in China where he had often worked gathering roots, bark, seeds and an assortment of fungi, all of which had to be ground, dried, smoked. steeped, preserved and packaged for the long trip back to China where Lei sold his goods. Song apprenticed beside him and learned to strip and dry frog skins and to squeeze their glands into distilled water. She also peeled, dried and powdered tree barks and helped to gather mushrooms.

King often helped his mother process herbs after home-school studies, which Song taught. It was not safe to have King in public school, because his heroic bridge story became a rumor that suggested the only reason why King survived the Japanese guards was because his family had collaborated with them. King was never again permitted to utter a word in English. Song also knew that she and her son would be sent to re-education camps if she did not do something to please the new government. She decided that King, at age sixteen, would volunteer for the army because enlistment would prove their family loyalty. In 1949, King joined, and later that year Mao enthusiasts threw his mother to her death out of a three-story window.

In North Korea, the Chosin reservoir and the Yalu River were beginning to freeze when King arrived by train at Namsan-ni, a mid-sized town on the Yalu. Part of his duties as a soldier was to dig holes in the ground and to act as a runner. Such holes were commonly used for punishment of soldiers who disobeyed. Commanding Officer Lee Wu's steady stream of conflicting orders and arrogance filled the holes and had a waiting list. Men under his command referred to Wu in whispers as Chop-Chop, a reference to the days when arrogant officials used their seal, in slang their "chop', to authorize everything from military orders to cargo manifests. It was a symbol of authority. Chop-Chop also came to mean "hurry-hurry" when used to describe endless authorizations by seal or chop to move approvals from one minor government tyrant to another. Lee Wu loved using his chop to authorize executions, whippings and routine military business, and he proudly wore it around his neck. Punishment of prisoners required stripping them naked with hands and arms tied behind their backs and placing a pole through the elbow loop and then connecting it to the feet. Prisoners were suspended for days at a time near the bottom of the holes they themselves were often forced to dig. At night, insects and rats ate away the skin and crawled into every orifice while prisoners prayed for death by freezing, which, in the fall of 1950, was a certainty, just never soon enough. Chop-Chop loved his work, and often poured buckets of water over prisoner's bodies to help the misery along.

***

Chinese troops were told that General MacArthur wanted for himself the dam and hydroelectric power plants on the Yalu River bordering Korea. The General, they were also told, was a capitalist warmonger, and his army was on its way to Peking to enslave all people of yellow skin. In September 1950, King's unit moved northeast to Ji-an, then to Manp'ojin fifty miles east of the Yalu River from the Chosin Reservoir. Near Manp'ojin were more than 350,000 of China's not so finest troops assembled to do Mao's work when the time eventually came to teach the General a lesson. The Yankees, soldiers learned, deserved to die, and all knew that the time was near.

Soldiers were commonly dressed in quilted jackets and pants that were too thin to keep out the wind. Many stuffed straw or grass inside their uniforms to keep out the cold, and while there was little to eat, the stuffing made them appear overfed. The majority of King's unit had been issued wood rifles and imitation grenades; twenty five percent of the soldiers had real weapons. The orders were simple. Charge the enemy position in waves, pick up the weapons of the dead and wounded and keep going until you were victorious. Turning back meant execution. And being taken prisoner by Yankees always resulted in a soldier's family being sent to a concentration camp. When King looked around and saw the sea of soldiers around him, he felt comfort in the attack logic.

Officer Lee Wu was the only one with a sheepskin long-coat. A political commissar issued them to those who strictly advocated all that was written in Mao's Little Red Book. A red star adorned his hat and he was equipped with a whistle and revolver. Otherwise, in the people's army, there were no other insignias of rank. King knew he would be safest as a runner close to Officer Lee Wu. In the rear areas, trucks moved supplies and ammunition forward, and marching men bellowed sing-song praises of the revolution and its hero. Medical personnel and supplies were almost non-existent because in Mao's China, life was expendable.

In November, they were ordered across the Yalu River for a night attack on a U.S. Marine division. The wind howled all that day and when night came, it stopped. King could then hear his footsteps in the snow and knew in his heart that the Marines could hear him coming. He couldn't help recalling the day on a Shanghai bridge when the distance between a Japanese guard and him became greater and greater. His skin crawled. Then he heard Chop-Chop blowing his whistle. With men screaming incoherently and dozens of whistles urging them forward, the regiment rose up and ran in waves of eight hundred toward the Marine positions. The whistles defeated any

Chinese advantage of surprise and the Marines mortared and machine-gunned row after row. Bodies stacked sometimes four high, but it did not stop the surge, and the attack rolled onward through the night. Among the first wave, King was one step behind his officer when a mortar blast blew Lee Wu's face away; his body flew backward onto King, knocking both to the ground.

King was struck in one eye with shrapnel and his entire rib cage hurt so badly he could barely breathe. He felt around his body and thought he had four broken ribs and a collarbone separated. He bled from several deep face and scalp wounds. He laid still under Chop-Chop for hours listening to the screams and the insane whistling of those around him. He waited for the Marines that he knew would come and kill him, or, if he were lucky, for his comrades to rescue him. No one came. The Marines withdrew from their defensive positions in anticipation of a Chinese artillery attack. The cold was so intense that King knew he would die in that sorry field if he did not get out of there.

Everything finally went still and King struggled painfully to move the dead body away. He stripped Chop-Chop of his sheepskin long-coat, revolver and whistle and put his own identity tag into the officer's neck wound. If King was going to be captured, he intended to be treated like an officer. King placed his own hat on top of Chop-Chop's head that no longer had a face. Now dressed like Chop-Chop, King rolled into the nearest shell hole.

What really interested King is what he found inside Chop-Chop's Little Red Book—an American $100 bill rolled into the binding. This was two years of officer's wages and an economic crime; owning American currency earned a death sentence. There was also a brief government letter stating that Lee Wu's family had died in a recent Yellow River flooding. King hid the $100 bill inside his pants lining before inching out of his hole and crawling past hundreds, then thousands, of frozen corpses.

Occasionally, he saw whiffs of breath oozing from snow mounds, showing where the still dying lay, but he was too weak to help. King stared into mutilated faces and bodies and thought back at the good fortune of those who died in the punishment holes with their bodies intact. The Chinese artillery barrage finally began, but it fell short of the Marine positions, and the arriving explosions came crashing among his dead comrades, making an unearthly chow mein of human parts, weapons and mud.

A series of explosions threw King upward into the air, and when he crashed back to earth, he disappeared into a dream of bright light and shining things at the end of a long tunnel. The Marines, believing the Chinese artillery attack was the prelude to another major assault, began to boil over that same ground with napalm and artillery of their own. When King was eventually found by Chinese troops, he was totally covered with kerosene-smelling soot. The officer whistle was clenched in his teeth, not because he was using it to urge the troops on, but because he was trying to attract attention to himself before disappearing into a white light. His saviors thought at the time that the cold might save one of King's eyes, so they packed his head with muddy snow and dirty rags and stretchered him back to where everyone had started. The immovable whistle, clenched in King's mouth, seemed proof to others, who were amazed at the carnage, that this was a man who had whistled and charged to the very end. Here was a hero, a sole survivor, one deserving of good treatment. And so it came to be.

Chapter Thirteen

The Pretenders

THE Chinese officer in the sheepskin coat, hero of the Sector 5 assault, had been asleep for several days. He was delirious and often mumbled in Chinese and English, but no one paid attention because there were thousands of wounded lying on the snow or on stretchers, and all of them moaned. Caretaker soldiers worried more about keeping themselves warm than taking care of wounded, and they often complained when ordered away from the fires to dump corpses into pre-dug ditches, making room for more wounded.

Allied prisoners with medical experience were fought over. Any Chinese soldier with rank who had a friend or relative deposited among the frozen acres used influence to get their favorites into a shelter attended by someone qualified.

Chinese soldiers were seldom provided with medical staff and supplies, and they understood that being wounded was close to a death sentence. When medic Jack Fischer, dressed in Mao quilts adorned with a medic's armband, was assigned to Hero Wu after arriving at Kanggye, sparks of hope were seen on the faces of the desperately wounded nearby. Jack's unusual orange-red hair and fair complexion stood out, and wounded who could walk would sometimes touch his hair. The eyes of the conscious wounded studied him. There was something about Jack's demeanor that gave the men hope. Oddly, being touched by this stranger also gave them a sense of ease.

Medic Jack Fischer unwrapped the filthy rags around King's head and saw that most of the left side of the face had peeled away from the scalp and hung below the jaw line. One eye was closed and swelling and the other eye had a shrapnel shard, which Jack removed with pliers. He washed King's face with rice wine as a disinfectant before lifting the skin back into place. The left side of the face, a puzzle of skin patches, was stitched wherever the pieces seemed to fit. Jack used horsetail hairs for sutures, a sharpened truck-seat spring became a handy if not very slim needle. Using rice wine rag-compresses, he bandaged everything back into place. Jack feared King would wake with a Frankenstein face and that could mean a mortal end to Jack's services.

***

When King awoke two weeks after the battle, he found an orange-red-haired man dressed in a quilted uniform staring down at him. Pretending to be asleep, he said nothing and was fearful when the strange man whispered into his ear in English.

"Officer, Wu," Jack said, in a low voice, hoping he could be heard. "Be careful when you wake. I'm your friend."

King heard, but thought he'd been discovered as an imposter. He moaned, hoping the man would go away.

"I know you're awake. I know who you are and I might be able to help."

An eyebrow rose and, with his good eye, King peeked again. He had never seen a redheaded man before.

Jack noticed King's shock, and in a whisper he explained that King had mumbled English during his delirium and that Jack had found King's $100 bill and would keep it safe for him.

"Who are you?" King asked, first looking carefully at his surroundings, using an official manner, hoping his sheepskin coat at the foot of his cot still credentialed him as an officer.

"My name is Jack; I'm American and a prisoner of war. I've been assigned to work in this casualty center and specifically on you." He waited for a reaction and hearing none, said, "don't worry about your sheepskin coat. No one will steal it."

The last thing King remembered was the artillery barrage. He had no way of knowing how he got where he was or that he'd become a hero. He had to ask questions, but to whom?

"Where am I?" he asked. "How did I get here?"

Jack told him how he, as Officer Lee Wu, became a hero and that he was being given special treatment. An English-speaking Chinese officer, with American money, would have been considered a spy, and King knew it. Jack also knew that this man knew it, and he now had leverage over a Chinese hero-officer who spoke English, and who also was not the person he was supposed to be.

King decided he had no choice but to trust Jack with the new life that had been handed to him back in Sector 5. Karma, he thought, was everything. He still had one good eye, and maybe the other eye would mend. He knew without looking into a mirror that Jack was no medicine man, but the work done, King felt, would heal and he would not be a Frankenstein. Oddly, that thought comforted him. Besides, the mid-sized village of Huadian, formally of Manchuria and far from the front lines, seemed a good place to be while he figured out what to do with his new identity.

***

Waking sporadically, Jin Jaing remembered being beaten with a pole by Officer Wu and refusing to utter a sound, seeing parts of his body tear away with each blow and then being left to die with the rats. He had no idea where he was or how he got there.

Jin Jaing lay on a blanket sixty feet from where King lay. His head, part of his face and most of his body were bandaged. Lee Wu was mentioned as a hero by wounded men nearby and that worried Jaing. Jin had been the only survivor of Chop-Chop's punishment holes and was discovered, partly buried, by replacement troops coming into the area vacated by officer Wu's men. Chop-Chop ordered the prisoners buried alive, but the amount of time before the attack on Sector 5 was short and the deed was only half completed.

Officer Wu spoke Cantonese, and Jin Jaing, who came from southwest China, did not. Jin misunderstood an order and in his confusion he failed to kowtow to Wu, who became enraged and ordered Jin stripped, tied and hung upside down directly over a punishment hole. Wu personally beat Jin for days with a five-foot wooden rod, taking care to aim at the most sensitive body parts. Eventually, flies matted Jin's cuts, bruises and peeling skin. When there seemed to be no life left, Wu cut the rope letting Jin fall onto his head into the hole. Chop-Chop thought it was funny and laughed while he kicked dirt from the rim and pissed over Jin's face before leaving for the front. Coming to know that Hero Wu was in a field hospital within a few feet gave Jin an opportunity to carry out a plan involving Wu's slow murder.

Jin would, of course, avoid being seen by Officer Wu, as it was possible that there was a mark on Jin's military record somewhere relating to his recent disobedience and punishment, and he did not want more trouble. Besides, Wu might recognize him. Time passed, and when Jin was well enough, a hospital assistant asked for his name.

Frightened to give his own name, Jin remembered Officer Lee Wu's runner, someone who surely had perished in the battle of Sector 5 or fighting Americans in some distant battlefield. He whispered it— *"King Poo Koo."*

Chapter Fourteen

Jin Jaing

JIN Jaing and his brother Qi came from the south of China, and both learned German and Russian from their stepfather, Rudolph Raurer, who married their mother in 1935. The Chinese could not form the letter "R," so when Rudolph suggested everyone call him Rudy Raurer, his name became Wudy Wawer and eventually just Woody. Woody left Germany for China because he no longer felt safe living there as a Swiss-German Jew. His family's machine works in Germany manufactured military rifles, ammunition and aircraft parts, and it was thought at the time that Woody living in China and drumming up business with the warlords was an ideal bit of luck. He planned for his mother and father to follow and leave Germany within five years. Meanwhile, Germany itself, he speculated, would be glad for the export business and for his Chinese connections to the various military factions.

He never knew if he would be murdered, kidnapped or even paid for his shipments of arms to a volatile warlord clientele. Woody did not like that part, but he did like that everyone fawned over him, believing he was an influential, behind-the-scenes mandarin. Guns were in high demand, and he enjoyed being wrapped with the aura of power and mystery. Woody lived for adventure, and its danger gave him a constant high, which he edged off by frequenting Shanghai's more exclusive clubs. That was how he met Jin's mother, Lily. Lily's then-husband owned a nightclub with gambling and prostitution, and she kept the books. Her husband was murdered in a turf war between gangs surging for control of the rackets in Shanghai's downtown area, and while Lily was well known, she was not equipped to run a gambling casino after the death of her husband. She needed to marry someone with connections to the warlords, and Woody wanted someone beautiful and influential. He also needed a wife who was a Chinese citizen, just in case Germany became difficult. The fact that Lily already had twin boys nine years old was of no consequence.

Lily was a good catch and a wedding was planned. A society event in those-war-threatened days was usually a gathering of risk takers, phonies, would-be politicians, the ambitious embassy types and some of the disenfranchised aristocracy from Russia. Established society itself had begun leaving the city a year before the Japanese army began creeping toward the capital. Ignoring the obvious, the new classes were oblivious to the dangers; mostly because they thought they had sufficient contacts with the Japanese that occupation would be an opportunity for wealth. Those who sought celebrity judged Lily's 1935 wedding a success.

The majority backed Chaing's armies and not the Japanese, and certainly not the Communists, whom they feared. Important people strove to expand their connections by meeting other important people, and some hedged their bets by secretly maintaining contacts with the Japanese and Communists as well.

Woody took over the twin's education and had them tutored at home. In addition, the boys worked at the office answering the telephone, typing cables and letters and handling financial arrangements. Inadvertently, they were immersed into the world of gun buyers and sellers, and by the time they were twelve years old, they knew the essential quality and caliber differences between guns, grenades and mortars. They could shoot well with all of them. One of the boys would always accompany Woody into warlord-held territories where they learned first-hand about orders, deliveries and payments, because it was something they grew up with, it was not especially exciting for the boys and they did not think much about it.

Woody knew that the Chinese battle against the Japanese would end with the Communists conquering of China, especially with a weak American president stopping his support of Chaing, the first leader to unite China. He knew that he could no longer live there. His son Jin's business trip to the southern border turned into a mistake. Mao's armies were in pursuit of Chaing Kai-shek, who was fleeing China for Formosa and taking his army with him. Jin, infatuated with a beautiful Russian girl, stayed longer than was wise and got swept into it. A Red Brigades unit caught him leaving what they considered a capitalist's home. When they investigated and learned that Jin Jaing, a Chinese, was with a *European* woman, they beat her to death with a heavy metal stove plate and dragged Jin through the streets, denouncing him as a Chaing sympathizer. Woody, his wife Lily and Jin's twin brother Qi fled. They waited to hear from Jin, but it had quickly become too dangerous. They left everything behind on the pretense that they were on a business trip and were expected to return. They disguised their intentions by traveling first to Hong Kong, which was still controlled by Great Britain, and from there to Formosa, in a fishing trawler sent from Japan. If Chaing Kai-shek's forces hadn't destroyed everything that could float as he exited China to prevent being chased or captured by Mao, Woody's family would never have made it.

With time running out and the family unable to reach Jin, little could be done for their son. But they deposited a revolver, a German Luger, travel and identification papers, instructions about the family's destination and American and German money under a doorstep at the entrance to their home. Each member of the family had previously been instructed to look there in an emergency.

After being rounded up by the Communists, Jin Jaing was drafted into the People's Army, which had already began making preparations to invade Formosa in pursuit of Chaing, an effort that was expected to take less than a year. Mao's army spent the summer building barges and boats for the coming attack. The men drank and washed in river water spilling into the nearby ocean. No one knew it at the time, but a parasite came with the water and soon tens of thousands of soldiers died from bursting bowels and fever. The invasion was aborted, and in 1950, Chairman Mao moved those weakened divisions to the North Korean border in anticipation of a full Chinese commitment to war. On arrival in Korea, Jin Jaing had the misfortune of being assigned to Chop-Chop on his first day.

Chapter Fifteen

Greetings

KING saw that Jack had a real talent for art when he produced a drawing of him lying on his cot with half his face bandaged. The caricature showed a pixie-like general propped up in a hospital bed, ordering champagne. The face emphasized King's wide-mouthed grin. It also showed a goofy bandage and exaggerated his one all-seeing eye. The picture did not project fear or authority. Instead, it exuded a good feeling, the sense of having known King from boyhood, and it brought smiles. Jack had the gift of capturing the essence of people's goodness. King saw this and decided to have a long talk with him to discuss business.

"Medic, you report to me tonight at seven o'clock," King barked loudly. "And bring a stack of those three-by-five-inch cards from the commissary and something to draw with."

"Do you want more pictures of plants and mushrooms?" Jack asked, as this was what he had done for King before.

King rose and pointed at Jack. "My orders don't need explanation, prisoner," King replied, and then turned to the small group of men who could not help overhearing. "If I order you to draw women with big tits, it is only to stimulate the men's morale. But, if the tits are too small you'll be sent to a punishment hole." He winked at the men and smiled.

Giggling, the Chinese didn't know what to make of that kind of familiarity, but they did begin thinking about women's tits.

Jumping to attention, Jack bellowed, "Yes, sir!" loudly and convincingly, making certain the superior officer and inferior prisoner relationship was observed. He knew King had difficulty acting officious, brutal, uncaring or threatening as a typical Chinese officer, so the charade was necessary. Otherwise, people would question.

When Jack arrived, King instructed him to draw selected

patients in likable poses on the cards. When each was completed, King wrote Chinese characters appropriate to each. "Wish you Were Here," "Good Fortune Today' and several Confucian proverbs. He asked patient's names and wrote them at the bottom of each card. He often signed them 'General MacArthur', which later, many thought amusing. Most of the men could not read or write but gleefully understood the importance of having someone do this for them.

"Now what?" Jack asked. "It was fun, but who's going to look at them?"

King replied. "You and I are going into the publishing business."

"What are you talking about?"

"I've given this a lot of thought; we need a ticket out of here and that takes money, right?"

Before Jack could raise questions, King took him by the arm and walked him into an outpatient ward where he presented the completed cards as gifts to those men Jack had drawn. With it came the suggestion that he would help print their family name and address on the reverse side of the card and also mail those cards through the military post. Patients looked confused, but by the third telling grins appeared. Men were amused, others surprised and some suspicious at the generosity. They passed the cards around many times before handing them back. King, as promised, sent them to their families. The demand to have one's own caricature on a card was born, and Jack, being a "famous" American artist and temporary prisoner, gave the cards added value.

King began accepting portrait appointments between five and ten o'clock every night except on Sundays, and everyone understood that there would be a three-cent charge for each sketch, which included delivery by the military post. King calculated that this activity would earn approximately $23.00 per month in American dollars, providing they averaged six drawings per hour. A big-city carpenter might make eight dollars per month working at the camp, and by that standard, Jack and King were on their way. In the beginning, a patient's price was reduced to two-cents. Soldiers paid three-cents. The cost of the cards and the post was free.

After the first month, the demand became so high that King held a sketching contest with the soldiers whose pay was less than $4 per month, offering them a $5 first prize, $3 second prize and a $1.50

third prize for artists equal to Jack. King and Jack managed five full-time artists who regularly visited hospitals and troop encampments in the district. The money attracted attention, but King easily made arrangements with key officers and political commissars for protection and for the necessary documents needed to travel between areas with his artists. The cost averaged about a third of the gross take, but King did not mind; he and Jack were putting away nearly three hundred dollars a month after expenses.

What King understood and Jack learned was that Chinese camps had phones, but not for soldiers to call home. Even if they had been available for that use, there were none anywhere in rural China where the soldiers' and patients' families might live. Communication with a family member was almost impossible, and a soldier often felt afraid to write anything that might be read by the censors. The caricature postcards, which for some reason the censors had no objection to, provided them with celebrity, a personality, contact with home, a means of personal expression and, most important, was proof to friends and family that their loved one at the front was still alive. Three cents was cheap for this service.

King introduced and charged for get well cards, birthdays were celebrated, military heroes were postured heroically, increases in rank were noted and loving pictures were created of the deceased. A hundred fifty thousand soldiers in nine divisions was a vast market without competition, so the publishing business grew enormously and where to put the money became a problem.

What King needed was some kind of banking system that took deposits in Korea or China and later transfer to a bank in either Hong Kong or Formosa. But, King had no banking knowledge or contacts with banks, and he was afraid. His false impersonation and his relationship with an American prisoner were potential problems, and there was a real risk that communist bankers, if he managed to find one somewhere, might report his deposits and transfers. Getting caught would mean death.

Jack and King did not change their life styles. They continued to dress the same, eat with the common soldier and both practiced extreme humility. King of course, was a hero officer, so he had privileges that Jack, as a prisoner, did not, and it was often difficult to protect Jack from guards and officials jealous of their prisoners' freedoms. King partially resolved this problem by obtaining a security clearance for Jack similar to that of an allied defector. In addition to these concerns, there was the real possibility that King could be transferred to another division or that Jack might disappear into the prison systems of Russia or China. With rumors running rampant, both men had reason to be anxious. Jack made learning to speak Chinese a priority.

***

Jack became familiar with captured western medical supplies and listed items monthly that would be needed. Antibiotics, disinfectants and bandages were ordered with little hope of delivery, but making such lists, in a Communist society, was equivalent to actually doing something. King also gave Jack a long list of Chinese herbs, roots, mushrooms and the like, and those items did arrive because King knew where to order because of the herbal lore and contacts he learned from his parents.

In one particular case a soldier's skin had been eaten raw by insect bites and he had horrific tear injuries to his skin and private parts. Jack had no idea what to do with his patient. While thinking about it, he noticed a room full of twenty-pound boxes of Arm and Hammer's Bicarbonate of Soda and recalled using it as an antacid after a hangover. He also knew that the alcohol in rice wine, which he had often used as a disinfectant, was dependable. Not knowing what else to try, Jack mixed the bicarbonate of soda with rice wine and stirred it into a thick paste. He cleaned the man's wounds with rice wine. He then cut and carefully stitched jagged bits of skin together and then covered the entire body with the white bicarbonate paste, applying several coats.

The new "white" man in the ward attracted the attention of other patients who were amazed at the sight. Some squinted at Jack half-believing him to be a witch doctor, in part because the Chinese were very superstitious, and spirits are depicted as being chalk white. Many jokes later, the man, who was afterwards remembered as Spirit Man by the Chinese, emerged from his near-death state with his skin scarred but still attached to his body.

The miracle of turning raw hamburger into human form made Jack's reputation as a can-do medic. Subsequently, he used the white paste or the ingredients separately to clean and disinfect the hospital areas. He also treated bad breath, bee and bug bites, bladder infections, body odor, nits, acid burns, canker sores, chicken pox, measles, heartburn, gum and dental care and various rashes. It all seemed to work, and Jack became so well-known for his white paste and rice wine treatment that patients would often pretend, in fun, to escape the "spirit maker" when he came into their wards.

Toward the end of the treatment of that badly tortured patient, Jack, for no particular reason, looked at the nametag tied to the patient's toe and was shocked to read—King Poo Koo. It described him as a runner for an officer named Lee Wu. Obviously there could not be two King Poo Koo's or two Lee Wu's in the same hospital, so Jack decided to quietly befriend this man, and began by offering him a small bag of ginger candies.

Jin Jaing saw that Jack was popular with the men, and that he was well-connected to Officer Wu, who, Jin feared, might one day recognize him from the punishment pit. Wu would have him executed, but this time for impersonating another soldier and for having escaped his previous punishment. The layers of bicarbonate of soda were a good disguise, but Jin knew he had little time. Lee Wu might not recognize or remember Jin Jaing, especially with his heavily scarred face, but he still had to die if Jin was to live, and Jack Fischer had the right access to make that possible.

Jin, now walking, but with a severe limp, asked Jack to sit with him and for an hour he described his contacts in China, Formosa and Hong Kong. Jin knew that this information could be used by Jack to denounce him as a capitalist dog, but he presented himself as a man Jack could approach for help with an escape idea. Days later, after the notion of escape had time to sit with Jack, Jin suggested he had a plan, but before he divulged the details, Jack would have to do something for him.

When asked what it was, Jin replied, "I want you to kill Officer Lee Wu."

"Why?" Jack asked in a lowered voice, glancing suspiciously at patients nearby.

"I have already talked too much about myself and I cannot tell you why I want Lee dead. If you denounce me, I will be executed and you will never escape this place, and I have heard rumors that most Allied prisoners are not going back home when the war ends." Jin paused and pointed to a life-sized poster of Mao on a wall. "They are being sent to labor camps inside China, but mostly to Russia, where you will never be heard from again. Many prisoners, I've heard, have already gone."

Jack had heard, but he did not want to believe it to be true.

"Why do you think there are Russian officers here in Korea?" Jin asked.

Jack did not reply nor did he look surprised at the question. He stared hard at Jin and left him.

After the meeting, Jin believed that Jack would indeed murder Lee Wu, and when it was over, all Jin had to do was bribe someone to have Jack shipped to Russia. When Jack was alone, he thought the chance of escape was slim, even disguised as a Russian, but he was also unnerved at the possibility of being sent to a slave labor camp. If he killed King, who was posing as Lee Wu, he would lose his only protector. Besides, there was no way to determine if Jin really had the connections he claimed, although Jack also knew that King had no outside contacts, and that Jin himself was an imposter.

In Jin's favor, Jack thought, Jin was in considerable jeopardy suggesting escape plans to an enemy soldier. Beyond that, King, Jin and Jack could easily be transferred together or separately, and if that happened, Jack's escape opportunity would be lost. Jack decided to tell King everything, for no reasons other than he liked and trusted him. King, he knew, also needed a way to disappear. They met and decided on using a ruse to flesh out who Jin Jaing was. Much depended upon it.

The plan was for King to pretend he had been murdered and for Jack to lead Jin to King's body at the hospital where there were plenty of corpses available. It would not be difficult to dress a dead man with Officer Wu's woolen greatcoat, place bandages on his face and attach a nametag to one of the toes. The real King Poo Koo would lie on an adjoining table covered with a sheet, ready to listen to Jin's reasons for wanting Officer Wu dead.

At the appointed time, less than a week after Jin's conversation with Jack, Jin was led to the hospital dead ward to witness Jack's handiwork.

Jin smiled with satisfaction as he gazed upon a corpse with a head and eye bandage.

"Jack, how did you do it?" he asked with a grin.

"Your English is pretty good," Jack replied without answering Jin's question.

"I traveled a lot and had to know it. All my family speaks English."

Jack decided to get on with the charade and smiled. "Simple, that shit likes his rice wine. I spiced it with what he thought was almond flavoring and an hour later he was convulsing. I looked after him to make sure everything worked properly and moved him here. Are you happy with the results?"

Jin reached for the dead hand he thought was Officer Wu's and felt it was cold. Satisfied, he turned to look at Jack expectantly.

"Now let's hear the story about why you wanted this man dead," Jack said. "And if you think you are leaving here without telling me, have a look around at those bodies covered beneath those sheets. One of them might rise up and kill you if I whistle."

Surprised, Jin quickly studied the bodies. None moved, but he could not be sure. He sat down at the base of the adjoining cadaver table and told the story of Chop-Chop, how Jin had been tortured and left for dead in a punishment hole, and why he adapted the name of Chop-Chop's runner, King Poo Koo. Jin was well into his story when a hand reached from under a sheet and shook his shoulder. Jin bolted to his feet and stood frozen with fright. A corpse in a sitting position grinned back at him. Confused, Jaing began backing toward the exit.

Smiling, Jack unmasked King's masquerade, by saying, "King Poo Koo, let me introduce you to the real King Poo Koo."

Jin stopped, looked carefully at Jack and the rising corpse, stooped low and made ready to attack. Jack continued to smile and raised both his hands in a peace gesture. Jin hesitated. Slowly he began to realize that he had been tricked. Jin stepped forward cautiously, extended his hand and said, "Gentlemen, my name is Jin Jaing. How did you know I was not King Poo Koo?"

Chapter Sixteen

Shanghai

AFTER three days, they met again.

"If I can get to Shanghai, my home town, traveling as King Poo Koo, perhaps as an officer of note, I could re-establish myself there as Jin Jaing. People know me. And I will see when I arrive which of my friends are still engaged in the banking system and determine if it is safe to open accounts."

"Don't you run the risk of being denounced by people you thought were your friends?" King Poo Koo asked.

"King," Jack replied, "Jin knows this and is trying to tell us that he is willing to run that risk. He could get caught and be executed as a spy, which of course might implicate us. We're all taking a chance here."

King thought a moment and then said. "You cannot leave here and return to your home using the name King Poo Koo. Eventually, some political commissar will look into that file and discover that the real King Poo Koo and his mother were not exactly glorified Communists. It is too risky, especially if we are seen as your friends. Once you are gone, Jack will remove that name from hospital records, and since you haven't already been sent back to your division, it is unlikely the name King Poo Koo exists anywhere else. Therefore, you will travel as Jin Jaing."

Jin asked, "How do we explain why Jin Jaing has been missing for all this time?"

"Easy," Jack answered. "Temporary identification is commonly issued in the hospital; especially in cases where the patient is unconscious or shell shocked. I would guess thirty percent of the casualties here are without identification. Jin, you didn't arrive here from the front; replacement troops discovered you in a hole and brought you here without knowing who you were. Anyone who might have known you from your old regiment is dead."

King agreed. "Jin must go to Shanghai with me as my assistant; I will go as Officer Wu, on the pretense of purchasing supplies for the division and prisoner camps. I can arrange all of that, but you will not come back here. Instead, I will make it appear that you have been transferred, maybe to the Russian border where no one will ever look for you. Jack will make up an extra identification tag with your name on it. If something unexpected comes up, he can attach it to a fresh corpse to prove your demise."

King paused and spoke while making notes. "Somehow we need to get you to Hong Kong where you might find a way for Jack and me to establish ourselves."

"My family," Jin replied, "are likely in Formosa. Getting there would be impossible now, even though I would pass very close to it en-route to Hong Kong. My family trades with Hong Kong and might arrange to make that possible with good documents, or failing that by smuggling you out."

King looked at Jin and thought, *This guy could slip away without being any help to us. Why should we trust him with our money?*

Jin noticed the unspoken questions forming on King's brow and replied, "Under a step at my old house in Shanghai there is a box buried. After I was drafted into the army, my family also thought they might be forced to leave China quickly and for that reason they took the precaution of hiding foreign passports and currencies, pistols, lists of contacts throughout China, Hong Kong and elsewhere, loose gemstones, some gold coins and gold wire. When we get there you can help dig up the box and are welcome to anything in it."

King, cautiously surprised, said, "Hmm. We will leave here in five day's time. I will be back here within three weeks, and you hopefully will be out of China by then. Jack and I will give you twelve thousand dollars for initial deposits, and the money will be for all of us in equal portion in more than one bank."

"That's pretty generous—I accept," Jin replied.

King continued. "Every seven days thereafter, we will deposit additional sums averaging approximately three thousand dollars. Lastly, we must be able to make these deposits from anywhere in China or Manchuria by courier. Do you think you can do all of that?"

"Yes," Jin replied. "I think there are several possibilities. The Indian banks have branches nearest to these borders, but the German and Russian banks are in the big cities and may be more useful in other ways. The way this will work is our deposits will be made using the local Chinese currency, but we will be given credits in foreign accounts in other currencies that accept Chinese money. The bank managers that I know will want ten percent of our money credited to them personally, in cash, as facilitators, before our deposits are recorded, plus there will be the normal bank charges. Foreign banks, and in particular European banks, have been doing this kind of thing for the elite within the Communist party for some time."

Jack and King nodded agreement. The men rose to leave, but in parting, Jack took Jin aside and asked him if he would contact his girlfriend in California, if ever that were possible, to let her know that he was still alive. He handed him the little four-leaf clover pendant.

"She will know I am alive when she sees this. I will also give you a letter and a sketch of myself." Jin wrote down the information and promised he would try. Jack felt he meant it, and his heart soared at the thought of Babe learning that he was alive.

It had been six years since he'd seen Babe.

Jack and King hid their cash in two ways—under the camp railroad ties and in boxes suspended beneath the officers' outhouse seats. Deposits were given numbers corresponding to the numbers on nearby rail yard switches. If a switch bore a number—say P189, and ran south and north, the coded reference would be P189W21S—this meant a money box was buried on the west side of the track, twenty-one rail ties south of switch 189. Toilet deposits were referred to as major one, two and so on. Some money was entrusted to a small group of men who had the responsibility of collecting money at artist events, paying bribes and acting as buffers between King and Jack and prison guards. These men collected and kept four percent of the total and became distribution captains. It would be these men who would make weekly deposits by direction when the time came.

It was decided that Jack would be in charge of all activities while King was gone, and that he would recruit help to lessen his medical responsibilities, preferably with allied prisoners. Before leaving, King introduced Jack to a Chinese intelligence officer assigned to the Russian military contingent, named Chin Xion. In exchange for access to the Russians, King paid him handsomely in money and young girls from nearby villages. Chin Xion would be the contact to reach King if anything unexpected arose. Chin also had access to both telex and telephone, which could be used sparingly, and he could provide Jack with travel papers within the POW camp system and Chinese Army camps. Near the camp entrance, during a howling storm, the men hugged, as Jin and King left for Shanghai.

***

They expected Shanghai to be crawling with troops, guards and road barriers, but no one prevented them from walking around the city quite freely; the war, as far as the people were concerned, was confined to Korea. Two week's time had been allotted to establishing bank accounts, retrieving the buried box at the Jaing residence, purchasing supplies for the base, taking passport photos and working out an escape plan for Jin. The pictures were completed at a coin-operated photo booth near the train station, but banking arrangements slowed when Jin learned that many old friends had been sent to re-education camps. However, the Warburg Bank, a German institution that had done business with Jin's family for decades, provided the necessary accounts. It also facilitated transfer accounts at the Bank of India that boasted of branches in China, Manchuria and Hong Kong. That business done, they headed for the buried box.

The old Jaing residence was in an exclusive area that was ideal for confiscation for Communist leaders, and most had security guards protecting their perimeters. Large trees lined the streets and surrounded the property, which made watching the house less conspicuous. No guards patrolled the grounds, but hiding behind trees, watching who came or went from the house, was proving to be too time consuming and they risked being discovered.

Jin, thinking out loud, said, "King, you're dressed like a military officer, go up to the front door and ask for me. Whoever answers the door will say that I don't live there anymore, but you will demand a search of the premises claiming Jin Jaing is wanted for desertion. You will get an idea of how many people are inside while I watch the street. If anyone approaches the house, I will break the side window on that car on the street and blow its horn."

"Good thinking," King replied. "Let's get going."

After ringing the bell, King stood away from the door. Anyone opening it would step out to see who was there. A middle-age manservant stepped out and King quickly won entry into the house after a brief discussion on the porch. Fifteen minutes later, King reported to Jin that the man was alone, but that the master of the house was expected within the hour. King suggested that he himself return to the house for a more detailed search of the basement area while Jin used an iron bar to pull the step boards and recover the box that was buried there. They agreed, and King disappeared inside again.

Jin had just pried the box loose from beneath the bottom step of the main entrance and was walking back toward the tree line when an open car with driver suddenly approached the house. Jin was too far from the street to reach the parked car's horn in time, and he would easily be seen re-crossing the driveway at the front of the house. Frantically, Jin ran back and broke open the box and reached for the nine millimeter German Luger pistol. He slapped a bullet magazine into it just as King was opening the front door preparing to leave. Jin recognized the uniformed officer in the car as a trusted friend and servant of the Jaing family, named Henry Gong. In that instant, Jin understood how his family had been compromised to the Communists. The driver who followed Henry Gong after parking the car he did not know.

Remembering how his family had treated Gong and his family for many years, Jin was outraged at seeing this obvious traitor. Without a second thought he raced to the front, but as he came up the walkway, Henry spun around, recognized Jin and tried reaching for his pistol. Before it cleared the holster, Jin pulled the trigger of his Luger, but without success. Jin was helpless. Henry, shocked and confused, saw his opportunity, but he and his driver were slow to act. Before they could complete the draw and fire at Jin, King had leaped forward like a tiger and savagely killed both with the only thing he could find near the entrance, a hammer.

King and Jin dragged the bodies inside the house and while Jin changed into Henry's uniform, King searched the house and found the servant hiding in a pantry. He tied the man's hands and asked him where Henry Gong kept his papers and money. Fearing for his life, the servant guided King to what turned out to be quite a lot of money, some very old jade pieces and a current passport enabling Henry Gong to travel to Hong Kong, Tibet and India.

"This is a miracle," Jin half whispered to King in awe. "We've got everything we need."

"I take it this Gong guy was with your family for a long time?" King said.

"Unfortunately we trusted him. He practically raised me and my brother."

"Why do you think it was him who denounced you and your family?"

"Well, we'd thought he'd joined the Communist party to insulate himself from its threats and abuses and to provide information to my father. His having this house proves they rewarded him for exemplary deeds, and I really don't need to know anymore than that."

"I agree," King said. "He would not have reached for his gun when he saw you if he was still your friend."

It took several hours to paste Jin's photo into Henry's passport.

King, acting as driver, drove the uniformed Jin Jaing to the Shanghai airport in Henry's car where he purchased a round-trip ticket to Bombay. Jin reasoned that it would have been suspicious to leave China with a one-way ticket. Before leaving, Jin promised to make arrangements for King's and Jack's escape from China.

Jin took with him one pistol, most of the German and American currencies, a blank British passport and all of the jade. The Chinese currency was no longer of value to Jin, so King kept that, the gold coins and wire, the rest of the foreign money, two guns found in the box and two from the dead men. He needed only one for himself, but the other pistols would command a good price. He also decided to keep Henry's and his driver's identification cards, hoping they might prove useful.

King said goodbye as he saw Jin pass through the passenger gates. He waited outside the airport entrance, like a chauffeur expecting a dignitary to arrive, and kept the motor running in case Jin was unable to board the Bombay flight and was forced to make a run for it. After waiting fifteen minutes past the departure time, King drove himself near the train station, abandoned the car and headed back to camp. Before Jin and King left the prison camp they had created a message system with Jack that used any Bank of India telex machine to send a coded transmission. If King received confirmation for orders or quotes for goods by a telex with Bank of India origination identification, he would know that Jin had something to say. If a telex arrived from the same bank, but from the Hong Kong office, King would know that Jin was wherever the cable originated. If King moved somewhere unexpectedly, he could originate a message to the Bombay branch of the Bank of India where it had prior instructions to forward it to Jin.

Chapter Seventeen

Zo Wu
1953

SINCE Jack's arrival at the POW camp three years before, he had seen Chinese soldiers sent down into North Korea in a steady stream. Replacements came and went, and camp personnel largely stayed the same. King, long returned from Shanghai, coexisted with the military. Jack became a genuine healer. Jin had been gone for over a year without word. But King and Jack's deposits were routinely accepted into Russian, German and Indian banks.

After returning from Shanghai, King arranged to be promoted to Colonel in charge of POW camp supplies and other needs for the military district. He also received a great deal of mail relating to that business, and both Jack and he opened it together. During those three years Jack learned Chinese and some Russian. He handled correspondence when King was away. One day Jack opened a letter addressed to Officer Lee Wu and signed by someone claiming to be Wu's brother, Zo. The letter requested Lee, now a hero with presumed influence, to write a letter to Zo's commanding officer requesting Zo's transfer to Lee's regiment. Neither Jack nor King knew anything about Lee Wu having a brother, but the one thing certain: Zo had to be prevented from ever arriving at camp and exposing King as his imposter.

Jack thought about it and decided to ask Captain Chin Xion to write a letter to Zo's commanding officer requesting a copy of his military and Communist party records. The letter's emphasis would appear as an inquiry into Zo's patriotism. When the information came back, Captain Xion provided it to Jack in exchange for six month's salary. Xion's grandparents died in Communist re-education camps two years before his arrival at camp, and he would have done

Jack's favor without the money, but Jack always insisted, and both would generally end their conversations jokingly with "Hey! It's for educational purposes."

The information in the file was extensive; it showed that Zo had no surviving family other than his brother Lee Wu, who was mentioned in the file as being a hero. There were entries suggesting a willingness to become involved in capitalist ways. Several offers of bribes to fellow comrades were noted along with a mention of trading in contraband American cigarettes. He had also been investigated for prostituting collective farm women. Most damning was an underscored entry: "Living in an apartment without sharing space with others. This guy obviously has connections." Mention was made of Zo's father, who had worked as a custom house agent for Chaing Kai-shek's government, implying Zo's loyalty was suspect, unlike his brother Lee, who cultivated higher-ups easily. A driving permit had been issued, which was unusual in a country with few automobiles, but he had become a card-carrying Party member on recommendation from high up, and they too were listed. No picture was included.

***

The Chinese army had pushed the Allied forces back toward the 38th parallel where the war had begun. Communist forces did not have the power to re-invade South Korea because their troop losses exceeded three hundred thousand. The Allies gained strength on the ground and frequently made deep incursions north of the parallel, often behind Chinese lines. They also controlled the eastern and western Korean coastlines with a powerful unopposed navy, and they dominated the air over the battlefields.

Both sides were weary of war, and pauses for negotiations offered hope for its end. A truce was finally held, with opposing armies separated by a buffer zone. Prisoners of war were exchanged, but not fully; more than one hundred thousand, mainly Chinese POWs, refused to be returned to China. The Allies saw this as a propaganda victory, but they were also sympathetic, especially so after recalling the forced repatriation of hundreds of thousands of Russian Cossack POWs, who committed suicide rather than be shipped back to the Soviet Union after World War II. A suspicious Stalin feared that their return might provide the basis for a counter-revolution, and he had them murdered or enslaved upon arrival in Russia. Press accounts of their fate stirred political storms among the Allies for having been facilitators of their murder, and they did not want to repeat that experience.

The Chinese would not agree to their soldiers not being returned to China, as that would imply to a world press that the Communist paradise was not a worthy homeland. China's Foreign Minister, Cho En-Lai, it was learned, had already signed an agreement with Stalin on September 19, 1952, to send twenty percent of captured Allied soldiers into Chinese labor camps and eighty percent into Russian slave labor camps. Many POWs had already been transported, and they could not round those men up for an exchange without exposing the slave camps.

Communist negotiators at first denied the existence of more than twelve thousand American and Allied prisoners, claiming death from wounds, voluntary defections to the glorious cause and the inability to be accurate about such matters in a war-torn countryside. Negotiations concluded with a percentage of Chinese POWs remaining in South Korea, eventually defecting to Formosa. Meanwhile, as settlement, the almost twelve thousand Allied prisoners still in Chinese Communists hands were distributed. Ninety percent were transferred to the Soviet Union and the rest rotted in China's labor camps, never to be seen again.

The Russians wanted both North Korean and Chinese prisoners to be sent to China to disappear. The Soviet Union could not allow word to reach its Warsaw Pact forces in Europe that troop defections to the West entailed nothing more than raising hands in surrender. For that reason, the bulk of Chinese POWs, who either refused or volunteered, were executed upon arrival to set an example, because they had been exposed to Western culture and were a liability to Communism.

It was probably a fair arrangement, considering that Russia supplied China with guns, tanks and ammunition and also provided the planes and pilots to pursue the war, so China sending thousands of Allied POWs to Russia would only be a small part of China's gratitude. The defenders of democracy also felt the bargain was expedient because elections were brewing in America and the Korean War was unpopular. Incumbents needed to claim success for bringing the war to an end. A final truce, without too many questions being asked about prisoners, was good politics. It was understood that resolution of the prisoners' issue would be kept secret by both sides.

Shortly after the POW exchange following the truce agreement, some American politicians, protesting the prisoner's abandonment, would prove to be no match for a slick cover-up by an administration swept to power on the basis of bringing the war to an end. Senator Joe McCarthy knew the truth and when he screamed at his fellow senators to "Give me a division of Marines and I'll go in there and get them out myself," the press printed outrageous headlines, "McCarthy to Invade China," "McCarthy, Power Mad." He was ridiculed instead of praised or listened to, and afterward the POW issue was safely buried.

***

King was in Harbin, Manchuria, buying camp and military supplies when news of the truce reached him; he hurried back to camp two weeks before he was due because he knew everything would change rapidly. Chinese military units would be returning home, prisoners of war would be repatriated. King and Jack might be assigned somewhere else and assets had to be gathered to affect an immediate escape for both. Before leaving Harbin, King sent a message to Jin at the Hong Kong branch of Bank of India, pleading for urgent action.

A day later, a message arrived: *"Confirming our order for dried red peppers and down feathers per previous telex. Please have shipment dockside at Nampo harbor, North Korea, October 28. Contact AA Pasha Company freight and customs agents there for documents. Make your remittances to the attention of Bombay Pacific Trading Partners: Mr. Vaswami. No reply needed. JJ."*

It took King six days to return to camp. Rail traffic had become impossible. Several times he bribed officials for a seat, but military traffic had priority and he did not want to test the pedigree of his officer's papers.

When Jack heard about the truce, instead of being cheered by it, he was frightened; too much was transpiring. What would happen to him now? Chinese troops were moving out of the area, Russians were becoming scarce and prisoners were being grouped into work-related categories, which was not consistent with being released. Jin and King were gone, new officers poured into the camps and Jack was genuinely scared he would be swept away, without a trace, toward another hell hole. Or if he were blessedly lucky, a bus back to Allied lines. The waiting uncertainty and fear wore at him.

King had been gone for twenty days and was not expected back for another three weeks. Worse, Lee Wu's brother, Zo, showed up two weeks after King left camp and demanded to be assigned to King's tent while he waited for his brother to return.

Jack was taken by surprise when Zo Wu barged into King's tent, but after a shaky start, Jack gathered his wits and explained that his brother would be back in two weeks. He then outlined some of the activities that Jack managed when Officer Lee Wu was away. Zo listened intently and was particularly interested in the part about the procuring of girls for important officers.

Zo, with a fake smile, studied Jack. "You are a useful fellow, aren't you?" he said. "I'm surprised my stupid brother had the sense to keep you around."

"Well, the war won't last forever and I try to be objective," Jack replied, wondering how he could influence the man.

Zo yawned and replied, "Look, I arrived here with no money—can you arrange for a small loan from my brother? I will pay him back when I see him."

"How much do you need?"

Zo, thinking fast, said, "I've got three months back pay coming—they owe me that."

Jack knew that a low-level officer earned far less than twenty dollars a month, and replied, flattering Zo with a presumption of higher rank in the process, "Major Wu, I will take care of the matter for you and return here in two hours. Will that be satisfactory?"

Zo was no Major, but he liked Jack thinking he was. "Yes, go now and let me rest."

"Did you just arrive here from the Russian border?" Jack asked, standing near the tent exit flap. "Your brother told me all about you."

"I have not been on the border for six months, but I managed to spend time in Shanghai and also in my hometown before coming here. Why?"

"Well," Jack replied. "I thought if you had been on the border for a long time you might need some female company. But, since you haven't been at the border for six months I won't bother with that."

Grinning with expectation, Zo laughed falsely, thinking of his smuggling activities at the border. "Consider me a border rat. Now get the hell out of here."

Jack left and returned two hours later with one thousand Yuan,

Chinese dollars, and handed it to Zo. "I am sorry this is all that was available on short notice, but I will manage the rest in a few days' time. I hope that will be alright, Sir?"

The blood drained from Zo's face. He could not believe his luck. *A thousand dollars!* he thought. *Why, that's more than three year's pay.* Privately, he also began to think of ways to take over this operation from his nitwit brother. *Imagine the luck of that jackass running into a jewel like Jack.*

Turning his back to Jack, trying to pretend that the money was not enough, Zo replied, "Yes, that will do for now. Incidentally, can you arrange for my uniform and boots to be repaired and cleaned? I'll need them tomorrow."

"Yes sir," Jack replied. "Put everything into your canvas bag and I will arrange for it to be done. You can wear your brother's things until I return."

Jack left the tent and raced over to the Korean prisoner's compound with Zo's bag and talked hurriedly to a trusted fellow prisoner.

"Kim," Jack pleaded. "I need the most important favor of my life and you are the only one who can do it."

"What is it, Yankee?"

"This uniform and everything in the bag must be cleaned like new by tomorrow."

"That's a life-time favor?" he asked sarcastically.

"No! Now listen carefully. I will bring some things that I want you to sew into the lining of the uniform and in the duffle bag; also I want to put something inside the soles of his shoes."

"Okay! When you coming back?"

"I'll be back before midnight."

At eleven o'clock, Jack met Kim and together they began the work. The American hundred dollar bill that King had found in Lee Wu's Little Red Book he slid into the uniform lapel and stitched it closed. Jin Jaing's military identification was placed between layers of shoe leather. Henry Gong's driver identification, a map of Shanghai showing a circle around the Jaing residence, and two thousand Chinese dollars were sewn into the leather end of the duffle bag. Finally, inside the hatband were directions leading to a money cache beneath a railroad tie inside the camp, and with that were contact names in Formosa.

Kim pretended to be amused, but he fully understood what Jack was doing. "I would have done this for free, but thanks for gold coin anyway."

Jack personally delivered the uniform in the morning. When he entered the tent he found it reeking of booze, and there was blood on the cot. He shuddered at what might have happened to the girl he had sent there. Silently he cursed into Zo's flabby pockmarked face.

"Good morning, Sir!" Jack beamed. "Did everything go well for you last night?"

Zo shrugged indifference. "She was a bitch. Drop that stuff over here and get out. I've got to get some sleep."

That day, an officer sent Jack to army headquarters ten miles away from camp to look after the pregnant "wife" of a general who had studied in America and trusted western science. In particular, he trusted a prisoner of war who would understand that the woman being treated was not his wife. Those duties took Jack almost four days. It was routine enough, but he worried that things back in camp might be chaotic, especially with Zo charging around. *What if King comes back early,* grated on Jack's mind.

When he returned, he discovered that King had arrived early and Zo had him arrested as an imposter. When Jack entered the tent he saw Zo sitting on a cot looking pleased.

"What's going on?" Jack asked. "Where is everybody?"

"That little cross-eyed rat didn't fool me and probably killed my brother. Tried to impersonate him. What a joke. Anyway, don't let that worry you. We will do business without that scum. You look after me and I look after you."

Jack protested. "What will become of him?"

"They will wait a couple of days—let him think about his crimes, maybe squeeze his balls a little—and when the truth comes out—bang—bang!"

Pretending to be impressed, Jack said, "Good work, Zo. We're going to be partners? That will be interesting."

"We'll talk about it later and don't forget the money for the rest of my pay. Now get out."

Dismayed, Jack pretended agreement and hurried back to his quarters to think. Visiting King in the stockade, for a POW, was not possible. He thought hard to find a way or someone he could get to pass a message inside, but no one came to mind. Sweating profusely, he decided to drop in on a friend.

"What do you need, Jack?" asked a smiling Chin Xion. He had heard about the arrest but did not risk an early visit until he heard from Jack.

"I've got this little problem with our friend and I think I have an idea how to solve it," Jack replied. "I need a telex from any Shanghai authority addressed to you that seeks information on a Jin Jaing in connection with a double murder in that City."

"Come on Jack, why do you need something like that?"

"Because that man, Zo Wu, who denounced our friend as an imposter is actually Jin Jaing the murderer. I remember treating him two years ago in this camp."

Chin replied cautiously. "How do *you* know about murders in Shanghai?"

"When our friend, the real Lee Wu, came back from Shanghai several months ago, he mentioned it was a big story. One of the victims was a party bigwig named Henry Gong. A Chaing Kai Shek agent was suspected of the murders because the killing took place in what had been the old Jaing residence. It was apparently in the papers. Don't you think it's strange that a Jin Jaing is in our camp and is the one who denounced our friend?"

"How do you know his name is Jin Jaing?"

"He gave me the name of Zo Wu, but when he asked to have his shoes repaired. I took them to Kim at the laundry; he found Jin Jaing's identification hidden between the soles. Kim asked me what to do about it. I told him to sew it up and forget it."

"Wow, that's pretty straightforward, Jack. Why not just let one of the officers know about it? Okay, I'll do it. But—well—is Lee Wu—is he really who we think he is?"

"I'll gamble this little stack of gold coins that he is. You want to hold the bet?"

"You'd better be right or my ass will..."

Jack interrupted, grinning, "What are friends for?"

***

Captain Xion "received" the cable from Shanghai, although it wasn't easy to arrange, and he promptly notified the military authorities. Zo was arrested and his possessions were searched. Overwhelming evidence emerged proving him to be a spy and a murderer. An unissued pistol was found under his cot. Viewed together, with the papers found in his shoes identifying him as Jin Jaing, Zo Wu's screamed denials failed to help him. The one thousand dollars Jack had given him was beyond explanation and his possessing it automatically made him guilty of economic crimes.

Jack was called to headquarters and asked if he had given Zo the money. Jack pretended fright and denied any involvement. "I am a prisoner of war with no money and no possessions. If I had a thousand dollars, I damn sure would not have given it to a complete stranger!" The camp commander agreed with that logic and released Jack to his barracks.

Zo was spending a lot of time trying to convince the authorities that he was not an agent sent from Formosa, but being suspected of being a foreign agent meant that he soon would be having *his* balls squeezed.

King looked terrible. He had cigarette burns all over his face and stomach, shadows under his eyes and he was limping from rods placed behind his knees and let to hang upside down. He had not been allowed to sleep. He was beaten repeatedly for three straight days and hollered mightily, but it did no good. He would gladly have confessed if it could have saved him the punishment, but his confession would have resulted in death. He had no choice other than to continue being an imposter and hope for the best. Upon release, incredibly, the army issued him a new uniform. They placed it on him, gave him an enthusiastic salute and carried him back to his tent. It was their clumsy way of reinstating a hero.

King tearfully hugged Jack with all of his might and said again and again how he marveled at Jack's ingenuity. Jack had saved his life and King was grateful, but it was time to head north to meet a ship that would take them both out of Korea and on to Hong Kong. They had to leave immediately.

King explained to Jack. "In China you don't get a trial like you do in America. Here it is up to you to prove you're innocent, but after a couple days of torture you confess to any crimes. Our problem with Zo," King continued, "is that he will confess and maybe someone will believe him. If that happens we need to be very far away from here."

The following day, King and Jack collected everything that

could be packed. An ambulance took them and their possessions to the camp's train station, compliments of Captain Xion. Just as King completed loading everything on board, four soldiers took Jack aside. A heated discussion was under way when King strutted over, like the officer he was, and demanded to know what authority they had to hold a POW doctor under his command.

"There are two trains leaving this platform beginning with that one over there," one soldier replied, pointing to a steam belcher on the far track. "All prisoners of war are being evacuated from this camp today and our job is to round them up. If you have a complaint, take it up with the Russians."

King, surprised, demanded, "The Russians? Why the Russians?"

The soldier shrugged. "Because everyone in this camp will be leaving on trains destined for Khabarovsk—that, Sir, is Russia."

King asked if he could talk to Jack privately before he was taken away. "Do whatever you want," the soldier replied, "but that train leaves in ten minutes and we are right over there."

Jack overheard and when King pulled him aside, he said, "I'm scared. I've heard about Siberia. No one comes back. What am I going to do about my girlfriend Babe?"

"I know, I know, Jack, but I don't have any idea what can be done about it."

Silence followed. Jack nervously replied, "King, if you get out of here and meet up with Jin, will you ask him to keep his promise to me about finding my girlfriend and letting her know I'm still alive?"

King's voice, choking to a whisper, wavered.

"You are my dearest friend. I will never forget you. My life is yours, I will do everything in my power to find you and—somehow—I will get you out, no matter where you are. Jin, you and me are brothers forever. Your girlfriend *will* be found and you *will* escape. I, King Poo Koo, personally pledge that *you will live*, no matter what the circumstances, because deep in your soul you will know that *we will move mountains* to keep our promise."

Tears streamed down both their faces. Before the train pulled out, King asked Jack to pick anything he wanted from the valuables, but understanding that he would be searched often, Jack reached for the small packet of gemstones that could be swallowed and be safe for short periods. With teeth clenched, King watched Jack being escorted to a column of prisoners waiting to board the train, a sight that crushed his heart and burned his belly.

Chapter Eighteen

Presumed Dead

WHILE the war in Korea raged, Babe prayed daily, often hourly, that Jack was alive. She wrote the War Department, the Marine Corps, the president of the United States and anyone else who could shed light on how it was determined that Jack Fischer was "missing," and what the basis was for the words "presumed dead." A truce stopped the war, prisoners were exchanged, but Jack was not among them. Some Marines, including a captain who was with Jack's company when he was captured, came to San Francisco to visit his family. These men were upset about the loss of life at Kojo—37 dead out of the original 117. They were also disturbed that prisoners like Jack were not repatriated, especially because rumors abounded that thousands of POWs were not returned home, that the American government knew about it and that it was not willing to risk continued war to demand their return. Officially the U.S. government denied the prisoners existed, and later when it did acknowledge that there *might* have been a few defectors, few believed it.

It was unheard of for people in North Beach to protest against the Federal Government, but that did not stop those who were outraged over the president's lack of response. POW protests were also stifled by Senate hearings in Washington concerning *Un-American Activities*. But Jack's mother, Rosemary, didn't care and was quick to become involved with prisoner-of-war groups protesting the government's unwillingness to act. In spite of demonstrations throughout America, the government stonewalled every attempt. One group called the Fighting Homefolks of Fighting Sons held a protest rally in Washington D.C. that received substantial press coverage. Government action did follow, but not the kind anyone expected. The FBI began visiting the organizers; Babe, Rosemary and Jack's brother Bob were taken separately to an FBI office in San Francisco for questioning about their anti-American activities and Communist sympathies. They were warned that an arrest would follow if they continued. The FBI also threatened to list Jack as a defector if the protests did not stop. Anti-Communist feelings had already swept America, and many people, guilty or not, were rounded up, held for questioning or became part of Washington's show trials.

Rosemary and Babe were frightened into inactivity and into waiting for their government to do the right thing. Neither wanted Jack falsely arrested, if he ever returned.

PART THREE

Chapter Nineteen

Tianna
1958

BABE moved in with her friend Tianna in 1955 after her father had left for Italy. She worked as a typist, doing general office work, and she was also employed at Blum's pastry and confection counter. She attended night school and learned to operate an Elliot Fischer electric calculator and a bookkeeping machine, and during her spare time she and Tianna made their own clothes. They also double-dated and experimented with interesting recipes in cookbooks.

Tia, or Tara, as she liked to be called, had known Jack during the years that Babe and he were together. Tara shared bouts of grief with Babe, unavoidable when a friend's loved one was missing.

***

Tianna's father, Jean Carmelita, had left France and immigrated to America where he married Rosarita Vasquez, a visiting Mexican citizen. Jean had discovered that girls liked his accent and he decided to create his own nickname. He was single and introduced himself as Frenchy. Rosarita did not like the implication and called him Jean. They got married and she gave birth to a girl, whom they named Tianna Tara Carmelita. Three years later, Jean was found floating in the San Francisco Bay with his pockets cut off—a symbol the Italian Mafia used on those who failed to pay a debt.

Unfortunately, Jean looked a great deal like his gambling friend Lou Sabella, and when Lou called asking to meet in front of La Rocca's bar on Columbus Avenue, Jean thought nothing of it. A sedan pulled to the curb and Jean hopped in thinking Sabella was picking him up. No one paid any attention to his pleas that he had never bet on a horse in his life. Jean's subsequent *accident* had given Lou time to disappear.

Rosarita held onto the family flat working two shifts at the

Mark Hopkins Hotel as a housemaid. She managed to send Tianna to Catholic schools, where Tianna met what would become her best friend, Babe Barsi. Tianna was not a good student and had difficulty keeping up with the work. Her problem was that she was too good-looking. She had matured far too soon, and the distractions that came with that were simply too much. When Tianna turned fifteen, she would arouse unwanted attention simply walking the two blocks from her flat on Filbert Street to Washington Square.

She often walked this route because her church—Saints Peter and Paul—was on the square, and Columbus Avenue, at the bottom of Filbert, was where she shopped every day. A bronze statue memorializing San Francisco's early fire fighters on Washington Square showed a fireman posturing heroically with a hose in one hand, and with the other pointing toward the sky. Frequently, that hand was seen embracing a whiskey bottle and on occasion a condom marked with the name of a neighborhood favorite. She pretended not to notice.

The neighborhood seemed to know when Tia hit the sidewalk. She could hear men whisper under their breath, as she passed, "Here she comes. Look! Look!" "Come here, quick." "Didn't I tell you?" "Mama Mia!"

She did her best to ignore them, but the more she blushed, the more it seemed to encourage them. Women stared at her as though she were a devil breaking into their homes to steal their husbands.

Tia had a sultry, almost vulgar look that caused men to fantasize being caught in her web, if given the chance. Many thought they would gladly die for the opportunity. She could walk a straight line down Filbert Street looking like a fashion model, even dressed in a school uniform. Unconsciously, she radiated enough sexual energy to move a truckload of pizza all the way up to Coit Tower. Blonde hair with reddish tones flowed down to Tia's waist, her brown eyes were almond shaped and she had a straight nose. At a distance, her highly arched eyebrows appeared painted on, but up close they had the soft look of mink. Men were often uncomfortable when she gazed at them through her long panther-like black eyelashes, and she was tall enough to be a model. In a world that worshipped Marilyn Monroe's body, Tia was her match. Eventually she came to enjoy the daily attention, and sometimes she would wave back at her admirers.

***

Carlo Bratsi was the assistant manager at Blum's Restaurant on the Geary Street side of Macy's Department store at Union Square. Tianna's mother Rosarita had been dating him. Carlo gave in to Rosarita's request to hire her daughter as a part-time cashier and that was the start of Tia's working life.

Blum's Restaurant created and sold the finest chocolates in San Francisco. They also specialized in beautiful European-style cakes, pastries and freshly ground coffees. They had an extensive soda fountain and a lunch menu that attracted retailers, shoppers and tourists. Blum's was where San Francisco elite came to parade their latest fashion acquisitions, and also where the male clientele met to discuss business. In contrast to the hippie girls who roamed San Francisco streets, Blum's women wore hats, veils and gloves. There, high fashion, power and wealth hovered over every table, and reservations were difficult to obtain unless you knew Carlos at the front desk.

Tia worked a four-hour shift on a cash register six days a week. Fortunately, she had been provided a uniform, because the only thing she had to wear was a school uniform, jeans or shorts. The lack of nice clothing made her particularly conscious of the endless stream of elegantly dressed women. Daily, she would imagine herself wearing the beautiful clothes that she saw on others, and found herself thinking. *Damn, if I had the money for an outfit like that, I'd have worn a green silk blouse with it. She's too fat for that suit; I'd have her wearing more loosely fitted things.* She could not afford such clothes, but eventually Tia purchased a used sewing machine and learned how to use it at the local high school evening class. She was not only good at it, she became obsessed. When she was not working at Blum's, she was out shopping for materials and accessories and found that she could complete a pleated skirt in a single night.

Finally, on her next day off with her plan in place, she walked into Blum's just before noon and demanded a table near where she knew the fashion people who worked next door at I. Magnin's department store always gathered. No one recognized Tia because she had on a gray hat, a black veil, gray gloves and a crushed-velvet pearl-gray skirted suit with a forest-green silk blouse adorned with a chained cross. The successful deception pleased her. The I. Magnin people did notice her, not only because of her attire, but also because of her unusual beauty.

Tia had previously arranged for a friend to telephone Blum's and have her paged near the end of the lunch hour to draw attention to her. When the call arrived, the public address system blared, "Telephone for Madam Carr, please." She rose dramatically and approached the front desk. As she got closer, Carlo Bratsi looked her over appreciatively and got the shock of his life when he recognized Tia behind the veil. He smiled mischievously and, deciding to go along with her theatrics, handed her the telephone and spoke loudly.

"Ah! Madam, how nice to see you so soon after your trip."

She listened, aware of the I. Magnin table nearby, and spoke into the phone.

"Yes I know. You need to talk to my agent about that." Then she paused. "Yes, I'll call you, dear. Bye!"

Carlo was impressed and nearly paternalistic when he noticed that fashion buyer Mary Carter had left the I. Magnin table to approach Tia.

"I want someone like you to model an unusual line that I've been flirting with," she said to Tia. When Tia raised her eyebrows and reached in her bag to pay her bill, Mary turned and said, "I'd like to buy your lunch if you have time to talk to me for a few minutes." Tia smiled and introduced herself.

After sitting in the foyer with Mary Carter, Tia approached Carlo and said, "Let's keep this our little secret, okay?" Carlo agreed but couldn't wait to get home to tell Rosarita.

Mary Carter was a fashion buyer during a time when styles coming out of Paris and New York had a typical cosmopolitan stamp. That worked well with the I. Magnin upper-class clientele, but Mary Carter felt there was a need to lean toward the fast-spreading hippie influence. She decided that the *look*, whatever it was, needed an up-market appeal to be compatible with the store's somewhat conservative staid image. Mary asked Tia to come into I. Magnin the following Monday to try out a series of mixes and matches with the hope of finding something thematic.

She was surprised when Tia, who introduced herself as Tara Carr, arrived wearing an autumn-colored silk sari, a headscarf and a red dot on her forehead. Tia, or rather Tara, also brought a bundle of clothes that she had either made or purchased at a Salvation Army store.

"What on earth do you think you're wearing, Tara?" Mary asked, horrified.

"Something to shock you," replied Tara. "Everything that people are wearing these days is worn for its shock value. It's about rebellion, that kind of thing. If you want to compete, you must shock back."

"How?" asked Mary, wondering what was coming next.

Tara, very confident, replied. "It is just as elitist to dress down as it is to dress up. Both styles are intended to give the wearer identity with a certain group, who, for whatever reason, the wearer has deemed to be the *in* crowd."

Tara produced a garment from her bag. "See this sack-cloth monk's outfit? If I put it on and adorn it with an expensive marijuana figure hanging from a cheap hardware store neck-chain, I would definitely be *in* because I am insulting religion, flaunting marijuana laws and cheapening the upper class by wearing hardware junk as a classy medallion. Rebellion, yes, and I *will* attract attention."

"We can't make money selling junk," Mary said, with a worried look on her face.

"No," Tara said. "But I. Magnin could invite an up-and-coming Indian guru to sit on pillows upstairs on the fifth floor offering customers advice on life hereafter, yoga, the meaning of love and consultations on the latest laid-back styles. While the guru keeps busy, we do a floor-wide promotion to sell saris, scarves, jewelry, sandals, candles, silver roach holders, bongo drums, incense, Sitar music and bath oils. Furthermore, we would invite that psychedelic drug freak, Professor Ken something or other. We can also hire a couple of North Beach poets to mix with our crowd and give it a bit of authenticity."

"Our *Bottom Line* is on the fifth," Mary chimed, her eyes brightening. "I can just see it."

Tara, pleased with herself, looked at Mary and said, "If I had drifted through Blum's dressed and perfumed like I am today, people would stare and they would wonder if I were scum dressed up like a Hippie or Mrs. Got-Rocks flirting with the new culture. The key is I would attract attention and that means women will buy what attracts people to look at them. If you doubt what I am saying, think back at your reaction when I walked in here. You were shocked—admit it—and you like it."

"You are right," Mary replied. "I want you to help me put together a range of saris and other Bohemian gear, and then I want you to model the line for our buyer's meeting, that's in ten days time. Can you do it?"

"That and more." Tara smiled. "I thank you for your confidence in me."

Tara gave notice to Blum's. She would now be working full-time for I. Magnin, earning the enormous sum of thirty-five dollars a day.

The buyers at first greeted Mary Carter's counter-culture ideas with contempt, and Mary thought she might have gone too far, but there were two things working for her. First, the corporate bean counters next door at Macy's were discussing ways to transform that location, then the San Francisco version of London's Harrods department store. They wanted to change it into a jeans-filled emporium of low-end buyers plowing for cheap goods with a patina of Macy's class. Second, fashion experts from all over the country and Europe, had already made fashion suggestions to I. Magnin. None had instilled an iota of enthusiasm.

Everyone at the buyer's meeting understood that Macy's plunging into jeans would spell the end of Macy's as they knew it, and that Blum's, on the main floor, might also disappear. But, I. Magnin needed to flirt with new lines to compete against a transformed Macy's just in case they succeeded. The buyers had nothing to put forward, and it was Mary's neck on the line, not theirs. For those reasons, after watching with some distaste as Tara displayed her line, they gave Mary their approval.

***

It took a frantic six weeks to get the Fifth Floor organized. Artist-drawn signs thematically and suggestively advertised areas of the floor: 'Christmas Is Coming' had several possible interpretations, while 'Get Down and Grab a Little Peace' had sexual overtones. Sitar music competed with Janis Joplin for the background. Gurus mumbled their way through the aisles, staff were dressed like refugees from the Haight-Ashbury hippie colony and the perfume counter was renamed the 'Drug Store', which is where exotic teas, incense, scented candles, bath oils and the like were featured. Fashion shows strutted their stuff at eleven in the morning and at two-thirty in the afternoon. Both were packed with the curious. People bought like crazy.

Tara herself modeled a gold-flecked white sari with a see-through blouse worn without a bra, and it did not take long for the ladies to see the potential for the new look. Later, she slithered down the walkway in a sackcloth skirt closed with an oversized clothesline clip to hold it in place. On her feet she wore sandals with bells. The peasant blouse Tara had chosen for this outfit was not only worn bra-less but with a beaded necklace that covered the vital spots every now and again as she walked.

Jerry Bunsen dropped by and was so impressed that the Chronicle Newspaper's Herb Caen column ran with it. *"Customers are bouncing off the ceiling on I. Magnin's Fifth Floor, with psychedelic gear."* It bellowed to its trendy readers. *"You got to see it to believe it."*

It was a huge success, and Tara was flown to Los Angeles to set up a similar program for another I. Magnin store. Before leaving Sarah Schlosberg, a San Francisco society matron, and a patron of the arts who sat on every worthwhile charity board, casually asked if Tara could suggest something she could wear to the opening night of the opera. Surprised, Tara studied her, and turned Sarah around slowly.

"Let me have a look at you," Tara said as she ushered her into a fitting room to take her measurements. She studied Sarah in the mirror and decided to take the plunge.

"You are obviously very brave to even think of dressing down for the opera, so I've decided to create something for you that no one has ever seen before—and believe me it will knock their socks off. Are you willing?"

Sarah Schlosberg, the queen of San Francisco's high society, didn't hesitate. "Can you have it ready by the end of the month?"

"Yes," Tara replied. "Here is my card, call me for a fitting in ten days."

Just thinking about doing the outrageous, Sarah left the floor with a look of anticipation and jubilation spreading across her face.

***

Puccini's La Bohème will never be the same after tonight, Sarah Schlosberg thought, as her chauffeur opened the rear door of her Bentley at the Opera House entrance. Regally, with her chin tilted upward toward the grand entrance, she paraded slowly down a red-carpeted aisle, past the glowing eyes of her contemporaries wearing the most exquisite ensembles. The press did not let her get that far; cameras, including television, held her captive.

Sarah wore a wide A-line princess-style skirt that flowed as she walked. It was a patchwork design with swatches of raw silk with predominantly orange tones highlighted by blues, yellows and reds. Gold rope hemmed her skirt and circled her waist. For a purse, she dangled a small chamois bag on her wrist. The gypsy-style, short-waisted bolero-style jacket, created from black-velvet trimmed with gold rope, was fitted at the front with crudely hammered gold buttons. A pale-green, see-through chiffon blouse, showing high on the collar, with long billowing sleeves hinting at Russian couture, was not only gorgeous, but also shockingly revealed ample breasts moving provocatively beneath. For jewelry, she wore a thin black hardware-store chain, wound three times around her neck and linked between her breasts by a small old-fashioned sink faucet.

"*Sarah turns them on at gala affair,*" led the Chronicle's society column. "*Making her entrance, Grand Dame Sarah Schlosberg stunned even Count Brownstein with an ensemble from new designer about town Tara Carr.*" Tara would soon have others clamoring for her attention.

Chapter Twenty

Peter Mattioli
1959

BABE had worked in offices as a typist in the years after Jack had left, but the pay was poor, it was boring and it was a dead end. She had wanted Jack to be proud of her, and wanted to live decently. So she borrowed the $46 dollars needed to enroll in an eight-week course learning to use the Elliot-Fisher bookkeeping machine. The demand for operators was high and she was good at it. This finally landed her an interview and a job working for the United Scavengers Association, the primary garbage collector in San Francisco. Peter Mattioli, in an office two floors above the accounting section, was vice president. It was his job to stay on top of financial matters.

Peter was struck by his new employee's smoky good looks and it made him uneasy to walk through her department, where he often found himself staring at her. Babe pretended not to notice, but their eyes met from time to time. Peter would later squirm for hours during the night, trying to figure out why all that staring was keeping him awake. He looked eerily like Jack Fischer, but a more elegant version of him. He had that northern Italian look with wavy reddish-blonde hair, pale skin and a patrician posture. When he talked he would swirl both hands in front of him, and his body would rock backward as he glanced up at the heavens. He arched his brows whenever he made a verbal point that needed emphasis. If his head tilted sideways, it meant he was questioning something. If it tilted back, it was a tacit approval. Everything about Peter oozed class except when he opened his mouth. When he did, he finished most words, names or sentences with either "Ugh" or "Ah."

"Whatcha-doin?" he would say. "You gonna have lunch-huh? I've got-ah tickets to the Seals Baseball-ugh game next Sat-tuh-day.

You wanna-ugh go?" He was not ignorant. In fact, he had gone to college in New York, only arriving in San Francisco two years before. Babe often recoiled internally when he spoke but eventually convinced herself it was cute. Peter's father owned fifty shares in the United Scavengers Association, which in 1963 was worth one hundred sixty thousand dollars per share and represented the controlling interest. Peter owned those shares now because his father died of an unattended infection.

Peter returned to San Francisco to take responsibility for the family business just in time to rescue him from his fascination with a New Jersey branch of gangster Mickey Cohen and his infamous bookmaking operation.

Babe Barsi had never attended a live theater performance, never set foot on a yacht and she certainly never went to world-class restaurants, as Peter did, often three times a week. Although she was a little bothered at receiving expensive gifts, the whirlwind of excitement brushed those reservations aside. This was a new, never-known life being discovered by Babe and she loved it. Unfortunately, Peter was very possessive and he often questioned the details of her whereabouts when she was not with him. When other men looked at Babe, Peter would hold her arm, kiss or embrace her to create the impression that she was all his. Sometimes he unexpectedly went shopping with her, choosing her clothes.

The garbage truck drivers were non-union, shareholders in a truck assigned to a particular route. Trucks were purchased by the company and rented to the group of drivers that operated them. The men became both minor shareholders and drivers. United Scavengers had the franchise rights to pick up city garbage, and the company made certain that newly elected city officials did not abridge those rights. Part of Peter's duties was to promote his firm's interests with the Board of Supervisors, the Mayor and many of its bureaucrats and business leaders.

Campaign contributions to competing candidates and parties were expected, financial gifts were given clandestinely. Entertaining the players was routinely done with lavish restaurant dates, sports and theater tickets, exotic travel trips and access to accommodating women. Peter was a celebrity fixture at restaurants such as The Shadows on Telegraph Hill, DiMaggio's and Scoma's at Fisherman's

Wharf, Jack's, Sam's and Domino's in the financial district. He held annual tickets for The Drunkard, a play on Green Street, that had run for eight straight years, and he had box seats at the Curran Theatre. Opera and symphony tickets were sent routinely to Peter, and party invitations in Pacific Heights were weekly arrivals. If anyone wanted to see celebrity entertainers, Peter could arrange it.

United Scavengers maintained permanent suites at the Huntington and Fairmont hotels on Nob Hill, which were almost always occupied by friends in need of discreet companionship. In fact, it was at the Huntington hotel that Peter's father maintained a separate suite for his mistress, and Peter, after his father's unusual demise, decided that this was also a good downtown location for him as well. He vacated that suite, planning that Babe would move in. But she refused, even though he sugar-coated the idea with the logic that it was just sitting there going to waste and that she might as well have the use of it.

"Peter, I'm not going to be your kept woman," Babe said. "Frankly I'm surprised that you would make such an offer."

"But it's empty and it's going to waste," he pleaded.

"The answer is a definite no."

Babe went everywhere with Peter. Once, when they were at the Gold Spike restaurant on Columbus Avenue with three other couples, the chef walked off the job. Babe rose to her feet and mimicked Peter.

"I've-ah got-ah look in-a kitchen sweet-heart, won't-ah be ah long." Somewhat confused, everyone laughed, but she moved so fast that Peter and his group were left waiting. He sat there vaguely pretending that Babe did this kind of thing every now and again. Thirty minutes later, he was amazed when the dishes came out and everyone raved about them. Peter read about the incident in a celebrity column the next morning and wasn't pleased. Babe's star began to rise.

One evening, waiting for her to get ready for a date, he noticed four shelves full of cookbooks in her apartment. He pulled a Bon Appetit magazine out and without thinking paged to a Chicken Marsala recipe. When Babe came into the room he made a point of noticing her interest in cooking. "My mother used to make the exact same dish." He said, showing her the magazine page. Peter, for the first time, actually began appreciating Babe in ways he had not been aware.

A week passed, Peter stopped to pick Babe up at her apartment on the way to a quiet evening at Paoli's restaurant in the Bank of America building on Montgomery Street. He had reservations in its very exclusive Captain's Room with two rare bottles of 1948 Pommard awaiting their arrival. Peter also arranged for three-dozen gold-brushed roses to be presented to Babe as they were seated. Babe learned of the reservation because her friend Mary worked at Paoli's. Babe had made other plans.

When Peter arrived, he found that Babe's apartment glowed with scented candles, soft music and Jade perfume. He told her they were late for dinner, but she poured him a glass of 1948 Pommard, sat him down and explained that she never had anyone to really cook for before. Jokingly, she pantomimed Peter's hand movements and said, "So ah—relax, okay?"

Babe wore a silver-threaded powder blue, full-length peasant skirt with an off-white Cossack-style, full-sleeved silk shirt cut to the hip and pinched at the waist with an antique silver cord. Her wrists were adorned with thin silver bracelets, her hair was combed long and down off the shoulders. She wore a beaded necklace with a small leather pouch floating between her breasts. Tiny bells adorned her Turkish sandals and they could be heard when she moved about.

Peter, still off balance from the switch in dinner plans said, "Honey, you look-ah beautiful, what's-ah in the pouch?"

She replied, "Oh, Peter! It's really nothing, just a little thought."

"Lem-me see, sweetheart," he said, as he reached gently for the little bag and opened it.

Inside was a fortune cookie-style message that read, "You will make someone very happy someday." Peter did not say much during the next hour. He picked at the appetizers and as he sipped the wine thoughtfully; he wondered at how lucky he was to be with Babe. He watched her perform like a Russian princess through an incredible gourmet event without her culinary labors ever interrupting the conversation. Peter wouldn't remember all the things she talked about, but he would remember how she expressed every thought with feeling, enthusiasm, fun and laughter. Peter never took his eyes off of her. He couldn't.

When the main course was ready, she handed him a stylishly

printed cream-colored parchment menu wrapped with a wide green silk ribbon, bonded together by a red-wax seal. Inside was the evening's menu written by hand in gold ink. Next to it was a color picture and recipe of the Chicken Marsala that Peter had remarked on. Babe had cut it from the Bon Appétit magazine, glued it in the center and framed it with oval shaped ivory lace. Peter sat silent, feeling himself being pulled by an undertow that was sweeping him away from land; he wanted to go wherever it took him. On this night, he knew there would never be anyone in his life like Babe, and now he knew what he was going to talk to Babe about at Paoli's. He felt a giddy combination of helplessness and elation. *Was he in love? Is this how love is? Must be.* With the menu still in his hand, feeling a little weepy, Peter coughed, his throat went dry. Out of his mouth stumbled the words, "Babe, would-ah you-ah like to be-ah my wife?"

"Yes, but only if you eat your asparagus."

They laughed, toasted, ate and went to bed. The next day, Mary called Babe. "Did he ask you?" she asked, "Honest? Oh! I'm so happy for you."

Chapter Twenty One

The Wedding
1960

THE wedding had to take place at Saints Peter and Paul Church on Washington Square in North Beach, which was the only thing definitely decided. Peter had wanted a society event held at Grace Cathedral on California Street, but Babe made a very strong argument against it.

"Everyone expects you to have the wedding there, everyone wants to be seen as being special friends, and there will be lots of important, very special friends there, but, what will they see?" She said to Peter. "Who will be seated on the bride's side of the aisle? Nobody! The only family I have is my mother in Hawaii and my two friends Mary and Tianna, and they would have to serve double duty as bridesmaids. Is that the picture you want to present to your society people?

"Don't you think a theatrical wedding at Grace Cathedral featuring me in the lead part for Pygmalion would cause tongues to wag, and wouldn't it be fertile ground for a lot of unfounded, negative rumors to be spread needlessly? Even your inner circle of friends will speculate that I might be a clever or lucky graduate from your Huntington Hotel stable."

He tried to interrupt.

"No!" she said to Peter. "This is our wedding and I don't want to share it with the gossip columns. We will invite people that are really important to us, and we will forever cherish that we held it in a place that is part of our roots and our heritage. The wedding will be at Saints Peter and Paul." Peter gave in and agreed.

The ceremony was set for the third Sunday of June 1960. It would be ten years since Jack was announced as Missing in Action.

Babe met her friends at the church for a wedding rehearsal—Mary and Tianna as bridesmaids and Peter's friend Joe Mazzoli as best man. Babe planned everything. She had rehearsed this dream for so long that she knew exactly what was needed. Bridesmaid dresses, printing, music and wedding dress had been decided a long time ago. Her white-on-white gown with a flowing fifteen-foot train was important. Babe also chose the flowers red and blue, except for the bridal bouquet, pure white.

"What's with the red, white and blue flower thing, Babe?" Tianna asked, surprised.

"Why? Don't you think that would be a good combination?"

"Hell, no! That's too patriotic. Might be good for the Fourth of July, though!"

Mary agreed with Tianna. "I think pink and pale blue is better. Besides, who do you think you're marrying, Jack Fischer, for Christ's sake?"

That bothered Babe. Later, sitting on the front steps of the church waiting for Peter to pick her up, she wondered about her choice of colors. Glancing across Washington Square toward the Palace Theater marquee, her thoughts drifted back to a different time and the very different world of ten years before. An old Ink Spots' refrain rolled silently through her head, repeating the words. *For all we know, we will never meet again...We'll come and go...like a ripple on a stream... So love me tonight...until the last minute...for all we know, we will never meet again...*She felt something break inside her, tears pulled at her as she looked up into the sun. Her heart was full to overflowing with such sadness she had never felt. Peter's car arrived at the curb.

Invitations were limited to one hundred sixty people. The reception would be held at Fugazi Hall on Green Street. Babe's only concession regarding the press was letting Peter invite Jerry Bunsen, who assisted columnist Herb Caen in producing his daily newspaper column. Jerry was a man who understood the world, his word was good, and when he wrote about the wedding of the year he would describe Babe as *"the Mystery Girl who was swept away by a not so mysterious garbage mogul with an 'un-canny' eye."*

The honeymoon itinerary was to be a secret, partly because Peter enjoyed the idea of having mysterious destinations unfold, but also because he did not want to be dogged by the press. Peter had his ninety-foot yacht, Gold Dawn, moved from the St. Francis Yacht Club in San Francisco down the coast to San Diego. Babe loved the yacht and she loved to sail and swim, so Peter planned to have them fly to San Diego to meet the boat and stay a few days. From there they would sail down the Baja to Mazatlan, Manzanillo, Acapulco and then on through the Panama Canal to Kingston, Jamaica. The two-month-long voyage would end there, and they would fly back to San Francisco to begin their married life in a newly purchased three-thousand-square-foot low-rise condominium overlooking the bay from Broadway Street. Peter put both of their names on the title.

Chapter Twenty Two

The Honeymoon

IT was after two in the afternoon when they arrived in San Diego to join the boat. They expected to be there for three days, but because the trip was a surprise, Babe had her trousseau and some boat clothes, but nothing to wear. Peter loved to take her shopping, and promptly after checking in to their hotel, escorted her to the Old Town section of the city to buy anything she wanted. Babe hesitated because she had never had the luxury of buying without thinking about the cost, but by the time the sun was near the horizon they had more bags than each could carry, and more were sent to the hotel.

Peter suggested they stop at one of the sidewalk cafes for a drink before heading back. She agreed. Babe was blushed with the excitement of recklessness, glorious and unaccountable spending; she felt guiltily loved and at the same time, absolutely loved. She also loved all of her purchases. The intimate small-talk between them was flirtatious, even foolish, but for Babe it was a new and different world and Peter was excited to see her so happy. He was especially proud that he had the financial ability to make it a reality. They sat at the cafe and ordered two very tall gin-fizzes and a bowl of apple fritters with ice cream scoops on the side. Lingering was fun.

Holding hands, and with their eyes embracing, the moment that both would remember most about their honeymoon was born, each for a different reason. After leaving the cafe they strolled past a small hotel next door. Something about it made her uncomfortable. She looked hard and then recognized it as the place she and Jack had stayed so many years ago. Her image reflected in the glass entranceway. She stiffened. It was all there. Nothing had changed. A ghost struggled to leave her body, she felt it. She resisted and wouldn't let it go. A whisper traveled through time. She heard his voice. Jack.

Peter noticed. "What is it, Babe?"

Guilt stared back at her. She knew life had to go on and that it was time to forget teenage promises. Still, in Peter's arms she squirmed uncomfortably, *Oh my god! Jack, please forgive me. I didn't know what to do. It's been so long.* She shivered again. *Where are you?* Somewhere in her universe a mirror broke.

Peter heard her suppressing tears and gratefully thought they were cries of happiness. "You okay, honey?" he said, hoping for a confirming answer. "Was it something I said?"

"No, no Peter, I think it's just—maybe I ate the ice cream too fast—or something. I'm okay. Please let's go back to the boat. Too much excitement."

"Ah, okay, sweetheart."

"You're such a good husband," she said, her eyes closed. "Thank you."

***

Gold Dawn left San Diego harbor and headed south toward Mazatlan. Peter expected they would deepwater sport fish and underwater spear dive during their three day visit. But when they arrived, Babe said she'd rather sail and sun bathe and that she'd rather not find new ways to kill fish. He went alone on his side trips.

Babe got to know the villagers who worked in the hotel who suggested she explore the town. On the streets she smelled and saw local fish wrapped in banana leaves barbecuing on open spits. She loved the smell and how it was presented. Sweet potatoes baked in clay ovens with hand-made tortillas. *What a great idea!* She thought, purchasing a small serving. Fresh beans cooking slowly over open fires in iron pots stirred by children and the sugar-rolled bananas tickled her imagination. She couldn't wait to imitate these things when she returned home. The smells and the sounds of preparations, the cooking itself, even the colorfully dressed peasant women peeling, chopping and talking with friends in Spanish, was all so romantic. She made a promise to herself to repeat the experience at a Mexican-themed dinner party when she returned home; filling her basket with everything she could reach.

On the second day, a beaming Peter arrived before noon with a hundred and fifty-pound swordfish. Babe took pictures of him with the fish and ordered him to hand it over.

He looked away from his catch. "Why? What are you going to do with it?"

She teased. "Never mind, just make sure you have an empty stomach for our farewell dinner tomorrow, and, no, you can't have it mounted over our fireplace at home!"

He laughed. "See what I have to put up with? Already I have a wife ordering me around and the honeymoon has just started!"

Babe met with the hotel staff and requested a beachside open-pit barbecue be arranged. She negotiated the use of the hotel's restaurant facilities for a farewell party. "Employees and their families," she said to the manager, "are invited to join the celebration dinner, as are you, the town folks and the mayor's entourage."

"I will attend to the invitations immediately," replied the manager.

"Thank you so much. And while you're at it, find me four of the best tortilla makers in town," Babe said. "I want them on pedestals in front of the main table so that everyone can watch tortillas being made the old fashioned way."

She pointed at Pablo, a junior manager. "We also need live Mariachi music." Babe put up prize money for the best dance couples and for the prettiest girls selected as Fiesta Queens.

Babe directed the kitchen staff to add jalapenos and cheddar cheese to the customary refried-beans. "Tomas," she said to the head chef, "add brown sugar and lemon juice to the barbecue sauce, for flavor."

"Mrs. Mattioli, I will take care of your every wish. Will there be anything else?"

"Yes, I want side dishes with rice featuring pork, beef, prawns, nuts, raisins or saffron with pineapple and sweet potatoes. Like these." She held one in her hand. "I want them baked, and their insides scooped out and mixed with the juice of freshly squeezed oranges. Make sure you save the orange halves. Combine the potato-orange mash with cinnamon, brown sugar and pineapple bits. Mix these together and scoop it into the orange halves and garnish with mint leaves."

Satisfied everyone understood, she added, "some of the orange cups will hide silver coins inside and be served on silver platters with banana leaves."

Babe was in the hotel kitchen by eight o'clock the next

morning. Organizing went smoothly except that she had yet to find a block of ice large enough to create a replica of Peter's fish. But, late in the day, find it she did, and by five o'clock that afternoon she personally had carved it into shape. Families, villagers and hotel guests began arriving. Music played, the couples' dance competition started and it was accompanied by a great deal of yelling and applause from supporters. The finest examples of Mexican blankets hung against the walls.

With dinner ready to be served and everyone seated, Babe walked to the head table and announced that the party was in celebration of love—and of the big fish! Pointing to Peter, and to the huge baked fish he had caught, she wryly left open which fish was the most important. Even Peter laughed. People had fun, Babe was in her element and Peter was amazed and very happy. Photos of the event were later passed among friends at home. Peter would often describe the happenings of that day and Babe's role in the affair.

Manzanillo and Acapulco spices added cultural differences to Babe's culinary explorations, and Peter, to her surprise, seemed to share her interest in these things. They discovered excellent Spanish and Mexican wines and thought enough of them to ship fifty cases back to San Francisco.

***

Gold Dawn raised anchor, left Mazatlan and traveled south towards Central America. The Panama Canal unfolded one rise at a time and with each elevation she felt a new respect for the ability of man to build such a marvel. Peter was struck by how small his boat seemed next to an ocean liner passing through the gates at the same time. At every port, Peter went off to find a telex machine, right up to their arrival at Kingston, Jamaica. Peter had a meeting in Kingston with three men from New York. She thought it strange that he didn't introduce her to them, but did not question him.

Chapter Twenty Three

Joy and Qi Jaing
1971

PETER and Babe returned from Jamaica, and Babe soon began hosting dinners at their apartment on Broadway. Every month her invitations celebrated different cultural themes, including an emphasis on the appropriate menus, which she prepared. Tara Carr was a frequent guest. Sometimes she came alone, but more often she arrived with a date or joined someone whom Babe arranged to escort her. She was also no slouch in the kitchen, especially south-of-the-border recipes, and Babe often relied on her. A rising star in San Francisco fashion circles, Tara was getting ready to launch her clothing collection.

Invitations to Babe's dinner parties were so sought after that Peter suggested they consider a larger home, but she suggested that he buy the adjoining unit instead. Peter agreed and thier apartment was soon enlarged by the purchase of the contiguous apartment on the same floor. With five thousand square feet to remodel, Babe selected a well-known design firm and together they created a French country-house look, featuring a large kitchen and dining area that became the envy of Pacific Heights society. The apartment was on the second floor and had nineteen parking spaces of its own beneath the building. It also had a panoramic north-looking view of San Francisco Bay. The apartment's home owners association permitted Babe to construct a three thousand square foot limestone covered patio onto her newly enlarged apartment. It also allowed the installation of a private, glass-enclosed elevator that traveled between the below ground garage and the new patio.

The apartment was both home and office to Babe. Here she hosted society events, political gatherings and private parties. Beyond that, her calendar listed The Palace Hotel as a breakfast meeting place for up-and-coming politicians on the first Wednesday of each month. A long list of restaurants, such as Julius Castle on Telegraph Hill, Paoli's, Amelia's, Ernie's, Jack's or Sam's in the downtown area, provided meeting grounds for business discussions, charity events, individual get-togethers and special celebrations.

***

Several people, including Babe, suggested to Peter that he run for a seat on the Board of Supervisors. It seemed silly to him in view of his business commitments, but Babe suggested that much of what he did was in the nature of maintaining his relationships with the city's power structure, and if he became part of that hierarchy, he would add a little insurance to his own company's future.

Peter agreed, primarily because he knew that Babe would be his campaign manager. She knew everyone by name and remembered things about each person she met. People felt that Babe thought them to be important and in turn made them feel important. When she called for volunteers, these friends often brought their own employees, offered the use of their business telephones and mailrooms or held fundraisers at their own homes. Babe, in the fourth year of her marriage, was five months pregnant when Peter was elected with a huge majority to the San Francisco Board of Supervisors.

***

Claudette Mattioli was baptized a Catholic. Peter hired a speech tutor to clean up his New York accent and Babe began planning his State Senate campaign.

Peter glowed with a pride and ambition he never knew he had, but he was also uneasy that he had become Babe's candidate rather than a leader in his own right. People went to her when they needed political or social advice. At functions it was always Babe who held center court, even when Peter became a senator and sat at the head of the table.

On a personal level, Babe felt she was happy enough with Peter, even though their relationship had become somewhat distant and his embrace began to mimic the kind of coolness exhibited by her father Quido. She rationalized that they were both busy and in the public eye, and that open displays of affection seemed out of place. Besides, Babe thought, she had everything any woman could want. When she saw couples who were obviously deeply in love, though, she would speculate how life could have been with Jack alive. One thing she kept to herself was that every time she had a private erotic thought, it was Jack who floated through her mind, not Peter. Sometimes that embarrassed her; sometimes it made her unbelievably sad.

Periodically, Babe talked about Jack with her friends Mary and Tara, because they had known him so well. Beyond that, she stayed in touch with Jack's mother Rosemary and his brother Bob, although she really did not understand why she did that either. After all, what was the point, other than sadness.

***

Time passed and Peter had somehow lost being his own man and did not quite know what to do about it. He often stayed, for more days than necessary, at the state Capitol in Sacramento where attentive and admiring women found a place at his side. These women, he rationalized, were just keeping him company. But inwardly, he knew they made him feel needed and important, and he loved dazzling them with expensive surprises. People who did not have Peter's best interests in mind followed and photographed him with beautiful women and even audio-taped him making love to a fifteen-year-old Brazilian visitor who needed his help obtaining a permanent residency card.

What Babe did not know was that Peter had become obsessed with another woman, a Chinese dancer named Joy Jaing, who was appearing at the Chinese Sky Room in Chinatown. She was Qi Jaing's daughter, and was born in Formosa two years after Qi and his family escaped from China.

Joy's father had sent her to San Francisco from Formosa to establish a family presence in the Bay Area as a hedge against Mainland China some day invading Taiwan. Qi Jaing, involved in the business of exporting sub-assembly parts to electronics plants, needed a family member to maintain personal contact with his buyers. He proposed providing her an apartment in San Francisco and connections to the wealthiest Silicon Valley entrepreneurs. Her beauty would make those kinds of contacts more possible, but she stubbornly refused to leave until Qi agreed to arrange a singing job for her at a famous nightclub in San Francisco's Chinatown.

Qi knew that his daughter had ambitions of being in the entertainment industry and that she would probably jump at the opportunity. Once she was there, he hoped she would take a more active role in furthering the family's future security.

***

Peter called his friend, Gordon Low, owner of the Chinese Sky Room, announcing that he might drop by for a drink. Gordon graciously invited him to hurry over. After hanging up the phone, Gordon took Joy aside and urged her to meet the state senator because the connection might be very fruitful for both. During the second show, Gordon Low pointed Joy out to Peter.

"She's the best-looking girl we have," he said. "Hell of a performer. Family's worth a fortune."

Peter did not seem interested in the new singer and was content to swirl his ice cubes. But, when Joy was introduced to Peter, he seemed, at first, to be at a loss for words and almost slipped back into his New York accent. He was impressed that she had very large breasts. *Unusual for Chinese girls*, he thought, beginning to speculate. They sat together in a booth and Joy declined the offer of a drink. Peter, sitting opposite, made small talk and waited for an opening. He knew instinctively not to come on to her, partly because her bearing exuded self-confidence, but also because he felt she would have rejected a barroom advance. Joy was surprisingly intelligent, Peter thought. She was different, and he imagined that she appeared interested in him.

When Peter suggested that she might enjoy a spin around the harbor on his yacht, she replied without a hint of an oriental accent.

"Mr. Senator, Gordon will tell you how to reach me during the day. I will think about it in the meantime." She excused herself and left the room.

During the next several months, Peter lavished attention on her and even arranged a screen test for Joy in two films. One was a sequel to an Ingrid Bergman film about the Pearl River in China titled "Yellow Dawn," a part she did not get. The other, a film about the Chinese-Italian race riots that roared across San Francisco's Broadway Street into North Beach and Chinatown, was based on events that took place right after World War II. This film, called "Concubine," was about an Italian businessman wanting to marry a beautiful Chinatown girl who was nearly killed by neighbors when her affair with a white man was discovered. Joy, with Peter's help, was accepted for the lead, and the movie was released during a San Francisco film festival to mixed reviews. Joy became a local celebrity, an icon in both the Chinese and

Italian neighborhoods, and she especially did not risk being seen with Peter.

Obsessed, Peter wanted to escort her to high profile restaurants and bars, saying he didn't give a damn about the potential notoriety, perhaps unconsciously hoping that he would be discovered. He installed her at the Huntington Hotel, in his private suite.

Joy, however, adamantly refused to be seen with him in public because he was a Caucasian and that would cause her to lose face in her community. Joy also could not risk being seen with Peter because her beauty could potentially translate into family connections when the right kind of person came into her life. That was fine with Peter. He need not run the risk of taking her out and he could still keep her like a bird in a gilded cage.

***

Anticipating a San Francisco weekend, Joy, who had been living in Peter's Huntington Hotel suite, had just dressed and was sitting on the bed putting on her lipstick and talking on the phone when she lost the top of her lipstick tube behind the bed. She hung up and searched—there it was behind the headboard. Pushing the bed away from the wall she saw something, a tiny transmitter. Joy had assembled similar devices and recognized its purpose immediately. She expected Peter to pick her up for a sailing date within minutes and quickly scribbled a note that read: "*Peter, this suite is electronically bugged. Don't say anything that would indicate discovery. Be normal.*"

Joy stopped him at the door. Peter read the note. They left the suite and rode silently down the elevator and instead of going sailing; now of little interest, they stopped for a drink at the Huntington bar.

Peter was physically shaking and his mind screamed out for answers as to who would plant such a device and why. Speaking softly, he said, "could Babe?" He thought not.

"Political enemies?" Peter added.

"Yes," Joy replied. "But which ones?"

"Partners in New Jersey?" Peter volunteered. "They have been a little unhappy with me expanding down into the Peninsula without them."

"Call Hal Lipset. You use his detective agency all the time. Have them check out the suite, your car, your office here and especially the one in Sacramento."

Peter thought it a good idea and telephoned the agency from the lobby.

Hal Lipset arrived three hours later with three electronics experts who promptly located taps on both the hotel line and the private telephone in the suite. Peter's car was clean, but his San Francisco office had two bugs, one in the conference room and another on his personal line. Before ordering the technicians to Sacramento, Peter asked Hal's advice.

Turning in his chair to look at Peter, Hal said, "Peter, we've collected more than two hundred files for you over the last twenty years. Some of those investigations include your partners, every politician you've ever met, and every bureaucrat you expected to make use of, every political donor of significance and every potentially troublesome female you had an encounter with. I suggest we go through all of these files together and look for clues. Meanwhile, see this olive with a toothpick in my martini?"

"Yes," Peter replied. "What about it?"

"Well, this will transmit our conversation from this room to another, within a two-block radius. Understand?" Hal Lipset loved new gadgets and he was often written up in the newspapers, extolling the merits of high technology in the surveillance business.

Peter was stunned. "You mean that they can do this as well as we can?" he asked.

***

Joy telephoned her father in Taiwan and discussed her relationship with Peter, her job at the Sky Room and the latest situation regarding the listening devices.

"Father," she said. "I don't feel personally threatened."

"You may not have considered the consequences," Qi said, being diplomatic.

"I'm not going to do anything to involve the family business in a scandal and definitely nothing that could compromise our reputation."

Qi suggested nothing be done with the relationship until he arrived in San Francisco the following month, but he strongly recommended that Joy move to an apartment nearby, perhaps on either Russian Hill or Telegraph Hill, and suggested a realtor friend to handle the search. She agreed, and later told Peter she thought it a good idea for her to have her own apartment again.

When Qi arrived in San Francisco, Joy had already rented an apartment in the Eichler Towers on Taylor on Russian Hill. When her father saw it, he insisted it be purchased immediately.

"I will put you on our corporate payroll, which will permit us to write off the cost of the purchase as a necessary business expense, Qi explained. "This will be the address that bears our letterhead in America and you can start becoming active in the business by meeting some of the clientele. Most have their offices on the Peninsula."

"What about my own career?"

"Look, you continue doing what you think is best to advance that ambition. I am only suggesting that you take an interest in our family business with a long-term view."

"Okay, father, she agreed reluctantly. "I'll give it my best, but you know I am not a business person."

During the month while her father was in San Francisco, he stayed with her and arranged for the purchase of the unit, introduced Joy to the company representatives, hired a private detective to look into the possible reasons for Peter's wiretaps and also got to know his daughter as the grown-up she had become.

The new closeness, and their shared interests, meant they would spend much of the day together as a result. Joy escorted him to all the restaurants she had learned to love in both Chinatown and in the greater Downtown. To her surprise, he preferred Scoma's Seafood Restaurant at Fisherman's Wharf and India House on Pacific Avenue more than the four-star Chinese restaurants. The India House particularly fascinated him because it replicated the Raffles Hotel Bar in Singapore with slowly rotating ceiling fans, oriental carpets, beaded curtained booths and bamboo furniture. The owner, whom clientele knew as Major Brown, dressed impeccably in a tan, British Army safari outfit, complete with pith helmet and swagger stick. He effortlessly organized his well-trained staff and uniformed them in typical Indian Army puttees with leg wrappings. The effect was transporting and the food was world class. Major Brown always remembered a name and often recommended the Pims Cup drinks he thought appropriate. Qi found the English Colonial atmosphere nostalgic and comforting. Its understated elegance, quality furnishings, service, polite efficiency and implied authority simply made Qi feel he was back in Shanghai.

Two days before her father left San Francisco, Joy asked him if he would be interested in watching her do a short television shoot for an advertising agency producing an ad promoting a travel agency in the city. The filming was scheduled at the rear of the Ferry Building at the foot of Market Street at eleven o'clock. He was pleased that she had asked and he looked forward to seeing his daughter perform. Midway through the shooting, a small helicopter landed on the helipad behind the building on a separate pier. Its eggbeater noise interrupted the sound track and the shoot stopped until after it took off again.

The helicopter had been chartered by San Francisco's KRON Channel 4 television station to cover the presidential motorcade crossing the Oakland Bay Bridge. The helicopter had landed to pick up a KRON news cameraman at the Ferry Building's helipad, but minutes into the flight, at three thousand feet, the engine stuttered and the helicopter swayed erratically, like a drunken bird. Thinking fast, Joy grabbed a studio camera operator and pulled him toward the helicopter pad, yelling at him to film her and the troubled helicopter.

At the edge of the helipad she spoke breathlessly into the camera microphone. "This is Joy Jaing, coming to you from the Ferry Building in downtown San Francisco where," she looked and pointed skyward, "right above my head," she panted, "is a helicopter in trouble."

She described the action being filmed and when the chopper's engine finally quit, it seemed to fall like a rock toward the Ferry Building.

Joy yelled into the microphone. "Oh, my God! Oh, my God. Ladies and gentlemen! The pilot is trying to return to this landing pad. Will he make it? Will he crash?" On camera, crouching with one arm protectively over her head, she anticipated a disaster. Joy understood drama.

The helicopter fell, but seconds before hitting the ground it flared, giving it enough lift for a very rough landing instead of a very hard crash. The camera caught the fall and the landing, but the sight of Joy continuing to broadcast while fighting the windstorm created by the whirling blades was stunning footage. She rushed toward the helicopter, and the bubble doors burst open. Her cameraman in tow, Joy yelled at the pilot and his passenger.

"Can you tell me what happened up there and what caused you to come crashing down?"

She finished the segment with a professional sign-off. "This is Joy Jaing coming to you for KRON Television News." Joy had seen the KRON marks on the TV camera inside the helicopter and gambled.

Her father was beside himself. "What the hell got into you?" he shouted. "Why would you take such a risk?"

He was too far away from the incident to know what happened, but when Joy suggested they watch the six o'clock news together, he was truly astonished.

Joy telephoned the news production manager at KRON to explain what had happened, what she had done and that she would drop the film at the station at four o'clock. She apologized for taking charge on a critical news story but explained that the station cameraman was up in the air and too preoccupied with survival to produce any footage.

"I was just trying to help," she said, "and maybe avoid an embarrassment."

"What do you mean by avoid an embarrassment?" the production manager said, annoyed.

"Well, I was careful not to mention that a KRON cameraman was in the helicopter, I only mentioned his name. You never know if the viewer might think the incident, how should I say it, amusing!" She meant to say embarrassing, but decided against it.

Surprised, the manager replied, "Joy, when you bring the film in, please ask for me personally."

The night of the broadcast and all the next day, the television station received calls asking about the beautiful Chinese newsperson. Several influential Chinese also directed their calls to the management suggesting it was about time the station had Chinese representation on its news coverage.

Joy was interviewed by KRON twice, screen-tested several times and the following week she became a regular on-the-scene reporter. She called her father at his home in Taiwan to tell him she was now on television.

"I'm so very proud of you," he said. "But I still think you were crazy to do what you did. And what about our other agreement?"

"Father, this is my big chance, let me go for it. Besides, having a company representative who is also a local celebrity might be even better."

"Okay, sweetheart, but given your potential for notoriety, I would break off with Peter. If a scandal leaks out, I don't want you involved. If you get caught up in something, your station won't like it."

She agreed.

Chapter Twenty Four

Paco 'Nick' Mateo

NORTH Beach was mostly an Italian neighborhood with very few Latinos, so it was unusual to have new neighbors like Paco "Nick" Mateo and his family. They arrived in San Francisco in 1947 from Nicaragua, just one step ahead of the deadly grip of that country's dictator, Somoza. Nick's father had stayed behind after sending his family away through Costa Rica and was never heard from again. A newspaper editor writing anti-Somoza articles ending up dead was not unusual. Growing up in Nicaragua, Paco went to the best schools and learned his studies well, and by the time he arrived in America he also spoke English, French and Portuguese in addition to his native Spanish.

The Mateo family moved into a flat behind the Fischer's apartment on Union Street, and it was inevitable that Jack, his brother Bob and his sister Carla would become friends with the Mateo family. Paco's first name became "Nick," which was short for Nicaragua. He liked to be called, Nick the Great. At sixteen, he strutted the streets with a duck's-ass hair cut, low-slung Levis and highly polished cordovan dyed shoes, just like the other American boys.

Nick and Jack were the same age and good friends. They went every weekend to Latin dances, a new thing for Jack, and they traded clothes and traveled by streetcar. Tianna attended a neighborhood Latin dance and when Nick spotted her, he became instantly obsessed. He followed her home without being noticed and was pleased to find that she lived just eight blocks from his place. From then on, Nick would find a reason to be on Filbert Street or in nearby Washington Park.

Only once did she notice Nick with a hint of recognition. He knew he had been caught and without knowing what to say he blurted,

"Ah, could I meet you one day at the park—or—maybe go to church—someday?"

She felt his discomfort and to his surprise she replied, "Yes, but come by and see if I am home and we will go together."

During the following week Nick's heart soared, and in his mind Tianna was a queen, actually, his queen. He dreamed every night about her and went to Filbert Street a dozen times before catching her at home. When he finally did, he said, "Hi, remember me? I'm Nick. You said you might like to go to the park one day if I came by."

"Oh! I remember," Tianna said. "But I can't go until two o'clock, can you come back then?"

Nick, amazed at his luck, replied, "okay, I'll come by in two hours."

He left and practically leapt as he ran up Union Street hoping to find a friend whose older brother sometimes helped the boys buy beer. Beer, he thought, would be just the thing to have, something to put her at ease. As luck would have it, Nick was soon in possession of a six-pack of Lucky Lager. Hurrying back to Filbert Street he began to have second thoughts; *if she sees me coming to the house with beer, she might not want to come with me.* Uneasy, he decided to cover the beer with some branches in Washington Park and casually stumble onto it walking through the park with Tianna.

The plan in place, Nick headed for Tia's house and rang the bell. She was waiting, stepped out and closed the door behind her. She took his hand down the stairs, causing him near paralysis. Never had such a beautiful creature looked at him, let alone touched him. He felt uncomfortably awkward and had no idea what to do with her hand. As they walked he held it slightly high and forward as if it were a grocery basket. She glanced at him, but refrained from saying anything.

At the park, Nick began rummaging behind a bush. Tia watched with some concern.

"Nick, what on earth are you doing?"

"I—ah—I think I may have lost something here," he said. But when he began shuffling behind another bush, she became irritated.

"Do you always act so strangely?"

He was horrified that she would think him strange, and even more horrified at the knowledge that his beer had been stolen and that his rutting around the bushes was obviously peculiar.

Not knowing what else to do, Nick plopped himself onto the bench next to her and told the story of his family's escape from Nicaragua. It was the one and only time Tia agreed to meet Nick, but the memory of that day burned in his mind. Worse, one day he telephoned to let her know that he now held a job at United Airlines as a spray painter. The attempt to impress her failed utterly.

"Nick," she replied softly, not wishing to hurt his feelings. "You are a nice boy and I am glad you have such a good job, but I want to have a relationship with someone who is older, more settled, perhaps maybe even an engineer or a doctor. I hope you understand. Perhaps we'll bump into each other someday."

He did understand and he cried after hanging up.

The phone call with Tia and the stupidity of wandering around the park looking for buried beer weighed heavily on Nick and he became determined that one day he would be some kind of professional, have smooth manners and lots of money. *Maybe I might bump into her someday,* he thought. *You never know.*

With single-minded determination, Nick enrolled at Heald College, a night school on Van Ness Avenue, to study electrical engineering. He quit going to dances, worked a full shift at the airlines to help his mother and studied seven days and nights a week. Nick graduated just as computers were becoming functional necessities in offices, and large firms found themselves in need of electrical engineers to help them with the coming age of electronics. Boeing Aircraft hired him into their antenna department and moved Nick to Seattle.

He was assigned to solving electrical engineering problems until he became well-grounded in how the company worked. Later, he became involved in commercial projects and also in secret antenna related programs. During a sales demonstration of how satellite communication could work for airlines, he spoke French to a high-ranking visitor and afterward Spanish to that country's head of Commerce and Trade. His technical ability, his language skills, and his way of making people feel that he could be trusted led visitors to Boeing to depend on his judgments and advice.

Nick's big break came when he was unexpectedly called to travel to Chile for a meeting with that country's president and advisors to discuss their purchasing of airplanes. Nick was told that he was being sent there to explain communications and fuselage electronics and to act as a technical interpreter for all parties. After each side asked questions, they would look at him and ask, "What do you think, Nick?"

He would tell them the technical reasons why they should buy Boeing, but he also could speak firsthand about the benefits of Chile depending on America for its aircraft. His reasoning: Chile needed both airplanes and political connections, Boeing had both and America was already supplying military equipment to adjoining countries. The logic worked. Nick became the point man with Boeing and was sent to Brazil, Venezuela, Argentina and Panama within the next six months.

The CIA enlisted Nick as an agent because they needed to know what the buyers of military electronics and airplanes were thinking around the world. At the American government's insistence, he became part of the Boeing sales team that traveled the globe. He refused to be paid by the spy agency for his efforts because it was his way of thanking America for having accepted him and for providing the opportunities he would never have had in his homeland. Eventually, Nick's job became one of knowing people in each country, keeping a continuous dialogue with them, establishing dependable trust relationships, hovering over their wishes when they came to the States, helping their families with contacts in America and promoting the interests of Boeing.

New planes were sold; older planes were traded. Often, they were of no value to Boeing. Nick arranged to have these unwanted planes privately sold to other countries, and toward that, he established an aircraft leasing company with funds provided by both the CIA and the son-in-law of Panama's president. Financing aircraft became a very large and profitable enterprise that sometimes involved Nick with unusual buyers. Some were drug cartels. Others ferried guns and ammunition to rogue states and insurgency groups, while still others were operators of small airlines. Regardless, second hand aircraft financing was an information bonanza for the CIA and a moneymaker for Nick. Boeing also found that contact with small airplane owners often led to the sale of larger aircraft.

Nick visited his mother, brother and sisters in San Francisco every chance he had. They were a tight-knit family, with strong religious values and an even stronger belief that hard work defined you. His mother continued to work as a housekeeper at the Mark

Hopkins Hotel. At fifty-eight years old she had no intention of quitting, no matter how much money Nick sent home.

On several occasions Nick tried to track Tianna down, but no one seemed to know where she had gone. She had changed her name unofficially to Tara Carr, but Nick had no way of knowing. He also tried to reach Babe Barsi and others in the old neighborhood, but that too was fruitless. One day, he glanced at a society column in the San Francisco Examiner, a section he hardly ever read. His eye caught the name Babe Mattioli. He made a mental note and had friends in Seattle look into it. *How many Babes could there be in San Francisco?* he thought.

The following month, Nick was surprised to see a message on his desk. *"Babe Mattioli. Maiden name: Babe Barsi. Married to Peter Mattioli, President of the United Scavengers Association, a garbage removal company."* The message described her activities, where she lived, her telephone number and copies of several society page articles.

Surprised at how nervous he felt, Nick dialed the number.

"Hello, my name is Paco Mateo. I'm calling from Seattle for a Babe Barsi Mattioli. Is she available?"

"Yes. One moment," a woman replied. Then Babe came on the line.

"Hello! This is Babe. Who did you say you were?"

"Babe its Nick! You know, Nick the Great from Union Street. I've been trying to find you for years."

"What!" Babe burst out. "I can't believe it! Is it really you Nick?"

"Yes," he replied. "I'm so eager to see you again. I live in Seattle now, but I get to San Francisco from time to time. It would be great to connect and say hi."

"So what are you doing in Seattle?"

"I'm the engineering vice president for both commercial and military aircraft sales for Boeing's overseas market. I'm on the road a lot."

"I'm having a small dinner party for four couples the last week of September, on a Saturday evening—can you make it then?"

"Yes," Nick replied. "Who's going to be there—a lot of stuffed shirts or will I be made to feel more at home with a root-beer float crowd?"

Babe laughed. "Nick, do you remember a girl from the neighborhood named Tianna?"

He nearly jumped out of his skin. "Yes, I remember her *very well*. Why?"

"Well," said Babe. "She just filed for a divorce, so *he* won't be at the dinner, and I just thought…"

Almost leaping through the telephone, Nick shouted, "Babe, *are you kidding*? I would walk all the way down there from here for an opportunity to sit next to Tianna for five minutes. But don't tell her that!"

"Oh? What's this I'm hearing, Nick? Is there something I should know?"

"Never mind, Babe, I'll talk to you about that later."

"Okay, Nick. Come in a tuxedo. And by the way, Tianna calls herself Tara Carr, and she is not only a clothing designer, she also has her own line called Tara-N-Things. It's a play on TNT."

"Good God, Babe! Say no more. I'll see you soon."

Nick cradled the telephone, his heart racing in disbelief. He could still feel like an out-of-control teenager after all of those years. He looked at his calendar and thought, *Paco Mateo, 1978 is a very good year indeed!*

***

Nick had decided to drive instead of fly to San Francisco, justifying it by rationalizing a need to stop in Portland, Oregon. The truth was he had just taken delivery of a new 1978 forest green Jaguar sedan, and he had it tricked out with a CB short wave radio, plus a top-of-the-line stereo system. *This time,* he thought, *I'm not taking any chances. I'm going to impress Tia right off her fashionable feet.*

Having called ahead for an appointment, Nick walked into San Francisco's Wilkes Bashford's elegant men's wear shop and was fitted with the grandest tuxedo he had ever seen. When he was satisfied that it would be ready in time, he stopped at a Grant Avenue jeweler.

"What can I do for you?" the sales girl asked.

Nick felt uneasy; he wanted to buy something special, but he had no idea what. "I am going to a dinner party this coming Saturday and someone I met many years ago will be there."

"Was she special to you then?" she asked.

"More than you can imagine, and I want to give her something that is simply great, but not overwhelming. Any ideas?"

"Okay, last question. Is this mystery women fashion conscious?"

"Are you kidding? She's Tara Carr. Ever heard of her?" Nick blurted.

"Are *you* kidding? She's famous."

Nick found himself looking at things he never knew existed, and according to the sales lady, every item had some special significance. Finally, he reached for a pair of black opal earrings surrounded by small diamonds.

"Oh!" the sales lady gushed. "You do have good taste. Any idea what they are?"

Nick shrugged his shoulders.

"These are very rare. They come from an area called Lightning Ridge in Australia," she explained. "Aborigines found them near the surface just after a rain."

"I'll take them," Nick announced. Something about finding a gem after a heavy rain struck a chord within him.

***

Babe greeted Nick at the door and they hugged for what seemed an eternity. He worried that the flowers he held might be crushed. Tara came up behind and tapped Babe's shoulder.

"Hey! When do I get to hug Wonder Boy?" Not knowing how to react, Nick turned, reached out and held both Tara's hands apart.

"You are more beautiful than I remember," he said. "And I don't mind telling you that I have been looking forward to seeing you again for about all of my life."

When Tara hugged him she noticed he had a nice smell and felt like a man who regularly worked out. His hand in hers, she pulled him toward the living room.

"Thank you for remembering me."

It should be more like 'thank you for even talking to me', he said to himself with a sappy smile.

Nick observed Babe moving about like a queen and Tara buzzing from quest to quest with the manners of a duchess. Sitting at the elegant dinner in a tuxedo, Nick couldn't help thinking, *It is too much like a dream*, remembering and comparing how things were when they were all in their teens. He listened to Babe's guests and tried falling in with their conversations, but was really not too interested. He kept following Tara with his eyes.

Sitting alone in a side chair in the lounge and sipping a Christian Brother's brandy, Nick gazed at the guests and thought the black and white tuxedos reminded him of piano keys. The brandy was good and he felt good being there. Peter Mattioli, Babe's husband, whom Nick decided he liked, looked an awful lot like Jack Fischer.

Both Babe and Tara wanted to have lunch with Nick the next day to learn more and to catch up on things. But as Nick was leaving the party, he asked Tara if he could pick her up for a drive to Marin County, for lunch, maybe at the Spinnaker in Sausalito.

"Come at eleven," she said. "And later I want to show you around my studios."

At the dinner party, Nick had completely forgotten about the earrings, and although he hadn't buried them in the park he felt as though he had when he got home and realized he had never even thought of them, so besotted was he with Tianna.

***

The Spinnaker, on a pier overlooking the Bay from Sausalito, was especially romantic. Their window table framed the sweeping panorama of moving boats, bright blue skies and Angel Island. Nick, suddenly shy about how to start a conversation, reached into his pocket and produced the earring box. Sunrays caught the opals at just the right angle making them sparkle like fire.

"I want you to have these, Tianna," he said, too quickly to be romantic. "I hope you like them."

Tara was surprised. "Nick! They're so lovely! Where did you get these?"

"They're from Australia," he said, sounding like an Aussie. "An Aborigine found them in the desert in a place called Lightning Ridge. They were right on top of the ground after a heavy rain. The morning sun was low and he caught a glint of the stones—almost missing it— thinking it was nothing more than reflections off a beer ring. On his way back to town he sold them to an opal dealer friend of mine named Phil Pearl, who brought them to Seattle. When I heard we were having dinner in September, I asked my friend's advice on what I might give you. The rest is, as they say, history." Nick cringed inwardly. *Why did I have to mention the beer can ring?*

Tara quietly clapped her hands, mimicking applause.

"Nick, you are the biggest liar I ever met, but I love them. I love that you would have thought me worthy of such a wonderful gift and that you have thought of me for a very long time, otherwise…" she trailed off. "Oh, never mind. Can I thank you with a kiss?"

Nick's legs turned to jelly. He stared at her without speaking, and when she scooted her chair close to his and kissed him, he nearly fainted.

***

The TNT sign on the building featured an explosion beginning at the main entrance and blossoming upward to the third floor. Nick thought it was corny, but he had to admit Tara got her message across. Inside, at ground level, merchandise showrooms filled the spaces behind a large reception counter. Twelve-foot-tall walls were covered with high-fashion photo blowups. On the next level were design studios, sample creation booths, new product development and special orders. The third floor featured attractive models sashaying TNT's latest offerings past a Parisian-style café that offered complimentary wines and cheese. The fourth floor handled the cutting, fabric storage and offices. On the fifth floor, Tara had what she called her downtown apartment.

Her place reminded him of a visit to the Vatican because the Spanish and Italian antiques were museum quality. Religious relics dominated the foyer. Everywhere he looked Persian carpets accented limestone floors and rust-colored Spanish floor tiles. Sixteenth-century tapestries hung against off-white, distressed stucco walls. Her king-sized bed wore silk sheets beneath a turned back brocaded antique bedcover from Morocco.

"I bought it because the seller told me it had once belonged to a harem favorite." She brought her scarf across the lower half of her face and batted her eyelashes at him. He thought to himself, *I could easily be her slave.* On a corner of the roof beyond the living room stood a glass-enclosed hot house where Tara grew orchids and begonias. A garden of vegetables, in large dun-colored ceramic pots covered a third of the rooftop.

Tara often plowed her hands into the soil or bathed in the shallow roof-top wading pool. Sometimes she would meditate or pray at her small shrine of the Virgin Mary for the people she loved most.

The contrast between the ground floor's "dynamited" entranceway and the sanctuary on the roof was remarkable. Nick had learned that Tara was a devout Catholic, a believer, like himself. She was also a modern-day warrior in a man's world, a world she not only brought energy and ideas to, but also one in which she set high moral and ethical standards for everyone around her. He also knew that he would not be testing the Moroccan bed covers until after they were married. Nick expected that would happen in June of 1979, although Tara did not know that yet.

For the month of October, Nick, Tara and Babe were inseparable. Many hours were idled away recalling old friends and their youthful explorations. The topic of Jack Fischer was something that Tara and Nick thought would make Babe uncomfortable under the circumstances, but for the love of him, Nick brought him up. To his surprise, Babe spoke so passionately about him that no one would have been surprised to see Jack walk through the front door. That was the first time Tara fully understood that Babe never forgot Jack and never would.

Tara held Babe in her eyes for a long moment and with the conviction of a gypsy fortuneteller she said, "Babe, when I get back to my garden I am going to pray for him. I am going to pray with all of my might that God will find a way for both of you to be together again."

Babe burst out crying, all three hugged, and they went on to other things.

Before Nick returned to Seattle, Babe invited them both for lunch at her apartment. She invited them to play tennis in the morning and suggested that maybe Peter might join them, but that he might also be in Sacramento on that Saturday. No one played well, every shot went somewhere else, and the first set became so fitfully funny that they could not lift a racket without bursting into laughter.

It was no use and they gave up the instant Babe yelled. "Hey! It's getting cold out here. How about going back to my place for a glass of hot wine with cinnamon sticks and lemon?"

Hugging Tara and laughing, Nick said, "lead the way. We're ready!"

The elevator was being serviced. They walked up to the second floor, and without thinking Babe picked up a large brown UPS envelope as she stepped through her door. It was heavy, postmarked

New York, and addressed to her. *Neighbor must have brought it in,* she thought. Curious, she opened it on the kitchen counter.

Out spilled large black and white photographs of Peter having intercourse with several women, including two that looked underage. Inside was an audio tape cassette. Babe, Tara and Nick understood what had just happened, but were too stunned to utter a word. Nick finally broke in.

"Babe, you probably want to be alone and that's understandable. I am also sure that you and Tara will be together, as always, when there is a problem."

"Thank you, Nick," Babe replied, warily eyeing the pile of photos.

Nick continued, cautiously. "Now, please, don't ask me any questions about what I am about to tell you. Promise?"

They nodded agreement, and he began to tell them about his secret life with the CIA. He swore them to secrecy and offered to take the envelope and pictures with him to Seattle to be analyzed for fingerprints. He also offered another suggestion.

"I recommend you say nothing about this, not even to Peter, because whoever is behind this probably did not send the pictures to the press yet. That means these were sent as a message."

"What kind of message?" Babe, asked.

"An enemy wants Peter to know, through your discovery of these photos and your expected outrage, that they have the power to destroy him. You see, they no doubt want him to do something he has refused doing in the past. Does that make sense to you?"

"Yes," Babe replied. "But what do they want him to do?"

"That will take some investigation, so be a little patient. Whatever you do, don't react, as they expect, with a noisy attack on Peter."

Tara looked at Nick as though she were seeing him for the first time, and said, "you are a pretty impressive fellow. I would never have dreamed."

PART FOUR

Chapter Twenty Five

Khabarovsk
1953

THE Russian City of Khabarovsk is north and inland from Vladivostok, and west of the Sikhote-Alin Mountains on the Manchurian-Russian border. The city is a rail hub through which prisoners are sent north to the Kolyma mining region, where life expectancy did not exceed three years. Luckier prisoners were sent west to Chita, above the Mongolian boarder, where they were often grouped and sent to Perm 36 near Novosibirsk or moved northwest to Archangelsk.

A rail spur from the main junction switched Private Jack Fischer's POW train to the east of Khabarovsk. Chugging slowly for much of the way, the train wound its way across Siberia. Prisoners eventually caught glimpses of what they assumed was their destination. Rusted barbed-wire fencing surrounded long lines of mud-splattered barracks. Guard towers intermittently straddled both sides of the train. Roughly painted signs marked prison compounds: USA, JAP and UN. Silently, Jack hoped cynically, without conviction and without prayer, that this was a collection point for repatriation.

The prisoners detrained outside the USA compound and were marched away from the platform. Emaciated American Negro soldiers, being herded toward the emptied train, marched past whispering to the new arrivals.

"We're being sent to Chita! Tell someone. Please!"

"Henry Jackson, Cincinnati."

"Private Kellogg, Dallas."

"Help us." Voices pleaded, hoping to be remembered by someone.

Jack understood immediately that those men knew they were

going to disappear into a deep hole and that POWs now arriving at camp USA would soon follow. He shrugged his shoulders and huddled with the rest of his group. The POWs were herded through a barbed gate and ordered to sit on the frozen ground in front of a small platform where a black man stood officiously.

"Wearing Chinese uniforms behind the lines is spying and a cause for immediate execution," yelled the camp indoctrinator, Sergeant Leroy Robinson. "But lucky for you, your lives have been spared because you chose to come to the Soviet Union for enlightenment. You have been sentenced to twenty-five years of hard labor for being war criminals."

Pleased with himself, Robinson continued with a smile. "The Peace Camp system in the Soviet Union is where criminals—like you—have an opportunity to participate in the cause of world Communism. The men you just passed were guests at our Peace Camp across the way." Sergeant Robinson pointed.

"And as Negros they should have understood the plight of the oppressed working classes; in particular they should have known, firsthand, the arrogance of racial discrimination by white capitalists."

Robinson paused to light a cigarette. "Those men were defiant and—*rejected* becoming part of the crusade to elevate and enrich the masses. For that reason they have been sent for re-education to copper mines near Chita—about 1,200 miles from here." Pausing for effect he pushed his chin forward. "Now! As to what happens to you!"

Sergeant Leroy Robinson beamed when he orated, but the POWs, hearing Communist bullshit for the first time coming out of the mouth of an American, were outraged.

"Prisoner exchanges ended months ago, the Allies have no record of your existence here and believe you are all dead," Robinson gleefully announced. "There will be no Red Cross packages or mail and if you die, it does not matter to us. Lastly, your sentences can be extended another twenty-five years when any guard files a complaint."

Silence hung heavily in the air while the threats were digested. "Follow the guards to your barracks!" Robinson barked. "Dismissed."

One Marine prisoner yelled, "Hey! We were forced to wear these uniforms."

No answer came from Sergeant Robinson. A voice in the ranks

whispered sarcastically, "let's find a lawyer."

"What the fuck was that all about?" muttered another.

A Hungarian Jew from New York got it right when he volunteered an answer to the chorus of voices. "Vee are dee slafes, und dot blick guy ist dee slafe master. Commies haffing fun mit us. See? Dot guy eats goot. You vant eat goot too? You kiss his ass!"

Jack paid little attention to the comments, his thoughts were of Babe.

***

Khabarovsk was a major interrogation center controlled by the Secret Police Agency or MGB, through which tens of thousands of prisoners from South Korea, United Nations armies and the American military flowed. The most prized prisoners were allied fighter pilots, navigators, radio operators, mechanics and tacticians. These prisoner categories were treated better than others. Allied pilots were forced to teach fighter tactics to Soviet pilots at Russian training camps. Radiomen taught their Soviet counterparts everything they knew about communications, electronic jamming and codes. These and other technical prisoners were sent to Soviet aircraft factories.

Another Russian objective was to convert Negro prisoners to Communism. Soviets believed that indoctrinated prisoners could be recruited to work for Russia as saboteurs and spies in America after their release, but first they must be made to believe Communism was their champion. It required extensive education and training. For practice, black prisoners lectured Soviet personnel on the evils of capitalism. They also created anti-American propaganda by participating in on-camera interviews, radio broadcasts and rallies. Reformed POWs, operating as spies in these roles, were expected to stir racial tension in America when they returned.

Prisoners and guards shared the same medical facility, which had been run by Major Joel Schwartz, a German doctor captured by the Russian army in June of 1943. Schwartz watched helplessly as German prisoners were shipped north to the Kolyma region and understood it as a death sentence. In Kolyma, the mining camps consumed one-third of their workforce each year. American prisoners now replaced the Germans and that reality shattered Major Schwartz's hopes of ever returning to Germany. Using twisted bandages, he hung himself from a doorway the morning Jack's train arrived, but not before cutting the throat of the camp's political commissar, whom he especially hated for stopping the mail eight years before. Jack was assigned to take over the major's medical responsibilities for two thousand nine hundred new men, plus the seven hundred Japanese soldiers the Soviets still held from World War II.

***

The hospital was a converted barracks. It had twenty-two beds, three coal-burning stoves and an operating room with two one hundred-watt light bulbs. Medical supplies were limited to bandages that were washed and re-used: disinfectant, splints, plaster and some herbs were available. For pain there was aspirin. Blood transfusions, without plasma, were done on a person-to-patient basis. No x-ray or sterilization equipment existed. A single microscope and the blood testing equipment intimidated Jack; everything else he could live with.

"Did the German patients go with that last shipment of Germans to Kolyma?" he asked a guard.

"No, they were shot the day before yesterday."

Trying to appear unaffected by the horror of what he just heard Jack asked, "What did the Major use for a medical reference book?"

"That stuff on the shelf," replied the guard.

"But it's all in German," Jack said. "I need books in English. Can you get some?"

"I'll see," he said, and left. Three days later the guard returned and had in tow an army corporal who had worked as a butcher's apprentice in Milwaukee. He had learned German because the shop was in a German neighborhood.

"Hi! My name is Thomas Obuchowski," the Corporal said, thrusting his hand forward. "Call me Obie! I'm a butcher from Milwaukee. Specialized in sausages. I understand you need a German translator? What do you want me to do?"

"Can you read German?" Jack asked, skeptically.

"If it has something to do with making sausages, I can do it," he replied.

Obie joined the medical staff as Jack's assistant.

Shortly afterward, a mine cave-in crushed the legs of three men, requiring amputations. Jack and Obie did their hurried best to translate anatomy charts and confusing surgery references while the victims screamed in the adjoining room. When the time arrived, vodka was given to the men, tourniquets were applied and a sympathetic guard struck the patient's skulls with his baton, killing only one. The cuts were made using both a rough wood saw and a hacksaw. Jack stitched everything he could see that bled, and then applied an overheated iron stovetop to sear the wounds. One man lived, but was later shot for not keeping up his work quota.

Three-foot-high tunneling shafts had been dug with hand picks laterally into coal walls, which fanned like spider webs and connected into work chambers. Two hundred prisoners in ten-hour shifts were given a 1,200-ton-per-day quota. Failure meant a proportionate cut in rations.

Men crawled into these tunnels on their backs, made more holes, kicked or passed coal backwards to men behind them who then filled wheeled buckets for collection in the chambers. If they were lucky, cabbage soup, the basic full ration, was slopped into bowls that were never washed. Mostly it was borscht soup, but sometimes Kapushka, a red cabbage salad, offered change. Camp quotas were seldom achieved and men starved to death. For this reason men ate rats raw and often did not report a dead comrade until body parts could be stored for later consumption.

The UN prisoners were sent into the shafts the night of their arrival. Quotas were not reached and they were given a half-share of soup. They never caught up on their backlogs and during the first month the men lost an average of forty-four pounds. Suicides became epidemic.

Attending an injured guard, Jack asked if the Germans died of starvation. "A lot of them did, but after the strike six months ago, the quotas were lowered and food got better," he replied.

"What? You mean they actually got away with a strike?"

"Yeah, we had to shoot a lot of them, but the mines were shut down and were beginning to flood and we didn't have any more prisoners, so those Germans had it pretty good from that time on. When word got out that Americans were coming, the quotas were changed back."

"Is that why the Germans were sent to Kolyma?"

The guard replied with a chuckle. "Probably. Mother Russia does not approve of strikes. At Kolyma no one strikes because no one has long to live."

The German strike had embarrassed prison authorities. Camp quotas fell behind and administrators, who did not forgive backlogs, executed prisoners to force compliance, which reduced the workforce and brought officials from other camps to investigate. The German prisoners understood the effect of their strike and they refused to work without improvements in their lives. They were successful only until word reached the camps that the Americans were coming. It was an act of vengeance that caused the Germans to be sent to Kolyma, and any future strike by Americans would be mindful of that.

It was the economic authorities outside of the camp system that established production quotas. Camp commanders simply divided the work out to the prisoners, knowing full well that it could not be accomplished. Commanders covered their shortfalls using creative bookkeeping and bribes, and also by maintaining a high death rate. If the cycle of death was to be broken, a new idea was needed and Jack thought he was onto one.

Jack called a meeting of the prisoners' own officers to describe his plan. First he told them what he knew about the relationship between strikes and quotas and their implications to survival.

"It is true that we don't get enough to eat, but even if we did, the quotas could not be met. I've been the medical guy in charge and I know what I see. The lower the production becomes, the more vicious the punishment, and medical attention is required more frequently."

The men laughed. "So what's news about that?"

"The news is that production is down because the men are down with fear, depression, loneliness and desperation. But, if we conquer that, we will reduce the death rate and eat better."

Captain Bruce Wiley broke in. "Private Fischer, you are full of shit. These pricks want to see us dead and half of our men already wish they were. What do you want us to do—invite the guards to Saturday night dances?"

"No! Now listen carefully. Each shift has groups of two hundred men in the shafts. Men coming off shift rest and doing other things. There are three shifts in a twenty-four hour day. I am proposing that the off-peak shift attend to the needs of the shift coming off the line."

"What needs?" asked Bruce, another prisoner.

"I want their bodies and clothes washed and the men rubbed down, fed and put to bed. I estimate that will occupy about a hundred men. The remaining hundred men will rotate administering massages to feet and sore muscles, they will manipulate the spine and other joints and some will cut hair and trim nails—whatever is needed."

A voice yelped, "Holy smokes! A whore house!"

Jack responded with a smile. "Call it what you like, but I want an end to depression, desperation and suicide. The only thing that works against that is love. I want the men to feel they belong to a group that really cares about them. My giving them a pill is not enough. I want them touched by real humans and I want them to feel their daily survival is a victory for all of us."

Beginning to see the possibilities, Captain Wiley spoke. "Jack, you might be on to something. How do you suggest we begin?"

"Make a list of men with skills in these areas; have them form teams who can be teachers. Do the simple things, like using smaller men to walk on the backs of those who need treatment for back, shoulder and leg pain. Find me men that can craft implements that I need in the infirmary, like crutches, splints and traction devices, for a start."

"Anything you're not telling us?" someone asked.

"Yes," Jack replied. "I want to include the guards in the program. If they are good to us, we will help to make them feel human too. Let's face it; this is shit duty for them and probably the end of their career paths, as well. Don't let them take it out on us. Make them whole again."

It took only a single day to organize the program on paper and inform the men what their schedules would be. On the second day, the plan was executed on the men coming off of the night shift and they could not believe it. Most hesitated and looked bewildered, but officers barked at them to get on with it. Many broke down and cried, some shook uncontrollably, and Jack began to sense the power of healing and brotherhood spreading through the ranks like electricity. The organizers themselves cried, and for days men hugged each other for no apparent reason. By the fifth day, a new spirit had been born and it was time to include the guards. Jack and Captain Wiley presented the idea to camp commander Alexander Ivanov, or Ivan the Terrible, as he was tritely known, carefully explaining how and why it should work. Ivanov agreed to try it with fifty guards as an experiment, although he did voice concern for the security of the prison. "I will do this if you guarantee it results in better production. You've got one month."

Ivanov, seeing further possibilities for his own possible wealth, introduced money in the form of barter chips, into the prison system to provide a basis for reward that was different from using starvation to force compliance. Those who worked hard received more money, and no one had their food rations shorted as punishment. A trading post, really just a room, was set up for the prisoners to purchase tobacco, tea, soap and the like, and it too operated at a profit for Ivanov and the inmates. Money in the hands of the prison population also bought favors from other inmates and guards. It was frequently used to buy the services of an enterprising group of prisoner homosexuals, who had found that the demand for their services made them too valuable to be working in the mine.

Jack responded to Ivanov's requests for a complete examination, or treatment, by reserving the hospital recovery room for clandestine meetings between the camp commander and a particular prisoner favorite. Men who shirked work found their money diminished, the touching process lessened. Some learned quickly and paid others to work, even musicians became a standard of prison society. Money had been a great innovation, and Ivanov basked in the success of his idea and loved showing visiting dignitaries through the compounds, although what particularly interested them was that the camp had become self-sufficient in providing a reliable source of food. Ivanov did not tell them he had introduced money.

Farmers among the prisoners, with Ivanov's permission, began planting peppers, tomatoes, potatoes and onions. Those crops eventually exceeded the needs of the camps and were sold for cash. This led to additional plantings of commercial foodstuffs such as sugar beets, cabbage, eggplant, garlic and soybeans. Taken together, farming became a hugely successful enterprise. The prisoners retained half the profit, the other half going to Ivanov. He parceled sums to various officers and guards and still had enough left over for a rainy day.

What he found most interesting was that camp inspectors simply assumed he was operating the prison successfully, the old-fashioned way of using force. When pressed he would shrug his shoulders and say, "it must be the Americans—this bunch do everything I tell them."

No one seriously questioned, but that would not last, and the problem with accumulating money was that Ivanov had no place to hide it. He also had to be careful not to show wealth or he would risk arrest as a capitalist.

A waterborne virus swept through the Japanese compound and overwhelmed their medical staff. Sixty-two men died, four times that many were down with high fevers. Prison officials shut everything down in the hopes of establishing quarantine, but men were dying far too fast. Fear stalked the American compound.

"What do you think we should do?" Ivanov asked Jack.

"If everyone suspects the water that's causing it, then they're probably right," Jack replied. "Our water wells go down about a hundred feet and the latrines maybe fifty feet. My guess is that the higher than normal spring rains have caused the water table to rise; at the same time shit is being washed downward. Put septic water next to clean water and you are going to have people dying."

"Hey! That's pretty good. What's the solution?" asked Ivanov.

Jack thought for a minute. "Stop everyone from drinking well water immediately. Drill other wells some distance from the camp and truck the new water into the compounds. I would also recommend a longer-term solution by building a water tower with lines running into the camps. It could also be useful for the farms."

"Too expensive and it would take too long," Ivanov said.

"I think we are in a race against death," Jack argued. "And all of our reputations are on the line. Get me one hundred fifty men, including the Japanese—it's about time we all worked together anyway. We will provide you with a list of materials, and I promise to complete the project in twelve days—if you promise to permit a camp celebration when we finish."

Smiling with good humor and slapping Jack's ass, he said in a mocking southern drawl, "You-all go git the job dun-son."

The Japanese were thrilled to be working side by side with every nationality in the United Nations playbook; in fact, it was a Japanese engineer who provided the most efficient design for the water tower and the distribution system. An American led construction team had built it in just ten days time The Canadian-British team tore down a hopelessly broken irrigation pump and made it functional for the project. Everyone held their breath each time they tried to start the old pump. But, it did start, every time. A feeble celebration followed, but it was enough and men saw laughter on the faces of others for the first time in ten years.

Unfortunately, men continued to die, and panic set in. Jack went to the Japanese compound and asked to see the men who had beaten the disease. They looked gaunt, but it was clear they would live. Jack approached their commander, Colonel Yashida, with an idea.

"I want to draw blood from these men and infuse some of it into those who are sick, and also those who are healthy."

A Japanese medic asked, "won't that kill them?"

"Maybe," Jack said. "But it might also work like an inoculation. There is something in their blood that fought the disease. Hopefully it will save the others as well."

"Will the white men object to using blood from a yellow man?" asked the medic.

Grinning, Jack said, "that's a possibility, but I am going to tell them that their particular blood transfusion came from Ivanov the Terrible, himself. That should be enough to cause the dead to rise."

Later that month the epidemic stopped, and though Jack protested that it probably had just run its course, he became known as a healer. In Russia, a healer, even one with no formal training was regarded with spiritual reverence. The Japanese, who were especially proud but did not show it, instead let loose a rumor.

"If you begin having more erections than you did before the transfusion, then you will know it was Japanese blood that provided the blessing," they were fond of saying.

Chapter Twenty Six

Molding the Future

THE original airport at Khabarovsk had a network of underground concrete bunkers surrounding the field. Built in 1944 by German and Romanian slave labor, it had become obsolete twelve years later when a larger airport replaced it south of the city. The bunkers were large enough to accommodate an infantry division of eight thousand men and their equipment, which Russia had once anticipated it might need to defend the rail junction against attack. Now it stood useless.

Prison farmers had turned the landing field itself into a hothouse complex that took advantage of black asphalt's ability to absorb sunlight during winter. Here, tomatoes, lemons, flowers and assorted vegetables flourished all year long, producing crops far in excess of camp needs. The abundance was traded to nearby market places and to the Trans-Siberian railway system. With increased demand, new hot houses had to be built. Existing hothouses already covered more than seventy-five acres.

A group of Japanese prisoners attended to Jack's own hothouses where he grew and processed medicinal herbs and other useful plants. One prisoner, curious about the concrete bunkers, broke through a rusted metal grate and wandered around for two days. Mold covered the floors, walls and ceilings and he could hardly pass from one room to another without running into blankets of spider webs. Snakes and rodents were also abundant. Excited with his inspection, he returned to camp to ask his officers to arrange a meeting with Jack to lay out a plan. Jack listened and was immediately absorbed.

"Growing mushrooms in the old bunkers? Who would have thought?" he said to the man, whose name was Yoshi. "I think it is brilliant—what do you need to get started?"

Yoshi described the racks necessary for growing and drying, and he included lists of furniture, tools and equipment needed for processing and storage of the finished products.

"Yoshi, I want you in charge of this operation and I also want you to do me a favor."

"What can I do for you?"

"I want an area set aside for fruits and melons that are allowed to decay."

"Why?" asked Yoshi.

"I read somewhere that ancient people scraped mold from fruit, mixed it into a poultice and applied it to open wounds. It apparently worked and we are desperate for this kind of medicine. I would like to experiment with the idea, maybe even create a mixture that can be injected." The men agreed and began cleaning out the bunkers that same day.

The underground bunkers were the ideal growing environment for the mushroom spores that the prisoners harvested from nearby forests. Fifty separate species were developed, ranging from the edible to the poisonous, and those that were useful in developing the kind of medicines that King Poo Koo had taught Jack in Manchuria. Mold poultices were used on victims of mining accidents and it did prevent wounds from becoming infected. Mold mixed with distilled water and injected into the body would be tried next. Yoshi had his own private project, which was the making of cheese out of goat's milk, and this too did well in the markets, but not nearly as well as did the wine made from the fruit.

Chapter Twenty Seven

Prison Commander Ivanov

LT. General Khan San Khu was in charge of three hundred special prison camps in the Soviet Union. When his son-in-law, Alexander Ivanov, was arrested for sodomy in Leningrad, the general had him sent to Khabarovsk to be in charge of prisoner transportation and the administration of a POW camp. The general had only one thing to say to Ivanov about the arrangements.

"If you embarrass me again I will see the end of you. Understand?"

Ivanov had listened to the murderous tales of camp life coming from the lips of his wife's father at family gatherings, and he understood there would be no second chance; his own life depended upon it.

***

Alexander Ivanov's narrow shoulders were hunched over, and he walked with small shuffling steps: It gave him the appearance of falling forward. A Mongol-style mustache hung from his upper lip and his amber eyes seemed to glow. Together they made his otherwise wrinkled head look like an eerie candle-lit Halloween pumpkin. Having a fat head on a large body would have been acceptable to him, but not on his small body. He knew it was grotesque, and for that reason he had taken to wearing jackets with extra shoulder pads to lessen the contrast. Unfortunately it gave him the appearance of a spinning-top, tottering forward.

He learned to hate attractive people, especially men he felt were superior, and if he could, he would denounce such a person to the Party or arrange for him to be fired. Ivanov would be filled with the excitement of revenge, often achieving erections just thinking about the next person he would denounce. His malevolent attentions eventually focused on handsome young homosexuals he admired in

Robert Fischer

Leningrad bars, where he discovered having money made it easier to meet compliant men. Some were tied or beaten before being victimized. His cruelties had lessened as the love act with men became more voluntary. Being arrested for such acts was an injustice in his mind.

"It was a bum-rap," he pleaded to his wife. He also vigorously protested to the police that he was married with two children and that his father-in-law was a powerful general, but it did no good. Ivanov's wife accepted the arrest as a politically motivated plot aimed at her father and never suspected that her husband really had another life away from her bed.

Ivanov avoided a long prison sentence by agreeing to move his family to Siberia, but his homosexual behavior, if discovered, threatened his marriage and freedom. The secret police, he felt certain, were monitoring his every move, but that proved to be the product of his imagination.

As the commander of a prison camp, he took to killing the young German boys who satisfied his urges. He did so not because he liked killing, he felt bad about that, but because he could not risk a discovery, a discovery that would have made him a prisoner as well. Killing was common enough, no one paid much attention. When the Germans went on strike he became frightened that they would reveal his sins to his superiors, but when the Americans arrived, it provided the opportunity to send the Germans to Kolyma.

Ivanov had agreed to Jack's schemes to use prison labor to attend to prisoner's needs because he had to find a better way to manage the prison without another strike, which if it ever happened again, would likely result in his execution. Miraculously, Jack created success that went far beyond expectation. Ivanov also knew that Jack intuitively understood his need for male companionship, and he was particularly appreciative of how the first encounter was arranged.

"I have a very unusual case at the hospital," Jack remarked, casually.

"Oh, is there something I can do?" Ivanov replied.

"Well, possibly. You see there is this British fellow who likes to act like a woman and yesterday he was beaten up. He is in my clinic and I need someone to attend to him without encouraging another assault. I really can't leave him alone."

Ivanov looked carefully into Jack's eyes searching for a hint of entrapment or guile. He replied carefully.

"Your work program is coming along very well and I would not want to see anything interrupt the harmony. Have the man sent to my office quarters and I will look in on him personally."

"Great," Jack replied. "I'll do it within the hour." And indeed the man, who had been especially picked, was groomed beautifully before being carried by stretcher to his new quarters. No questions were asked, nothing was said, and when Ivanov understood that confidences could be kept, Jack approached him with the idea of permitting the homosexuals to be grouped together so that they could organize what he described was a vital, humanitarian and very confidential service. Ivanov pretended hesitancy, but gave his approval—for the prisoners' well-being.

***

The Soviets held allied POWs in separate compounds, away from Russian prisoners. However, guards, administrators and vendors were often transferred between areas, a practice that did not prevent word from leaking. Women prisoners were also held in permanent camps, but many were in crammed transit camps where they awaited transfer to camps with labor needs or high death rates.

The Russian officers in charge of one overcrowded women's camp decided to vent their anti-American feelings by grouping sixty women they considered the ugliest or sickest into a boxcar and sending it, un-announced, to the US compound. The fun part was that before loading the women into the freight car, they first immersed them over their heads into the ground-level tank filled with shit and urine from the building.

"Say hello to those American assholes for us," yelled one of the officers as the rail car pulled away. It was a safe prank because prisoners sent to a secret POW camp would never be seen again.

Shortly afterward, the freight car arrived at its destination. It surprised Ivanov, who had no idea what it was about. But on inspection he could see and smell that there was something more to it. He tried telephoning anyone in charge at the factory the women had described, but was told that the officers were not available. Puzzled and fearing the prisoners might carry an infectious disease, he had the women questioned by the staff, but it was Obie, Jack's medical assistant, who understood that this was an anti-American gesture and made a suggestion.

"This is just their way of saying, 'shit on you.'"

Looking at Ivanov and holding a rag to his nose, Jack said, "this is a top secret compound where no Russian prisoners are allowed to mix, and that would include these women. Whoever did this must be crazy."

Ivanov, gagging on the stink, replied, "well they are here. No one claims responsibility and I can't really send them back now that they have seen Americans. Not without risking my own ass." A sly smile formed on his listener's lips.

"I'm beginning to feel like stuffing sausages again—let's keep em," Obie said with enthusiasm.

"We have nearly three thousand men in these compounds and no women. Sixty of them might cause more trouble than they are worth," Jack replied.

Ivanov suggested an idea. "I am going to arrest them—to keep my records clear—for attempting to escape from somewhere or another and for seeing American POWs."

Jack joined the plot. "Hell! Don't stop there; let's find out where they got dumped into the shit and round up the rest of the women."

Thinking out loud, Ivanov advanced another thought. "As Commander, I will have all of their guards and officers arrested for breach of National Security. That way, my ass is covered and we might round up a couple hundred more women in the bargain."

Obie, almost beside himself, yelped, "Let's dump some of the guards into the shit when we get hold of them."

Everyone agreed and Jack directed Obie to have the women cleaned up, issued new clothes and given their own barracks. One woman, a Greek, who was abducted in 1963 from Athens by the Soviet NKVD, was sitting at the edge of the boxcar door covered in wet shit, watching the discussions. She could not hear the voices, but she understood the body language as meaning that she would not be raped today and, judging by the look of that bearded red-head, probably not tomorrow either.

Ivanov chose forty of his most trusted men and sent them down the line to arrest the factory guards with their officers. Taken by surprise, they were rounded up and placed into the same excrement-smeared rail car that had previously held the women. Upon arrival at the US compound, the guards were stripped of all identity, each were given POW uniforms and ordered to work in the mines for the next twenty-five years. The two hundred twenty-five additional women who had come to camp were now clean and safe from abuse for the first time in many years. Even their hair was allowed to grow because lice were not a problem at this camp. They also came to realize that as long as the Americans lived, they could not be released, but for the present they cared little about that.

Chapter Twenty Eight

Cognac
1967

THE German Army had captured Cognac in Romania in late 1943 and transported him to Poland. He had pleaded for his release.

"I am Egyptian, not Jewish. When my ancestors fled the homeland centuries ago and arrived in Romania they shortened the name from Egyptian to gypsy and that is why I am now known as a gypsy." Before the war, he traveled from village to village in his covered two-wheeled donkey cart calling himself Cognac, which he explained was French, and that he had no other name. He also proudly claimed to be a descendant of an Egyptian prince. It was a good story, and the Germans appreciated creativity and hung a sign around his neck stating that he was Cognac the Egyptian Prince. German guards amused themselves by calling him Schnapsy, slang for an affable village drunk.

Cognac was a six-foot giant with black shoulder-length hair, who had sang with a deep melancholy voice through a string of villages in exchange for offerings, but when these were meager he practiced painless dentistry using hypnosis.

"Come sleep with me—for your own good," he would say, with a wink to the girls, as he pulled his wagon through the marketplace. A cloth sign on the clapboard siding of his cart also advertised the same message with a sense of humor—"Cognac can put you out of your misery."

He was fun and people loved him, but the Germans had different ideas and sent him to a concentration camp in Poland. The Russian Army liberated him, saving his life and transported him to a Siberian Gulag for twenty five years. It was nothing against him personally; They imprisoned everyone that the Germans held: Americans, Poles,

Jews and Russian POWs, it did not matter.

Twenty four years later, in 1967, on a twenty degree below zero day, Cognac was marched alongside a rail line with two hundred other prisoners who were told to drop their pants and await the next train. When it arrived, the boxcar doors slid open revealing a cargo of recently abducted women from Hungary, still dressed in their city finery, including some with high-heeled shoes. The men cheered. The women were horrified at the sight of filthy bearded men with their pants down, lined along the tracks. Guards pushed the women out of the cars onto the snow.

A bullhorn announced, "You've got ten minutes."

Women screamed and ran, but sex-starved prisoners howled and smothered them with their stink and sex. Guards filmed the event for later viewing by future women prisoners, who might be hesitant to confess their crimes against the State. Cognac met Ati Niarcos in that way. She literally fell on him from the train.

Luck brought them together and luck assigned Ati to Cognac's dental clinic, where he taught her the arts of hypnosis and pulling teeth. During their five-year relationship she gave birth to a boy, who she understood could not be kept. But when it was taken away, she fought to keep him and a guard smashed her face with a rifle. Cognac leaped to her defense, striking at the guard. He was immediately overpowered and dragged to an outhouse toilet.

Cognac was tied onto the toilet seat; one arm was pushed through a newly sawn hole in the door, tied to a tree and held in that position throughout the night. Guards regularly pissed on his arm to assure it would freeze solid. In the morning the offended guard walked over to Cognac.

"This is the arm that struck me and you will now learn a lesson." The rifle came down on the frozen arm, snapping it off like an icicle. After beating Cognac with the frozen limb, guards tied him by his feet and attached the rope to the back of a truck and dragged him over the ice, while bets were made on how long the head would stay on. Ati was sent to Khabarovsk.

Chapter Twenty Nine

Ati
1973

OBIE entered the office and pulled Jack aside.

"Hey, look at this new 3 x 5 card that just came in."

"Read it."

"Attica Niarcos, age 27, worked two years as a perfume maker's assistant and several years as a dentist using hypnosis—says she can sing too. Been in the Gulag for ten years. It also says she was abducted from Greece in 1963."

Jack thought for a minute and decided. "Bring her in next week. I'd like to see if she can help out here."

Jack was astonished when Ati walked into the infirmary. For a moment he thought he was seeing Babe standing before him, even with her hair shaved. Tears swelled his throat, forcing a stutter.

"Plea…se sit down," he managed to say.

He reached for her hand and guided her to the chair. When they touched, something deep inside made his heart race. She sat very still, and when Jack did not say a word for several terribly long minutes, he began to feel foolish. Apologizing, he said, "I'm sorry to stare at you—I just lost control of myself for a minute. You, ah, you look almost exactly like my sweetheart in America. It was so unexpected…"

"Never mind. When did you last see her?" Ati asked.

"Twenty-three years ago in 1950."

"You obviously still love her."

"Yes, I do," Jack whispered.

***

For the next five years, Ati shared Jack's bed and they lived each day as lovers, companions and workmates. They had a child together that they named John. She taught Jack the hypnosis he had clumsily tried before in crude dental procedures. She also involved him in her passion for making perfume. Jack brought her into the world of medicinal herbs and the arts of healing, and together they sang, for themselves and for prison events: songs by Nat King Cole, Vaughn Monroe and the Ink Spots. The one song that everyone, including the Japanese, repeatedly called for was "Sentimental Journey" and behind that, "Answer Me My Love."

Life was idyllic in a macabre sort of way. They and other prisoners never ceased to wonder at what they had created together and how proud it had made them. They had good medical care, food was abundant, collectively and individually they had more money than could reasonably be hidden and the work itself was a fulfilling activity. The program of touching and caring for one another never ceased being important. It was the love-thread that wove them together as a community.

Chapter Thirty

Colonel Pavlovsky
1978

A hospital expansion to add another forty beds and other facilities was under way when an Australian private pulled a board from the floor beneath the operating table, revealing what appeared to be two rolls of toilet paper. He brought it to Captain Wiley, who deduced that they were lists of Axis prisoners held since the end of World War II. The names had obviously been placed there for someone to find; someone wanted these men not to be forgotten, someone wanted to leave proof of their existence, and that thought began to eat away at the officers seated around the table.

"We could be on a list just like that," said the Captain.

"If that German major hadn't killed himself when we arrived here, maybe he'd planned to escape with it," someone volunteered.

"Truth is—we are never getting out of here. We'll be just like them," chimed another.

Captain Wiley said, "This really gives me a knot in my stomach. I suggest we form a committee to look at a possible escape or for finding a way to get the word out to the West that we are here."

Everyone agreed, but not enthusiastically. Russia itself was a vast prison camp and no one ever escaped. But, they reasoned, things might be more lax now. Most had been prisoners for more than twenty years and the prospect of risking their lives was thought not to bother many, at least not yet.

"We need maps of the area and of potential escape routes through adjoining countries," barked someone.

Another injected a superb idea of creating secret time capsules, within which lists of prisoners would be buried along with their military numbers, facial caricatures and one-paragraph stories behind each picture. That idea was adapted with enthusiasm and within six months there were five such capsules buried within the city center of Khabarovsk, at regional crossroads and at camps that had easily identifiable landmarks, such as a water tower.

The capsule project was intense because it offered some hope of recognition or immortality, perhaps even rescue, but when the Australians announced that they could get their hands on two thousand bottles, with the intent of launching them into the sea—four hundred miles away—with messages from prisoners, the officers had to stop it. Any thinking man would know it was more likely that a Russian would recover a bottle launched near its shores, and it would not be long before their little Shangri-La would be shut down and the prisoners dispersed to other camps.

Some escape plans, while ingenious, never came to anything because the men knew that the prisoners could not escape en masse, and those left behind would face torture and then a firing squad for simply knowing about it. Logistically, escaping with the entire camp would require thirty airplanes with a capacity for more than three hundred passengers each or one long train load of prisoners dressed as Russian soldiers heading off to some border, no doubt with a band playing. Those fantasies would have ended in disaster. More importantly, even an unsuccessful attempt would end camp life as they knew it, and few would risk being transferred to a death camp. The only other option was for one of them, perhaps someone like Jack, whose special status and language skills could theoretically get him through to another country where he could notify the American government that POWs were still alive, to take off on his own. But, they also feared that Western governments might suggest to the Russians that they get rid of everyone in the camps and erase all evidence of Allied prisoners ever existing, to prevent a scandal from reaching the newspapers in either country. The men did not want to think that their own country had abandoned them, but they were no longer sure.

Jack and Ivanov talked openly about escape possibilities, because any escape would result in the camp commander's execution. Ivanov also knew that he and or Jack could be transferred to another part of the Gulag at any moment at the whims of anyone with a grudge. Men had a way of disappearing after being denounced by someone anonymous and he did not want to be one of them. Any escape would require money, and the first step was to somehow funnel their money into a foreign bank.

"Find us the nearest branch of the Bank of India or the German Warburg Bank, and I will arrange for you to have an account that no one in Russia will know anything about," Jack said. "It won't be easy."

"You can do that?" replied Ivanov.

"Yes," Jack answered. "In fact, I already have an account in a foreign bank and it's possible, even after all these years, they will trust the opening of another account. It's the Bank of India, they have branches everywhere."

Ivanov looked at Jack questioningly but said he would get a list of bank locations and once the information arrived, they could plan how to make the trip.

The City of Vladivostok is the Soviet Union's only all-weather seaport on their eastern border and, as a consequence, business with the rest of the world was done there. It had branches of both banks and more. Jack instructed Ivanov to send a telex, but only from central Khabarovsk, to be less conspicuous, announcing the arrival of #11036720, during the first week of August 1978. It would be dangerous to be seen waiting at a foreign bank, not knowing if they were under surveillance, but Jack estimated the business and deposits could be made within a one-hour period, limiting their exposure. His telegram through Ivanov would insist that documents be ready for signature when they arrived.

Jack boarded the train using the identification of a guard lieutenant captured at the factory some years before. Two railcars would separate Jack from Ivanov, and they would not talk to each other until after arrival at Vladivostok, in three days. Both wore holstered standard issue 9mm pistols.

After arrival, Jack planned to follow Ivanov; both would check into the same hotel, but into different rooms. One hour later, they would appear on the street with Ivanov leading the way toward the Bank of India. Jack would enter first to confirm the arrangements while Ivanov waited outside for any possible trouble.

Ten minutes into the wait, Jack tapped Ivanov on the shoulder and said, "Come inside, I would like to introduce you to the bank manager."

Sweating and shaky, Ivanov seated himself and went through the motions of setting up an account without ever taking his eyes away from the front entrance. Jack deposited the Russian ruble equivalent of $46,000 in American money and requested that his deposit be noted to the Bank of India's branch in Hong Kong, along with a message to be forwarded to a Mr. King Poo Koo. Ivanov deposited almost three hundred thousand dollars into his own numbered account.

"Were you some kind of big shot in the old days? I was shocked when you talked about an account in Hong Kong. What's the story?" Ivanov asked later, at a teashop.

"No, I'm no big shot—I will tell you the story later. For now, I suggest we eat, and then you walk over to that post office and telephone the camp. Make sure everything is alright." Jack replied.

They ate in silence, knowing they had just put a fortune into a foreign bank and that they had no place to go but back to a prison camp. There was something surreal about that. They sipped their vodkas and studied each other for hints of fear. Finally Jack spoke.

"Better go across the street, Ivanov—get going."

He agreed, but when he arrived back, a half-hour later, he was ghost white.

"You make the phone call?" Jack asked, alarmed.

"Yes!" Ivanov replied in a shaky voice. "I got through to my second in command and he informed me that the camp is crawling with inspectors investigating evidence of capitalist crimes against the State."

"What evidence?" Jack asked urgently.

"A camp guard had one of the prisoner's weekly newsletters with him when he visited a relative, who happens to be Colonel Sergei Pavlovsky," Ivanov explained. "He was the prick in charge of transportation and part of his jurisdiction included the brick factory. Remember, we gave him a big headache when we took all of his women and imprisoned some of his guards? He has been gunning for me ever since."

"He can't do anything about that anymore; it's been more than five years. By now he would have made his paper work accommodate for the missing people."

"That's true, but he makes money selling female prisoners to camps up the line, and we put a dent into his operation," explained

Ivanov.

Surprised, Jack said, "Bullshit. He receives a cut on everything we deliver to Trans-Siberian rail."

"Don't you see, Jack? He wants to take over the bunkers and the hothouses on the old airfield. Technically—you know—they are closer to his command than to mine. All he needs to do is get me out of the picture and seize what he wants."

"Alex, he can't do that with a copy of our newsletter. Be realistic," Jack replied, hiding his own concern.

"Yes, he can," Ivanov said. "It outlines every activity from dances with women no one knows anything about, to what this week's menu will be. Cabbage soup isn't on it, but upcoming bingo prizes are!"

"So what do you want to do, Alex?"

"Oh! That's simple. You of all people know I'm a coward. I'm finding my way out of this fucked-up country. I am not going back to get shot for no good reason and I think $300,000 in my pocket is too hard to come by to risk on the whim of a biased investigator."

Jack was not surprised at the answer. He knew the fear that permeated the whole Communist system, and he felt sympathy for the man sitting across from him. Ivanov would never see his family again if he fled, and without help getting out of the country, he would probably be caught, the scandal would reach his father-in-law and he would be a lucky man if they only shot him. Jack thought for a long while and looked Ivanov in the eyes.

"You are going back on tomorrow morning's train and nothing is going to happen to you. Now, let's get out of here and go some place where we can discuss an idea!" At Ivanov's panicky look, Jack said, "no, no, no, Alex. Don't say a word until you hear what I have to say."

They left the teashop and walked toward the center of town as Jack outlined a convoluted plot that started with Ivanov withdrawing one hundred ten thousand dollars from the bank account he had just opened.

"After you board the train back to camp, I will use one hundred thousand dollars of this money to deposit into a Russian bank in the name of Colonel Sergei Pavlovsky from Khabarovsk, and I will obtain a receipt for it. Two thousand dollars will be placed as a credit for a one-week stay at the end of this month in that fancy hotel across the street with accommodations that will include a prostitute. The rest of the money will go with me on the train one day later, but I will not come directly to camp. Instead, I will stay in a hotel at Khabarovsk. From there, I will telephone you to ask how many men the colonel has left behind at his headquarters, and who is in charge there. You will find this out before I get there. Subsequently, I will arrive at his headquarters and ask to speak privately to the officer in charge."

"Good God, Jack, what do they have to do with it?" asked Ivanov, surprised and frightened.

"Before I arrive at those headquarters, I will have already notified the NKVD, anonymously, that I have information about a certain colonel who recently opened a huge bank account eight hundred miles away in Vladivostok. Then I will speak earnestly to the officer in charge. I will tell him that I am his friend coming to warn of the impending arrest of Colonel Pavlovsky and I am going to suggest he accept four thousand dollars in cash to smooth his own departure before that happens." Jack paused. "I will explain to him that the secret police know everything about the kickbacks on the Trans-Siberia rail account, the bribery coming from the bunkers, the selling of women prisoners, and obviously, by implication, I also know about those activities. I will suggest to him that I think it would be wise if the headquarters building burned to the ground, just in case there is incriminating evidence of these criminal activities."

"Why in the hell would he do any of those things?"

"Because I will be telling him the truth and he will know that these kickbacks are happening. Besides, how could he argue with another colonel who tells him things he already knows?"

"What other colonel?" Ivanov asked.

"Me!" Jack explained. "I will be wearing your colonel's shoulder boards. If he is still unconvinced, I will simply shoot him."

"You are risking your life. Are you nuts?"

Laughing, Jack said, "Well, all they can do is shoot me or put me in prison. I am already in prison so my odds are pretty good."

"How do we explain your role in all of this, particularly if it is you that shows up with the bank deposit receipt and hotel reservation?" Ivanov asked.

"I am going to claim Colonel Pavlovsky approached me to make the deposits because he did not want to risk doing it himself. I am well known in the area and I have substantial liberties of movement relating to medical needs of his soldiers. I will allege that he also did not trust me to go alone, because, I will state, the very lieutenant I am now impersonating came along with me. Of course he did not find the lieutenant, because he does exist, that's me, under arrest at your camp. But that will appear to the NKVD as something the colonel pre-arranged to cover his own story.

"Further," Jack continued, "the NKVD will see me as the fall guy in the colonel's scheme. They are likely to assume, if I do get caught, that they would expect Pavlovsky to say I escaped with payroll money from his safe—or something like that."

Ivanov looked completely confused. "You're giving me a headache," he protested.

"Naturally, they would also expect him to attempt killing me in an effort to cover his tracks."

"That's pretty much the way the NKVD would think," Ivanov said. "A hundred thousand dollars is more than twenty years of that shit's salary, and they would never believe you had stolen the money, because the colonel would have to prove he had it to begin with. Very clever."

"Okay! The last and most critical step is for you to wait for my second telephone call from the train station. This will tell you that I have arrived near the station and have finished my work at the colonel's headquarters. You will then telephone the NKVD explaining that you have used one of your prisoners to do something illegal. And that you have a Private Jack Fischer under your guard because he fears for his life, and that he is now en-route back to camp. That, Alex, is how the bank receipts get into your hands to produce as evidence."

"Very well thought out," Ivanov replied. "And just to make sure it is my men that arrest you, I will have them at the station immediately after my return from Vladivostok."

An hour before the train left, Ivanov withdrew the money and handed it to Jack saying, "I don't mind admitting your plan is good, but frankly, I am scared. If something goes wrong—I don't even want to think about it."

"It's our best chance Ivanov. We are in this thing together."

Ivanov arrived by train back at the POW compound and noticed that Colonel Pavlovsky had occupied his personal offices and that there were twenty-two men with him guarding all entrances. There was no NKVD in sight. He realized that Pavlovsky had no intention of involving them, and their absence was proof that this investigation was nothing more than a shakedown, a matter that would require negotiations. It was also clear that Pavlovsky thought he had Ivanov under his control.

"Greetings, Sergei!" Ivanov said, as he reached for the colonel's hand. "It has been a long time, but I see that you have made yourself comfortable in my absence. So, why don't we forget about this newsletter bullshit and get down to the business of why you are really here?"

Sergei sneered. "You are a smart fellow and I will do that, but first I want to kill as many of your men as those that disappeared from my command five years ago."

"Ah! Sorry about that, but you will remember I was having a rather shitty day. But if you want your fellows back, I'll arrange it and we can forget about the shooting."

"I don't want them back. I have no way of accounting for them and you know it, so fuck you, and let's stick to the subject of my shooting some of your men."

"Okay, Sergei, you win, but let's not hurry with that just yet, it's late in the day, and I have already made plans to hand control over the bunkers to you—the day after tomorrow."

"Why wait?" Sergei complained. "All I need from you is a signed order, that's it."

"Let's put it this way, asshole," Ivanov said, leering into his face. "You aren't going to call in the NKVD, because that would not result in your obtaining a piece of the action, and you are not going to shoot me because you could not get away with it. That leaves you the option of wandering around here with gunmen that can't force me to sign an order."

Holding the palm of his hand toward Pavlovsky's face, Ivanov continued. "In other words, you can fuck up the whole operation and get nothing or strike a deal with me that I would have to adhere to, because I know that an asshole like you can, in fact, bring everything down if he doesn't get what he wants. Am I not correct?"

Sergei was a little surprised at Ivanov's balls and having never seen him in that light before, replied flippantly, "so make me an offer!"

Ivanov offered a partnership in the bunker and hothouse operations in exchange for shared control of Pavlovsky's transportation and army supplies business. It was also agreed that the new headquarters would be in the US compound where outside scrutiny was less likely. The colonel accepted and a celebration was planned. Ivanov knew that once Sergei moved in, it would not be long before he would reach for complete control.

As planned, Jack's telephone call arrived the night of the celebration and his arrest by Ivanov's men followed shortly after Jack visited Sergei's headquarters. Jack was placed into a cell at camp until the NKVD came. When the Internal Security men arrived at the main gate, Ivanov asked Sergei to come to his office to examine some interesting things recently discovered.

"Sit down, sit down. Make yourself comfortable," Ivanov casually remarked to Pavlovsky, "Too bad about the fire burning down your headquarters building. I hear nothing is left."

"What?" Pavlovsky, who had just sat down, jumped up. "Who did it?"

"Actually, I arranged for it, but it seems the NKVD is asking the same question. In fact, they are on their way here to question one of our prisoners, someone who claims you sent him to open a one hundred thousand dollar bank account in Vladivostok—in *your* name—and as you know, doing such a thing is completely illegal."

"Impossible!" shouted Sergei Pavlovsky.

Ivanov spoke menacingly, breathing into Sergei's face. "I have the bank receipt that says differently, and I also have a receipt for your hotel reservations there—a very fancy place, I might add. The prostitute you had waiting for your arrival, incidentally, has also been arrested."

Shocked, and realizing that a trap had been sprung, Pavlovsky grabbed the telephone and demanded to be connected to his headquarters.

"Forget about it, your officers have all bugged off, and let's hope for your sake that they are not caught, because they have a great deal of money on them."

"You prick!" Sergei yelled. "You will never get away with it.

This is all bullshit."

"Yes, yes, of course it is all bullshit, but the NKVD likes bullshit," Ivanov replied. "In fact, they are here in this very building as we speak."

Sergei whirled toward the door, anticipating something horrible coming through it. "Sergei? " Ivanov said. As he turned, four pistol shots hurtled him to the ground.

"You should never have tried to escape, asshole," a sweating Ivanov said to the dead colonel.

Chapter Thirty One

Chita

"COLONEL Pavlovsky is dead," Ivanov said when Jack arrived at his office.

"What happened?"

"When he didn't call State Security, I realized his mission here was purely extortion. If I refused his demands, I would be in the shit the moment he left camp. I couldn't risk it."

Jack thought for a moment. "The KGB already knows about Pavlovsky's bank account in Vladivostok. It won't be long before they find their way here."

"I don't think so. We moved his body near his burned-out headquarters building. The men he came with have been tattooed with prisoner numbers and are being transported to a Moscow hospital where they will be used as guinea pigs."

Jack shifted his shoulders over the table between them. "Why do they need people for experiments?"

Ivanov rose from the table. "I couldn't tell you before because I couldn't risk riots, a prisoner strike and mass relocation of inmates to other camps, most likely Kolyma or killings to quell a disturbance."

"Tell me," Jack said.

"Remember those guards we arrested at the brick factory? Do you recall prisoners moving in and out of this camp? Didn't you ever wonder where these people go, and don't you wonder who controls these camps?"

"I just assumed this camp and others like it were established to make use of POWs for slave labor. The compounds are secret because the government doesn't want the West to know."

Ivanov gripped both of Jack's arms and said, "in your wildest imagination, you'd never imagine the truth of what I tell you. It must be kept a secret."

"You have my word."

"In Moscow, there is the Institute for Nuclear Medicine or INM. It accounts for around two thousand POWs per year. Most come from the Khabarovsk region. They investigate the effects of chemical agents, drugs, biological organisms and nuclear radiation on prisoners. A transfer to Moscow is a death sentence."

"No, I wouldn't have imagined that. I had no idea."

"Allied pilots train Soviet pilots in tactics, aircraft performance, communication and codes. Aircraft mechanics, military intelligence personnel, medical specialists, you name it, if the prisoner has a skill, he'd be sent to the Moscow Institute for Nuclear Medicine."

"This is bigger than I thought."

Ivanov didn't stop. "Our region imprisons fifty thousand. In our own compound are Vietnam and Korean War POWs. I know for a fact there are approximately thirty-five thousand Americans from World War II spread throughout the Soviet Union.

"Before your arrival, we had seven hundred German soldiers who were shipped to Kolyma after the strike. We still have Japanese troops. You may not know this, but after World War II, more than a million Japanese soldiers were captured in Manchuria by the Soviet Union, which decided to keep them, but many thousands committed suicide in protest. Under pressure from world press and high suicides, two-thirds were returned to Japan, but the rest, like the ones in our camp, will never leave Russia alive. Non-Russian are the Greeks, Bulgarians, Poles, Hungarians and those stolen off the streets, like your Ati, by the KGB. Most are rounded up after a demonstration somewhere."

Jack started to interrupt, but decided not to speak.

"Requests for prisoners for experiments come in all the time, and we keep their transportation secret. Imagine what would happen if the prison population found out they were not being sent to other work camps, but instead were being used for experiments. There would be a revolt: I would lose my job and maybe my freedom. Anything that we administrators do that is in any way unusual becomes cause for denouncement, and the ease by which one reverts from being a respected officer of the Soviet Union Army to a prisoner in the Gulag is truly frightening. Greed, fear and cruelty are so common in our officer ranks that discussions about prisoner abuse are often accompanied by laughter at examples of the most recent heinous punishment meted out to some poor soul for the slightest infraction. We turn on the prisoners, we denounce one another, we all survive by knowing people higher up on the food chain, and before them we grovel, plead and bribe away our existence until we are lucky enough to be transferred to a regular army unit or retire.

"Our late Colonel Pavlovsky knew that my camp operated in a far different manner, was profitable and humane, and he could easily take effective control in behalf of his general by setting the stage for a denouncement for crimes of capitalism. They could not take actual control of my command without rubbing against my father-in- law, a general in charge of three hundred prison camps, so they elected a not too subtle shakedown. It would have succeeded if you had not come up with the plan to eliminate the Colonel, but don't rest too easy with that. His general will know that the disappearance of Pavlovsky and his entire headquarters would have something to do with Colonel Alexander Ivanov. It is only a matter of time before more of the General's front men arrive from the KGB, GRU or other security operation to pay me a visit. Having you here leaves open the possibility of your arrest and torture and that will bring both of us down. Therefore, I must send you away."

Jack was about to say something, but Ivanov waved him silent.

"I do not know where to send you and still retain the ability to have you returned. If I make a mistake and you are transported to the mines or timber cutting areas you'll be worked to death. The State of Khabarovsk is half the size of America and is one giant prison, and every village, harbor, road or factory is part of the prison system. It would be impossible to bypass thousands of checkpoints without being noticed. If you somehow did escape by virtue of local help, they'd risk being forced to finish your sentence. You would be shot."

Jack understood, but still felt it was not fair to have won the battle with Pavlovsky only to be rewarded with a dire future. "Where is this place you are thinking to send me?" he asked.

"Chita is a city much like Khabarovsk. It is more than a thousand miles west and two hundred miles north of the Mongolian border. It's a junction for the Trans-Siberian Rail system. Around

Chita there are prisoner camps for both Russian and non-Russian prisoners. Most are held there to work in the mines. In the main, this is a collection point for prisoners that are to be assigned according to which region has the greatest need for labor. I know an officer there who is in charge of prisoner allocations. He was the one who provided us with an un-recorded group of the almost six hundred women in our camp. The bribe cost me twenty-five thousand U.S. dollars and another two hundred dollars a head to transport them here. Let's say I have a big investment in females, but I wanted a higher man-to-woman ratio. My friend might locate you to another camp as a healer. It follows that for a few more rubles your return here could be assured when the heat dies down."

"What about Ati and my son John?"

"They too must disappear. You can't be together because it is against prison rules and if they are here when trouble comes, they will be at risk. I could hide the boy at my home and send Ati to a nearby camp—as a dentist, on loan for say six months. If I do everything right, you should all be back together within a year."

Jack shrugged. "I accept your judgment and now appreciate the risks you have been taking on our behalf. You can count on me not to tell the other prisoners about the medical experiments. Meanwhile, as I await transportation, I would like you to consider another plan that might mitigate the threat of your own arrest or removal."

"Christ, Jack, don't you ever sleep. What is it this time?"

"Alex, the entire prison system is based upon fear. You cannot trust your fellow officers and administrators, and you never know from day to day if you will be denounced. Therefore, I suggest several programs be put in place. The most important is to establish a network of spies or informers throughout the region, all the way to Moscow, if possible. The information will give you a handle on what the anti-Ivanov trends are. Just as important, you can provide information that affects your Soviet colleagues' well-being. This will make them dependent upon you; open the door to their advocating your promotion and for your continued placement here. The organization would also provide the basis for a quid pro quo program, whereby it exchanges knowledge and services for others' knowledge and services. In effect, I want you to establish your own secret police. You have plenty of money and the talent to promote the idea, and it is better than sitting here waiting for the axe to fall."

"That would be very useful to me. Keep going," Ivanov replied with enthusiasm.

"You will also need a paramilitary force that operates parallel to your command. Enforcers, if you want to call them that. These men will come from the best prisoner warriors we have. They can be trained and ready to carry tasks like bugging, extortion, sabotage and assassinations. This force, which will include your own soldiers, would also be responsible for arming and training all of the prisoners. Don't worry; they aren't going to break out. You said yourself that a single escapee could not get out of the area, so have no fear that an armed prison camp would fare any better. No, the idea is to have more guns than your adversary, and the day may come when you will need it. Lastly, you should create an underground network of tunnels and chambers that lead to key defense points inside and beyond the camp's perimeters. The network should be large enough to house all the females and children that we're not supposed to have, whenever an inspection is anticipated. The underground areas will also be useful to establish manufacturing capabilities."

"I'm having a hard time getting my mind around prisoners being my defender, but go on," Ivanov pointed out.

"For example, the Japanese used what they called a knee-mortar. I want these made in our own machine shop. The shell can be made to explode tin foil strips in the air. Our men could infiltrate the countryside and fire those rounds above the electric transmission lines. The foil falls and contacts the wires, shorting out the power grid for hundreds of miles. That kind of chaos might provide an escape opportunity, but primarily it would give you and the rest of the men time to don Russian uniforms and melt into the taiga."

There was a lot to think about and to do, but Jack was right. Waiting for another Pavlovsky was not smart.

***

Before leaving for Chita, Jack had breakfast with Ivanov. They talked at length about the successes in camp: the boost to morale when women became part of everyone's lives again, the rich bounty from their agricultural pursuits and their fears for Ati and Jack's son, John. Alex did his best to reassure him that everything would be alright and it would only take a year for them to be back together. Jack did his best to hide his fear of what lay ahead. Finally, a car arrived. Ivanov dropped a bomb saying.

"Jack, I feel guilty for even telling you this and I have avoided the subject for a long time, but I must tell you now because I don't want you to do anything reckless, like trying to reach an American or other country's consulate."

Surprised, Jack asked, "What are you talking about, for Christ's sake?"

Alex looked at Jack. "The Western governments know you are here. They know you are prisoners. You've been written off. You have become slave labor because your government felt it was more important to end truce negotiations than it was to hold out for your return. None of you exist, and if you suddenly appear, you will be turned back to the Soviets because they too won't risk the embarrassment of American POWs surfacing inconveniently with such a dishonorable story."

With complete recognition of this fact, Jack stood, speechless, his heart in the pit of his stomach. Ivanov continued. "We are on our own, Jack. No one is coming to the rescue. Exposing the truth will not set you free, but together, for different reasons, we will find our ways home. Depend on me."

***

Ati was sent to a camp along the Amur River that harvested timber. She worked there as a dentist, but three months later, in sub-zero temperature, she was maliciously and carelessly assigned to a tree cutting unit that failed to reach its quota because trees were frozen too hard for cutting. The punishment was being left in the open all night. No one was allowed to return to camp without making up for the original quota, and the subsequent day's quota that followed. A week later, two hundred twenty cutters, along with two-dozen guards, were retrieved frozen solid. When Ivanov heard the news, he knew it was a subtle message aimed at him, a form of retaliation by some faceless bureaucrat. For the first time since his conversation with Jack, he became utterly determined to create a powerful intelligence force. Ati's killing would not go unpunished.

Chapter Thirty Two

He's Alive

THE war was trying to end with a truce in 1953 and King was on the move. The Indian freighter taking King Poo Koo out of Nampo harbor in North Korea toward freedom was a Liberty ship built in 1942. It barely made seven knots and at that speed he estimated the trip to Hong Kong would take seven days in good sea conditions. King kept his valuables in waist and ankle pouches.

The ship's position at the time it was hit was one-hundred miles south of Nampo and approximately fifty miles west of Seoul, the closest safe harbor. The five-inch cannon rounds, from a Chinese destroyer, blew away the communications and holed the ship twice near the waterline. The slap of heavy seas against the ship sides slowly filled the lower bulkheads with seawater.

All the bridge officers were dead, leaving command to an engine room ensign who raced to a map table to determine what his options might be. The destroyer had come alongside but moved off and made no attempt at rescue when they realized the stricken ship's radio had been wrecked and its sinking would likely be recorded as an unexplained event. They reasoned that the truce negotiations between the Allies and China, being held in Panmunjom, would probably not appreciate the deliberate sinking of an Indian ship within reach of the South Korean coastline and friendly to the United Kingdom.

The warship stood off until it was certain the freighter, aided by an upcoming storm from the west, would sink. It then left the area.

Ensign Sikar Pushta already had the pumps running, but in heavy seas he knew the ship would sink, perhaps within three to eight hours, depending on the force of the wind, Pushta pointed the ship toward Inchon, hoping the westerly storm behind them would blow him toward the Korean coastline. He also thought the new heading would diminish the effect of the waves broadsiding his vessel.

Down below, King organized an attempt to close the hole closest to the waterline using fifty-pound bags of dried peppers lashed together with netting, but the effort was failing. Running topside, King explained the problem to Pushta and a new scheme was contrived to make use of the aft crane to lift cargo pallets wired together and lower them as a patch outside the hole. On the first try, the pallets slid down the side of the ship. Trailing ropes, attached to the pallets, were pulled through the hole by the crew below decks, who tied them firmly in place. Canvas cargo covers were lowered over the side and tied to prevent swells from entering the hold. Metal plates were cut from the demolished bridge and welded into place outside and inside the bulkhead. The gap closed just enough leaks for the pumps to have an effect.

Inchon harbor, outside of Seoul, came into sight twelve hours into their run for the coast, but when they attempted entry, Pushta realized the tide leaving the harbor was stronger and faster than his four-knot headway. Afraid to be swept back out to sea, he dropped anchor and hoped it would hold. During the night, the crew watched the water recede and were amazed to find themselves stuck in a mud flat that spread for miles. Inchon harbor was used only during certain times of the day as retreating tides emptying into the basin routinely stranded ships in mud. In the morning, the Liberty ship re-floated and Pushta flagged a South Korean cutter bearing his way, in response to his SOS. Hours later they were on land.

***

King sent a telex to Jin Jaing in Hong Kong, informing him that he had escaped and explained his arrival at Seoul, South Korea. The cable also explained that the cargo was a write-off, that there might be some salvage value, and that King did not have papers to enter Hong Kong. Jin had originally planned to bring King into Hong Kong illegally from a ship under his control, but now new plans would be necessary. King talked for almost an hour on the telephone telling Jin about Jack being sent to Russia.

King finally said, "Jin, why don't I just stay in South Korea for a while? Maybe set up some kind of business that we can both benefit by."

"Can you stay there legally?" asked Jin.

"This is just another shithole with a lot of confusion," King replied. "So I think it won't be a problem. I've already seen the Americans about rehabilitating either a bombed-out coal mine or a war-damaged cement factory, outside of Seoul."

Jin said, "Just like that? Didn't you being Chinese get in the way of their cooperation?"

"Nah!" King replied. "I speak Pidgin English—learned from Jack. Hell, they nearly hired me for two different jobs; a cook on board a ship, if you can believe that, and as an interpreter."

Jin laughed. "King, you were always a good bullshit artist. How did you explain what you were doing on that Indian ship?"

"Told them I was a business passenger from India overseeing the quality of the feathers and peppers, that I bunked with the officers and that the evil Chinese Navy blew them away along with all of my papers."

"Good story," Jin said. "So what happened next?"

King affected what he thought was a southern drawl and said, "Ah solt em what wuz left of dee fedders, dey all wish'd me luk and tol me to contaxt dem if'n I be needen any-ole-thing!"

Jin laughed, and King felt that maybe he really was free after all.

***

The war-torn city of Seoul, its Kimpo airport and the smashed factory buildings along the Han River were in desperate need of locally produced raw materials. The American military had neither the time nor the will to establish those infrastructures, especially in light of the potential for the Chinese army to invade the border again. The current cessation of hostilities could fall apart at any minute. Needed cement, steel, lumber and power tools would have to come from the States by ship. King made a request to the U.S. Navy for a small launch tour of Inchon Harbor and the Han River, a trip he could not have made without their approval because the area was a military district. He explained his interest in establishing a cement factory and to his surprise they agreed to show him around.

The tour revealed great stockpiles of imported raw materials from America, but nothing was produced locally. The main reason for the lack of infrastructure or local supplies was security concerns. There were no military or other police, and the North Korean army had slaughtered half the civilian population with a rage that was beyond belief. The population was scared. King inspected a gravel quarry littered with the skeletons of eight thousand dead civilians and he couldn't get away quickly enough. Ironically, it was the site best-suited for his purposes and it could be bought for almost nothing if he offered to remove the remains.

He agreed and set to work on the grisly task by hiring off-duty American servicemen who could drive bulldozers and trucks.

Once the site had been cleared, King erected a rock crusher he found at another wrecked facility and crafted new sifting screens and mixers. He constructed storage areas and built housing for his workers. He knew that worker and family housing would be a key to obtaining and keeping good employees and he did not have far to look to find what he needed. Unassembled, pre-fabricated American barracks were stacked everywhere.

Less than a year after King began his Korean adventure, Jin arrived in Seoul and was astonished to see a walled enclosure consisting of a one-hundred-acre facility that crushed gravel, sifted sand and made bagged and wet cement for a fleet of thirty cement delivery trucks. At one end was housing sufficient for three hundred workers, a community kitchen and a recreation area. King also paid employees top money for their loyalty and a good day's work. At the Han River's edge, molds were under construction to build cement boats, concrete panels, cement blocks, septic tanks and a strange-looking igloo King thought was just the thing for farm housing.

"I had a fair amount of money from the China operations and some came from the salvage sale of the peppers and feathers, but if the truth be known, Jin, I actually did not need a penny of it to start all of this," King explained, showing Jin around for the first time.

"How did you do that?"

"Control of the Kimpo Airport was being handed back to the civilian government because the American military no longer wanted to run it," King explained. "But the Korean government refused ownership. It did not want the responsibility of improving roads, buildings and infrastructure. The U.S. decided to go forward with the improvements and came to me for cement that I did not have—at least not yet."

"They believed you could deliver? Incredible," Jin said.

"Yes, and I demanded a firm contract with a big deposit. With that in hand I got the Korean government to fund it for me—that is how I started."

"I imagine the government borrowed the money they loaned to you from the U.S. military?"

"That's exactly right," King, said with a chuckle.

Korea Cement Ltd. expanded and became South Korea's largest post-war materials manufacturer. Over the following twenty-four years, it also became a construction giant with development contracts in Saudi Arabia, Kuwait, the Emirates, Hong Kong and Australia. King was on top of the world. He married a Korean woman, Soon Yee, fathered three children and held seats on government boards.

During the same period, Jin developed an interest in plastic injection molding equipment, which he manufactured in Korea in partnership with King. He also had the notion that they should manufacture the products that came out of these machines.

"What kind of products do you have in mind, Jin?" King asked, during a company meeting in the spring.

"To start, I'm thinking personal care items like hair dryers, combs, curlers, pins, lipstick tubes and the like."

"You want to make this stuff here in Korea or back in Taiwan?"

"Neither!" said Jin. "I want to establish injection molding companies throughout Mainland China, the farther away from the big cities the better."

"Why?"

"Look, President Nixon has been to China. It's opening up, you'll see. We know it needs technical expertise that we can give it, and we are Chinese, which should help. They have cheap labor, we have the capital and we can teach the workforce what is needed. We will export these products at prices that are cheaper than either Korea or Taiwan can make them. Most importantly, we become part of the emerging China."

"And the reason for staying away from the big cities?" asked King.

"Well, it is a lot easier to pay off small-time mayors and local officials than it would be in the likes in Canton or Peking."

King thought about the idea. "Would we be limited to personal care products?"

"Hell, no!" Jin replied. "Anything that can be made from plastic, we do it in China. Automotive parts, office equipment, anything we can think of."

"Are you hedging your bets against Taiwan's long-term future, Jin?"

"Frankly, yes," Jin replied. "I don't like to say this, but we don't think it's wise to trust America to stand by its treaty obligations with Taiwan. That would leave us at the mercy of China, so it's better for us to be established there as well."

The logic rang a bell in King's mind. "Jin, there are thousands of Americans in slave camps in Russia and China, and America does nothing to get them back. In fact, they deny these men exist, but you and I know different. So, yes, I agree, any government that would sell out its own would do the same with treaty obligations."

***

By 1978, King and Jin had established a wide network of plastics fabrication factories that brought them into China many times. A visit there was never complete without making inquiries as to what happened to Jack in Russia. In their effort to find him, private investigators, high-ranking officials and well-connected business people were enlisted. King actually interviewed men who had been guards on the train that took Jack to Khabarovsk. Ex-soldiers who were stationed in Manchuria witnessed American prisoners being herded onto trains going to Russia. A Turkish trader claims to have seen a red-haired man being held prisoner, with others, around the Chita area of Siberia, and that the prisoners had American accents. The information was not very useful, but enough to keep on with the search.

In August of 1978, the Vladivostok Bank of India transferred $46,000 from a numbered account to its Hong Kong branch into the account of King Poo Koo. The bank manager telephoned King.

"I have a numbered account from our bank in Vladivostok transferring a large sum of money into your account without identifying what the payment or deposit was intended to pay in this transaction. Do you know anything about it?"

"I may," King replied. His mind reeled at the possibilities. Gathering his composure, he said, "what is the identity of the depositor in Vladivostok who made the transfer to my account?"

"It's a Jack Fischer," the manager replied. "Do you know him?"

***

Confirmation that Jack was alive and had been in Vladivostok only a week ago electrified King's and Jin's efforts to pinpoint his location. Their investigation focused on the rail networks connecting regions that might reveal the existence of prison complexes. In addition, inquiries were made through the National Bank of Korea, the Bank of Warburg and the Bank of India.

Jin offered seven year's salary, or fifty thousand dollars, as an incentive for bank managers to provide information about POW camps in their region and if possible the names of the officers in charge. Jin made it clear he wanted verifiable information and that managers were in competition to deliver it. The information was not difficult to find for the Bank of India's manager in Vladivostok. He had recently opened a three hundred thousand dollar account for an Alexander Ivanov located near Khabarovsk, but without an address. The manager suspected Ivanov was in charge of POW camps, a poorly kept secret in the area, because when the account opened, it was an American—a Jack Fischer—who vouched for him. In Vladivostok, there were no Americans walking around the city.

Jin thanked the manager for the information. "There is no way to verify the information unless I see copies of what you have. In addition, I want a meeting with that man, face to face, and I want you to arrange it."

"That could be difficult. This city is the center of a military region and arranging such a meeting here might be impossible. I also think the man is a colonel. He didn't introduce himself that way, but he had insignia on his shirt."

Jin thought for a second.

"Do foreign passenger ships or freighters enter that harbor?"

"Yes, they do."

"Good! I will arrange for a large yacht to arrive in port. On board will be our trade commissioner, several South Korean industrialists, including King Poo Koo and myself. We are looking to establish business in Russia. And in particular with commodities prison camps are likely to produce. Meetings will take place in broad daylight on board the yacht."

"It's a good idea," the manager said. "The earliest I can arrange it will be some time in October, can you live with that?"

"I will have to. Telex me your best date and allow me a week to get the yacht in place. Please let the colonel know that I value his time and we are willing to compensate him with another twenty thousand dollars," Jin said, before hanging up.

King called fellow capitalists and enlisted their participation in the trade mission. He was truthful with them, but he also suggested it might be worthwhile establishing capital and trade opportunities in Vladivostok. In spite of short notice the one hundred eighty foot yacht named Prince of Tithes, with all dignitaries aboard, arrived on the clear cold day of October 12, 1978. The mayor arranged a tour of the city, meetings took place between government officials and the Korean tycoons, and Colonel Alexander Ivanov arrived. He was immediately met in a closed session with both Jin and King, who came right to the point.

"Colonel, it was good of you to come on such short notice," Jin said, handing him twenty thousand U.S. dollars in four bundles.

"Call me Alex," suggested Ivanov, smiling, but nervous.

King explained the quest to find Jack and that they were here to find a way for him to escape. Ivanov described what Jack had accomplished at the prison and showed photos he had taken, with a box camera that fascinated him, of the US compound and pictures of Jack and of Ati with their three-year-old son.

Ivanov explained. "I can't let you have these because American POWs are not supposed to exist. You understand that, don't you?"

It was an amazing story. Jack was not supposed to exist. Ati and the child also officially did not exist. And the POW compound was not on any Russian map.

"Where is he and what can we do to get him, Ati and the boy out?" Jin asked.

"You are a little late, I'm afraid. August last year a transport commander's headquarters was burned down and the officer in charge killed. Jack was not involved in the affair, but I sent him to Chita in early September to keep him safe from investigations that I felt were certain. At that time the plan was for him to return in six months."

"Did you lose track of him?" Jin asked.

"Yes. He did get to Chita, that we do know, but afterwards he disappeared."

"What about Ati and the boy?" asked King.

Ivanov rose and paced the floor as he spoke. "Russia has a policy. Prisoners are not allowed to have children. It was impossible to conceal the boy's existence during the investigation that followed. The authorities, angry to find a woman in my compound, ordered me to send Ati to another camp. I have requested her return. I have the boy at my home." Pausing a moment, he then continued. "There was so much going on at the same time, too many important people to avoid. We did our best, but we'll get more into the circumstances later."

"What would you suggest we do now?" King asked again.

"I suggest that you both come with me to Khabarovsk, I will show you what the region produces and manufactures. Even if you do not buy anything, your visit will provide the basis for having continued contact with each other."

"Good idea, Ivanov. Why are you sticking your neck out?" Jin asked.

He took a long time before answering.

"I came to admire Jack, he was my best friend. He helped to turn my command into the most productive facility in the Soviet system. He also saved my life."

"Is that all there is to this, Alex?"

"Mostly it is," Ivanov replied, pensively. "But, you are my first real contact with the outside world and I would like to think that you will be useful to me; that is, if I ever get the courage to leave this fucked-up place."

"Okay, Colonel," King said. "Find where they're keeping him. Get information on the officers in charge and the logistics of the area. If you can, also try to locate Ati. Meanwhile hang onto the boy."

Ivanov stood to shake King's hand. "I've already started. I anticipated the real purpose of this meeting when my bank manager called to inform me that a Korean bank was making inquiries. As to Ati, that will be more difficult, but I will try."

The following day, King and Jin flew with Ivanov to Khabarovsk where they were given a tour of the Trans-Siberian rail junction, the city and the surrounding coal, tin and iron mines, masking the true intent of the visit. When Alex thought it safe, they made a dash to the

US compound, a very dangerous thing for Ivanov to do, but he needed to be certain they understood he would risk exposure in exchange for their trust. After all, that was all there was to rely on.

King smiled when he inspected the bunkers, noting the herbs, spices, mushrooms, perfumes and cheeses. *Jack, you learned well, I'm proud of you,* he thought.

The hothouses were of particular interest because Jin recognized them as a potential source of fruit and vegetables for South Korea. He questioned Ivanov. "Can you increase capacity in these hothouses to accommodate the export of food to South Korea during the winter?"

"Yes, but it must be flown out from Khabarovsk. Rail and ship transport would be too slow and this is not a government-sanctioned business. It will involve local marketers who have a way with these matters."

"Great," Jin agreed. "I will have a letter of credit guaranteeing payment to you for weekly shipments throughout the winter months, of melons, strawberries, tomatoes, peppers and peaches, if you have them. Tell me the quantities I can expect. I will take all of it."

Delighted, Ivanov agreed. "I will have the figures before you leave for Vladivostok in the morning."

King explored another thought with Ivanov. "We will pay you an extra ten percent on each shipment. This money will be deposited into a South Korean bank no one will know anything about, so when you quote, be mindful of that."

Ivanov began to think he had arrived in heaven. Nothing like this, he thought, was ever possible. "I can't tell you how glad I am to meet you."

"One more point," Jin said. "All instructions will state that our letters of credit are only valid if Colonel Alexander Ivanov signs all shipping documents personally, and that the letters be witnessed by an authorized agent appointed by us. Later, we will insist that you accompany selected shipments into South Korea to receive payment, CIF Seoul."

Ivanov nearly pirouetted across the room with pleasure. He had the biggest smile his huge head could wear.

"You guys are geniuses. You've just wrote my ticket out of here and guaranteed that the Commie fucks won't kill or transfer me."

King sat Ivanov down again. "You risked your life bringing us to the POW camp and we want you to know that we will get you out of here, just as soon as you trace where Jack is. We want him out too," he said.

Jin telephoned his brother Qi Jaing in Taiwan to tell him the news about Jack, that he was definitely still alive and a prisoner. He urged Qi to make every effort to find Jack's girlfriend Babe Barsi.

Chapter Thirty Three

Babe & Joy
1978

THE only person Babe recognized in the photos she had found on her doorstep was Joy Jaing, the KRON television news anchor, which did not make sense, especially since their paths had crossed many times over the years. *Why would Peter be involved with such a high-profile female?* she asked herself. *Why so reckless with her and all of the others in the photos?* Babe decided to see Joy in person and called the station for an appointment.

"Hello, Joy? This is Babe Mattioli. We met at last year's Opera Ball."

"Yes, I remember you very well," Joy answered. "What can I do for you?"

Babe suggested lunch on Friday at the Iron Horse restaurant on Maiden Lane and Joy agreed. She had no idea what Babe had in mind but assumed it would have something to do with the upcoming Film Festival or the grassroots effort to tear down the Embarcadero Freeway.

Babe was already in a booth when Joy arrived.

"I'm glad to have an opportunity to meet with you like this. You know, I watch you on the news almost every night," Babe began.

"Thank you, I recommend the crab salad, by the way."

They both ordered salad and a glass of white wine.

"Let me get right to the point, Joy. Someone dropped a black and white photo of you and my husband together in a compromising position and I'm going to guess that the event took place at the Huntington Hotel. I asked for this meeting to find out what went on between you."

Joy's faced flashed a pained expression. "I guess you could

have embarrassed me professionally with a revelation like this, but since you did not, I assume we can talk freely."

Leaning a hand on her fork, Babe explained. "I never thought Peter would do this kind of thing. Obviously that was a mistake, but what I would like to know, really, is why he did?"

"First of all, those photos must be at least five years old, because I broke off the affair that long ago, but that is irrelevant."

Joy then described how the affair began, highlighting the fact that she would never permit them to be seen in public and how the bugging devices played a role in terminating the relationship. While the revelations spun on for perhaps fifteen minutes, Babe, conscious of studying Joy's face and body language, decided she liked her in spite of the circumstances. Oddly, once the subject of the conversation had exhausted itself, both fell into asking questions about each other and talking about current events in the city.

"So you were born in San Francisco?" Joy asked.

"Yes, I was," Babe replied. "Right here in North Beach."

"And your dad, was he an immigrant?"

"Yes, my dad came from a small town in northern Italy and arrived in San Francisco around 1928."

"Was he an interesting man—I mean, you have such a fabulous personality, I wonder who you got it from?"

Babe smiled. "Quido Barsi knew everyone in the neighborhood and everyone knew him, so I guess I took after him."

Joy nearly leapt across the table. "Barsi, was that your maiden name?"

Slightly taken aback, Babe replied, "yes, it was Babe Barsi. Why?"

Exhaling a deep breath, Joy said, "Oh my God, oh, my, God. My father has been looking for you for over twenty years."

Babe was stunned. "For heaven's sake why?"

Joy could hardly get the words out fast enough.

"My father's twin brother was in the same prisoner camp in Manchuria with Jack Fischer. When he escaped in 1953, Jack gave him a message to give to you."

Thirty years of repressed longing surged through Babe's body; she looked wildly at Joy's face, moaned and then fainted. Joy frantically yelled at the restaurant owner.

"Sam! Quick, get me an ambulance! I don't know what's wrong with her! Maybe a heart attack!"

Joy rode to the hospital with Babe and stayed until she was certain Babe would be alright. Joy had a chance to reflect on what happened at the restaurant. The look in Babe's eyes before she fainted was something Joy would never forget. They had a wide, wild, haunted look that frightened Joy. *Like an animal protecting its young.*

She telephoned her dad, who was in Portland on business, from the hospital lobby and when she told him about finding Babe Babe Barsi, he was excited beyond words. He got the next flight to San Francisco.

The following morning, Qi Jaing arrived at San Francisco General Hospital and was greeted by his daughter in the lobby. Together, he and Joy went up to the third floor to visit Babe, who the doctors said was doing well. Apparently, the doctor explained, she had been under stress, and something must have happened at the restaurant that overloaded her emotionally. It triggered a severe angina attack. Joy ushered her father into the private room where Babe was propped up in her bed, looking gray but good.

"Boy am I glad to see you looking so good, Babe. Let me introduce you to my father, Qi Jaing. He lives in Taiwan but spends a lot of time here in San Francisco with me and our family business."

Qi walked over to the bed, gripped Babe's hand with tears in his eyes and said, "I have been searching for you for over twenty years. We looked everywhere, even Italy, but that, too, was a dead end."

Babe did not let go of his hand. "Were you a prisoner with Jack?"

"No, I was never in the Chinese Army. My family escaped just ahead of the Communists. We fled to Formosa, which is now, of course, Taiwan." Qi began to tell the story of King Poo Koo, Jack as a medic and caricature artist, of his brother Jin's harrowing escape from Shanghai, how King got out of North Korea by ship and what he was doing now. When he got to the part where he described Jack asking Jin Jaing to take a message from him to his girlfriend Babe, she began to sob.

Qi, having previously obtained Jack's letter and four-leaf clover from his brother Jin, reached into his jacket pocket and pulled out an envelope. It contained a handwritten letter to Babe, Jack's picture drawn in caricature and the four-leaf clover pendant she had given Jack twenty-eight years before. He passed these things to Babe, who was crying so much she could barely see what was in her hands. She rubbed and rubbed the pendant and thanked Qi for not ever giving up.

"Babe, I could never give up. My brother and King owe their lives to Jack, and they have made a commitment to find him in Russia and get him out. Their promise to find you and bring both of you back together is our family oath of honor."

Joy moved closer to the bed and said, "Babe, would you like to be alone for a while so you can read Jack's letter and sort out your thoughts?"

"Yes, thank you. I expect to be home by tomorrow; perhaps we can get together later?"

Sept 9, 1953

Dearest Babe,

I don't have much time to write. If you get this, it will mean that Jin escaped from Shanghai. When you hold the four-leaf clover you will know that I am alive. My friend King and I are hoping to escape or maybe our country will do something to get us released. Anyway there is hope on this end and I pray that you are okay. I can't tell you how many times I think about you, how I miss you and how foolish I feel for having joined the Marine Corps. Anyway there are maybe 12,000 other Americans here with the same story. That's all past and I can't help what happened. Babe I love you with all my heart. I will never forget you and I will not die before finding my way back to you. Love,
Jack

Jack's letter written in 1953 and only now reaching her in 1978 coursed a surge of love through her heart, but waves of guilt for not waiting for him tugged at her. There was nothing now that would alter the past and crying just made happiness harder to bear. Jack was alive and the world must know. She would go to Russia herself to find him or die trying. *Twenty five years is too long, Jack. I'm coming, don't you worry.*

Babe returned home completely drained of any emotion for Peter. When he came home from Sacramento, she did not say a word as she passed the photocopied pictures to him. She did not care any longer what his reaction would be.

Peter just stared at the photos, shaking his head in disbelief. Then he looked at her without looking into her eyes.

"You can have this flat, free and clear, in your name. I will also transfer the Santa Rosa house and vineyard to you and provide a cash settlement of four million dollars, prior to a divorce agreement being recorded," he said.

He continued without waiting for a response from Babe. "I am up for an appointment as Lieutenant Governor in a year and a half. I would appreciate it if you would not record our divorce until after the election. I will move out by the weekend."

"That's very generous of you. I accept."

The two girls, Claudette, eleven years old, and Jenna, born just two years ago, would go with Babe. Looking down at his feet, Peter said, "I really blew it, didn't I?"

"Yes, you did Peter, and right now I don't know who is more sorry—me or you." Peter was silent. Babe continued. "I won't tell you who is helping me, but I will tell you that the originals of these photos are being examined for fingerprints. My friend suspects you are surrounded by some very bad people and I think we would all like to know who they are."

Surprised at Babe's resourcefulness, Peter replied, "I know I have been followed, my offices and apartments have been bugged and my investigation into who is behind this effort has come up with nothing, so I would be very interested. Especially since these kinds of revelations could affect an election."

There it was. Peter was only concerned about his public persona. He had no thought or anxiety about how such photos, if made public, would affect her or the children's reputation.

"When did I stop loving you, Babe? Was it obvious to you?"

Without thinking, Babe said, "my father used to pretend. He would hug me and tell me he loved me, but as I got older I realized he was just going through the motions, and that behind those hugs there was nothing. About eleven years ago, you made me feel just like my father did and that was about the time that you won a seat on the

Board of Supervisors. Maybe power became your mistress. I don't really know, but I feel that you clearly do not love me now and haven't for a very long time."

Peter rose. "Before I go, would you mind if I hugged you?"

Babe stepped back and said, "Peter, I just don't have it in me."

***

Babe met Qi and Joy Jaing again, this time at her Broadway Street apartment, for breakfast.

The day after visiting Babe at the hospital, Qi telephoned his twin brother Jin in Korea to inform him that Babe had been found and also to hear if King had learned anything. Qi could not wait to tell Babe all he knew and looked forward to their meeting.

Joy discussed with her father the ironic circumstances of her meeting with Babe at the Iron Horse, how the truth of the affair with Peter Mattioli surfaced and how that revelation led to the discovery of Babe Barsi. They both agreed that there would be no point in that subject ever coming up again and that the breakfast meeting would focus only on Jack Fischer.

***

"Eggs Benedict," Qi said, as he spooned another portion. "This is my favorite breakfast. You would be surprised how rarely you see it on hotel menus, almost never in restaurants, and in Asia, well, don't bother to ask."

"I'm glad you like them, they go especially well with the fizzes, don't you think?"

"I have heard about this apartment for years," Joy said, "and your dinner parties. I've had a mental picture of it being hidden in a huge wine cellar with golden doors."

Laughing, Babe said, "that's really funny, Joy, but considering the way the society pages describe events here, I'm not surprised."

Qi changed the subject. "Babe, I am thrilled to have been the one that handed you Jack's letter and the four-leaf clover, but the truth is it was my brother that brought it out of China and so the credit goes to him."

"But you never gave up the search for me and that's just as important, isn't it?"

"I am trying to be humble, Babe, because what I am going to tell you today is really going to be an even bigger shock."

"Oh, Dad!" Joy butted in. "Get on with it—tell Babe what you found out."

"You better make it fast," Babe said, "or I'm taking the Eggs Benedict away."

"Oh! No! Not that, I couldn't bear it. Okay, I will confess."

With that, he announced that they obtained proof Jack was still alive one year ago in August. He went on to describe the $46,000 deposit transfer from the Bank of India in Vladivostok to King Poo Koo's account in the same bank, but in a Hong Kong branch, and that King traced the origin of the deposit to Jack Fischer. Babe sat quietly, tears flowing down her cheeks. Qi continued.

"My brother and King have since found in which camp he had been held prisoner and who its commander is. They've arranged to meet with him on a yacht." Babe's blood rushed furiously, her eyes flashed. The news was stunning; hopes began to soar as they all speculated on the possibilities of an escape. Babe wanted to go to the press or bring the evidence that was available to the U.S. authorities, but Joy cautioned against the idea.

"If ordinary citizens can make this kind of progress, you have to assume that our government could also do the same with little effort. The fact is, they haven't. We have to assume they do not want the story of POWs held in slave labor camps in Russia getting out. Babe, think of what a story like that would do to the morale in our military. Why, men would never join the forces knowing that."

"I frankly don't give a damn about the morale of a military that knowingly leaves its soldiers behind to be herded into labor camps," Babe said.

"That's true enough," Joy added. "And maybe that was a poor example, but realistically anything that might embarrass our government could prompt them to cover up the story, especially in an election year."

"What do you mean by that?" asked Babe.

"What Joy is trying to tell you, Babe, is that if you ask for help from the U.S. government, it might well result in the death of all prisoners still being held, and that would include Jack," Qi said softly.

"I can't believe that."

"Believe it, Babe. Your government covered up the enslavement by Russia of over thirty thousand GIs after World War II. They knew it and did nothing. Now you come along with proof of government crimes from the Korean War. How long do you think that *you* will be tolerated?"

"Me?" cried Babe. "They wouldn't do anything to me, would they?"

"There is a good chance of it. Remember telling me how the FBI threatened you with arrest for protesting the POW issue back in the 1950s, and didn't they also suggest that Jack might be a defector or possibly a traitor, even after his being awarded the Silver Star? Well, consider that, and while you're at it, begin believing that the Chinese and Soviet governments would not hesitate to kill everyone to remove such an embarrassment and that *could* include you!"

"My God!" Babe gasped. "All three governments against my poor Jack. Who would believe such a thing?"

"Let me suggest," Qi said, summing up, "that we plan his escape first and then think about the merits of exposing the government's crimes later."

They agreed to meet again. Joy and her father left and Babe began immediately to learn all she could about American POWs held in Russia and China.

***

"Hi, Babe, it's Nick. I'm calling from Seattle to report on that little matter we discussed before I left San Francisco."

"Great. Thanks for getting back to me so quickly. What did you find out?"

"It looks like Peter has been partners with the New Jersey Mafia for many years. In fact, soon after his father started United Scavengers they offered him cash and permission to run a non-union operation. They also provided help eliminating competition."

"But all the truck drivers are shareholders in the company."

"That's how it was set up to avoid a union. The Mafia never controlled California the way they did the eastern states. When Peter's dad needed help, both the Chicago and New Jersey mobs came in and wound up with a forty percent share of United Scavengers."

"Why two mobs?" Babe asked.

"In those days, everyone wanted a piece of the action in California. They also wanted to avoid clashes before they got started, and operating as a friendly joint venture, they were seen as turning over a new leaf."

"How do you know all this, Nick?"

"The fingerprints on the photos are from a mid-level New Jersey mobster named Armando Battaglia. He works for the Luca family, whose boss is Dino Luca. Among other things, they control all the sanitation franchises in the State of New Jersey."

Nick continued. "In 1960, the federal government subpoenaed testimony before one of those televised trials from a Chicago mobster named Johnny Rossetti. Part of the way through his testimony, his chopped-up body was found in a fish bait container placed in front of the Florida governor's mansion.

"The New Jersey mob removed their Chicago partners out of the sanitation business in California in a violent campaign in late 1962, but the bloodshed attracted attention from the state authorities. The Luca family decided to run your husband's United Scavengers on the up-and-up and that meant legitimate management. Peter had been schooled in New York and was known to have underworld friends, especially in horse betting. They kept him away from that activity and made sure Peter focused on his business degree."

"And I was married to him all these years and never knew," Babe said, feeling like a fool.

"At the time Peter's father died, the Luca family indirectly guided the operation, using Peter as a proper CEO, knowing that the skill Peter lacked most was the ability to make people want to seek him out. It was always the other way around with him, his idea of making contacts was shuffling cash-filled white envelopes to the faithful at city hall and giving theater tickets and supplying hookers, until you came into his life. Within a short time, his marriage to you led Peter to becoming a politician, an accepted member of high society and a soon-to-be elected lieutenant governor. In other words, Peter now had real contacts and that translated into renewed city and state agreements and lots of open doors."

"I was helping a crook get elected, wasn't I?"

"Riding on his new success," Nick continued, "Peter started another scavenger operation in Silicon Valley, neglecting to include his old partners, and that incensed them. The mob really could not eliminate Peter because that would erase the political clout they needed for the garbage company and for their other endeavors. And that, Babe, was the reason for the photographs and the bugging of his residences. Translation: leverage. The mob reasoned that Peter's bad habits with women could be relied upon to give them the compromising material they needed. It was intended to convince him that it was better to be partners with them than being a disgraced politician. Most interesting is that since the day those photos surfaced on your doorstep, the New Jersey mob, through an offshore corporation, obtained a forty percent share in the Silicon Valley operation. In other words, Peter buckled."

"Jesus, Nick."

"Babe, I'm telling you these things in the strictest of confidence. You are not to indicate to Peter or anyone else that you know anything about his affairs. Furthermore, let him think you're stupid when he asks about the fingerprints on the photos. Tell him they were inconclusive."

"It won't be difficult playing stupid. I feel stupid. Anyway, Nick, do you still have a couple of minute's time while I have you on the telephone?"

"Sure, go ahead."

Babe then told him about Joy, the Iron Horse, Qi Jaing, the $46,000 deposit coming out of Vladivostok from Jack Fischer and the general discussion she had with Joy and her father about what to do next.

Nick was stunned. "Wow! Jack's alive! Oh, Babe, this is the best news I've ever heard."

"I too am alive, Nick, after all these years," Babe said, tears in her voice. "But there's more, and I need some help from you."

When she finished telling Nick the general discussion she had with Joy and her father about what to do next, he said, "I'm glad you told me. I think you're asking me if I can look into the subject of abandoned American POWs. Am I right?"

"Yes."

"Jack and I were the closest of buddies when we were young. The news of him being alive makes me happy and at the same time my blood boils. As an American patriot, and a friend, I will do everything I can."

Chapter Thirty Four

Korea-Siberia

"HELLO, Qi, it's Babe here. I'm calling from San Francisco. How are you?"

Qi Jaing, back in Taiwan, replied, "I'm fine. Thanks for returning my call. I want to give you an update on what transpired at the meeting between my brother Jin, King Poo Koo and the trade delegation in Vladivostok."

"Yes, please do," Babe said. "Although, when I first heard the idea I thought it pretty far-fetched. How did it turn out? Did anyone important show up?"

"It was successful beyond what anyone expected." Qi explained how the Bank of India's manager had been bribed to uncover who had transferred the $46,000 deposit into King's Hong Kong account, and how eventually that led to a meeting with Jack's prison camp commander in Vladivostok. He described the city of Khabarovsk, the US prison camp and finally the proposal to ship produce from there to South Korea.

"But where did he go? Where did they take Jack?" Babe asked. "Is there any way I can meet your brother and King Poo Koo? I am willing to fly to Korea or anywhere else. I feel we are all committed and I want us to be together in this effort. Is that possible?"

"We don't know exactly where Jack is, but we feel we're close. We've already discussed meeting with you and they can't wait. They're going to be in San Francisco next month. Is that soon enough?"

Jin Jaing and King Poo Koo arrived in San Francisco and checked into the St. Francis Hotel at Union Square. Jin had been to the city often and chose this hotel because of its downtown location, within walking distance to Chinatown and the financial district. It would be King's first visit and although he looked forward to seeing some of the things he had heard about the city, he was really only eager to meet Babe. He could not help reflecting on the crisis that led to Jack being transported to Russia and that Jack's only thought, under those horrific circumstances, was of his love, Babe. King thought how it must feel to have known that kind of love. His own leap into that arena was more blessed by his absence than his presence.

Babe made reservations at Alfred's restaurant in North Beach. It was the only eatery in town that had private booths large enough to seat eight people, four across, and it featured floor length curtains that could be drawn to ensure privacy. She had been there many times and knew that the owner would do anything he could to please her.

Babe telephoned the St. Francis Hotel and was connected to King's room. She wanted him to know that lunch would be at Alfred's and for him to arrive by taxi at twelve o'clock, but when he answered the phone she could not get a word out for her tears. She kept repeating, "Hello, Mr. King?" Each time she tried to speak, tears gushed uncontrollably, until she finally heard King between her sobs.

"Hello, Babe."

She hiccupped, calmed herself and listened.

"I can't tell you how many times I have thought of you and wished for this day to come true," King explained. "Don't cry anymore. We are here and we love you." There was a long pause on the telephone while King caught his own breath to break his own sobs. "Where can we meet? Do you know a good Chinese restaurant in this town?"

Babe had to chuckle. "I've made special arrangements at a restaurant that lets me bring some of my own dishes for special occasions—I wanted to do something really—well—you know…"

King broke in and said, "okay, tell me where this place is before I break out in tears myself."

Babe laughed and said, "thanks." She gave him directions.

Alfred's Restaurant, on Merchant Street seventy years in business, was Italian cuisine at its finest. Babe knew the proprietor and together they planned a spectacular lunch for a very special occasion. It was not the Chinese meal that King asked for, but she felt it was a meal for Jack Fischer. Babe also organized a photographer to take pictures of the event and have them returned after lunch.

Joy and her father, Qi Jaing, arrived early, but within minutes, the eager Jin and King exited their taxi, and before its door could slam, they were hugging and kissing in the restaurant's entryway. King, Babe observed, was more Italian acting than Chinese. He couldn't say a word without his arms and hands swirling in the air, and each sentence spoken was additionally punctuated with side-to-side boxing movements of a politician making a point. Jin, like his twin brother Qi, was reserved in his appearance. His hands were warm and his eyes— well, they scanned the room as if searching for enemies, but when they landed on Babe, they made her feel like she was a sister worthy of his personal protection and that Jin was a warrior and defender of family honor. She instantly felt that she could rely on him. It was in his eyes; she trusted him.

Jin and King recounted the story of their pretending to be someone else at the prison hospital in Manchuria. King described Jack pretending to be a medic, and himself acting as if he were an officer wearing a ridiculous-looking sheepskin long-coat. And of Jin, the murderer to-be, trying to claim he was King Poo Koo. It was hilarious in the telling and when King described the meeting at the camp's morgue, with King pretending to be a dead man reaching for Jin's shoulder in the dark, it brought peals of laughter.

The story of Zo Wu was so vividly told by King that everyone seated could feel themselves being marched to a firing squad. The description of what Jack had done to rescue King amazed Babe; she had never thought about Jack doing things like that, and it also made her proud. Two hours went by quickly; the photos arrived, triggering revelations by Jin of how Jack and King got into the greeting card business and other endeavors. Jin did not mention using village girls to exploit various opportunities.

Jin, unlike King, did not move his body when he spoke. When he worked his way through the story about the Shanghai killings and his escape, his still posture added severity and drama. By the time he described himself boarding the airplane leaving Shanghai, there was not a dry palm in the booth.

The men were busy talking between themselves when Joy spoke to Babe, completely changing the subject.

"Why don't you do your own cooking show?" Joy said, hoping to lighten the conversation. "You have the looks and the panache to make it a winner. Everyone knows your name—I mean—you've been in the newspapers almost every week for years."

Babe looked at Joy as if she were from Mars. "Start a cooking show? We're talking about Jack," Babe replied with incredulity. "Thanks Joy, but I'm not in any of this for celebrity or for that matter the money. My interest is making myself useful in finding Jack."

"Sorry Babe, I got carried away," Joy politely replied.

"Food does bring people together, I understand that. I love people and I want them to experience something memorable. I want to make a difference in their lives and to be remembered as one that cared enough to make that effort. Take this luncheon, for example. I know the restaurant has soup and desserts, but when was the last time you ate in a restaurant where the customer created part of the meal? It is something you will remember—and you will know that I did it because I wanted to leave something of myself in your hearts."

Joy turned to the others and said, "did you guys know that Babe made the soup and dessert and brought it down here for the restaurant to serve?"

"No kidding?" Qi remarked. "Maybe you should go into the restaurant business?" Joy nodded her head in silent applause and hoped the cooking show suggestion might find its way into opening an international restaurant in Vladivostok.

Babe, feeling completely foolish and misunderstood, explained that she had thought about a restaurant, but that she would not want the involvement in an everyday business and that she had a love for the art of cooking itself.

King told her that the Americans in Seoul, Korea, had almost hired him as a cook on a ship and didn't even care if he knew how to boil water. He laughed at the thought and then explained how he had got into the cement business and how it had prospered during the last twenty years. In telling his story, Babe could sense that money was not King's motivation for success. She could see that his enthusiasm soared when he described a problem or how it was solved and was positively emoting when describing the prosperity of his workers. King, she thought, was an entrepreneur who acted on his beliefs and was clever enough to hire people who were good managers.

"Why don't you come visit me in Korea, Babe? I'll show you around."

"I'd like that very much," Babe responded. "You probably know enough about the Inchon invasion and the capture of Seoul by the Marines to take me through what would have been Jack's own steps?"

King laughed. "I will have an expert there and I will come along, too, because Jack told me about it. He was in a battle in some cement factory there—so it should be interesting to see."

Jin joined the conversation. "Why stop there? If we are going to do this tour, let's include a stop in Khabarovsk. Believe me, Siberia is something to see, and you won't ever forget it. We have to go there in September anyway. Babe could come along as one of our vice presidents, and while she's there, it might be possible for her to see the boy."

"What boy?"

Jin had forgotten that he and King agreed not to mention Jack's son by another woman until the timing was right. He was now embarrassed and hurriedly blurted that Jack had a six year old boy, born from a Greek woman who had been a prisoner with him, and that she had apparently been murdered in another camp when she and Jack were separated. It was a rough story, but he got through it, and when King emphasized that the boy was in good hands with Alexander Ivanov. Babe was surprised to hear the new information but she was ecstatic.

"I want to see the boy as soon as possible. Jin, can you make arrangements for me to obtain a visa? And yes—I will be going to Korea, and yes, I will also be going to Khabarovsk—if it's the last thing I do in life."

Qi also agreed with the idea. "You will have to leave your little girl here while you are gone. It would be too difficult otherwise. How old is she anyway?"

"My daughter Jenna is just a little over three years old and I have a nanny for her. I don't think it will be a problem."

"Maybe your oldest daughter can look in on her. What was her name again?"

"Her name is Claudette and she's sixteen years old. A troubled teen, I'm afraid. I have her in a boarding school in Menlo Park. I think she likes it there. At least I hope she does."

King had been thinking about the Russian visa problem and

realized that an American in Siberia, especially a woman, would draw too much attention. Also, the Cold War politics between Russia and America would make her purpose for a visit suspect, to say the least. "Do you speak Italian? Because if you do, I think we can arrange for you to travel using an Argentine passport. A large part of that country speaks Italian and that might be acceptable to the Russians."

Babe rattled off a full minute of Italian, complete with traditional arm and hand movements. King and Jin applauded the effort and mimicked her. "Hey, keed! You-a-gonna be-a-all right!" King said.

Looking at her father, Joy added, "the passport must be attended to right away, Father. You have contacts in Argentina, don't you?"

Qi replied, "I'll get right on it."

While discussing passports, Babe thought that Nick Mateo might just be the person who could facilitate such a thing. "I may know someone who has been selling the Argentineans aircraft for many years and knows most of the leadership. I'll give him a call," Babe said.

During the following five days, Babe hosted both Jaing brothers and King to extravagant tours of San Francisco, the wine country of Sonoma and the newly emerging electronics center of Silicon Valley, of which Qi knew some, but not all. Qi had already put into motion his effort to obtain an Argentine passport.

Babe telephoned Nick to see what he could do.

Tentative plans for her arrival in Seoul, Korea, were made for September. She intended to spend a week in North Korea and three weeks in Siberia. The plan was for her to be the vice president of a new enterprise named Pacific Foods, Inc., which would appear as a joint venture between Korean Cement and Zanussi Equipment, Ltd. of Italy. Zanussi, a major Italian firm specializing in high-quality food processing equipment, was dominant in Argentina as well.

Babe marveled at how business got done when everyone had the same goals; she wondered where these men obtained the knowledge. None were Harvard graduates and would have been lucky to have made it through high school. Jin probably framed the answer best when he said to her, "Success is nothing more than racing from one failure to the next—with enthusiasm. I heard it somewhere."

He laughed at his own pronouncement, but there was truth to his observation. Jin, she thought, spoke for the millions of people who made the extra effort, no matter what the failure. They wanted to survive, to live, and during times when desire might not have been sufficient motivation, there was always the prospect of prison or death to spur them on. She admired them; she admired her Jack, the man she thought of as her husband, her mate, her love. How was he able to do all those things these people said he did? She felt humbled by his life, his ingenuity, his kindnesses and his torturous experience compared to hers.

Chapter Thirty Five

Babe in Korea and Siberia
1979

BEFORE she left for Korea, Babe briefed Tara Carr and Nick on all that transpired with the Chinese boys. Arriving at Seoul's Kimpo Airport, King greeted her, then drove to his home and installed her in a large guesthouse. The English Tudor-style home, screened by massive iron gates with a flagpole flying an American and Korean flag, sat on a hilltop overlooking a river. It seemed out of place in a neighborhood dominated by oriental architecture, but King loved the sedate Colonial English consulate appearance he had admired in Shanghai.

The plan was for Babe and King to be accompanied by a captain who had been with the U.S. First Marine Division when it landed at Inchon. They would take a motor launch and follow the steps that Jack Fischer took, starting with the invasion of the beach at Inchon and ending at Seoul.

The Marine captain explained, as they moved through the approach to Inchon harbor on the Salee River, just how the invasion took place. He described the bombing and shelling of Wolmi-Do Island at the harbor entrance, the Marine landings at what were called Red, Green and Blue beaches, the mounting of a seawall with make-shift ladders, crossing the Han River and the taking of Yongdungpo. Later, Babe actually walked inside the cement warehouse that Jack described in his letter to an Aunt in Milwaukee, which said he "got eleven of them." The warehouse still had the pockmarks of battle and was currently used to store farm equipment. She could barely breathe as she stood inside the warehouse, envisioning what she knew from Jack and what she'd heard from his friends. How could anyone have lived through such a barrage of mortar and bullets and cement dust and confusion? She wanted to fall to her knees and weep, but she did not. Jack hadn't; how could she?

From there they went by car up the Inchon-Seoul Highway, repeating Marine General "Chesty" Puller's 1950 advance, bypassing the smaller cities of Kansong-Ni and Ascom. Finally, they toured the actual streets that Jack's B Company fought through in house-to-house combat. She felt closer to Jack, stood where he stood, with death everywhere, death without end, without purpose. Looking at the rebuilt capital, she could not help think what a waste war was.

On the fourth day, King took Babe through his first cement factory. Afterward she had an opportunity to see what a vast empire he had built, and she was proud to know him. King constantly said things, sometimes in broken English, about Jack during the tour. "Jack—he never cheat." Or, "he save life." And he often retold the story of the last time he saw Jack at the train station. It was obvious to her that he loved him.

"What did he look like?" she pried, searching for answers.

"He looked okay. I mean he was thin, you understand, but he had a beard, kind of a ginger beard," King said.

"Healthy, right King?"

"Considering, yes."

"Was he scared when you were separated?"

"We both were," King explained. "It was real fear and a terrible moment in my life that I'll never forget. I watched him march off to that awful train to Russia. It was terrible."

Babe saw King's eyes tear and hugged him.

Jin Jaing arrived in Seoul on the fifth day of Babe's visit and handed her business cards stating that she was Babe Barsi, Production Vice President of Pacific Foods, Inc. The card had addresses, telephone and telex numbers in Argentina, Korea and Italy. On the backside were pictures of food processing equipment. He also gave her color brochures showing the kinds of equipment Pacific Foods sold.

Jin asked, "Babe, how did you get the Argentine passport so quickly? I could have gotten it done as well, but not that fast. Who do you know?"

Babe described Nick Mateo, his job at Boeing Aircraft and the airplane leasing business.

"Jin," she said, "all Nick had to do was send my information and photos down to Buenos Aires on a direct flight, and the passport was made up right at the airport. In his business, this is not unusual because the government often needs experts related to aircraft and military equipment, and when they need someone or something, it means right away."

"Babe, you have to introduce me to this fellow. I think we can do business together."

"Oh, Jin, come up for air once in a while. Everything in the world is not centered on business." She laughed and continued, "but, I will make sure that you two meet."

***

The Siberian city of Khabarovsk's International Airport services a city of approximately six hundred thousand people. It is situated in a valley between two mountainous areas. Looking out of the window, Babe could see the Amur River, the massive rail networks coming together and the countless brick chimneys spewing smoke, making it obvious that this was a thriving industrial center.

On the ground, the pilot announced that the plane would be stopping twice. Babe could see the second airport center at a distance which she learned later was used by the general public. It was an awful, solemn, grey, cement and barbed wire building with long lines of shuffling people. She shuddered at the thought of their plane stopping there. The airplane turned right and Babe saw a smaller, well-guarded terminal, blistering with razor wires around its perimeter. This, Babe learned, was the VIP terminal and that it was dedicated to foreign dignitaries, business people like their group, military or KGB brass. The aircraft pulled forward and stopped. Aluminum steps we pushed up to the fuselage. A frayed and dirty red-carpet rolled out to greet them. Filthy old Soviet flags stood limply at the entrance to the VIP terminal.

Inside, a large picture of Stalin hung prominently on a wall. The décor was of frocked-velvet papered walls, red and black upholstered seating areas and a sturdy-looking bar that ironically featured American whiskeys. The vodka and whiskey, without ice, were free and there was no customs barrier to pass through.

The second stop the airplane normally would make was to the public terminal. At best, this terminal had the allure and appearance of visitor's day at Leavenworth Prison. Every thing she could see was intimidating. Police, razor wire, long lines of unhappy travelers, layers of customs inspectors, gray concrete, iron bars and employees who made you feel it might be time to confess to something. Scores of Communist red flags sagged wearily everywhere.

As their luggage was loaded into a Mercedes limousine at the front of the VIP terminal, Jin noted that a small strip of electrician's tape that he had placed over the suitcase hasps had been breached. He did not expect less, and whispered into Babe's ear. "We cannot talk openly unless we are outdoors—assume everyone works for the KGB or Militia, including drivers, guides, cleaners and hotel staff."

Nodding agreement, she glanced at her surroundings and remembered spying on her husband. It didn't feel good.

King and Jin had been to Khabarovsk before and knew what to expect, but both Jin and Babe were taken by surprise when King opened his carry-on bag and began calling out the names of employees at the VIP terminal. By design, he remembered their names and started handing out pens, transistor radios, stuffed toys and perfumes. With each giving, he would explain why he thought each item was something special for that particular person. It was an education to Babe. People beamed and so did King. It was something, Babe discovered, he did everywhere he went, and loved that he could remember everyone's name.

Jin smiled at his partner. "So this is what you are up to when you travel alone."

The Hotel Moscow, in Khabarovsk, was built in the early 1950s, but the architecture was no different from structures constructed thirty years later. The stone lobby entrance featured a wall-sized picture of Russia's latest ruler, faded red flags drooped on both sides of a red-carpeted runway aimed at the front desk and every piece of furniture and counter was clad in worn-out cream-colored wood veneers. Modern architecture, perhaps born in the Soviet Union, made a point of simplicity. No gargoyles, carved columns or other art adornments that could be associated with wealth were permitted. Instead, the plain prison look was celebrated as an economic design for the workers, for the State persona. Embellishments were limited to the obligatory statue of Lenin in heroic pose, rows of small flags that advanced the notion that the Soviet Union and all of its friendly neighbors heralded your arrival.

At the far end of the hotel desk was a foreign currency

exchange booth where guests changed their good American dollars for near worthless rubles; even then an appointment was necessary for the fleecing. But, there were compensations; after all, this was an international hotel. If Babe wanted her laundry done, a housemaid came to her quarters, washed those things in the room sink and hung them up on a clothesline strung across the seating area. This was the Russian version of good service and they did not expect a tip. Vodka of course was plentiful, not Russian but American vodka, Wolfschmidts, because it was imported and therefore a more elite beverage than the local offerings.

"Ice, please," Babe had asked the woman who did her laundry.

"Nyet, not in Siberia," the woman answered. This made Babe laugh, as she'd always thought of Siberia as the frozen tundra.

Russia encouraged foreign investment, especially in Siberia, by countries viewed as pro-Soviet and willing to trade in barter. South American, Indian and Japanese companies were favored. Jin arranged for a car and driver to tour them through the countryside for at least fifty miles in each direction from the city. He didn't care if the secret police kept them in view. Everyone wanted to see firsthand how people lived and worked; they expected the effort to take four days. Outside the city, the main roads, while paved, were poorly maintained and often forced detours around large potholes and road erosions. Other roads leading to small villages were constructed of crushed rock from the many mining operations in the area; these too suffered from lack of maintenance. The surrounding views were of huge forests, thick with larch, spruce and fir, spilling down from snowcapped mountains and cascading into valleys below where farms under threat from the approaching winter sat peacefully. Siberia at a distance was beautiful. Up close it was awash with the tears of human suffering.

Dirty concrete, as if it were a popular color on a Russian painter's palette, was splashed lavishly on Siberia's beauty along with endless concrete block structures and rust-stained barbed wire. Seeing a black limousine approach a village always promised trouble for someone. The country people were like deer in the forest that become rigid when a threat is heard; entire villages disappeared behind closed doors to watch warily through darkened windows.

Guard towers and road checkpoints were a common sight,

as were dour men in ill-fitting uniforms. Farm fields lay unharvested because the collective farm system did not provide an adequate network of storage. There were no silos, warehouses or refrigeration depots, and the potatoes, beets and corn lay rotting in the fields until soldiers came to gather what was urgently needed.

Babe turned to Jin.

"I find it depressing. I can see that common folk have no automobiles or trucks to bring the fruits of their labors to market and their homes have no indoor toilets, telephones or televisions. Nothing resembling a tavern or pub exists anywhere," she said.

Turning the car heater up a notch, Jin replied, "I thought I'd get used to it, but it never changes. These people are afraid, they're hungry and they have little hope."

"I hope we can make a difference here."

A fish processing factory, a cannery and a can manufacturer had all been closed after the fish died from poisons flowing from the mines. Government stores that were actually open had almost nothing on their shelves, and long lines of people waited endlessly for anything that might be left when it was their turn.

"It's not a pretty drive, is it?" Babe said casually.

Jin pointed to a store without a name or windows. "Babe, that's where the privileged do their shopping," he said. "It's a not-so-secret store that has everything, but excludes the peasantry. It's for Party members only, sorry folks."

By now, Babe thought she could sense the presence of the KGB, whether they were close or not. She didn't answer Jin. *The KGB is just like the wild Siberian tigers in the forest,* she thought. *They have no natural predator, they watch and wait and without sound, they take what they want from the unwary while everyone else is too frightened to do anything, pretending not to see.* As they drove, Babe wondered in silence about the misery of the people and of Jack's prospects for surviving an even harsher environment. *Somewhere out there*, she thought. *Maybe he's close by.* Goosebumps rose on her arms.

King had arranged for Babe to meet Alexander Ivanov on a Saturday at his home three miles from the US POW compound that he commanded. Babe could not wait to see Jack's little boy John Fischer. When she was introduced to Ivanov she thought his head looked like a large Halloween pumpkin, but she kept those thoughts to herself.

"Call me Alex," he said. "I have heard so much about you from Jack that I have looked forward to this day."

Babe smiled at him. "King and Jin have told me a great deal about you too. Let me be the first to thank you for all that you have done for my Jack."

"Ah-ha. No thanks are needed," Alex said. "By the way, little John will be down in just a few minutes. Can I offer you a martini?"

She could hardly imagine anyone making a martini in Siberia and wondered where he possibly could have picked up the taste for it.

"No thanks, water or juice if you have it will be fine."

Alex showed them through his home, which was not very large, because if it were, he would come under suspicion for economic crimes. The house struggled to be ornate enough not to look like a prison. It was a two-story surrounded by an eight-foot brick fence and a central wrought iron entranceway. Everything else was stucco. The new Turkish carpets in the hallways and dining area were decoration enough for visitors, in Ivanov's mind. If some idiot from Moscow showed up he could always roll them up.

Six year old John Fischer, born in 1973, could be heard bouncing down the stairs with enthusiasm until he reached the living room where he stopped and turned solemnly toward the adults. He was introduced to Babe and the others. His big blue eyes got bigger and he rounded the room with his gaze, wondering who everyone was, why he was shaking hands. Babe instinctively reached down and picked him up, held him close, breathed in his scent and choked back her tears. She just stared at him. He was a wonder, an auburn-haired version of Jack Fischer. She cried outright, the tears streaming down her face unheeded.

"How old are you, little boy?" Babe asked, trying to keep him from squirming loose. It did not matter who asked John questions about his age, school or toys. His answer was always, "Da" or "Nyet," and he spat those words faster than the questions could be asked.

Alex explained to Babe that John was doing well with his English language studies. "John doesn't have much opportunity to speak it around the house, but if you speak slowly, he will understand."

Babe held John in front of her and said slowly, "just who do you think you look like, young man?"

"My daddy, Jack. That's what Uncle Alex says."

"Would you like to come to America with me?"

"Nyet!" He bellowed and squirmed to pick up a shoe that had squeezed off his foot. Babe and the boy then spent the next several hours together in his room and in the garden, while Jin, King and Alex met in the study.

Babe and John played in the courtyard, but through a window in the study she heard Alex explain that Jack had gone to the city of Chita two hundred miles north of the Mongolian border, more than a thousand miles from Khabarovsk.

"He was to have been met by a reliable friend who was to hold Jack for six months and then return him. Unfortunately, Jack's train was diverted to a prisoner transit center near the city of Manzhouli, near the Wall of Genghis Khan and from there he disappeared without a trace."

Babe poked her head through the window and cried out. "Oh my God, Alex, this can't be. Not after all this time. Surely you know people that can help."

"Can't your friend help?" King quickly added.

"The problem," Alex said, "is that Manzhouli, to my knowledge, handles both POW and Russian prisoners, and that once corralled there, Jack could have been sent to any one of five thousand camps in the Soviet Union."

"Christ-all-mighty," King lamented. "What can we do now?"

Alex was deeply upset at the news of Jack's disappearance. "I sent three of our recently trained operatives to interrogate, somewhat forcefully, my friend in Chita. It turned out that he was telling the truth. I directed him to offer a reward of five thousand dollars for Jack's return."

"That should get someone to talk," King said.

"Yes and no. The reward has also attracted the attention of the KGB. They want to know who is behind the reward. Fortunately, my friend was able to deny everything. It was close."

"What if I just put an ad in the newspapers in that area?" Babe said, hopefully.

Alex's eyes rolled upward. "Babe, such a thing would be reckless. Russia cannot permit foreigners to run missing POW ads and would make sure you never left Russia."

"Sorry, I guess I wasn't thinking."

Unfolding a map of Siberia, Alex pointed to the Mongolian border and said. "communication from here to Chita is difficult because it is monitored by Internal Security. I have to be careful what is said to people there. It is not the best, I am afraid, but I am forced to rely upon my own undercover men to travel a thousand miles in each direction."

The men pondered various schemes related to finding Jack and then discussed a host of other topics. Alex explained in detail the arming and training of his prisoner population.

"I've never heard of such a thing," Babe said.

"It was Jack's idea. He implemented the creation of an underground labyrinth beneath the entire camp."

"Whatever is it for?"

"Basically, it's a place to hide what we don't want the authorities to see."

"Like?"

"Families, arms, supplies, you name it. It is also where we are developing an intelligence force."

Explaining further, Alex said, "the intelligence corps is fairly new as we speak, but I can tell you there are already positive results. We have two telex operators on our payroll that work at the main Khabarovsk train station. They automatically send us copies of military and political traffic, and we have begun an intelligence data bank on the command structure in the region. One especially juicy plum arriving three weeks ago was a series of photos showing a KGB general in drag being screwed by a gorilla of a man inside his own office. The pictures are explicit and should prove useful at some point." Alex grinned in a way that made Babe squirm.

"Do you need small eavesdropping and camera recording equipment?" Jin asked, breaking his silence.

"Yes," Alex replied. "I need a few of those new fax machines and some computers I've been hearing about. Can you get them for me without getting me arrested?"

Laughing, Jin replied, "this kind of business I know. Don't you worry about being arrested. When we start receiving hothouse produce from you this winter we will pay for it partly in cash and the rest will be paid with legitimate cargo. Gradually each shipment to you will include what you have requested, but it will be packed in a very careful manner."

Looking much happier, Alex put forth his wish list. "I would like about a thousand live American turkeys to start a breeding program. We need sugar, snowmobiles, printing and etching equipment sufficient for us to make our own passports—maybe even a few rubles—some good cameras and machine tools. You want me to go on?"

King listened and agreed with everything that was asked for. He was surprised that he was not surprised at being involved in what was potentially a very dangerous enterprise. Not a person in that room needed the money or the risk. This, King thought, was the magic of friendship, and perhaps the brandy brightened the picture. Regardless, the room was warm with comradeship and it crackled with ideas, plans and goodwill.

Near the end of the briefing, Babe, now also in the study said, "I have been thinking a great deal about what might be possible for me to do to get Jack back. I will discuss this with you in a few days after I have had a chance to weigh the facts. Meanwhile, I have to assume that failure is a possibility; therefore, I want to find a way to get John out of this country and back to America. I want to raise him as my own. Can you understand that?

"I'm going to need your help to make that happen," she continued. "There is no way I could possibly live without him now that I've been with him. He's Jack's boy."

They did understand. They knew long before arriving in Russia that they would be helping Babe get Jack's child to the States.

***

King invited the Mayor of Khabarovsk, his employees, the police chief, the KGB officer corps, consular members from China, Japan and India, all with their wives, to a dinner at the largest Chinese restaurant in the city, named China Gate. King met with their manager and chef to organize a banquet for five hundred people and explained it was to be done with panache and that money would not be a problem. Together Babe, King and Jin went into the market to place orders for the delivery of fresh whole fish from Lake Baikal, ice blocks for carving, fresh vegetables, fruits, foreign beers, whole piglets for the rotisseries, barbecued duck, assorted dim-sims, nuts, many other foods, party decorations and favors. Georgian and Hungarian wine would dominate the drink list, along with the obligatory vodka.

More help would be required and Babe would participate in the organization. In spite of shortages of food ordered, everything appeared miraculously when payment was offered in American dollars. Music would include Russian balalaika, Indian sitar and a boogie-woogie piano, bass and trumpet trio from Japan. Nine photographers would take pictures of the guests posing with Jin, King and Babe, and many taxis would be contracted to stand by as needed. The Friday party was expected to begin at eight in the evening, last until four o'clock in the morning and would cost almost fifteen thousand U.S. dollars, including a large tip for the management and staff. For the restaurant, this was truly a surprise because the Communist Party elite abusively ordered people around and never left a tip, and the proprietor would consider himself lucky if he didn't lose a good deal of his silverware in the process.

The guest speakers would include the mayor, of course. King Poo Koo, through an interpreter, would be introduced. The head of the State Economic Board, Ivanov's favorite KGB general and the Japanese Counsel General would sit at the head table. Babe placed ten tables at the entrance for guests to register their names, their occupations and contact information. These would later be developed into a go-to list. With each name she gave tickets for a drawing to be held at midnight. First prize: an all-expense paid round trip to Kolyma. This prize was added as a joke because everyone shuddered at the prospect of going anywhere close to the place, but if the winner did not want to go, he could convert the travel ticket to cash. Second prize: an Italian Vespa. Following these were another hundred prizes ranging from fruit baskets, free dinner tickets and vodka, to free accommodations at the Moscow Hotel. Finally, Jin would be responsible for press invitations, security and the printing of menus describing the meals, speakers, entertainment, music, prizes and, most important, their company name and contact information. Babe would give away hundreds of autographed photos of their group posing with the dignitaries.

The party took place the week before Babe's group expected to return home. Zabo Babka, the winner of the first prize, had so much fun with the notion that someone had to be lucky to win a trip to Kolyma, akin to vacationing on the North Pole that he decided to make the trip so he could return with "the story." And as it turned out, it was quite a story. Press accounts of Babka's win reached Kolyma before his arrival, and he was met at the airport by a limousine driven by the mayor himself. Marching bands paraded him down the main street and he was hosted to non-stop parties for a week. The local press enjoyed featuring Babka on their front pages in summer beach poses lying atop snow mounds spiked with fake palm trees. They followed him all the way to his departure flight to Khabarovsk; afterward the press headlined his return arrival. *"Babka Back From Kolyma."* Such was the nature of humor in the Soviet Union.

King made himself busy during their final week in Siberia by meeting personally with those he thought represented the ruling elite. Jin staffed a permanent information booth inside the Moscow Hotel to facilitate connection between the local business community and their company. During all of this, Babe obtained passport photos of John Fischer with the intent of having him included on her Argentine and American passports.

Chapter Thirty Six

Soup's On

IT had been a busy final week in Siberia, during which Jin and King met with Babe to discuss her idea that until then had only been hinted at.

Babe started by asking, "do you remember our driving through all those farm areas where the harvests lay in the fields to rot? These people can't feed themselves and most of what they eat arrives from the western regions. Skilled employees are so scarce that Moscow commonly offers workers four times their normal salary to work anywhere in Siberia. Even then, they must be promised that it will be for a very short time. The farmers themselves are dispirited, suspicious and very much afraid of the secret police. They have no incentive to work productively in the collective farms and the only source of spending money is selling fresh produce grown on home plots and sold in the marketplace."

"Yes, that's about the sum of it, but there isn't anything we can do about it, King said. I'll be able to do some business by making use of my newfound friends, but frankly, this is something of a hell hole and if I were you, I wouldn't be enthusiastic about it."

"We need some kind of presence here besides Ivanov," Jin injected. "If we depend on him to find Jack on his own, I am afraid he could fail, he already has a lot on his plate. Besides, he may be looking out for number-one first and always."

"Do you recall my saying I was thinking of a plan that could lead to finding Jack?" Babe added.

Everyone nodded.

"Now that the Soviets are allowing foreigners and bartered commerce in here, my plan is to literally change the system from within. First we purchase the closed fish canning factory and the can-making operation next to it. I don't imagine we'll have any competition on that score, so it will be cheap. We schedule it to be operational by the spring of next year and begin producing two sizes of empty cans in anticipation of the fall harvest. Our office in Khabarovsk will offer cash for potatoes, as a start, and we will begin manufacturing thick potato soup in many flavors, such as cheese with paprika, bacon and onion, seafood and capers, plain or with sausage and so on. I envision expanding that line the following year with split pea soups, then chicken and corn varieties. No one makes canned soup anywhere around here. In fact, the railroad must cook up its own on board for passenger meals. That has to be very inefficient."

"What about the equipment for processing raw potatoes into soup?" King replied. "Do you know anything about food processing, Babe?"

"Yes, King, let me explain. The Italian firm Zanussi & Co are specialists. There is no doubt they can lay out the equipment, power needs, water and storage estimates, and they can provide technical expertise as well. I've already telephoned them to describe what my needs might be, and by the time we return to San Francisco I will have a food-processing plan in hand. It's also true that much of what we might need could possibly come from here, but I don't want the maintenance headaches that go along with Russian equipment."

Babe paced the floor as she spoke. "The brand name will be 'Siberia Jack' and labels on each can will feature a picture of Jack. I intend using an aged version of the drawing he did of himself and beneath each picture will be printed the question '*Do you know my last name?*' Lastly, the label will give instructions on where to send a photo and a suggested last name. The unsuccessful entries will receive a can opener. If we are lucky someone out there will know that the winning last name is Fischer—and that will put us back on the trail again. The successful entry will receive fifty thousand rubles, which is many, many years of average salary. It will be our way of casting the search to every corner of Russia while disguising it as a product promotion."

Jin raised questions about running a private enterprise without being harassed by the KGB. Babe replied.

"Ivanov's favorite KGB general will be a silent partner. If he becomes unruly, Alex has leverage over him and from what I'm hearing he also has the ability to put the general in the hospital for a long time. Although, I'm sure that won't be necessary. The general also will claim that our operation is ideally suited to extending the KGB's information networks, but of course he won't know that we will in fact be using the distribution system as our own intelligence operation."

"Your mind works just like Jack's," King said. "You have it all worked out in your head and you have no doubt it will lead you to him. I admire you for that. I would love to think that my wife would go to the same lengths, but I'm afraid her enthusiasm would end when my money ran out. By the way, it is one thing to make soup and another to sell it. What do you have in mind for the marketing?"

"Everything that moves uses the Trans-Siberian Railroad, and so will we. I met the local director of the railroad at the party and he could not have been nicer to me. I suggested that I would like to discuss a little business with him; he expressed interest. My plan is to give him five rubles for each sign spiked and maintained at half-mile intervals alongside the rails. A Burma Shave-style advertising campaign with many messages: DO—YOU—KNOW—MY—LAST—NAME?—SIBERIA JACK'S SOUPS, or GIVE—YOUR—WIFE—A—BREAK—TODAY—GIVE HER—A LITTLE—blank—SOUP. You get the idea. The slogans will attract people to the soup and in turn will bring attention to the name contest. Beyond that, marketing to hotels, restaurants, camps, the military and the airport is something we can also do locally."

"What do you think all of this will cost, Babe?"

"If you figure that a Russian electrician makes, at most, twenty dollars a month in comparable American currency, you know then that skilled labor is cheap. My estimate for operating capital, new equipment installed by experts and the purchase of the cannery won't be more than three hundred thousand dollars. I am prepared to put all of it up myself if either of you have any doubts."

"Geez, Babe, you really are born for this, aren't you?" Jim said.

"No, I have never done anything remotely like this, but one thing I do know is that love conquers all. You guys know how I feel. My Jack, as God is my maker, is coming back to us."

"Necessity is the mother of all invention," King said without thinking. "You know," he continued, "I really admire you. Truth is, you and Jack have a lot in common and somehow I almost feel he is in the room with us."

Neither Jin nor King hesitated a minute before joining Babe in the proposed venture.

Chapter Thirty Seven

Khilok
1978

JACK'S train stopped at Manzhouli. When the prisoners were ordered off the train, Jack figured they would not be continuing on to Chita. But, when they were herded into open-air corrals where they stood for hours in a slush of frozen mud in a driving snow, Jack feared the worst. He and the other prisoners learned that the mines around the area were short of men, that Manzhouli was a prisoner collection and disbursement area south of Chita and that they were destined to work in the mines. The prisoners had been hijacked by New Russia's labor racketeers.

When Forestry or Coal Ministries needed labor they bribed officials in the Transport department to shunt trainloads of prisoners to whomever paid the most money. No one cared how long a prisoner served in another camp or even if he had already served out his sentence. What was important to the production managers was keeping up with their appalling death rates and still maintaining quotas. Consequently, large shipments of prisoners were routinely hijacked and trucked into labor camps where they would begin another twenty-five year sentence. Thousands of prisoners' identifications were stamped deceased. It was the administration's way of accounting for missing men who were still alive but working in a coal mine or forest for the benefit of a new class of crooks called Cleptocrats.

The prisoners were loaded onto trucks and initially driven toward Chita, but halfway through the ten-hour journey, the convoy moved west into the Yablonovy Mountains to the small city of Khilok east of Irkutsk and Lake Baikai, between Irkutsk on the west and Chita four hundred miles east.

Silent and corralled like cattle, the men stood eating cold

cabbage soup while snow flurries howled across Lake Baikai. They blew breath onto their gloveless hands to keep warm and huddled together, but it did not help. Beyond the corral, men stared at thousands of logs, cut too late in the season, lying partially submerged in lake-ice or stacked along banks, apparently waiting for spring and the sawmills. Nearby, a plywood factory stood empty for the winter. Discarded from making plywood, wood cores destined for the cast-iron stoves inside a row of barracks were stacked against the dilapidated structures.

The region held the largest coal deposit in Russia and it was more efficient to use coal to fuel these stoves, even though this would result in the plywood cores becoming useless. Russia tolerated inexplicable inefficiencies, and by somebody's direction, the cores would not be used for heat. In the distance Jack could see another factory that appeared to be almost three blocks long and on it was a sign—CHAIRS. He wondered if other buildings had signs marked COAL, WOOD, and COPPER. It was strange, he thought, that a factory of that size did not have a proper name such as The Moscow Chair Factory. *This is probably where all the chairs in Russia come from*, he thought.

It took three days to process the new prisoners and assign them, at least temporarily, to the barracks. Mens' names were not important, only the numbers tattooed on their shoulders. These were recorded alongside definitions of each man's work backgrounds. Collecting names, if they ever became important afterward, would be someone else's job. These lists determined where prisoners were sent, but since they no longer officially existed, copies were unnecessary.

In perfect Russian, Jack described himself as a healer from Khabarovsk who had been sent to Chita to attend a high-ranking officer. He explained that he did not know who that officer was, but that he was to have been met at the Chita station by a personal friend of Lt. General Alexander Ivanov. Jack desperately threw out names and ranks in an effort to impress the clerk. It seemed to have little effect.

Finally, the man yawned and said, "where are your medicines?"

Jack, feigning authority, replied, "back at the train yard where some idiot has probably left them in the mud and snow. Perhaps the officer I was to meet in Chita will stumble upon them and bring them here."

The clerk got up and left the room. Ten minutes later he returned, pointed out of the window and said, "you go Chair Factory. Next!"

The Soviet Union needed chairs and this factory had been designated to make a captain's chair that featured a curved armrest and upright back, supported by wooden spindles. Only one style chair was available in only one color, a brown varnish, and there was only one factory in Russia making that chair, a chair that it promised to deliver within two years from the time it received an order. In reality, it often took twice that amount of time for customers who were not well-connected.

Three hundred prison workers at the Chair Factory did all of the work by hand. Spindles and legs were turned on individual lathes rather than on automatic machines. The seat planks were shaped using hand routers, templates, chisels and band saws. Painting was done one chair at a time when the sun was shining, instead of on a production belt carrying chairs though a dryer. Raw timber came into the factory at one end and came out the other as finished chairs at the quota rate of three hundred per day. If the factory ran out of kiln-dried wood, they used wet wood, which warped the end product and caused the chairs to sit unevenly on the floor. It did not matter. They were shipped anyway, because it took time before the warping began and the administration could then blame the buyer.

Product rejects, if they were truly impossible to ship, could be found everywhere—in the barracks, the infirmary or screwed down onto boards and fastened to trailers for prison transport. Rejects considered either salvageable or useful for parts were stacked exposed to the weather at the rear of the factory, where the snow-covered chair piles, over time, took on the appearance of an archaeological dig of man's earliest captain's chairs. If it were not for the potbelly stoves, the rejects would have over-run the camp like a mold. Regardless, the administration carried rejects as available inventory. Periodically, these would go up in smoke, on paper, as a result of accidental fires, balancing the books.

Jack had been assigned to what passed as the factory clinic, although the entire camp used it. The waiting room had twenty captain's chairs, the hallway another dozen and his surgery held six more. There were also eight beds, several wood benches that doubled as surgery tables and a microscope. Jack had a small kitchen and his own bed. In comparison to what other prisoners suffered, Jack had it made. The medical supplies, which had been left at the train station, were recovered by no less than the KGB itself from a village sixty miles away from the train yard; Jack concluded that name-dropping had some effect.

Men working fourteen hour days often complained about back and neck pain, so Jack created a roller device for people with those problems. It was a log core from the plywood factory, cut into two round pieces and wrapped with layers of felt and placed on the floor. A patient would move his back and body over the roller. It was an effective means of manipulating the spine and of loosening sore muscles. He fastened clamps high on a wall and used them to hang patients by their ankles to stretch legs, back and hips. He also fashioned a padded sling hung from a pulley on the ceiling. This contraption stretched the neck and took pressure off the head. A workday's success, for Jack, was measured by the popularity of these innovations and by adding new medicines or herbs to his apothecary. Jack's own personal factory chair reject had loose armrests and crooked upright spindles. The factory's warranty, he assumed, had expired. He had the rear of his chair carved with the words CHIEF HEALER.

One day a Mongol prison guard arrived at the clinic for removal of a ten-inch wood splinter from his buttock. The patient lying on the table had an empty stare, Jack noticed, and he decided to try hypnosis on what appeared to be a very good subject. It worked and the extraction went painlessly. The Mongol was still deep in a trance after the operation and Jack thought he might try an experiment. He placed the man between two chairs with his head placed on one and his feet on the other. The rigid Mongol was suspended between the chairs when patients in the adjoining waiting room peered through the door with wide-eyed astonishment. When Jack noticed he had an audience he sat on the guard's stomach. The man felt no pain nor did his body collapse under Jack's weight. It was an interesting experiment, but for those watching, giggling and whispering in the next room, it was proof of magical powers, and from that day forward hypnosis became a standard part of Jack's medical practice.

Jack settled into his new environment at Khilok. It was a vastly different life than he had in Khabarovsk. There he had essentially been

Commander Ivanov's partner. Now, he was his own boss, but had no real friends. The officers were friendly, but Jack was never able to repeat the magic that he had accomplished in his previous location. Weeks became months. Months became years. The years passed. Jack's one constant remained Babe. He faithfully continued his noon vigils when he could get outside at midday. He wondered where Babe was and how she was. He believed she was thinking of him and wish he was in her arms. He could not afford to believe anything else.

Chapter Thirty Eight

Yuri Senya
1998

YURI Senya had arrived from Central Asia ten years before Jack's appearance at the Khilok camp. He had come from the Rostov-on-Don, the Crimean section of Russia, where he preached a mixture of astrology, Greek Orthodox religion, card tricks and sexual freedoms. The latter got him chauffeured on a military truck headed for Tashkent's collective farms with a prison sentence of twenty-five years; from there he was transferred as a political dissident to the harsher climates of Siberia's city of Khilok.

His grossly pockmarked face was putty colored and his unbroken bushy brows protruded above his eyes and across his forehead like a visor. With the overhanging brow and the downcast eyes, Yuri was often thought to be looking at people's private parts. This won him few advocates, except among women. Yuri's hair, until recently, had been pure black and he had too much of it. At age fifty-five, he now had gray-streaked tuffs protruding from his wrists, above his collar, his ears and in a dirty unkempt beard. Women in the settlements were attracted to him anyway, mostly because he exuded an earthy animal magnetism. When a woman interested him, he dilated his eyes into large penetrating orbits, visually copulating with her. Unfortunately, these attributes were of little value to him among all-male fellow inmates.

Yuri preached repentance among the men and the hereafter. He often warbled verbally about his wrongful imprisonment. His "ministry" would have been comical in any other place but a Russian prison camp where religion was prohibited. There, Yuri developed a skeptical but willing following. In spite of the religious ban, he was allowed to continue to preach to a spiritually hungry populace. Some prisoners came to believe that he could speak to the dead on their behalf, if his mood was just right. He also made astrological predictions and performed ceremonies for the recently dead in exchange for small fees or favors.

Yuri earned his place in the prison population because no one else even pretended to give a damn. He earned a tolerable life tending his flock. Prisoners held him in awe when he performed his card tricks, which they believed to be feats of mental telepathy, or when he spoke in tongues. What he did not like was the emergence of the Healer, Jack Fischer, on his turf and was particularly alarmed by prisoners claiming enthusiastically that Fischer's patients were seen flying through the air without visible support.

***

Cognac had taught Ati two illusions that he used as part of his fortune-telling routine and she taught them to Jack, but there was never an opportunity or the need for Jack to make use of them until now. He became aware of Yuri Senya through word of mouth and never thought much more about the man, but in Khilok, as the years passed, word whispered back that Senya thought Jack was a fraud. This did not really matter to Jack because by now he was a true healer and hypnotist. But, he thought, it did not help for these rumors to go unchallenged. Jack's own credibility with the prison administration could not be put at risk. It was time to meet this man in person.

The Khilok camp is a series of compounds organized to provide labor for the mining of coal, zinc and copper, the harvesting of timber and the manufacture of related products. A central administration controlled a system that spread a hundred miles in every direction.

Senya was imprisoned in the copper-producing area near Ulan-Ude, thirty-five miles northwest of Khilok. It would not be easy for Jack to get there, but Senya might be made to come to Khilok under some pretense. Perhaps an urgent need could be contrived, such as the death of a popular official. Something, Jack thought, would come along.

The beloved wife of prison director, Yakir Petrov, died giving birth to their sixth child, and Petrov had become deeply depressed. His wife had been an obsession and he felt responsible for her death; it caused him to brood incessantly. *If I could only speak to her one more time,* he often thought. Because of their closeness, he half believed it might be possible.

The camp guard director came to see Jack to describe the situation with Petrov. "Can you communicate with the dead? Do you know someone who could?"

"I have done it twice before, but only under the strictest of circumstance," Jack replied thoughtfully.

"But, the director is important; he could do things for you. You must try."

"If I try and fail with your leader, bad things could happen to me, and I am unwilling to take that chance. Although, I hear there is a fellow by the name of Yuri Senya who other people claim speaks to the dead and he is not far from here; perhaps he could come?"

The officer thought for a moment and agreed that Senya could be sent for. "Both you and this fellow will make separate attempts," he ordered.

"I'm not sure," Jack said with hesitation.

"It is important to me," the officer replied, "for something to be done. Commander Yakir is also my very good friend, and even if it all fails I am sure he will appreciate the effort. Of course no word of this must ever leak out. You understand, don't you?"

"I can assure you," Jack replied, with sincerity, "this matter will be handled with the strictest confidence and secrecy."

Jack began practicing the two illusions he would need to perform when Senya arrived, spending hours every night familiarizing himself with his props. The first trick, a mind-reading illusion, needed nothing more than plain white 4 x 5 inch cards and very black tea or coffee in a broad-mouthed white cup. These he placed on the wood table in front of his chair.

The stack of white cards he placed at the center of the table, the black coffee cup he positioned near where his left hand would be. He would ask the person seated at his right to take one card and draw a name or number on it, while Jack looked away or was blindfolded. He then instructed that person to turn the marked card face down and hand it to him. Jack would pass it to the person seated on his left. The purpose of this move was for the person on the left to hold the marked white card and later verify that Jack had guessed correctly. After the card had been passed to the left, Jack would then ask the man on the right to mentally concentrate on what he had written.

Jack's task was to pretend communication with the man's

concentration and correctly identify what had been marked on the white card, now held by the man on the left. After a great deal of practice, Jack guessed correctly every time. The trick was to take the white card face down from the man on the right, then hand it to the man on the left, passing the card over the black coffee in the white cup. What was written on that card could be seen by Jack reflected on the surface of the black coffee. Success of this illusion would leave the impression that Jack, under special circumstances, could read the minds of others, and if people began to believe, his power would increase and an escape opportunity might develop.

A nervous Senya arrived at the chair factory in Khilok in the spring of 1998. He was given his own quarters in an unused office above the blacksmith shop. He sat for several days before being summoned to an interview with Yakir Petrov, where he did his best to give the impression that he was a holy man with mysterious powers.

"Mr. Senya, are you a mind reader?" asked Commander Petrov.

"There are men," replied Senya, "who live in the forests who can speak to the animals and they can smell and hear like a dog. But, if such a man is taken out of the forest to live in a village his sensual and communicating powers will go away. I have come from the forest— and it will take me a little while to adjust to my new surroundings."

"Does that mean you will be able to communicate with the dead after you have been here a while?" Petrov asked.

Becoming uncomfortable, Senya mumbled, "I hope the powers around us come together at the right moment—we will try."

A little surprised, Petrov asked, "Who is we?"

His feet were already sweating. Senya tried again to foil the inquiry.

"I was hoping to work with the Healer here in your camp. We have heard of his great powers—it would be a means for me to channel my energies through a soul who already knows the way."

Yakir Petrov seemed pleased enough with that answer and directed his assistant to bring Senya to Jack's infirmary.

Jack thought that Senya, from a history book he recalled, looked like a hunched-back hairy version of Russia's famous Rasputin. They stood looking at each other for several minutes when finally Senya spoke.

"So you are the famous one who can communicate with the dead?"

Jack, not wanting to take Senya's place in the hot seat with Petrov said,"Oh no! I am a healer and hypnotist, although I am familiar with the art to which you refer. Perhaps you can explain to me how you will attend to our Commander's wishes."

"It is just something that comes to me in an intuitive form," Senya explained, "and I cannot guarantee a good connection with the spirit world—unless everything is just right."

Satisfied, Jack offered to show Senya around the camp and allowed him to watch his healing procedures and surgeries. Senya, in turn, showed Jack how he used astrology to predict the future for fearful patients and how card tricks appeared as mind-reading stunts. It became obvious to Jack that these skills would be of no help to him when it was time for Senya to communicate with Petrov's dead wife. He felt sympathy for the man, who he now called by his first name, Yuri, mostly because it was Jack who put him into this precarious situation.

Fluorescent paint was widely used at the lumber mills and plywood factories to mark the butt-end of timbers, skid pallets, directional signs and as container markers. Jack turned to his now very troubled friend and said, "do you believe that men can actually speak with the dead?"

"As a matter of fact, I don't." Yuri shrugged. "But that isn't going to help me with Petrov. I'm in the shit if he thinks I'm a fraud. Why do you care?"

Relieved to hear him speak honestly, Jack replied.

"I tell you what—you come to my infirmary tonight. Bring a little fluorescent paint. You'll need the paint to mark objects, objects that belong to someone who has died. It could be a locket, a book, anything. Preferably someone close to you. Will you do that?"

Yuri looked at Jack suspiciously at first, but he couldn't shake his despair for the challenge facing him with the commander and decided.

"I will come tonight, Jack, but the only thing I have to connect me with the dead is this neck scarf, it belonged to my mother, and this little prayer book that belonged to my sister. When the Germans left the Crimea they took her with them and I have not heard from her since 1944. Maybe she is still alive."

"Those items are perfect," Jack said. "If you have a small purse or a cloth it will be useful to place a written message describing what you desire the most."

"What are you going to do, Jack, speak to the dead for me? That's my job, remember?"

"Don't worry, Yuri. If I can speak to the dead tonight you will be the first to know it, now won't you?"

Yuri arrived at Jack's infirmary at ten o'clock that evening and was instructed by Jack to daub a little fluorescent paint on each of the objects he wished to speak through. Jack had removed everything from one room, leaving only two captain chairs, a simple wood table and a small bell. He asked Yuri to inspect everything in the room for wires, mirrors, recording devices or anything else that might be used to fake the arrival of a dead person's spirit. Yuri examined the two chairs, picked them up and shook them. Then he turned the table upside down and examined it for secret compartments. Satisfied, he turned to Jack.

"You pick a chair." Jack did and Yuri said, "good choice. Now, I will take the one that you picked."

"Yuri, you are getting paranoid in your old age," Jack chided.

He instructed Yuri to tie his wrists to the chair's armrests to prevent any hint of fakery. In addition, Yuri was asked to place the fluorescent-marked prayer book, scarf and small purse on the wood table. Lastly, the bell with a wooden handle was set on the floor adjoining the table. It would ring if spirits entered the room.

"Okay Yuri, when you put out the light, come back to the table, feel that my arms are still tied, then place both of your feet on top of mine. In that way you will know if I move." Yuri complied and was satisfied that Jack was not going anywhere.

"Yuri, I want you to concentrate first on your mother. If you do that clearly, she will tell us she is here by ringing that bell on the floor. Once we establish contact you can ask her questions. We will do the same with your sister."

Ten minutes had gone by in the darkness when Jack asked if Yuri was concentrating. He claimed that he was and as he spoke, the bell on the floor rang several times. Stunned, Yuri leaped up from his chair and turned on the light. Jack was still tied to his chair and there was nobody else in the room.

"Yuri," said Jack, "if you bolt up like that again, I will end this session. Agreed?"

Jack began to call out to Yuri's sister by begging her to make her presence known once more. Again the bell rang, but this time more vigorously. Jack told Yuri it was alright to start now.

"Yuri, when you ask a question of your sister, suggest that she move the prayer book sideways if the answer is yes, and if the answer is no, ask her to lift the book into the air."

Yuri began. "Dahran, my sweet little sister, are you still alive?" Moments passed and suddenly Yuri could see the fluorescent-marked prayer book move side to side on the table. His tongue became dry.

"Are you in Russia, Dahran?" Yuri pleaded. The answer came when the prayer book floated into the air. Yuri was stupefied. Jack urged him to press his good fortune by bringing his mother in at the same time. Yuri concentrated and loudly urged his mother to make her presence known to him. Again the bell not only rang furiously, but this time it sailed through the air hitting a wall before rolling back. Sweating, Yuri asked both if they were happy and if they remembered him with love. The scarf and the prayer book floated upward and stood suspended in the air. Feeling rejected, he asked to be forgiven for leaving them when the Germans came. This time the bell hit the opposite wall.

Desperate for forgiveness, he began to sob. Jack interrupted, suggesting that the spirits were beginning to fade, and for Yuri to ask a final couple of questions.

"Is there something I can do to redeem myself with you before I die?" Yuri begged to the spirits in the room. "If that is impossible, say yes or no!" Slowly the book and scarf floated upward indicating that it was not impossible. Suddenly the small purse spun on the table making fast circular movements before it flew through the air, striking the ceiling. Silence followed. Jack suggested that the spirits had gone away, but that they might come back at another time.

"Please, Yuri, put the lights back on," Jack urged, but Yuri could not move. He was frozen into his chair. "For Christ's sake, Yuri, I'm tied to this chair. What do you want me to do—fly to the light switch?" It took almost ten minutes of Jack's soft-talking to get Yuri to move. Finally the lights went on and Jack could see that Yuri was ghost white.

"Sorry about the purse," Jack said. "I hope that whatever message you had in it gets answered. Where is it, by the way?"

Yuri walked across the room and picked up the purse as Jack protested that he wanted to be untied. "Wait a minute, Jack, I'll be right there." And as he said that, Yuri opened the purse and could see that the message he had written was no longer there. A different message lay in its place.

"What the hell!" Yuri yelled. "This is not my message. What happened?"

"God damn it, either read it or untie me. What does it say, anyway?" Jack replied.

Yuri reached into the purse for a white linen strip of cloth.

"You must free the Healer from Russia. That is your destiny."

***

Yuri was listless for days after the session with Jack and when he did bump into him, he could only stare at him in wonder.

"How were you able to do that, Jack?" Yuri asked humbly. "Do spirits come to you often in that way?"

Jack looked hard at the suffering man and said, "I have only done it twice before. Why?"

"I have been a fraud all of my life, Jack, and have only pretended to read minds and call up the spirits. But you, you have the real touch. If I could do what you can, I would be the most famous man in Russia."

"Yuri, if I help you to communicate with the dead, will you help me to escape from here?"

"Good heavens, Jack, you are asking me if I want to be God? The answer is yes, but frankly I have no idea how to help with your escape."

"Come tomorrow tonight, Yuri. We will talk and I will make you the god you want to be."

That evening Jack reconstructed the scene of the séance and again asked Yuri to tie his wrists to the chair. The lights remained on and Jack asked Yuri to watch closely. To his amazement Jack's tied arms lifted into the air. He held both arms up to demonstrate that the chair armrests were still attached to his arms but removed from the chair itself.

"How did you do that?" yelped Yuri.

"Simple. The only thing that holds the armrests in place is a little metal pin that looks like a nail and fastens the armrest to the upright spindle; you would not have paid any mind to it. Before sitting I pushed the pins out using a small nail. You would have already inspected the chair and table."

"But how did you make things fly through the air?"

With his arms still attached to the armrests, Jack reached inside two spindles of the armrest, which had been hollowed out, and pulled out two telescoping radio aerials that were painted black. He extended them to full length and proceeded to move everything on the table. Yuri was wide-eyed.

"How did you get that message into my purse and ring the bell?"

"Well, I asked you to put both of your feet on top of my shoes. What you did not know was that the toes of my shoes had a wooden top covered in felt. They looked just like yours, didn't they? While your feet pressed hard on the phony shoes I moved my feet out to ring the bell with my toes—you would not notice. As to the message in the purse, that was easy. You were too preoccupied to notice my opening the purse. I had used cloth earlier to scribe the message so it made a soundless transfer."

"Why are you telling me this, Jack?" Yuri blurted. "You could become a legend using this trick on your own."

Jack understood that Yuri had a problem attempting to convince the prison commander that he could communicate with the dead and that failure using his current bag of tricks might have bad consequences. On the other hand, if Yuri successfully performed the trick, he would become the God he so fervently desired to be.

"Yuri," Jack said. "I want you to perform that trick successfully, but the message I want you to put into Petrov's purse will read *'You must free the Healer from Russia. That is your destiny.'* The simple truth is that if the Healer puts that message into the purse and also performs the trick, it would be suspect. Far better if someone else performs the trick and that I become the beneficiary of the message."

"What if I do the trick and don't put your message into his purse?" Yuri questioned. "Won't I still be just as famous afterwards?"

Jack thought for a moment and replied.

"I will know if my message has not been delivered and make

it my business to explain to Petrov how the illusion works. Afterward I will need reservations for a seat at your hanging. And let's face it; I am solving a big problem for you with this trick. I know you have nothing else and Petrov wants to see you next week. You don't have much time to practice."

Yes, he thought nodding his head in agreement. Rising to leave he reached for Jack's hand. It was the first time he'd ever touched the hand of an American. *I wonder why Jack was so kind and helpful. I would have ruined him if the situation were reversed.* He needed Jack and he didn't like it, but at the same time he felt touched, even appreciated. How strange.

Chapter Thirty Nine

A New Mafia
1999

IT took a year longer than Babe anticipated getting Siberia Jack's Soups up and running. Equipment and installation delays were the order of the day. Frustrated, in 1981, she arranged for a team from Italy's Zanussi Company to complete the work. Potatoes and peas, generally left in the field to rot, were harvested in surplus quantities before the scheduled factory opening, and Babe was forced to add drying equipment to manufacture instant potatoes and peas. The ability to store and convert surplus to other uses led to Siberia Jack's contracting with farmers for crops at guaranteed prices, which also created an abundance of fresh quality products that could dependably be distributed to the railroad and throughout the region.

Babe had been impressed by the way King ingratiated himself with everyone at the airport when they arrived. Now, like him, each time she arrived in Siberia she brought along a large bag of gifts for customs and airport employees. And she was good at remembering every name. On a return trip to San Francisco, at the end of her third year of setting up shop in Siberia, Babe was able to bring John out of Russia. Jin, with some financial encouragement, had John listed on her Argentine passport as having arrived with Babe the first time she entered Russia; he then had her passport updated with current photos. When Khabarovsk customs officials saw them leaving together, no questions were asked. John Fischer was ten years old when he left Siberia in 1983.

Siberia Jack's Soups opened a roadside tasting room near the factory entrance and began by handing out samples of potato soups in flavors such as bacon and onion, cheddar, Mexican pepper and onion, cream of clam, fish and capers. The unexpected favorite was bacon and mustard. Neither the general public nor potential commercial buyers had ever been to a soup tasting before. Being seen there, for many, was cause for celebrity. It became so popular that items such as locally baked breads, handmade sweaters, pies and sausages and painted dolls were added. Within a year, the tasting room became a restaurant and trading post and in later years its format would be replicated throughout Eastern Siberia as Siberia Jack's Trading Posts.

In the spring of 1984, Siberia Jack's Soups' sales soared past three hundred thousand gallons per month; the five-color labels featuring Jack's picture were spread far and wide. Requests for the label came from as far away as Leningrad, and it became obvious that people kept them in their wallets, just in case they ran into the mystery man and discovered his last name.

After meeting with King and Jin, it was decided that the very technical manufacturing and maintenance process be managed by Jin until a professional could be hired for the job. Babe, it was agreed, would handle public relations. Siberia Jack's, everyone agreed, needed a seat at the table in dealing with the Trans-Siberian Railroad, politicians, graft riddled government agencies and the mafia.

Years and many trips throughout Russia later, Babe's efforts became pivotal in Siberia Jack's existence and expansion. She became proficient in speaking Russian and produced and appeared on Russia's first television cooking show, which was widely viewed. She used many of her own products, but was careful to provide visibility and attention to other food processors. During her travels she explored ideas and tips on where Jack might be held. And, almost every day, she looked up at the sun and thought; *I'll find you, Jack. Hang on, I'll find you.* Babe also worried that she spent much more time in Russia than she did in America.

Contest entry forms with pictures of a proposed Siberia Jack winner poured in at an average of ten thousand per month, which resulted in a full-time contest staff. Thousands of can openers and free samples of instant potatoes, beans and peas were shipped weekly to all contest respondents. In Russia, nobody got anything free, so the give-away items were prized, desperately wanted, a delight to people. The demand for these items in turn led to the opening of another department specializing in catalog sales. However, theft became such a large factor with the Soviet postal system that catalog sales had to be stopped.

Siberia Jack's also employed a full-time photographer because the great numbers of men who would appear at the factory claiming to be the mystery man were unforeseeable. All of them believed they were Siberia Jack and rather than disappoint them, they were treated like celebrities. As a result, hundreds of Siberia Jack look-a-likes adorned walls of the tasting room. Often, entire families of the hopefuls would arrive, and they too were showered with soups and candy.

The Trans-Siberian Railroad stopped making their own soups and began to purchase large quantities from Babe's company. One problem that she had to resolve was that they would purchase several flavors, but by the time the soups were loaded onto the trains, their labels would be missing and no one knew what was in the can. She solved the problem; in part by providing contest information packets placed at the back of each passenger seat, and by rubber-stamping the top of each can describing its content. Contest labels led to sales into regions that Babe never expected the product to reach so quickly; some soup shipments even went to the North Pole in nuclear powered submarines.

Raw material needs were a constant problem because roads to farms were often impassable, and potato farmers under contract with Siberia Jack's Soups often failed to deliver. On one of Babe's many return trips to America, she followed through with an idea she had for some time. She contacted an organization dedicated to saving wild horses from being killed and ground into dog food. Those horses, mostly Mustangs, were offered to anyone in America for fifty dollars, provided a good home for the animal was assured.

Babe joined the organization and subsequently requested five hundred horses, which she received incrementally over an eighteen month period, and transported them, using Argentine invoices, to Khabarovsk. Prior to the arrival of the horses, her agents fanned the countryside, requesting farmers to be at the soup factory during the first week of September 1990 for a drawing. The lucky ones would win a horse and with it they could increase farm production and transport to the factory. With five hundred fresh horses imported each year; coupled with their expected offspring, Babe estimated her program would produce almost ten thousand horses and would enable connection between remote villages. Her trading posts became an ideal network for Ivanov's intelligence network.

At first, the concept of getting something for nothing was difficult to sell in a society steeped in fear and suspicion. But when explained that the factory itself was the biggest beneficiary, they understood and went away happy, always taking a bundle of contest entry forms and free can openers with them.

The soup factory's success inevitably attracted the criminal element, in particular the KGB. They wanted a piece of the action and farmers became vulnerable. Babe asked her minority KGB partner, General Olov, what she should do. His advice was to leave everything to him, which proved to be a worthless promise. Instead of finding means of protecting the farmers, and therefore the factory lifeline, he set up a protection racket to enforce payoffs. This was tolerable for the short term, but Babe knew it would not be long before General Olov decided to take over Siberia Jack's itself.

Jin Jaing and Alexander Ivanov had been working together for several years, and one of Alex's objectives, learned long ago from Jack, was establishing counter intelligence against the KGB in the Khabarovsk area. This he did so successfully that Ivanov's influence now exceeded his original ambition. Babe had become close to Alex, especially because of his involvement with Jack's son and for his help with little John's escape to America. During a lunch with Alex, Babe described her problem and the ramifications of not doing anything about it.

"How is little John doing in America?" Alex asked.

"He started school a week after he arrived and fit right in. Although English was spoken too quickly for him, his teacher says he'll be just fine. Last month, before I left, Valentine's Day was near and John asked me for a heart-shaped box of chocolates. I asked him why and he said that he wanted to give them to my youngest daughter Jenna. I think there is going to be a budding romance there, so I will keep my eye on him."

"Well," replied Alex, "you never know. You were all that meant anything to Jack, and you were really very young when you met. If I had the power to somehow bring you two together—I would do anything. Perhaps it is fated that if you and Jack don't find each other, maybe it will be John and Jenna's destiny to live out that dream."

"Geez, Alex. What are you trying to do, make me cry? I had no idea you were such a sentimental guy."

Alex smiled. "I never used to be. In fact, I am not proud of many of the things I've done. When Jack came into my life, he did so in such an unexpected way. He made such an enormous impact on how I related to people that I will always love him. A day does not pass without my wishing the two of you to be together. And you know what? I actually believe we will find him. Incidentally, I have already started looking at General Orlov's activities. It seems he has ambitions to take over this region when the Communists and their Cleptocrats collapse."

Babe was a little surprised at that and asked him what he thought would happen in the Soviet Union.

"A lot of us wanted President Reagan to get tough. We in Siberia know the Communist system cannot work much longer and that it won't take much of a push for it to collapse. We've been continuously surprised that previous American presidents never called our bluff. Just look around you. The whole country is a joke. When you have to wait two years to buy a chair or ten years to buy an automobile, there is not much to recommend the system."

Alex shrugged wearily and continued. "Those fellows with the guns—the KGB, the police and the military are all out looking for ways to steal from their country and from individuals. Huge quantities of steel, oil and timber have already disappeared into the hands of these thugs, and many of them have yachts in the Mediterranean. They'll be the ones running things around here. What we call the Cleptocrats. I have been watching this develop. Even before the Berlin Wall came down, we had begun several programs, originating in the POW camps that were aimed at making ourselves economically self sufficient and militarily a force to be reckoned with."

"I thought you wanted to get out of this country, Alex. When did all this happen to you? What changed your mind?"

"I've come to realize that there is nothing for me in the West. Here I'm what the Chinese call a warlord. People around here are not aware of our potential because we've been secretive about our affairs, but I believe we're the only organized body that can take over the state and keep it from being raped by people like General Orlov. You'll no doubt be surprised to know that our activities paralleling your soup company have permitted us to expand our network of operatives throughout the state very effectively. On your next visit I promise to show you things that will amaze you."

***

General Orlov had created a network of enforcers himself. Farmers, small businessmen and vendors at the market place, who, if they did not make the KGB their partners or pay them cash for protection, were murdered in the most gruesome ways. Their defense against the criminal elements had been the police, but they too were often part of Orlov's organization. Alexander Ivanov knew each and every one of the general's enforcers and it was only a matter of making the decision to begin effecting changes.

Before the snows began in 1993, Babe returned to America. Ivanov had organized farmers to stage a harvest celebration at a large soccer field within the city of Khabarovsk. The perimeter of the playing field held booths for a farmers market and the center was left for marching bands, dancers and other entertainment. Later, there would be speeches and a free banquet.

The KGB, military and the police officer elites sat in bleachers that featured a very long speaker's table, which was replete with the customary red cloth, banners, hero portraits and flags. More than a thousand admirers and sycophants of the elite sat as close to the podium as possible. The farmers with their families sat in the opposite bleachers and waited obediently for the boring speeches to begin. These were about to start when General Orlov received a handwritten message marked urgent. The message directed the general to meet *immediately* with General Dimitri Gustavson, a KGB commander of three neighboring states, at the soccer field entrance behind the bleachers.

His exit from the podium was obvious because he sat at its center. It was also conspicuous that he left just as the speeches were to begin. No one at the time thought much about it because everyone knew how dreary those monologues would be. But, when six hundred pounds of mining dynamite blew up beneath the leadership side of the bleachers, killing almost everyone, General Orlov's departure from the podium, which saved his life, appeared suspicious. He would need new friends if he expected to live, and from that day forward, General Orlov hired only men associated with Alexander Ivanov. The note from General Gustavson turned out to be false. At the time of the bombing he was in the Bahamas. The newspapers blamed the explosion on the Russian Mafia. Ivanov was pleased to put the blame on his competition, as they were becoming an irritation.

Ivanov's operatives made certain that every farmhouse was connected by CB radio, and several were equipped with fax machines. A telephone system had been installed years before. Ostensibly, this effort was to facilitate communication between them and the soup factories. However, Ivanov used the network to broadcast news, events, farming tips and the latest happenings in politics. The farmers, using their own handle, could also notify others of KGB or Russian Mafia efforts to make criminal inroads. Ivanov's men would then eliminate the threat before it developed.

The Soviets had taken guns out of the hands of its citizens to ensure that only their own gunmen held the upper hand. In Khabarovsk, the police, KGB and the military had weapons, but farmers did not. Ivanov quietly exchanged farm products for scope mounted semi-automatic rifles and ammunition. He had read American history and was impressed with the idea of the Minutemen preparing themselves to be ready to defend the land against an oppressive government or an invading army. He understood that such a system, unique in the world, guaranteed that leadership could govern only with the consent of the peasantry.

Shooting contests were held in the countryside every three months and featured prizes such as American turkeys, which were hugely popular, pairs of breeding pigs, cans of soup, small engine farm implements, travel arrangements to the big city and cash. At any given time, Ivanov could summon two hundred marksmen, each being capable of hitting a watermelon at a thousand yards. These contests, along with other rural programs that educated the farmers, were extremely popular because it brought people together, which was a new experience for those who in the past feared saying hello to their neighbors.

Ivanov established a communications center that included the CB radio network, but the real focus was the wire-tapping of important leaders, computer surveillance of the military and KGB, computer interception of messages relating to transportation and electronic sabotage. It took him only four years to make these networks proficient. The impressive information flow, he thought, would be decisive. His confidence was at an all time high.

Most important was the creation of a technical force that could sabotage computers that controlled dams, electric power grids, transportation links, airport communication towers and telephone systems. Their assignment, if the need ever arose, would be to shut down the state of Khabarovsk itself and create confusion all the way to Moscow. Specialists were trained to mimic the voices and handwritings of high-ranking military officers, KGB and the bosses of the railroad system. Other operatives had the ability to create bogus orders aimed at turning one military unit against another. They were brilliant at impersonating officers and their orders coming from Moscow and using them to initiate false commands. It promised to become an art form.

The underground facilities at the POW compounds stored military equipment, food, ammunition and medical supplies. To defend against supply interruptions, there were thirty Honda four-wheel-drive motorcycle-powered all-terrain vehicles, which were large enough to carry a driver and an anti-tank gun operator. Parked at ground level and camouflaged, they looked like freight containers from the air.

Because of Perestroika, the Soviet Union had largely disbanded their infamous Gulag. Russian prisoners had either been sent home or confined to prison cities. American and other foreign POWs, however, remained imprisoned. Ivanov thought that it would soon be the right time to start the mass escape of his prisoners to the West. He had the power to defend against Moscow's outrage, and he had the ability to facilitate the movement of thousands of prisoners down the Ussuri River, through Promorsky Kray toward Vladivostok.

Ivanov's officers were asked to make lists of those who wished to escape to the West and those who would stay because of age, fragility, personal reasons, and those choosing to fight with Ivanov. In any case, their wives and families would be with them, wherever they went. Out of a total prison population of six thousand five hundred, including families, less than half elected to escape. The organizers considered that the extreme cold would keep the enemy indoors, and the target date was set for January 10, 2000. It was time to contact Jin Jaing and King Poo Koo.

Chapter Forty

Chair Man of the Bored
1999

COMMUNICATING with his dead wife was not all that Petrov had on his mind. Fur buyers were due in Khilok in two weeks, and a virus had broken out killing half of the sable and mink raised at the prison. He was depending on those sales to finance a new dacha and was behind on his payment schedule for the construction. His girlfriend Sasha had been spending money lavishly in Germany for home appliances, an entertainment center, furniture, windows, doors and, of course, a new wardrobe. The sick animals were killed and made into pelts, but Petrov knew the traders would reject the fur's lack of luster. If he were lucky, the pelts might be sold three for the price of one.

Fortunately for Petrov, in 1999, the new Russia was beginning to emerge. For the first time, an economic summit was to be held in Tashkent. What made this summit different from the Soviet-style meetings was that it would be based on competitive price and quality of products, not on typical five-year plans that focused on quotas. The conference would be attended by all of the former Soviet Republic states, giving Mother Russia an opportunity to show that it was just like America, proving at long last that it could make quality goods at competitive prices. Russia intended to send a message that it could be a reliable supplier and potential partner.

Delegates from Chita would be attending, and it was their representatives' connections with Moscow that resulted in Petrov's nearby factory receiving a rush order for three thousand two hundred captain's chairs. Petrov's chairs would be sat on at the conference by the elite, a real opportunity to put his company's name where everyone could see it.

It was truly now his company, at least in his mind. He, like others of the ruling class in Russia, simply appropriated factories without payment. He called his "The Petrov Chair Factory". Yuri Senya blessed the factory for Petrov, provided him with an astrological prediction of success and promised him a séance the day the chairs were to be shipped.

It was decided that, to build all the chairs in time for the conference, they must add night shifts. Petrov picked the best men, selected only the finest kiln-dried lumber and put the finishing department on notice that rejects would be tolerated.

Petrov estimated production needed was no less than one hundred chairs per day, or 3,200 total in thirty two days, but to be certain of quality he could not afford mixing the order with regular production, which often suffered accidents and delays. He knew the night shift could easily handle one hundred per day and be free of interference Shipping time to Tashkent was an additional fourteen days, and he forecast their arrival, inside of the conference center, three days ahead of schedule, on January 15, 2000.

The work went well and the finished product was by far the best the factory had ever produced. Petrov was proud and elated. He knew in his bones that from this order would come more business and from that more profit. It would no longer matter that the pelt business could not pay the bills, because one order for chairs like the one going to Tashkent, when he received payment would put his finances well ahead of his obligations.

The shipment left the factory on schedule and it was truly a time to celebrate. Yuri Senya was summoned to perform the séance.

At the lavish celebration party, Senya, frightened as he was, skillfully executed card tricks for Petrov's guests and even performed the mind-reading trick that Jack had taught him. Yuri Senya was blindfolded by guards before Petrov wrote the word TASHKENT on a small white card. Now without the blindfold, Senya took the card and passed it face-down to the observer on his left. He pretended to summon his telepathic powers by chanting gibberish and rolling his eyes heavenward, and then with a sweep of showmanship he announced that the hidden word beneath the card was TASHKENT. The applause was deafening. He was sweating. It was a close call. In the cold, steam from hot coffee rose and almost obscured his ability to see the card reflected in the cup as he passed over it.

Tashkent, now the capital of Uzbekistan, was far below

freezing when the chairs arrived; they were hurried to the Hotel Navoi conference center on the Boulevard of Parades and placed into storage until the following day when the delegates would meet.

The president of mighty Russia, Vladimir Kruchlov, and his staff occupied the hotel's top floor. They were informed of the chair's arrival and the president was pleased to hear the report praising their quality. Products from Russia and the newly independent states were being exhibited at the Pakhtor Stadium, which now featured an all-weather dome that covered the field, compliments of Russia's Ministry of Engineering. Products ranged from cranes to dinnerware, and each item represented the best that could be produced in Russia. The competition for orders and reputation was an all-out effort by every participant.

The Lenin Conference Room was constructed in a series of tiers for tables and chairs with a speaker's platform below. It could accommodate four thousand people. The building itself was not heated until an hour before the meeting. But it warmed up soon enough, and the bodies spread their own heat through the cavernous room.

President Kruchlov gave the opening address; he spoke passionately about the hope of all the states to work as one, to compete with the West as a single economic block and above all to emphasize a high standard of quality and workmanship. Leaders of six other states followed and largely mimicked Kruchlov's central theme.

The heat in the large room had been on for three hours, delegates could see ice melting from the exterior windows. And Petrov's chairs began to fall apart.

Arm rests fell from their upright spindles, legs randomly collapsed, and on the speaker's platform, several chair seats split open spilling their occupants onto the floor. Replacement chairs from the hotel were rushed in, but as fast as they arrived, more Petrov chairs disintegrated. People were falling so often the scene became comical. Many were outraged, still others burst out laughing. When sixty percent of the speakers remained standing for lack of a chair, the meeting was called off. Russia's efforts to rehabilitate its image in the marketplace had been shattered, and the president of Russia turned black with rage that would soon be felt in Khilok.

Poor Petrov did not know that chairs manufactured during night shifts, when it was much colder, might fall apart: glue cannot be used when temperatures fall below fifty degrees Fahrenheit. If used, the end product will stick together for a time and appear perfectly normal, but after being transported in a warm and vibrating freight car or being sat on in a warm conference room, the glue would simply lose its bond. No one read the instructions, if there were any.

Chapter Forty One

Les Misérables
1999

DESU Ursala had graduated from the Moscow Film Institute five years earlier, a product of the new Russia which was copying the West as madly as possible. In 1997, he found work making documentaries. One, in particular, gained notoriety in the West because it unveiled the horrible state of the Russian National Health System. Unfortunately, the current president of Russia did not share the enthusiasm for the exposé, and Desu found himself on a working trip to Khabarovsk, Siberia, to further his studies and to film a series on Siberian wildlife.

Ursala had noticed the Siberia Jack's contest material before, but he didn't think anything of it until he found himself working as a cook's assistant on a train headed east. Slowly, an idea began to take shape in his head and before long he found he could not wait to get to Khabarovsk. He had no money, no connections and not much experience, but the idea was going to make him as rich as any Hollywood film producer. At least that was his hope and plan.

Upon arrival, Ursala went directly to Siberia Jack's main headquarters and asked to speak with the manager. He was not successful. A day later he stopped at a T-shirt shop and had one printed with the words, *"I know Siberia Jack."* He wore it while parading in front of the entry doors. When people asked, "Who is Siberia Jack?" he would reply, "I can only reveal that to the owners of the factory." A considerable crowd milled around Ursala, all repeating the same questions. Babe's son John Fischer, now a grown man of twenty-three and already in Siberia for much of his life, noticed the melee.

He noticed the T-shirt and walked up to Desu. "Come inside, young man," John said as he put his hand on Ursala's shoulder.

"You have the look of a madman in your eyes, so I daresay you have something important for me to hear."

"I do have something, yes!" Desu said in English.

They sat at a table in the restaurant of the factory and John offered Ursala a grand meal. When he was partly finished, Ursala began.

"You are from America, yes?"

"Yes, I am," John replied. "Although, I was born in Russia."

"You know the French play Les Misérables?"

"Yes, I saw it just last year in San Francisco. What about it?"

"It's about a prisoner, yes? He is always on the run from his past and there is a police inspector always chasing him. An American film with Harrison Ford, 'The Fugitive,' used the same theme."

John, becoming puzzled, asked, "What does this have to do with Siberia Jack?"

Desu explained his film background, that he had no money and was unpopular with the ruling elite. His idea began to unfold.

"I see your mysterious Siberia Jack as the fugitive in a weekly television series. In each episode he will be involved in some drama where he is a hero and helps people in all sorts of situations. At the end of each story he departs for a new destination, just ahead of the evil inspector who is hot on his trail, leaving the question in people's minds, 'Who was that man and what is his real name?'" Desu, now truly excited, went on. "I think it would be a great story; particularly if it hints that Jack might have been a prisoner in the Gulag. A lot of people can relate to that and maybe he could even have an American accent. That's big in Russia right now—everybody wants to talk American, you know."

John Fischer was on it immediately. It was downright devious, and he could see the brilliance in it. Until then, Siberia Jack advertising could not suggest that Jack might be a prisoner without offending Russian leadership and bringing their ire right down on the heads of the Siberia Jack enterprise. Perestroika may have shut down the general prison camps of the Gulag, but not those that held foreign POWs.

"It's a superb and absolutely astonishing concept. What do you want from us, Desu?" John asked.

"I want my own production company with you as my partner.

I'll produce the show, and who knows, perhaps someone will find this Siberia Jack, if he ever existed."

"I'm not at liberty to discuss whether there is a Siberia Jack, but for now I will agree, so long as you never treat this like a joke. Not that you have."

John faxed the proposal to Babe in San Francisco, who was also enthusiastic and urged production to begin immediately.

Ursala Productions rolled out its first episode to Russian television audiences in late 1998, and the show became an instant hit. Mesmerized viewers everywhere began wondering in earnest just who Siberia Jack actually was. Everyone hated the faceless inspector, and soup sales went through the roof.

Months later, a red-haired fur trader, often mistaken for Siberia Jack, who purchased pelts in Khilok, caught a glimpse of the Healer. He knew instinctively that this man could be Siberia Jack. If he was, the prize money, which had become enormous, was enough for a man to live the rest of his life in luxury. The problem he had was trying to devise a way to control the Healer and transport him to the soup factory. Of course he had to guess right, but he had heard that the Healer had an American accent and so did the character in the television show. *Surely*, he thought, *it was a deliberately planted clue.* His thinking was that if he did anything less than obtain absolute control over the Healer he would risk losing the prize money. Any official could claim it was he who had been the discoverer of Siberia Jack and could steal the prize. *You couldn't trust anyone in Russia*, he lamented to himself. And it was a long way to Khabarovsk.

Fur trader Ivan Guk did get close enough to the Healer to say a few greeting words in English. Jack turned, looked startled and asked, "Who are you?" Guk did not understand the question and moved on, knowing with certainty that the Healer just spoke English. Hair on the back of Jack's neck bristled. He sensed something.

Prisoners raised sable and mink on Petrov's commercial farm and Guk came to know Petrov well. On this trip, Guk offered a higher price for the pelts than the current market, and during negotiations with Petrov he also offered to purchase the Healer for fifty thousand rubles.

"Why do you want to buy him?" Petrov asked.

"The Healer is clearly not a Russian prisoner or he would have been released with the closing of the Gulag. I think he is an

American POW. Don't worry, I have seen many others all through this region and it is none of my business. So, let's say he has 'special status' and cannot be released, and if that is so then perhaps my offer might provide an inducement. How you handle the paperwork is your business."

The notion of buying an individual came as a surprise to Petrov, especially because it was Jack.

"I'll have to think about it," Petrov said. "Why do you want this man?"

Guk had developed an elaborate story he hoped was believable.

"There is a religious sect, east of here, whose leader recently died. Now that religion is no longer illegal, I thought the Healer would be a good replacement. The sect is fairly large, financially well off, and I suspect they will pay well for the right man because it would increase their membership. I would be paid a fee for my trouble, and, given the Healer's reputation, I expect the fee to exceed what I give to you."

"What do you want me to do, connect him with a chain to you?" Petrov asked.

"No, that is not necessary," Guk replied. "It will be sufficient for you to simply sign his transfer out of here, appointing me as his official guide."

"I have to say, Guk; this is a suspect request. I'll get back to you next week when you come for the pelts."

"By the way, Petrov, what is his real name?" Guk asked before departing.

"Jack Fischer," Petrov answered and turned away.

Thrilled with his progress, Guk sent a fax from the post office to the management of Siberia Jack's Soups that read:

Pursuant to your contest, I hereby submit the name of Jack Fischer as being the true identity of Siberia Jack. I can be contacted at Post Office Box 186 in Khilok. Ivan Guk. Fur Trader.

The message arrived at the soup factory early in January and was received with jubilation. Babe was contacted by fax immediately with the following message.

Siberia Jack's last name is FISCHER! We are heading to Khilok to find the person that provided the name. Staff will stay on the alert for further contact from that man. Will keep you informed. Your son, John.

***

Babe received the message at three o'clock in the morning in San Francisco. Her heart racing, she called Joy with the news and within an hour her dad offered his corporate jet to her for as long as she needed it. She left that night for Siberia.

Yakir Petrov, the prison camp commander at Khilok, had received his séance from Yuri Senya when the chairs were shipped in December 1999. Yuri performed brilliantly. Petrov spoke passionately to his dead wife, she forgave him, he wept, and he opened the little bag and read that the message was to free the Healer, Jack Fischer. Petrov had sworn to do that.

Petrov had in his hand fifty thousand rubles from the fur trader to turn Jack over to him, but Petrov worried that this might lead to Jack's imprisonment somewhere else, and while he wanted the money from Ivan Guk, his promise would not permit it. Petrov knew that his dead wife would *know* he had broken his promise and he could not risk upsetting the spirit. While pondering the issue, he received a telephone call from Tashkent that shook the very floor he stood on. All of his chairs had failed, the conference failed and it was entirely his fault. He had no idea why those chairs collapsed and immediately suspected sabotage. He would not receive a penny for the shipment, his personal finances were now in the red zone and there was no doubt more trouble was on the way. Perhaps he would be arrested or worse. He did not know. He could barely think for the sudden fear.

Petrov knew trouble was coming and he had to flee, but he was torn between his promise to his dead wife and the $50,000 rubles he desperately needed. Finally he made a decision and summoned Jack to his office.

He explained the proposition he had received from the fur trader and announced his decision to free Jack, but permitted him to weigh whether he wanted to take the risk and go with Ivan Guk or not. If Jack decided not to go with Guk, Petrov promised to give Jack Ivan Guk's identification papers, his passport with a visa stamp permitting him to appear at a New York furrier's show, his plane ticket to get there, plus whatever money Guk might have on him. Petrov would detain Guk for three weeks before letting him go, leaving Jack plenty of time to escape from Russia.

Petrov recommended using Guk's internal passport to get Jack into Mongolia and advised him to go to the British, not the American, consulate in the capital, Ulan Bator. He had heard that escaped POWs who found their way into the American Consulate were returned to the Russian prison from which they came. There was no point running the risk if the rumor was true.

"How do I get out of Mongolia?" Jack asked Petrov.

"They have a little more independence down there than we do in Siberia. Therefore, the Red Cross will not be as politicized. The British Consulate there will either fly you out using their own air service or if they think you are too hot to handle, they will pass you on to the Red Cross—with them you will not need a passport. After that no one will care what happens to you. However, if for some reason you decide to use Guk's ticket and passport and head for New York on your own, without announcing yourself to a Western consulate, that is up to you."

"I've made my decision," Jack said. "Ivan Guk was going to buy me like a slave. Let Ivan Guk rot in hell. I want out of here by tomorrow morning. Can you do that?"

"Yes," Petrov replied. "I'll see you off personally. My driver will take you to Chita; from there the train ride is only a day's travel to Ulan Bator. God be with you." In the morning Ivan Guk still sat in his cell.

***

John Fischer, on the seemingly hot trail of his father, arrived in Khilok three days after receiving Guk's message and went directly to the Post Office to inquire if anyone knew where to reach the man named Ivan Guk. No one knew where he lived, but a clerk suggested that John go over to the old prison compounds where sable and mink were raised, suggesting that a fur trader might well be doing business in that area. John thanked him with a large tip and left.

It did not take long to locate Yakir Petrov. John introduced himself, explaining that he represented Siberia Jack's Soups and asked if Petrov was familiar with the contest to identify Siberia Jack's last name.

"Yes, I watch that program every week and of course I see the soup cans everywhere. Why?" Petrov said.

"Well," John replied, "a man named Ivan Guk correctly

identified the last name as being Fischer. We haven't heard from the man since Guk contacted us. I am here searching for him. He's a fur trader and I had hoped you might know where he is. Perhaps he has come here to buy pelts?"

"That's very interesting," Petrov remarked. "How much is the prize money now?"

"It has grown every year for almost seventeen years and it's now five hundred eighty thousand dollars. Mr. Guk will be a very happy man."

"Did you say your last name is Fischer?"

"Yes. Siberia Jack is my father."

A long silence followed. *This is a miracle,* Petrov thought. He asked to be excused and hurried to Guk's cell. Standing at the bars, seething with rage, Guk began howling at Petrov to get him out of there. Calming him down, Petrov brought over a stool and talked in earnest with his prisoner.

"You have violated Russian law. It is illegal to bribe a government official and it is also a criminal act to conspire in a kidnapping. My office is equipped with a sound recorder and I have all the evidence I need to put you away for a long time."

Guk could not quite believe what he was hearing, but it began to worry him. In particular, Guk's big concern was for the Siberia Jack prize money. If he did not get back to the post box or if he failed to bring the Healer to Khabarovsk, all that money would be lost. His guts wrenching, he looked at Petrov.

"Cut the bullshit, Yakir. You've already stolen all of my money and my passport, what do you want now?"

"Ah! Mr. Guk, I am glad to see that you are an intelligent man. What I want is for you to sign this little piece of paper stating that it was both you and I who discovered Siberia Jack's last name. We will share the prize money and you will go free. I could kill you and take all the money, but unfortunately they already know your name."

"You prick," Guk yelled. "How did you find out?" *You see,* Guk thought, *you can't trust anyone in Russia.*

Pushing the paper into the cell and handing Guk a pen, Petrov said, "that's none of your business. After you sign that piece of paper I may tell you—I don't know yet. In any case, I must hold you for another day."

Petrov returned to his office with Guk's signature in hand. He explained to John that he helped Jack Fischer leave the camp two days before and then proudly told the whole story about Guk wanting to buy Jack, how Petrov put him in jail for this crime and how they had agreed to share in the prize money.

John asked to use the telephone and called his home office. He directed a check be made out to both Guk and Petrov for having guessed right. "The only other contest requirement is the winners must come to Khabarovsk to collect their checks and be part of a publicity program, John said, turning to Petrov. "National television, that sort of thing."

"Who pays for the trip?" Yakir asked, knowing he had to leave the factory in a hurry.

"We can provide you air tickets or if you like, both of you can come with us now. That is, if you have the time."

"You have your own airplane or did you arrive by train?"

"We have our own plane."

"I'll go and talk to my partner," Yakir said with a smile on his face.

***

John telephoned his mother explaining that they had just missed Jack by two days, that he was probably in Ulan Baton and that all efforts would be made to find him.

"How did he get out of prison?" Babe asked.

"His commander received a message through a spiritual medium suggesting that he release him. It's a long story. The commander's name is Yakir Petrov and he actually drove Dad to the City of Chita where he boarded a train for Ulan Bator. He doesn't know where Jack went afterward."

Babe could not believe they had been so close to finding Jack and now were losing him. "What did this Petrov man say Jack might do when he got to Mongolia?" She wanted to scream her frustration into the phone.

"He suggested that Jack go to the British Consulate or the Red Cross. I already have the telephone number of the consulate—I'll be calling them after we hang up."

The twin engine Apache could seat five, and to Petrov's disgust, Guk was also onboard. The prospect of being flown to Khabarovsk in a private plane was something Petrov could not turn down. Besides, he thought, the chair business is finished; Moscow would be breathing on him very soon, and the quicker he got his hands on the prize money, the faster he would disappear.

The Russian pilot had difficulty flying toward Khabarovsk. The radio was silent for much of the trip. Flying past Chita, John noticed that all its lights were out. Further into the flight, they discovered that all the cities and villages along the way were dark and without power. Twice, military jets came alongside the Piper Apache, looking it over carefully. Everyone on board was edgy and wanted to know what was going on. He could not raise anyone at the tower and Khabarovsk and the surrounding area was all dark.

The pilot flew the small company plane into Khabarovsk. The blacked-out city and the airport concerned him. As he landed he saw military vehicles near the terminal with their headlights on. General Orlov's men escorted them into the terminal where they were greeted by the soup company manager. The relief was immense.

After introductions, the manager answered the questions. "The electrical grids throughout Khabarovsk and the adjoining states are down, there is no power anywhere. Several dam gates have been opened and water is flooding into the valleys north of here. Warplanes are in the air, troops are maneuvering at cross-purposes with one another and an ammunition dump south of here blew up two hours ago. You are all welcome to stay at the Soup Factory's guest cottages until this trouble is over. By the way, John, your mother will be here in the morning."

"Do you have power in the cottages?" Petrov asked.

"Yes," the manager replied. "Generators were installed fifteen years ago because power in Siberia was too unreliable. We'll turn the lights on when we're sure there is no military emergency."

For the rest of the day and into the night John speculated what was happening, but suspected that Ivanov had initiated a coup.

The following morning, Babe arrived. She too, had difficulty getting into Khabarovsk, but this was a flight she had waited a lifetime for, and she intended to be part of every effort to locate her Jack.

That evening over dinner, Petrov described Jack's life during the past years and Babe listened intently. *Jack the healer? A hypnotist? Hey! Maybe he really did hypnotize me when we were young.* It would take days for Babe to hear the whole story. She had time, there was no safe way to get into Mongolia with the power down, and every aircraft was suspect as an intruder. In Petrov's telling of Jack's story, he learned of Babe's relentless search and marveled at the power of love. How he wished his wife were still alive.

An army motorcycle driven by Yoshi, the man in charge of raising mushrooms at Ivanov's POW camp, stopped and hand delivered a sealed envelope to Babe and John. She opened it and read out loud:

I have evacuated twenty seven hundred POWs from the prison compounds. Twenty one hundred are on their way to a small port just north of Vladivostok where a ship, disguised as a Russian vessel, will take them to San Francisco. King is on board and directing that effort. The remaining six hundred are on their way to Japan. Jin Jaing is with them. Return home at once. We will need your support there with the press. Future communication will be to your home fax number. Do not attempt to contact me or discuss this with anyone. Time is of the essence. POWs expect to arrive in San Francisco Feb 18, 2000. Alex Ivanov.

John spoke first. "Alex has been planning to do something like this for years, Mom. I think you know that."

"Why now, and why wasn't I informed?"

"I think he understood that the naming of Fischer in the soup contest would be a winner and it would be widely carried by the international press. He would know that this kind of publicity could lead Russia's rulers toward the killing of all POWs held in China and Russia to cover up the truth."

"I'm sure they would do that to erase any evidence of live POWs being used as slave labor," Babe sighed. "Revelations like that would not be good politics."

***

Any effort to follow Jack into Mongolia would be time-consuming and hampered by the lack of telephones and power. If Petrov's story was true, then Jack would be heading for the British Consulate in Ulan Bator or he would be going to New York using Ivan Guk's plane ticket. Babe fought the almost physical urge to plunge after Jack, but after discussing the options with John, she realized she could contact the consulate from her Gulfstream when telephones in Ulan Bator came back on line. If Jack were there, she could return to pick him up; if not she would be more useful to him in America.

PART FIVE

Chapter Forty Two

Escape
2000

JACK found that using Ivan Guk's internal passport was not a problem because he already resembled the fur trader. Buying the train ticket was easy. Trouble surfaced crossing the border into Mongolia when all the passengers were ordered off of the train for customs inspections. Jack was not prepared for this; he had assumed his ticket would take him through. Now sweat began to pour out of his body as he waited his turn. Mongol border guards examined his papers and demanded the Mongolian equivalent of a visa. Out of the corner of his eye, Jack watched several passengers being herded into a nearby metal building. They looked anxious. Jack thought fast and said in a slow, unconcerned Russian voice.

"These are my air tickets into New York—I must get to the American Consulate in Ulan Bator to obtain visa papers. It is the closest consulate. Otherwise, I would have to send all of my documents to Moscow—that could take months. My plane trip would have to be cancelled if I did that."

One of the officials asked, "do you trade regularly with Mongolia?"

"No," Jack replied. "I thought of establishing business in the country. I have been told that our common borders were sympathetic to accommodate those ends."

"A lot of Russian criminal types try to cross the border here to make trouble," the soldier replied. "Our country does not want them, but it seems you have air tickets to America and that makes you an exception. This time we will let you pass, but in the future you must first obtain an entry permit."

"Thank you," Jack replied. He looked up into the sky and

thought, *Babe that was too close. But I'm on my way.*

His confidence, he knew, had been shattered. As the train pulled out of the station, he thought, *what if word that I am not Ivan Guk reaches the Capitol before I get there?* Climbing into a high valley surrounded by the ragged ridges of the Khenti Mountains, struggling, the train slowed to a crawl. Jack looked down through the window at the Tuul River flowing past Ulan Bator, and wondered if freedom or prison awaited his arrival.

Jack asked directions and located the British Consulate six blocks from the station. He set out with some uncertainty. Ivanov and Petrov's words rang in his ears, urging him not to approach the U.S. Consulate because they were known to betray prisoners back to their captors. If there were the slightest suspicion, Jack thought, he would find a way to get out.

The British Consulate building was not the grand structure Jack had imagined. It was a crudely shaped three-story affair resembling a miniature Great Wall of China fashioned from mud-bricks and adorned with narrow windows that had been gun slots in years past. He entered and requested the person in charge, refusing to discuss his business with anyone else. Finally, a tall man dressed in khaki and wearing a patch over one eye entered the room.

"Haydon Skudder is my name," he said. "I am the Consul General here in Ulan Bator. What is your name and how can I help you?"

Jack really did not know how to start and blurted, "my name is Jack Fischer. I am an American. I was captured in Korea in 1950 and have been held prisoner in Russia until two days ago when I made my escape."

A consular office deals with visas, trade documents and on rare occasions assists British citizens with travel or police problems. Haydon Skudder had simply never handled a problem like this before and his first instinct was to tell Jack he had come to the wrong consulate. But Jack's luck had finally turned. Skudder was also a military man who had once been a prisoner in Malaysia during an insurgency. There he had an ankle crushed and an eye blinded by a thirteen year old boy-soldier having a little fun. When Jack said he was a prisoner of war for almost fifty years, Haydon Skudder felt a deep compassion for the man in front of him.

"Nice to meet you." He held out his hand. "Can I call you Jack?"

"Yes, if I can call you Haydon."

Reaching for the telephone, Skudder instructed his secretary to call the local restaurant and have them bring food for both. He also requested that they not be disturbed for the rest of the afternoon.

Haydon, turning to Jack said, "please come into my office and take tea while we talk. I expect you have a lot to say."

The office, like the reception area, had a round iron stove with a top plate supporting a steaming teapot. Haydon pulled the teapot to the center of the plate to increase the heat, and reached into his desk for a tin of butter cookies. "These will do while we wait for a real Mongolian lunch."

Jack told his story without interruption. The more he spoke, the more Haydon's interest intensified. He asked many questions and Jack answered them.

Finally Haydon asked, "Why did you come to the British Consulate rather than the American?"

"It is the belief of other POWs and of my own prison commanders that the American escapees are returned to Russia. First we thought it was for money, but later we realized it was because our government did not want our story out."

Haydon thought for a moment and speculated whether there was any truth to what Jack said and decided that he did not know enough to make that judgment; he would therefore err in Jack's favor and say nothing to the American Consulate.

"Jack, if I put you on board a plane with British travel documents and something blows up on the POW issue back in America; I might become a convenient scapegoat, that is, if you are right about your allegations."

"What are my other options?"

"You could claim to be defecting from Russia, to us here in Ulan Bator, as Ivan Guk, but if that became widely known, it's possible you may not get out of Mongolia because every means of transport from here must cross either Russia or China. Besides, we are really still in Russia, regardless of independence or consulate sovereignty."

"I could leave here for New York as Ivan Guk. I have travel papers and a ticket."

"Right now, for reasons I don't know, and it doesn't seem you do either, all the power is down around Khabarovsk. The real Ivan Guk is not dead, according to you, and you admit to having his money and ticket. If word of your escape reached here before your departure, and before the power failures clear, then you might not get past the airport terminal without being arrested. This man Guk may already be in a police station filing a complaint."

"Okay, Consular, what would you suggest?"

Haydon explained that he had a lady friend who administered the Red Cross center locally, that she was also British and that she was leaving Ulan Bator in five days for a conference in Sweden.

"My friend will have to telephone Sweden," Haydon said. "She will explain to her superiors that there is a very important refugee she wishes to bring to Stockholm, and that he has a British passport. She will claim you are a nuclear scientist with an interest in staying in the West, but not necessarily in Sweden."

"Why would she do that, Haydon?"

"We are close; if she thinks it's important to me she will make the effort. I would guess we get a yes or no from Sweden within three working days. In the meantime, you will stay at my home. Nothing will be said of this to anyone until long after you're gone."

Haydon arranged a new wardrobe for Jack, including a business suit and leather luggage. Jack got his hair cut and new shoes to complement Haydon's gift. The Bank of India had allowed Jack to deposit $46,000 in Vladivostok and to send a commercial message. Now, Jack worried about withdrawing ten thousand dollars in cash based simply upon his numbered account—an account that had been alive for forty-seven years. Jack feared that sending a non-commercial message from Ulan Bator, at the same time he was attempting a withdrawal, would be noticed, and it was not worth the risk. Haydon listened to Jack describe the problem and thought for a minute.

"I think the answer might be to direct the Bank of India to transfer $10,000 to my account here in Ulan Bator. Once received, I will provide you with the cash," he said.

While Jack listened he glanced through a window to see the sun and briefly thought of Babe. *This can't be true; I'm really on my way,* he thought.

Noticing Jack staring out of the window, Haydon stood up and said, "come along, old chap, let's get this business done."

***

The Swedish government apparently liked the idea of an atomic scientist fleeing an unstable Russia for the West because a few days later they got an answer that granted a temporary visa to Ivan Guk without difficulty. Using that name would attract less attention than Jack's own, although it did have its risks. After six days of waiting, Jack said goodbye to his new friend Haydon and boarded a propeller-driven aircraft in the service of Air Mongolia. It would fly west; refuel in Ankara and again in Krakow before making the final dash for Stockholm.

Upon arrival in Sweden, Jack checked into a downtown hotel and stayed three nights. Before officials had a chance to react to news stories that Ivan Guk was not a nuclear scientist, but rather an escaped POW named Jack Fischer, he had left the country on a fishing boat headed for Denmark. From there, he would travel on to New York.

Chapter Forty Three

Mass Escape

IN the year 2000, New Russia's greatest fear was that it could lose all or part of the Siberian territories to insurgency movements financed by China. Air and rail links were the threads that held Siberia together, and as the Russian economy collapsed further, fewer resources were available to defend and maintain those corridors or the garrisons they connected.

Ivanov had control of the regional KGB through General Orlov, but the army was a different matter. There were two linked military districts that cut across state boundaries, one in Khabarovsk, the other in Vladivostok. These districts had been compromised by the creation of duplicate command structures staffed by Ivanov's men who resembled the real officers in physical appearance. The duplicate, or ghost staff, had been tutored on each of their target officer's families, military history, mistresses, sexual preferences and exploitable weaknesses. Plus Ivanov's intelligence organization was privy to all military communications. The ghost staff's job was to replace the existing army command structure using rehearsed tactics.

Politically, Ivanov followed the American President Lincoln's lead. Ivanov too intended to 'free the slaves' and would announce it when he was certain the prisoners were out of the country. His plan was to seize control of the state by force, not as another criminal opportunist, but as a reformer, and freeing prisoners would strike the right note in a country that had long been a giant prison.

A mass escape of POWs from Russia to America would create an international publicity firestorm, and Ivanov needed to hold the moral high ground. In his judgment, Moscow would be in the uncomfortable position of trying to kill him for what he had done but not being able to because he would be an international hero. Ivanov did not intend to threaten Russia with a move toward independence. Instead, he planned to be the governor in perpetuity of a state that was part of Russia and economically healthy, relatively Mafia free.

After forty nine years of captivity, many POWs and their families had decided to stay in Siberia. They had long ago given up the hope of their government rescuing them, and even if they had not, there was nothing back home for these men. The prisoners had become families, they were safe with Alexander Ivanov in control, and they saw no point risking what they had for something most could barely remember. The decision to stay came with the responsibility to help those who would escape. But if the attempt failed, there could be ramifications. Every prisoner, whether he stayed or went, would receive shares in the commercial activities they helped create.

Vietnam POWs accounted for almost five hundred of the twenty seven hundred prisoners who decided to leave. They would leave from Llinka, south of Khabarovsk, on the same day as the main body of prisoners left for Vladivostok by train. Those who were born in camp and of combat age would fight alongside the Vietnam POWs, if it came to that.

Six hundred POWs boarded two heavily armed riverboats and departed from Khabarovsk on the Amur and Ussuri Rivers and moved unnoticed northeast to Nikolayevsk, a small port exiting into the sea opposite the Sakhalin Islands. A Brazilian destroyer, procured by Jin Jaing and flying a Japanese flag, would escort them to Japan. The escapees were sixty percent Japanese and the rest American and Australian.

The ruse pretended that the two riverboats were transporting replacements for rotating troops at the garrison of Chumikan, a military town northwest of Nikolayevsk, on the Russian mainland. The risk, apart from being stopped, was there would be no way to determine beforehand if the harbor was clear of ice when they arrived.

**

The largest group of twenty one hundred had the longest journey. They would travel by train, forty cars long, to the small harbor city of Artem, forty miles north of Vladivostok and a distance of twelve hundred miles from Russia's military controlled rail junctions. It was expected to take several days to reach Artem. From there they would transport by ship into the Sea of Japan, through the Straits of Hokkaido and on into the Pacific Ocean. The pretense would be that they were to reinforce the Russian-occupied Japanese island of Sakhalin. The dangers were that the train might be stopped or that the Russian Navy could intercept the ship at sea or at the loading point.

Each group would impersonate specific Russian army units. They would be uniformed and armed accordingly and acting under orders from the military commanders of both the states of Khabarovsk and of Primorsky.

***

Jin Jaing had leased a Brazilian destroyer, which included a captain and his staff, for twelve weeks from a Brazilian Navy representative who believed it would eventually lead to a sale. Jin convinced the representative that a Polish shipyard was building a similar craft for the Cook Islands and that their crews needed to practice on a similar vessel before taking delivery. If Jaing failed to return the destroyer, his letter of credit would easily purchase a new replacement. The warship, flying the Japanese flag, would rendezvous with the POW riverboats at sea near Nikolayevsk.

King Poo Koo purchased the formally Russian ship, the Azov, a 27,000-ton troop transport, from the independent state of Latvia, which had almost no use for it, King exchanged farm tractors and machine tools for the vessel, made it seaworthy and had it crewed with South Korean seamen. The ship, already registered as Latvian, would make its way to Vladivostok to load twenty one hundred men with their families and move them to Sakhalin Island pretending to replace rotated Russian troops.

Chapter Forty Four

Going Home

JACK Fischer stepped out of the Swedish mini-bus onto a snow-flecked dock near Stockholm. A rusty and well-used fishing boat waited to take him to Denmark. Once there, he was to meet a Red Cross official who would put him on an airplane bound for New York. It was March and fifty years had passed since Jack had joined the United States Marine Corps and left America for the Korean War. Jack climbed aboard the boat, his hopes rising. He did not feel his age. Instead he felt a glowing wonder at the world around him, that he might truly be escaping, and that he might see Babe and his family again.

***

Three days later, the fishing boat arrived at a small village near Koge on the Danish east coast. From there, Jack traveled by rail to the Copenhagen airport. But in transit, he became nervous and then frightened after seeing newspaper headlines about his escape from a Russian POW camp. *How the hell did the newspapers know?* he wondered, after all those years in the Soviet Gulag without his government making any effort to obtain his release and denying that POWs existed, it made no sense that suddenly he was important. Or even noticed. The warnings he had been given at the Mongolian Consulate regarding Western government feelings about unreturned POWs echoed in his mind. He began to believe he might now be a troublesome inconvenience.

Still masquerading as Ivan Guk, Jack made it through the Copenhagen airport and boarded his airplane. He hunkered down in his airplane seat and prayed that his route out of Denmark had not been discovered. If he were found, he was certain he would be sent back to Russia, maybe even by his own countrymen. If that happened, it would finish what strength he still had. He concentrated his thoughts on Babe and how he would find her. He longed to feel the airplane leave ground and begin what would at least feel like a much more irreversible trek back into America.

Once in the air, and finally heading for New York, Jack twisted in his seat gawking at every detail inside the MD-11 jetliner. It was huge, futuristic and unbelievable. He caught an air-conditioned flow of air with his hand and wondered how that was possible. The cabin attendant handed Jack a plastic packet with earphones and noticed his confusion. She demonstrated the headset for him and plugged it into his armrest. He grinned, pretending he understood, and when she left he pressed buttons and was surprised to hear music. He figured out how to change the positions in his seat and sank deep, his feet slightly elevated; music flowed through his head without static and he dreamed. All the other passengers seemed oblivious to the wonders, but Jack was floating, filled with the sounds and smells of a world he never knew existed.

Glancing around the cabin, Jack Fischer attached his curiosity to people's clothes, conversations, their strangely stiff hairstyles and amazing politeness. Almost everyone smiled, and he wondered why. People often said things like "thank you," "excuse me," "have a good day" or "I hope you are comfortable," phrases he had forgotten even existed. He also noted with some interest how overweight many of them were. Never had he seen such fat and over-perfumed people, even the young ones, and he wondered if all Americans would be the same. The plane that had taken him from Mongolia to Sweden had been a Russian propeller-driven antique. The aircraft, in which he now cruised noiselessly at thirty thousand feet was a stark testimony to what he had missed in confinement.

Leafing through the in-flight magazine, Jack examined the wonders of wheeled luggage, hotels featuring exotically shaped pools, Polynesian, Italian, French and American restaurants displaying foods he'd never seen before, beachside condominiums, or "flats" in his understanding, all for sale at prices only a Soviet politician could afford. A Mont Blanc fountain pen for "only" US $350 got his attention. He remembered the fountain pen he found when he was young and wondered how much it had cost back then. Turning a page he stopped and studied an electric massage chair and couldn't help thinking how much money he could make back in Siberia, charging people for a thirty-minute session, but the $4,000 price reduced to only $2,500? *It wouldn't pay for itself,* he thought. A gold-plated .45 caliber Colt Celebration pistol was also for sale along with women's steam hair curlers. He mused about buying a gun from a catalogue and why anybody would want one in the States. A strange looking pillow with arm and back rests appeared on the next page. Jack laughed, imagining people carrying it around. *What's it for?* he thought. *Damn if it doesn't come with a small light to read with.* He saw himself in the forest wearing the contraption around his waist, using the light to see in the dark, searching for a place to sit. He couldn't help chuckle. *America,* he thought. *America, America, America, I love you.*

The aroma of hot food pulled Jack to the present, and he ate greedily. He found himself trying to be polite and at the same time make up for fifty years of prison rations. He ate two main-course trays, one with chicken, the other beef, and he drank six vodkas without ice. The attendants were so courteous, Jack observed. Nobody in Russia was polite, and he instinctively tried to rise up from his seat each time one came by with a meal, a drink or a pillow.

Ironically, a movie about an American who escaped from a Soviet Gulag began showing after the meal. Jack remembered the big movie projectors of his youth and tried to imagine cramming them into compartments over the heads of the passengers. *Seeing a movie in an airplane—really, unbelievable!* Jack thought the actor had a close resemblance to him; he even combed his hair the same way and had the same fair complexion, except his hair was black. Did anyone on the plane recognize him? Jack's story had apparently been making news in Europe, and he was impressed by the airplane company, paying attention to current events enough to provide a movie in which life—his life in this case—imitated art. But as much as the traveling public liked a good escape story, he was uncomfortable that it was being shown. As he got caught up in the plot, Jack wondered about his own story. *How would it feel to be that guy in the film, to still be young and handsome?*

As the jet moved quietly through the air, he could imagine himself fleeing across the Russian wasteland, escaping evil men, rushing tearfully into the arms of his long lost Babe. His escape was much more mundane. *But I did it,* he thought, and shivered at his audacity, his luck. *Ah, what a dream to have come true.* He had made a tolerable life for himself in the Gulag; with not many years left in life, he wondered if his escape was going to turn into a foolish joke. He turned off the sound from the movie. *Where will I go if this fails? Babe could be dead or married with a family and maybe not want to see me, or worse, see me out of sympathy. I'm sixty-nine years old, my stomach hurts from bad food, I sweat when I think I could be an embarrassment to her, and I'm an old, old fool who still thinks he's a teenager. What an idiot I am!*

Returning to Siberia was out of the question, but what if returning to the States was also? Unconsciously, Jack's hands clutched the armrests. *Babe, help me!*

Jack had given Babe's name to the Mongolian Red Cross, as well as her address. He also gave them his parents' home phone number and address. Maybe his brother, sister or parents were still around. Maybe a neighbor would know where to look. Red Cross officials had only promised that it would take time and told him to get in touch when he reached San Francisco.

Jack rested his head against the cabin window and gazed blankly outside, letting time drift backward thinking of the days of his youth.

San Francisco.

Babe.

He found himself replaying his favorite memories of meeting, courting and winning Babe's love. The Palace Theater dominated his memory and flashed through his mind again. He could still feel the softness of her sweater and taste the salt of her skin. In his mind, he kissed her. *Such a long time ago,* he thought, *an entire lifetime.*

Another Vodka arrived as the in-flight Gulag movie ended. *The Palace Theater had changed everything*, Jack thought. He could recall so clearly how he then felt attached to someone who did not withdraw physically or make sarcastic remarks, even in fun. That feeling was something so unexpected it had felt for the first time that he could trust someone not to reject him and that it was okay for him to be silly or stupid. *Imagine,* Jack thought; *if the Palace had never happened. What would I have been able to think, believe or depend upon over all the years?*

He had long ago figured out why his father had behaved the way he did, a man with only one emotional oar in the water, void of any love from his wife. Jack realized a thousand times over that he would have died long ago without Babe. The Palace Theater always brought tears to Jack's eyes. But for these memories, there had been no reason for living.

That he was on an airplane going home was a miracle he had thought to be never possible. He couldn't help but to think about the scores of escape plans that had come to nothing. Yet, he was here, and expectation made his heart sing and his mind race—*where can you possibly be now when I am finally coming home to you? Did you wait for me? What was your life like? Was it possible that you got pregnant in San Diego? How will I ever find you?* Jack closed his eyes, leaned back in his airplane seat, and struggled to sleep. Instead, he found himself half awake throughout the flight, reliving and remembering, not about the Gulag, but about his Babe.

Chapter Forty Five

New Era

MESSAGES were sent to Army Generals Sikorsky and Vadir ordering that they be present at a military conference relating to the updating of codes and procedures for internal terrorism and insurrection. The meeting would be held at the KGB headquarters building in Khabarovsk. They were to bring key officers, current contingency plans relating to the conference, code applications and lists of communications assets. KGB General Orlov would host the three-day affair. He had telephoned and personally promised each general, not only a good time, but brand new Mercedes four-wheel drive off-roaders, compliments of stolen vehicles from Europe. Jack Fischer, by this time, was on his way to Mongolia.

Generals Sikorsky and Vadir and their staffs were arrested upon arrival. Ivanov's hand-picked imposters assumed their positions and carried on communications with their bases as normal. The imposters gave orders directing other key officers to destinations where they in turn were arrested and replaced by imposters. Within seventy-two hours, Ivanov's team had the army under its control. Ivanov's false orders were then sent to the respective bases through the imposters, outlining maneuvers and communication alternatives necessary to defeat an internal uprising. The military were told that a test would take place during the upcoming days and that it would last a week. Subordinates were urged to achieve high marks for performance because the entire East Siberian command structure would be watching.

The army takeover was followed by Ivanov's POW communications compound using its computers to shut down the electrical grids, open key flood gates and sabotage military computers controlling transport and communications throughout the states of

Khabarovsk and Primorsky. Simultaneously, teams already in place used mortars to hurl foil strips and long lengths of copper wire along a patchwork of power transmission lines. Ghost commanders ordered military convoys away from the POW escape routes.

The escaping groups began moving when the power went down and were already in their third day of travel when John Fischer's plane flew into Khabarovsk with Ivan Guk and Yakir Petrov. Three days later, Babe received the hand-delivered message from Ivanov to return to America, and both POW groups made contact with the ships that would become their final links with freedom.

***

The smaller POW force, led by Captain Wiley, had no trouble reaching the ice-free harbor area of Nikolayevsk. From there, the riverboats chugged forty miles east to rendezvous with Jin Jaing's destroyer. Weather forecasts predicted twenty-foot swells. Six hundred escapees boarded the Brazilian destroyer and arrived at Hokkaido, Japan, during a howling storm. At three o'clock in the morning, a very puzzled Japanese Navy Marine guard unit was signaled by the destroyer to come aboard.

Captain Wiley then met with the Japanese Navy base commander and explained his cargo of escaped Japanese, Australian and British POWs from Siberia. He urged that their presence in Japan be kept secret until the second group fleeing from Vladivostok by river boats reached safety in America.

The Navy commander listened with amazement, as Wiley explained.

"Publicity is critical, and if the Japanese announce prematurely it could create risks for the POWs still aboard the Azov."

The Japanese government became involved, and Captain Wiley pointed out to its representatives that a premature announcement could also doom thousands of Japanese POWs still held in Russia. The Japanese had no doubt a Russian submarine would sink the Azov if it knew of its cargo. They also understood that such events could also result in the death of all other prisoners, Americans included. Captain Wiley argued that such a result would push blame onto the Japanese government unnecessarily. Especially so, because each escaping group had names, photos and histories of all prisoners left behind and was also bringing unearthed time capsules that held lists of thousands who had perished in the camps. The Japanese government agreed not to announce until the Azov docked in San Francisco.

"If both POW groups had attempted the escape together and failed it would have led to their execution. However, with two groups, only one needed to succeed, because an international publicity spotlight will follow," Captain Wiley explained. "And that would militate against the possibility of the murder of the ones who were not successful or of their being returned to a Siberian prison."

***

Further south, King Poo Koo's ship, Azov, timed its arrival to coincide with the POW train arrival near Vladivostok. The Azov had proper documents and knew Russian Navy signals. It waited a day for the escape train, which had been held up without challenge at the rail junction of Artem by priority military traffic. The off-loading of the men and their families at port was uneventful. They formed up and marched with their own military band, ten-abreast, toward the Azov. They had no trouble boarding ship or leaving the harbor.

John and Babe were en route to America, Jack Fischer had just flown over Greenland on his way to New York and the Brazilian destroyer was docked in Japan.

Chapter Forty Six

"Go Jack Go"

THE Gulfstream landed at the Nandi airport in the Fiji Islands to refuel and to sit out an approaching tropical storm, which was expected to ground them for two days. Using the satellite telephone to make their calls, Babe discovered, after talking with Haydon Skudder at the British Consulate at Ulan Bator, that Jack had left that very morning and was heading for New York. The next telephone call was to Khabarovsk.

Siberia Jack's managing director answered.

"Babe! Am I glad you called. Things are really jumping around here."

"Why? What's happening?"

"Well, we held a press conference introducing Ivan Guk and Yakir Petrov as the winners of the contest. We had the checks blown up for the cameras. Each winner was asked how he came to realize that Siberia Jack's last name was *FISCHER*. I tried to stop that line of questioning, but it was too late. Petrov apparently loves the camera, so he blurted that the weekly television show had hinted that Siberia Jack might be an American because of the accent."

Babe wondered why the fuss and said, "well, we did hint that, didn't we?"

"Yes, but no one dreamed that Petrov would announce on national television that Jack Fischer was an American prisoner of war held in a Russian prison camp for forty-nine years. And that the owner of Siberia Jack's soup company, a Miss Babe Barsi, was Jack's long lost love, that she created the company just to find him and that she had never given up believing him to be alive."

Babe was stunned and blurted. "Oh, my God! What was the press reaction?"

"You can't believe it. If you had a television capable of receiving Russian TV, you would be hearing not only the story of your quest to find Jack, but there are demonstrations everywhere chanting 'Go Jack Go!' It's incredible."

"Why are they yelling that?" Babe asked, slightly confused.

"Russians can identify with prison life for one thing, that's my guess," suggested the manager. "Petrov told the press that Jack was trying desperately to escape Russia and that he was already on his way, hopefully to America. He also identified himself as Jack's prison commander and as the one who helped Jack get out from Khilok."

Babe was shocked. "Is this going to make it more dangerous for Jack to get away? What do you think?"

"I can't answer that, but I can tell you the international press is not just looking for Jack Fischer right now, they are looking for the heroine in the story—Babe Barsi. Your picture has already been on the news. I can tell you that the story has touched a very raw nerve here in Russia. Nearly everyone around here can identify with escaping from a prison and positively everyone has fallen in love with the idea that your love quest will soon be fulfilled. The story is now front page internationally. Babe, this is better than Romeo and Juliet. And just for your information, our ordering dept can't keep up with demands for pictures of both of you. Soup, of course, is selling so fast we started a twenty-four-hour production effort."

"Is that all of it?" Babe asked, a little shaken by the unforeseen turn of events.

"No. Desu independently announced to the press that the mysterious inspector, who had been chasing Jack in each weekly episode of the TV series, wasn't an inspector after all. It was his girlfriend trying to find him all of those years, and that the girlfriend is you, the owner of Siberia Jack's Soups."

"Why did he go so far, I wonder?" Babe replied, trying to suppress a sob.

"I don't know, but the revelation that you were the inspector in the series has hit the television audience by storm. Right now they are running repeats of each episode four times a day, and the viewers are watching with a dedication that is completely unknown to me. Between the series and the television news, along with the newspapers, there is a national frenzy to find Jack and to bring you two together."

Pausing for a moment, the manager asked Babe to hold on for a minute while he turned up his television. He held the telephone receiver to it and Babe could hear the near hysterical chanting coming from the television. *"Go Jack Go—Go Jack Go—Go Jack Go!"*

Babe burst into tears.

"Hey, Babe, don't hang up, there's more," the director pleaded.

Babe stayed on the line, but could not speak and barely managed to murmur an acknowledgment.

The director continued. "Ursala Productions received a telephone call from an international film star named Natasha Kerensky. She wants to play your part in the movie version of our weekly television series now that you have emerged as the heroine, and she won't take no for an answer. She just called Desu from her Lear jet and is heading for Khabarovsk as we speak."

Babe hung up sobbing.

A short while later, Babe composed herself, telephoned Tara Carr and told her of Jack's escape and the publicity storm that was heading toward America.

"What is it you want me to do, Babe?"

"Please, get through to Nick. Have him meet me at my place in San Francisco. Tell him I need to know everything he knows on the politics of the POW issue, and also ask him for his help in contacting Jack."

"I'll do it, Babe, I'll do it. Anything else?"

"Yes. There is no doubt that Jack is heading for San Francisco to find me. I need some kind of plan for us to locate him and at the same time not enlist the help of our government."

"Are you afraid of our government, Babe?"

"Tara, I am so afraid of them my guts shake every time I think of what they might do to stop a forty-nine year Gulag POW emerging from Russia during an election year. You know that Senator George McBain is running against our current vice president, Allen Hurst. McBain's a war hero and an ex-POW. He has been after the administration for years to release uncensored Korea and Vietnam documents. They, along with Congressman Bob Dornan and Senator Bob Smith and others are also trying, but they have been stonewalled. Since president Conklin is a draft dodger and Hurst has a suspect military record and both are on record denying that such prisoners exist—well, you get the picture."

"Okay, Babe, I'll get on it right away. I'll get in touch with McBain's office for you. By the way, while you were talking, I had an idea of how to find Jack or make it possible for him to find you."

"Tell me about it, Tara."

"We start running newspaper and TV ads asking for Jack Fischer to call you on a hotline that we set up. Our phone bank will ask only one question of the callers, and there will be a lot of callers. *'What personal item did Babe give you before you went overseas?'* Only one person would know that it was your four-leaf clover pendant."

"Tara, you are a genius."

Chapter Forty Seven

New York to San Francisco

JACK passed through customs in New York posing as Ivan Guk without a problem. He toted his carry-on bag and strolled through the airport wondering what to do next and decided to have vodka at one of the bars perched along the terminal walkways. Ordering a drink in English felt strange to him, as did all the English language signs and television sets blaring CNN news. A television set at the bar got his attention. He heard a chant coming from it, broadcasting the words, "Go Jack Go." As he focused, a newsreader delivered the latest news.

What you are hearing in the background is a chant that is being heard throughout Europe. People everywhere are urging Jack Fischer—an American POW held for forty-nine years in the Russian Gulag—success in his escape attempt, which took place last week from a secret POW compound in Siberia. No one knows exactly where he is at the moment, but one thing they do know, he is trying to reach his lifetime love, Babe Barsi, who lives somewhere in San Francisco. What makes this story so sensational is that Ms. Barsi has been in Siberia searching for Jack Fischer for all of these past years—and—if you can believe it—just missed finding him two days before Fischer made his own escape. Both are now heading for America and absolutely everyone is looking for them. A television special, tonight at seven o'clock, will be dedicated to describing Babe Barsi's lifetime quest to find her Jack.

The Russians, as might be expected, are denying that Jack Fischer ever existed, and that if he did, he would have been a defector who chose to live in the USSR voluntarily and that his current flight from Russia may have something to do with crimes against their state. We will keep you up to date as information comes to hand. This is Paula Jones for CNN personally saying 'Go Jack Go' wherever you are.

Jack was so overwhelmed he could barely breathe. He had no idea that Babe had been trying to find him all those years. The thought brought tears to his eyes. He had so many questions now that he had never dreamed of before. His body shook uncontrollably and between sobs he wondered. *How did she get to Siberia, what did she do there and how did she just miss me?* One thing was certain, she was alive, she still loved him and she was heading for San Francisco and he would find her. Jack's head was filled with emotion, but he forced himself to think over his feelings. *I damn well promised I'd come back, didn't I?*

The broadcast clearly hinted at how the Russians intended to handle his escape. They would discredit him if he became a public icon. The way the system worked, Jack knew they would kill him if they could find him. He also knew he had to leave the airport immediately.

***

Jack took a taxi to the Amtrak station and booked a first-class seat to Oakland, California using a false name. He purchased several newspapers and while he waited, overhead television sets continued to blare out the story of his escape. All of the pay telephones at the station were busy and when he was finally able to use one, the information operator told him there was no listing for a Nella or Babe Barsi in San Francisco. After boarding, the telephones on the train were of no use; Jack did not have a credit card.

Newspapers all carried the same headline themes: *"BABE & JACK,"* read one, *"JACK ESCAPES,"* another. Babe's last name was Mattioli, he read, and she was divorced with two daughters born from that marriage and a son named John. Jack's mind leaped at that. He wondered if it was at all possible that this was his own son John Fischer, but dismissed the idea as being too fantastic to be real.

Reading further, Jack saw that the American government was already matching the Kremlin's response to his escape. *"Washington, DC. NY Times, sources have disclosed that Marine Pvt. Jack Fischer defected to the North Koreans in November of 1950 and had subsequently become a Soviet citizen. Other defectors corroborate the story. Fischer was last seen in Denmark. If he did return to the USA he would likely by charged with treason."* He became more bitter as he read and wondered how he would avoid his own government putting him in jail before he got the chance to see Babe at least one more time. And who saw him in Denmark? His skin crawled with the old familiar fear he had lived with for half a century.

Chapter Forty Eight

The Kremlin

A disgusted President Vladimir Kruchlov heard sporadic chants of 'Go Jack Go' coming up from Red Square. He closed the window as his First Secretary Vasili Mitrokhin entered the room.

"I brought that tape you requested on the Petrov press conference in Khabarovsk."

"Well, play it."

The tape began. A spokesman with Siberia Jack's Soups explained the long history of the contest and how the prize money had increased each year. Yakir Petrov and Ivan Guk each received oversized checks for two hundred ninety thousand dollars. The spokesman tried repeatedly to continue the program, but the roar of approval from the audience made it impossible.

The crowd carried both Petrov and Guk on their shoulders around the stage area while the press, ignoring the spokesman, obtained interviews from them. Petrov spilled to the ground and was caught by a European network reporter who bellowed on camera, "tell me Mr. Petrov, we now know that Siberia Jack is Jack Fischer, but who is Jack Fischer?"

Now a celebrity, Petrov blurted, "oh! He is an American captured during the Korean War. He was held for twenty years in a POW camp near Khabarovsk—that's in Siberia—and then he was sent to me. You see, I am the prison commander at Khilok, near Chita. That's in Siberia, too."

"Why was he a prisoner long after the war was over?"

"I don't know anything about the politics of this kind of thing. Thousands of American POWs came through my area, but under the old Soviet system you did not ask questions."

"Are there still American POWs being held in Russia?"

"Are you kidding? There are plenty of Americans—that is true, but there are also Germans, Japanese, Australians, Turks, you name it, we've got them!"

"Isn't that illegal? I mean, aren't these men covered by the Geneva Convention?"

"The Soviets didn't care about that. They needed men to work the forests and the mines so they kept them, but don't be too critical of them for doing it; China has them, too. I've heard plenty."

Another camera focused on Petrov. Ivan Guk joined him. The reporter attempted to ask POW-related questions to Guk, but he clammed up immediately. Finally, a female reporter asked the question for either to answer.

"Who is behind this quest for Jack Fischer? Is it an American? Is it a family member?"

Guk said nothing. He wanted out of there, but Petrov loved the moment and replied.

"The person behind Siberia Jack's Soup Company established it to run the Siberia Jack contest. That person is Jack Fischer's first and only love, Miss Babe Barsi, the company's owner," he said, pointing to a large photograph of her. "They were separated by the Korean War. Since then, she has retraced his steps in both Korea and Russia in an effort to find him—and she missed doing that several days ago."

"Tell me, Mr. Petrov. How did she miss him? I would think that after almost fifty years of searching for her lover, that a near miss would have been a traumatic event?"

"Well, I didn't know she was looking for him at the time that I arranged for his escape, but when her son John showed up at my headquarters I realized the gravity of the situation."

"Mr. Petrov, would you say that the Soviet Union stood in the way of these two lovers finding each other?"

"Of course, of course, any damn fool knows that! But not for long—Mr. Fischer is heading for America and his girlfriend Babe is racing back there to find him."

A spokesman for the company was horrified. This was not part of the script and there would damn sure be ramifications from the Kremlin. He was worrying about those things when another reporter pointed her microphone at him and asked, "If Jack Fischer could hear you now, what would you like to say to him?"

After a long pause looking the camera straight on, and with a clenched fist held high he began yelling with a burst of emotion. "Go Jack Go—this is your life now—Go! Go! Go!" The crowd repeated the chant as the cameras faded to black.

President Kruchlov was on his feet pacing the floor pondering the enormity of what he had just seen. He turned to Mitrokhin.

"Shit, we'll be hearing from every damned country on the planet! Why does that name Petrov sound familiar to me, Vasili?"

"You aren't going to like this—but he is the one who sent us those fucked-up chairs in Tashkent. We didn't pay him for them, of course."

"That prick! What the fuck is that son of a bitch doing in front of a camera disclosing all that POW shit?"

"I don't know, Mr. President, but I am at your command."

"First, kill him, then if there is anymore bullshit about the POWs we have, kill them, too."

"Yes, sir! But what about the Americans or the Germans, what do we say to them?"

"The same as we always say. The prisoners don't exist, never have, and that the subject arose only because of the presidential election. They want to make the vice president look bad because of his draft record."

"That's a good idea. It has worked before. But what if it creates pressure for President Conklin?"

"Fuck President Conklin. Tell him to deny everything. Tell that shit we will discredit their precious Jack Fischer as being a deserter who moved to Russia on his own, who then killed someone and that is the reason why he was in prison."

"Good thinking, Mr. President."

"Okay, now get out of here. But one more thing, let our overseas people know we want Fischer neutralized and, for that matters, that fucking woman as well. Got it?"

"Yes, sir!

President Kruchlov slumped into his chair and poured himself a water glass-sized vodka.

Chapter Forty Nine

The White House

"**T**HAT fucking McBain! Did you see this morning's press conference in North Carolina?" President Conklin yelled at his political security advisor, Greig Rivers.

"If you mean the one where he had boxes of Freedom of Information Act files on POWs held in China and Russia and showed documents that were ninety percent redacted and marked 'Top Secret?' Yes, I have," Greig Rivers said. "Are you up on the Jack Fischer and Babe Barsi story?"

"A little, what's the latest?"

"I've had a wire tap on Senator McBain's office ever since he announced his candidacy for the Presidency. We just picked up a telephone conversation between him and one of Barsi's people, a woman named Tara Carr. She wants to put a press conference together with McBain as soon as Babe Barsi arrives back in America."

"Fucking great. That asshole gets to play war hero again with a romance angle, that's going to play just great with the soccer moms."

"That's not all," Rivers explained. "McBain's office has calls into Ex-Congressman Bob Dornan's and Senator Bob Smith's offices. He wants to establish a national board of inquiry alleging our administration covered up the POW story. Collectively, those two guys have been a pain in the ass, always trying to dig into the trash—you know the type."

"Okay. Tell the vice president to dress up his Vietnam War record. Find anyone or anything that will make him look good, then have him do a press conference in front of the Freedom of Information Office demanding the POW files for previous administrations. We get a head of steam on this push and we can blame the Republicans for the whole thing."

Pausing to think for a moment, the president added, "have the vice president set up a blue ribbon investigative body that reports only to him on POW facts, and tell my secretary to book about a dozen events for me. You know the kind of thing that's needed—speeches before Veterans groups, some kind of performance at the Tomb of the Unknown Soldier, meetings with relatives who are active on POW issues. Greig, we, have to stand in tall grass on this thing."

"That's great, but the big inquiry is going to be on what we didn't do during our terms in office, that's what we have to deflect. What do you think?"

"Shit, that's easy," Conklin replied. "We claim that past Republican presidents have buried the truth so deep that we could not possibly have known about it, and proof of that is going to be asshole McBain's own press conference with those POW files. We just point to them and say, you see, it takes a Republican war hero to uncover Republican wrongdoings. Once we're on high ground we can bury the issue."

"Good stuff, Mr. President. Meanwhile, I've got the military scouring the records for defectors who will claim Jack Fischer was a traitor."

"Hey Greig, that's the kind of forward thinking we need," the president said, as he rose to shake hands.

"Thank you, sir!"

Chapter Fifty

Sergeant Leroy Robinson

WHEN the war started, the North Korean Army swept down the Korean peninsula with such speed they overran many U.S. Army units until they were stopped at Pusan. The US Army's 24th division had been destroyed and American POWs were taken to the North Korean capital of Pyongyang.

POW Sergeant Leroy Robinson met his first Russian officer at a special indoctrination camp at Pak's Palace, northeast of Pyongyang. He was taken aside and taught that black men were equal to white men. Pak's Palace had been established to teach men like Robinson that Communism was a true revolution of the oppressed.

Being from Alabama, Robinson liked what they had to say and quickly became a convert. His newfound Communist rhetoric was so convincing to others that the Russians sent him to other POW camps to hold educational meetings with the prisoners. Leroy rose to the equivalent rank of a Russian junior officer. His educational efforts included sorting out new prisoners and determining whether men would continue their education in Russia or be passed on to the labor camps. Those sent to labor camps, he thought, had it coming, because evidence of their war crimes was everywhere in Korea.

Robinson was transferred to the Bunkers at Chiktang, southeast of Pyongyang, a camp that was expecting a large number of POWs. Leroy was part of the reception committee and was the one who gave the welcome speech to Jack Fischer's grubby batch of men. While Leroy did not make much of an impression on the new arrivals, he loved being the overseer and routinely separated Negro men for better treatment. Revenge was a great motivator.

During his two years at the Bunkers, Private Fischer treated Robinson several times for sickness. Robinson witnessed the prison camp as a death camp transformed into a place where love and individual feelings of freedom were dominant. He also saw how Fischer and Commander Ivanov brought together Japanese, Koreans, Americans and Australians as equals, and how successful the camp had become, especially when compared to others. Robinson was impressed with the notion that freedom and capitalism prospered behind prison walls, but he thought, it was probably an isolated experiment.

After training in Leningrad, defector Robinson was sent to America with a false passport. There he operated as a spy for the Soviet Union. His handlers ordered him to California as a provocateur stirring racial discord in Oakland, Sacramento and Los Angeles. He loved the work and he was good.

In 1969 during the Watts riots in California, Robinson's job was to cause panic by shooting recklessly into crowds of black people, enlisting their return fire. He also firebombed several factories. His organization marched on City Hall demanding equality and justice. The Russians did not care about the methods used, their only interest was to show the world, on international television, how oppressed the workers in America were, especially the minorities. Robinson received a Soviet Medal for his Watts efforts.

At first, Robinson was exhilarated to be part of the new American Revolution, but upon returning to the Soviet Union and seeing that their revolution had resulted in the creation of a prison state, he again returned to America but ceased being a Russian operative and disappeared into Georgia. There, he married, returned to California and settled in Oakland. He had not been in touch with a Russian for thirty years.

The Jack Fischer story was on the television and Leroy Robinson followed it avidly. He knew Jack, but when the news hinted that Jack Fischer was a traitor, defector or possibly even a murderer, his mood turned dark. Leroy knew better, and the thought that Jack had spent forty-nine years in prison while his girlfriend spent her life trying to find him really bothered Leroy. He also felt guilty for not having come forward years before with his firsthand knowledge of live POWs held in Russia and China.

Leroy Robinson had been a defector and a spy, but he was not, in his mind, a man without character, and Jack's story began to make him feel he owed something to America and to Private Fischer. The thought frightened him because he could not come forward to stand up for Jack without revealing his past, and that could mean going to jail for a long time or maybe losing his wife, who knew nothing of his true past.

Chapter Fifty One

America the Beautiful

BETWEEN Fiji and San Francisco, Babe could not keep Jack out of her thoughts. She wondered where he was, how he would attempt to contact her and what help, if any, he had. If he surfaced and the press got to him first, they would adopt the White House line with questions. She could hear it. *"When did you defect to the Soviet Union?"* *"How many years did you serve for the murder of your wife?"* *"Why didn't you turn yourself in at an American consulate in Mongolia, Sweden or Denmark?"*

If he voiced fear of his own government, no one would believe him. Babe was convinced of this. She knew he would have no experience in these matters and would probably assume that once he was in America that the nation would greet him as a hero. On the other hand, she reflected, if Jack did make those assumptions, he would have surfaced in the press the instant he landed in New York. Maybe, she thought, Jack was savvier than she gave him credit for.

The Gulfstream's pilot spoke on the cabin telephone, informing Babe and John that there was a huge crowd gathering at San Francisco Airport waiting her arrival. He asked for suggestions.

"How long before we land?" Babe asked.

"Three and a half hours."

"We can't avoid the press, but we can insist on speaking only through Joy Jaing. Radio that message ahead. I will attempt to reach her by telephone."

Joy had just arrived at her station when the call was put through. "Joy, this is Babe. There's a crowd at the airport waiting to interview me. I want our story to be told as news, not slanted by newscaster's opinions giving the White House an opportunity to edge in their discredits."

"I know what you mean. We get filtered here a lot ourselves. What you need is a spokesperson who answers all the main questions. You do the appearances and they do the rest."

"Can you do this for me, Joy?"

"I can and I will. My station might have a shit fit, but I'm on my way to the airport. When you land have your pilot radio the tower requesting that only I approach the aircraft. I'll join you, we will disembark together and I will take care of the press."

"Thanks Joy. I'll call. See you in a couple of hours."

John called his half-sister, Jenna Mattioli, letting her know of their mother's arrival in San Francisco and for her to call her mother later.

He also called his older half-sister, Claudette Mattioli, whom Babe had not seen for three years. John thought the current events might be an opportunity for her to reconcile with her mother. Claudette did not answer the phone and John left a message announcing their arrival.

Television and print reporters mobbed San Francisco Airport's private aircraft terminal. Crowds of demonstrators were shouting "Go Jack Go!" Over the din of shouts, the public address system repeatedly requested that Joy Jaing pick up a white courtesy telephone. Joy rushed to the nearest white telephone and picked it up.

"Hi, Babe, this is Joy. I'm cleared to approach your aircraft. Have the pilot let down the ramp when I'm near the plane."

The pilot shut down the engines and when Joy appeared on the tarmac he let down the stairs and Joy climbed up quickly. The steps retreated back into the aircraft. Joy and Babe hugged, Babe clinging to her friend.

"Joy, how much negative stuff is there being broadcast about Jack?" Babe asked.

"Well, your side of the story has been silent, so they're having a field day speculating whether Jack is a criminal or a hero. I suggest we put your story forward the moment the terminal doors swing open."

"Is there anything I should emphasize or not mention?"

"Tell them what Jack meant to you, that you have never forgotten him and always believed he was alive, that you received confirmation he was still alive in 1978 and that he was being held in a Soviet POW camp. Describe how you followed Jack's tracks throughout Korea and Siberia and how you established the Siberia Jack contest. Tell them you have met personally with the prison commanders at both Khabarovsk and at another camp near Chita and that you have verified his escape through Mongolia.

Babe thought for a minute and replied, "if they ask me how I received confirmation that he was still alive in 1978 or what I had learned from the prison commanders, what should I say?"

"Refer all further questions to me. Tell them you are tired and anxious about finding a way to establish contact with Jack. Plead for their forgiveness and promise them you will appear on television for an hour if they wish. Ask them to pray for Jack's safe return to you and enlist their help in finding him."

The interview in front of the terminal took only fifteen minutes, but it was moving. Dozens of cameras floated before her and questions were asked before others were answered. She told her story, and as she did she realized that it was a subject she never discussed with anyone other than very close friends. Before this day, she had been accused of being overly romantic or someone who pursued a fantasy to make up for something missing in her own life. She wondered, at times, if she were obsessed and if her dreams substituted for the many voids in her married life.

As she spoke and the details unfolded, her heart relived the memories, the stress and the yearning of all the years of uncertainty. To the listening press, Jack and Babe became the boy and girl next door separated by the cruel winds of fate. Their story, that of a long-lost love, perhaps found once more, was again fanned with new hope. Every person there became determined to play a role in bringing them back together.

Babe's face blushed, her eyes flashed brightly, her arms reached out and her voice rose. She pleaded for their help and as she did an Arab woman in the audience let out a continuous high-pitched, tongue-vibrating wail that in her desert homeland would have been heard far across the mountains and brought men running. Her mournful cry, now being broadcast in the background of Babe's delivery, sent a chill across the television world, urging what seemed to be a call to arms against evil. People tried to shush the ululating woman, to no affect. The keening seemed to announce the presence of justice on earth. It filled listeners hearts with greatness, and in that instant, two hundred fifty million viewers became kindred spirits.

Above the wail, with tears running down her cheeks, Babe continued in a broken voice.

"I want to thank each and every one of you for making it possible for me to be in the national spotlight—and for making it possible to tell the world—Jack, I love you. I never stopped loving you. Come home—come home to me. Please!"

The cheering mob followed her to the limousine that Joy had arranged and roared its approval. As it pulled from the curb, leaving Joy to finish up the questions from the crowd, she could hear the chant 'Go Jack Go,' and she couldn't stop crying.

Chapter Fifty Two

America For Sale

THIRTY minutes from her Broadway Street home, traveling north on Highway 101, Babe telephoned Tara Carr to see what she had found out.

"Wow, Babe, the whole world just saw your press conference. You've got the entire nation in tears, including me. And not a single negative question was asked. You are going to get the Academy Award for that performance. Where are you now?"

"John and I are just approaching South San Francisco."

"Look, I have Nick here with me and he would like to talk to you as soon as possible. I've also been in touch with Senator George McBain. You will be close to my office in a few minutes, why don't you stop here first before going home?"

"I'm emotionally drained, but since I'm so close, I might as well stop. I could probably do with a good martini anyway."

Tara Carr's TNT building was on Howard Street, and when Babe's limousine pulled to the curb an employee opened the doors and ushered Babe and John toward the elevator to Tara's penthouse.

Tara greeted them dressed in a rough-cotton floor-length robe with a gold-silk scarf tied around her waist, a gold fez hat and a big smile. Nick Mateo stood behind her. She grabbed Babe by the hand and swirled her around in a circle declaring, "and to the winner for best performance by a female actress, may I have the envelope—please?"

"Oh! Tara, you know I wasn't acting. I was shaking in my boots the whole time. I was so afraid of doing something wrong. Before I knew it words just kept spilling out, I didn't even look up until I heard that Arab woman's wail. That sent a chill through me like I have never experienced before."

Nick agreed. "It was eerie alright, I felt it. Whoever was watching felt it."

"Well," Tara joined in, "we're off to a good start and that's what's important. I'll fetch the martinis. You and Nick go ahead and get started."

Nick hugged both Babe and John, they sat down, and he began.

"You asked me to look into the POW issue and to find out why most of the material relating to captured servicemen is either still stamped SECRET or is so censored it is of little value."

"Yes," Babe replied. "What did you find?"

"I've heard things through the grapevine and I *am* warning you. You must decide if being together with Jack is more important than creating a lot of publicity about live POWs, because that will feed into Senator McBain's run for the Presidency. In fact, there have been many sightings in the Soviet Union of what are believed to be missing POWs. Your press conference today electrified the nation, for that matter the world, and it put the administration in a bind. The vice president isn't going to win an election against McBain if you succeed in mortally wounding him with the POW issue."

"Pretty scary, Nick," John said. "I get the picture, but it all seems so improbable."

Tara entered the room with a frosted Aladdin-shaped, crystal container of martinis and poured its contents into tall pre-frosted glasses. Babe could not help but smile. Tara, she thought, never did things in half measures.

Nick, eyeing the container, said, "I'm expecting a genie to waft into the air."

"Nick," Tara said, pouring and ignoring Nick's smart-ass crack, "I've made arrangements for Babe to meet with Senator McBain the day after tomorrow. That's important; she needs to have him on her side."

"She needs him alright," Nick said, "but if it has the appearance of endorsing him, Babe could get herself in trouble."

"What do you advise, Nick?" asked Tara.

"Make any contact with Jack a private matter. Don't push their face into it. Let McBain support you; let him be the one that advocates POW issues and he can use you as an example. But you will not make joint press calls with him. Instead, we develop contacts with the White House. Perhaps suggest to them that you might be willing to do a joint press conference if they stop their discrediting efforts. That would open the door to you and Jack reuniting quietly and I might add, safely."

Babe sipped her martini and nodded.

"Remember that the administration has a problem too," Nick continued. "The Russian and Chinese governments don't want to be embarrassed with revelations about slave labor camps. That would affect the trade relations with America and open up inquiries into other dealings. I'm certain they have agreed between each other to deny and discredit and I am equally sure they would kill any remaining prisoners if publicity turned against them."

"Your thinking is good, Nick and, I agree," Babe replied. "But if anything happens to hurt me, my family or Jack or if there is the slightest interference with my effort to find him, let them know that I will be America's Joan of Arc."

"I have a good relationship with a senator. I'll call her right now, so don't leave just yet."

Nick dialed a telephone number and asked to speak to Senator Leslie Slator. She came to the telephone.

"Hi Nick, this is a surprise. What's up?"

"I'll make it short Leslie. This Jack Fischer story isn't going to help the good politicians that we both know, and your president is putting himself into a bind. I'm calling to let you know that I have full authority to speak on behalf of Babe Mattioli. She is willing to appear at a joint press conference with the president and you, of course, to show her support for his policies. In exchange she wants the administration to cut the bullshit aimed at discrediting Jack Fischer."

"Nick, your client is a very, very intelligent woman. You have offered the perfect solution. I owe you. Hang up now, I will be through to the White House within the next two minutes."

"Thanks Leslie. I'll see you at your next fund raiser."

She laughed and said, "I hope I survive long enough to see that."

John and Babe left Tara's penthouse after almost two hours of discussion and headed for home.

Chapter Fifty Three

Daddy's Little Girl

FROM the day she was born, Claudette Mattioli had been Daddy's little girl. Peter had doted and took her everywhere, even to his office. He never forgot a birthday, went shopping with her and eventually turned Claudette into a rival to her mother for his affection. When Peter embraced Babe, Claudette would sometimes conveniently move between them. Babe discussed the problem with Peter frequently and he pretended to understand.

"Babe, I can't help it if being a good father makes Claudette look up to me," he would explain. "Maybe if you didn't entertain so much. I'm not criticizing, but all those phonies on the hill—are they more important than your daughter?"

"My entertaining always included you and it helped you get elected to the Board of Supervisors, the State Senate and now elected a lieutenant governor. Why is it alright for you and not for Claudette?"

"She's a child and needs nurturing," Peter replied with an insincere smile.

"I never heard you complain when it got you where you wanted to go."

"Look, Babe, she'll grow out of it. What am I supposed to do, push her away?"

Babe looked Peter squarely in the eyes. "You could start by being more openly affectionate to me. Demonstrate to her that I come first. Make sure I'm the one who sits next to you at dinner and at parties."

"That will only drive her away from the house altogether. Just let it be. A little patience is all that is needed. She'll grow up," Peter said, hoping the conversation would go away and liking getting the better of Babe for a change.

Peter loved taunting Babe by occupying the high ground. He knew full well that he had usurped Claudette's affections and that he used that relationship to put Babe down as an absentee mother. His actions were always defensible as a loving effort to make his older child happy. It was his way of counterbalancing Babe's popularity and he often subtly hinted to others that Babe, under her smiling exterior, was really a cold fish. Rumors of his dalliances with other women would then seem more reasonable.

This day, though, Babe was not as easily suppressed. "Peter, I know that you set out deliberately to turn Claudette against me and you've succeeded. It makes me unhappy and I am sure that is part of the reason you're doing it, but what do you think it's doing to her?"

"She looks pretty happy to me." Peter said smugly.

"She is at an age, for a long time now, when she subconsciously cannot understand why you, the superman in her life, don't take her into your bedroom to substitute for me in the fullest sense."

"That's outrageous. I'm not encouraging her to go to bed with me."

"You are if you make yourself into the only man in her life. For her it's the next most natural thing to do."

"You should see a shrink, Babe. You're sick and your imagination is running wild."

Angry, Babe replied, "Claudette already feels guilty bringing her dates home. She pretends they are really not important to her because she feels that she is being disloyal—in effect, cheating on you. Her relationships suffer as a result."

Inwardly, Peter knew that Babe was telling the truth, but he couldn't bring himself to admit it and wasn't going to let her off the hook.

"Well, maybe I should have an affair with her to confirm your worst suspicions."

"You are a sick son of a bitch, Peter. Go ahead and spew that garbage at me. I really don't care anymore. But do me a favor; think through how this will end for Claudette and how it will affect her self-esteem."

"Don't get carried away. She has so many boyfriends she has to beat them off with a stick."

"Yes, she is beautiful, but when her father doesn't fully love her she makes an extra effort to be sexy, to attract men who praise her and take her to bed. The more she lies with strangers, the more reassurance she needs. One-night stands or short-term flings never end in a true relationship. You, asshole, have stolen that from her. Not only that, but she can't even confide in me because I'm her competition for your precious affection. She's not stupid. She knows you whore around. The rest of our world knows, and she no doubt thinks she needs to do the same to make you jealous."

Babe's words rang a note of truth in Peter and he could see himself screwing around town, coming home to be smothered by Claudette for his affection, taking her to special dinners and never taking her to bed. He felt a sharp sense of guilt and shame.

"There may be some truth to what you say, Babe. Lord knows I'm not perfect. I sincerely thought I was doing the right thing—if there is something you think I should do, I'll do it."

"I've already told you what I think you should do. The question is, are you capable?"

"I'll try," Peter answered.

Claudette continued to race from one lover to another. She experimented with drugs and psychotherapy and discovered in the process that everything that was wrong with her was her mother's fault. She moved away, drank heavily and cursed Babe's memory. Often, when she was in some drug-induced haze, she would call her father vaguely hoping to find a missing key, enlist some genuine affection or maybe find an emotional ledge to lean on while catching her balance.

Peter would just send money or change the subject by offering her the world. "I'm always here for you sweetheart, you know that," he often said. "What can I get you? How about a trip to Switzerland?"

The truth was Peter's money was always there for her, but he had no time to share. He didn't know what to do with her anymore and in his mind he had already done everything a good parent could do. He sent her to drug therapy, alcohol recovery, psychologists, and foreign countries and even secretly paid a high profile movie actor to squire her around and promise marriage. Marriage, that was what she needed, he thought. But, it turned out; such efforts would not be the key to her salvation.

***

Claudette had been working steadily for almost two years without being fired. It was her crowning achievement; she had come to love work and going to night school. Computers were her world and the people in it were driven to a single cause—perfection, and she loved it. Nothing turned her on more than crashing at co-workers' pads to crank out another sixty-hour week or to accomplish some breakthrough task. Her fixation with lovers had disappeared, she had quit drinking and had almost stopped using drugs, but that was something she felt she would save for last.

She had bought her own car without Dad's money, and shared a San Francisco flat with a girlfriend from work, who, like Claudette, was a beautiful malcontent. When they went to dinner together they had a lot to talk about and both shared a passion for belonging to something that was bigger than they were. Work enshrined them, worshipped them and it made them feel important and useful. It transformed everything, and when attractive men approached, the girls saw themselves differently.

Chapter Fifty Four

Smokey the Bear

THE Russian ship Azov had shed its yellow-brown camouflage and had been repainted the gray-blue and black of an American Navy vessel. A new name was painted on its sides calling it the USS Montana. On the fore and aft decks, painted canvas covered two five-inch guns and the Stars and Stripes flew on the mast.

King was three days out from San Francisco when Ivanov relayed an intercepted Russian Navy message. It said as follows:

Latvian transport ship Azov headed to the West Coast of the United States with two thousand escaped POWs. Destroy it. Moscow Naval Intelligence.

King ordered canvas stretched across features of the vessel to distort its silhouette. He also began shooting practice with the two cannons and ordered five Stinger missile soldiers to remain on the upper deck until they docked in San Francisco. Seven marksmen armed with the latest 50-caliber single-shot rifles headed topside to practice. Loaded with armor-piercing explosive shells, these rifles could immobilize a tank. Wire-guided shoulder-fired anti-tank missile launchers were placed forward and aft.

By previous agreement with Ivanov, King began sending computer-scanned copies of each POW name to the Matt Drudge news. The only message attached to these files was:

National Security issue. Do not destroy or put onto your website until you receive an explanation from us within the next three days. Please e-mail your acceptance. King Poo Koo.

Each file outlined the prisoner's history, including his photograph, military identification and list of relatives. An outline of POW camps, their locations and a personal message was included. Drudge understood exactly what it was. He kept his word and replied to the sender.

Thanks for choosing me. I'm honored. Contact me when you are ready. Unless I hear otherwise, after the third day of this message, I will release the files onto the Internet and presume that is what you intended. Good luck!

A Russian submarine on routine patrol picked up the USS Montana three days out of San Francisco. Through the periscope it looked like an ordinary U.S. Navy transport ship. The ship's sonar pinged the submarine.

Men dressed in American Navy uniforms flooded the deck looking seaward in the direction of the submarine, hoping its periscope would observe the costume party and go away. Both five-inch cannons traversed in the same direction, a canvas screen covered their turrets and muzzles. Speed: 11 knots. Radio messages from the ship to American Navy headquarters tapped in open key.

USS Montana reports unidentified submarine shadowing 1500 yards. Please advise on secure transmission.

King knew his only chance of defending his ship was to allow the submarine to approach within two thousand yards. Meanwhile, he continued to broadcast the Montana's alarm and requests for a destroyer. He also knew the Americans would be more than a little curious about his messages and would quickly investigate by air.

The submarine captain decided not to approach the Montana until dark. The sun fell on the horizon and he slipped close enough to use his searchlights and if necessary dispose of the ship using his repeater cannon.

The submarine searchlight struck the Montana's bridge, raking the length of the ship. Sailors scurried to port side creating the impression of curiosity. A Russian accented voice blared over a megaphone.

"Identify yourself and prepare for a boarding party."

"We are the USS Montana and refuse your request for boarding."

The submarine's automatic cannon swung toward the ship. It was too close for the Montana's cannons to depress enough to shoot, and the Stinger missiles needed more distance to arm, but the Montana was still moving fast and was close enough to execute a turn and ram. A decision had to be made quickly.

"Anti-tank weapons fire immediately on the submarine's cannon. Don't stop until it is destroyed, then hit the conning tower," King yelled.

High atop the Montana's crow's nest, Tom Obuchowski aimed his 50-caliber sniper rifle. He looked down the sub's open tower and could see men pouring out onto the deck. When the order came for his weapon's group to concentrate their fire into the rotating cannon, Obie decided to take a couple of quick shots at the inside of the tower. His first shot rocketed down the tower's ladder and exploded inside. The second shot jammed the hatch cover and his third blew a chunk of the periscope section away. No one else could have seen those targets in the dark, but from above, the sub's own searchlight bounced off of the Montana's port side illuminating the submarine's topside.

Another shot took out the searchlight. The Montana beamed its own lights onto the sub and King noticed a large hole beginning to form forward of the tower near the waterline, below the cannon. The submarine responded by accelerating away putting distance between itself and the Montana. It did not need much room to launch a torpedo.

The riflemen were effective up to seven hundred yards, but as the distance between the two vessels widened, the Stingers and anti-tank missiles were brought to bear and they too found their mark. Fire was seen coming from a forward hatch. Men were climbing out and running, an inflatable boat popped open on deck. The sub had moved away and a torpedo shot became a certainty. The firing continued and the Montana turned to ram. The sub could move at twice their speed, and the Montana turned sharply to starboard aborting the ram and moving away at a right angle to the submarine. Night closed in again. The fire onboard the submarine was no longer visible and the Montana plowed desperately away at full speed. King's radiomen could hear a steady stream of coded radio messages coming from the submarine.

Sonar and radar lost contact with the sub. It was gone and the Montana resumed course for San Francisco. Overhead an American aircraft was told what had happened and the identity of the submarine, but when asked whom they were, King deflected the question by broadcasting:

We have been hit and may have critical damage below. There are electric and power problems. Request destroyer escort to San Francisco. Conserving batteries. Thanks for the assistance.

"Well," said King to his helmsman, "we are going into San Francisco with an escort. Couldn't be better. I'll radio ahead and request Bay Marine Harbor tugs to start pumping water into the air as soon as we sail beneath Golden Gate Bridge." He loved being a mystery ship and felt a secret pride—deflecting an enemy sub. He could imagine what headlines in America would be saying when he got there.

Chapter Fifty Five

Claudette

CLAUDETTE Mattioli had been out of touch with her mother for almost three years and while sitting in a hairdresser's chair getting her dirty-blonde hair streaked with gray highlights, she thought about it. Maybe she blamed her mother for the divorce from her father, but she wasn't sure anymore. News coverage of the Jack and Babe story put an entirely new light on how she saw her mother.

Under the dryer, she moved her head just enough to call her mom's home on her cell phone. John's message on the answering machine got her thinking. A television in the salon was turned on, and it seemed that everyone was watching a replay of Babe's press interview at the airport. Claudette watched her mother cry and sincerely plead to the world to bring her Jack safely home. Ill feelings for her mother washed away in a swirl of guilt for having been so juvenile. For the first time in many years, she was proud to look like her mother.

The beauty salon on Union Street was only five minutes from her mom's Broadway Street home. She cut her appointment short and raced for her car. Claudette Mattioli had decided that she loved her mother and wanted to see her right away.

She had hoped her mother was at home and wanted to tell her how proud she was of her television interview. Claudette also wanted her to know that she would be part of the effort to bring Jack back and she also wanted to make amends to John for the lousy things she had done and said to him.

***

Seventy five year old Ron Goldberg was a little forgetful but not so bad that he couldn't work every day. He loved leaving the front door dressed in a business suit and briefcase. Typically, he walked a block up Broadway Street and then returned, a good day's work behind him at the office. Martha, his wife, watched him from their fourth-floor balcony to make sure he did not stray. On his return to the building entrance, she would call to him through the intercom and ring the buzzer, letting him back into the building. Ron didn't know what keys were for anymore.

The Goldbergs had lived upstairs from Babe for fifteen years and had come to love both Claudette and Jenna. Ron and Martha never had children of their own and often babysat the girls whenever Babe would let them. Both missed not having seen Claudette in recent years.

Mr. Goldberg still had a full head of hair and a beard white with age. His blue eyes were intense and looked sharp, but they masked the confusion that came with being forgetful. He had just completed his walk and as he turned to come into the building he waved at Martha standing on their front balcony. A multi-colored flower delivery van sat on the curb opposite the building's front entrance; its motor running. In that neighborhood, flowers were often delivered.

Claudette pulled into the restricted white-zone just behind the flower van and walked to the entrance. As she did, Ron met her on the walkway. He was so delighted to see her he beamed and hugged her with all of his might and together they approached the entry door.

Seeing Ron Goldberg on the sidewalk made her smile. She was so glad to see him. It was like a homecoming, and she could not help embracing him.

"That's them all right. Gray hair, gray-streaked hair, blue eyes, an elderly, loving couple—she looks good for her age. Let's go," said the driver to his companion. They scooped up a large bouquet of flowers and ran up behind Claudette and Ron just as Martha hit the door entry buzzer. When they came within four feet of the couple, one man said, "Ms. Mattioli?"

Claudette turned and nodded agreement, but looked confused. She saw the large bouquet of flowers moving in her direction, but something wasn't right.

"Greetings from Russia. Have a nice day," one man said.

The silenced guns shot both in the forehead and behind the ear. The men calmly retreated to the van and pulled away from the curb just as Babe and John's limousine arrived to take the space they were vacating.

The stolen flower delivery van rolled down Broadway Street, stopping at the crest of Taylor Street to call Washington D.C. using a stolen cell phone.

"Greig Rivers please."

"Hello, this is Mr. Rivers."

"This is San Francisco calling. We got lucky. Both Jack Fischer and Babe Mattioli are dead. We staked out her place after the press conference and sure enough, they both arrived at the same time."

"Was it messy?"

"We couldn't fake a car accident. Everything happened too fast, so we delivered a bouquet of flowers and shot them when they reached for it."

"When did this happen?"

"Less than three minutes ago."

"Okay!"

Greig Rivers thoroughly believed he was helping the administration solve a political problem without his boss knowing it. He had contacts with the Russians and when he learned that they wanted Jack and Babe removed, Greig had done everything in his power to curry favor with them. He spun his deep leather chair toward his window and gazed at the Washington Monument. *Damn, I'm good,* he thought, pleased.

The telephone was destroyed. The van was ditched and the men disappeared. A private detective, hired by a society matron to investigate her husband's infidelities with a high-class prostitute on Broadway, sat in his car a half-block from the murder. He did not see it happen, but had picked up the cell phone call on his scanner. His equipment recorded the conversation of the killers.

Chapter Fifty Six

Tape Worm

BABE and John leaped out of their limousine and ran toward the entrance to her home on Broadway. They had no idea why two people were lying on the floor at the entrance, but as they came near and saw the pools of blood, recognition and horror screamed out at them.

"Oh, my God," screamed Babe. "Quick, call 9-1-1!"

John used his cell phone to call and felt both bodies for a pulse. There was none. The building's intercom screeched loudly in his ears.

"Ronny, Ronny, talk to me. What's happening down there? Should I call the police?" It was Martha screaming hysterically.

Babe cradled Claudette's head and tried to talk to her, to bring her back to life. Blood oozed, covering Babe. Martha ran downstairs, slipped on the blood and slid, crashing her head on the tiles, momentarily stunning her. She rose covered in blood and threw herself on Ron as if to protect him from an assailant.

"Why? Why her? Why Ron?" Babe cried and rocked her dead daughter's body. "Who would want to do this?" And as her questions repeated, her tearful gaze fell on the gray-silver highlight streak in Claudette's hair, it rang a bell subconsciously, and finally she could not blot the thought any longer.

"It was me they were after, me and my Jack!" The truth burned her soul. "Oh! Why couldn't it have been me? What could I have done differently? I would have given my life for her."

The ambulance and police arrived at the same time and the bodies were rushed to Shrine Memorial Hospital nearby. Detectives took pictures, asked questions; they secured the area with yellow tape and tried calming Babe and Mrs. Goldberg. One interviewed Martha.

"Mrs. Goldberg, did you see or hear anything from the balcony or hear anything on the intercom when you buzzed your husband inside."

"There was a flower delivery van at the curb when I left the balcony," Martha recalled. "I kept buzzing Ronny in; sometimes that took a long time, but he didn't say anything. Although I heard two male voices."

"Was it anyone you recognized?"

"No."

"What did they say?"

"One of them asked if she was Ms. Mattioli. The other said something about Russia."

"Was anything else said?" The detective was scribbling furiously.

"I could hear noises. They sounded like a soda pop bottle opening. I think I heard it three or four times. Then there was a crashing sound. I suppose that's when they fell."

"Do you remember what the men in the van looked like?"

"I didn't see them. I had already left the balcony." Martha paused and then her face lit up. She turned and said excited, "the security cameras might have picked them up! Why don't you have a look? The association just put them in last month. Vandals in the neighborhood, you know."

"This could be a big break, Mrs. Goldberg. Can you take me to the camera system?"

That same night the Examiner Newspaper had pictures of the assassins on their front page with a headline, "*MATTIOLI MURDERED.*" Television news carried the same pictures along with one of Babe on the entry floor holding Claudette's dead body. Reports hinted at a White House or Russian conspiracy, which infuriated the administration. Martha repeated on camera the words about the Russian language spoken. The next morning, Joy Jaing received a telephone call from an old friend at the Lipset Detective Agency. She broke the story by televising a detective's taped conversations between the killers and Greig Rivers before the police had an opportunity to hear it. The tape was a sensation and it was repeated hourly during prime time across the world.

Chapter Fifty Seven

Queen of Hearts

CLAUDETTE'S body was held at the coroner's office during the investigation. Babe and John arrived there the next day. They sat in a drab room waiting to formally certify and identify the body.

"You know, John, in a million years, I would never have thought something like this was possible. Either the Administration, the Russians or the Chinese have murdered my poor Claudette. Now here we are mourning the fact that she never had the chance to live. Damn it, every flower is entitled to its day in the sun. And to make matters worse it was Jack and me that they intended to kill. It makes me feel guilty they killed my daughter instead—I would have given my life for her."

"I know you would," John replied. "But right now, we have to stay alive and somehow bring those criminals to justice."

"You remember what Nick said about my life and Jack's being at risk if we made any waves that might embarrass the administration?"

John walked Babe away from the waiting room and replied, "they are not going to risk you shooting your mouth off at another press conference. They'll blame someone else for Claudette's killing and for your death as well, and if that happens it will be blamed on overzealous patriots, mysterious Russians—that sort of thing. You can believe the White House will be in high-gear right now discrediting Dad as a traitor or defector, and you will be pictured as a whore who not only slept around during your marriage to Peter, but who had an unhealthy and possibly treasonous relationship with Russia. Your death will be the result of dark forces that are peculiar to the world of spies."

Surprised, Babe replied, "I'm not a spy and they could never prove I slept with a single man during my marriage to Peter."

"You don't have to be a spy or a whore. It is enough for them to allege that you are. Weren't you the one that went to Russia, when it was illegal, using an Argentine passport? Don't you have business and personal relationships with shadowy foreign business people in Taiwan, Korea and China? I can see the headlines now. 'MYSTERY WOMAN MURDERED'."

Babe felt agitated, but not afraid. "I am not going to get in bed with them so they can cover their rear-ends on the murder of my daughter. If that means fighting them at the risk of losing my life, well, I would have given it gladly to have Claudette back anyway. And from what I know about Jack, he would want me to fight as well. I know firsthand about his courage and I would be ashamed of myself for not doing the right thing."

They were nearing the entrance to the lobby of the coroner's building when a limousine pulled to the curb. Senator George McBain and aides piled out and were climbing the stairs when two television station vans pulled alongside. Cameramen peeled out of their vans and rushed behind McBain's party.

"Babe, look outside," John said. "Do you see what I see? Isn't that Senator McBain? What's he doing here, I wonder?"

"I don't know," Babe replied, showing surprise.

McBain rushed into the lobby and saw John and Babe at the entrance. He reached both arms forward to hug her and said, "I am so glad I found you here. We were to meet later in the day, but recent events dictate that we show the world that we will not stand for murder and anarchy in our country." Babe winced at the political innuendo, but her emotions were still running high.

"Senator McBain, you are a sight for sore eyes. John and I were just talking about you. What do you have in mind?"

"The press is just outside. I want to replay the audiotape of those two murderers. The reporters are willing to run the security camera video clip of the shooters' faces at the same time. With national press coverage, especially with you on screen, we might be able to find those mongrels. The caller used the name 'Greig Rivers' so clearly the Administration is now associated with the murders. It will be the first time the camera and audio tapes are played together."

"I'd like to see that happen," Babe replied. "But that's not the only reason they are here, is it?"

"No, it isn't. I am a politician running for the office of the president against a vice president who looks to be involved in a criminal enterprise. If I can prove it, I stand a chance of being elected. I have never wanted to be president of the United States more than I do now. The American people deserve better. Someone has to stop the vice president from acting like he is innocent of the scandals and crimes we are all familiar with."

"I think you are an honest man, George, and we are all for supporting your effort, but, what about my Jack Fischer? He is out there somewhere and I don't want him killed, too."

"I've thought about that as well. When we make a joint appearance to those cameras outside, you and I will ask America at large to help protect him from being killed."

"Wow! That's going to throw a lot of feathers into the air in Washington."

"That's the idea. Are you ready to step outside?"

"With every fiber of my being I will make this my personal holy crusade. I know the American people's hearts are with me." McBain stepped back and looked at her.

"You sound like you intend to become the next Joan of Arc."

"No, George. I expect to win because I am, to the depths of my soul, their Queen of Hearts. We will march on Washington and together we will see love triumph over evil."

"That's my pledge as well, Babe. Will you repeat what you just said to me about the Queen of Hearts to those cameras outside?"

"Lead me to them, George," Babe replied confidently.

Chapter Fifty Eight

White House Spin

THE president of the United States turned off the television after watching the rerun of the press conference at the San Francisco airport.

"Get Allen on the phone," he bellowed to his secretary.

"Vice President Allen Hurst?

"Yes, damn it. Who else is named Allen?"

"Yes, sir. Connecting."

"Hi, Al," said the President.

"It looks like this POW thing is going to be behind us. Is this another one of your master strokes?" the vice President responded.

"Not exactly. We just heard from California Senator Leslie Slator. She's made arrangements for Babe Mattioli to give a joint press conference with me in the White House. Mattioli's going to support us and, of course, we are going to support her. The whole thing should go away quietly and frankly I welcome the return of Private Fischer."

"Anything you want me to do, Joel?"

"Yeah! Set up the conference. I want you to be there. After all, you're the one running for president next year and it will be an opportunity for you to piss on McBain."

"I'll do it."

Two hours later, Greig Rivers asked urgently to be connected to the president. He had difficulty getting through because President Conklin felt he had the Fischer problem solved and could get back to Greig later. However, Rivers persisted.

"Mr. President, I can confirm to you that both Jack Fischer and Babe Mattioli are dead. The Russians got them just as they met for the first time in close to fifty years, right on her doorstep. They were hugging at the time and never knew what hit them."

"Holy shit!" replied Conklin. "She was coming over to our side and was scheduled to give a press conference with Al and me. People are going to think we had something to do with it."

"You need me for anything else?" Greig asked.

"I have to think about this for a minute. Don't go anywhere. I'll get right back to you when I see how the press reports the story."

"Okay, I'll be in the office."

Greig Rivers hung up the phone and sat back in his chair feeling very good about himself. He was clearly at the top of his game. The president depended upon him and he did his job well. Maybe he did it too well, but in this business you had to be tough. The president's comment about seeing how the shooting played out in the press bothered him some, but he put it out of his mind. He turned his attention to the FBI files on Korean War defectors Christian Zanier, Joel Gardner and an interesting guy named Leroy Robinson. Some documents suggested that he had become a spy for the Soviet Union. Maybe there was some shit on him somewhere.

The television set in River's office was always on as background and tuned to CNN, but the sound was muted. He had watched Babe Mattioli's press conference at the San Francisco Airport and turned up the volume. It really disturbed him. He couldn't help being surprised at how powerful one little woman could be under the right circumstances.

An hour later, Greig's secretary buzzed him.

"Are you watching TV?"

"No, but I'll turn it on." He had watched part of the initial coverage of the shooting and shrugged. *You have to break a few eggs to make a good omelet and a high profile shooting would certainly make news,* he thought. *But there's nothing to connect it with the White House. Bingo! A good omelet.*

But then, things went awry. The first horror of the day came when the press announced that the victims were not Jack Fischer and Babe Mattioli but her daughter Claudette and a neighbor named Ron Goldberg.

Greig River's telephone began ringing. The first call was from the vice president.

"What the fuck happened in San Francisco?"

"I just saw it on the news. I don't know. The Russians or

somebody must have been certain of the identity or they would not have done it."

The vice president, in an agitated voice, said, "look, Greig, even if they don't have proof, those conspiracy types are going to try connecting it to us."

"There is absolutely no proof, Al—we had nothing to do with it, trust me."

"Okay. Well it's your neck, isn't it?" The vice president hung up sharply before Greig could reply.

Greig tried calling the men who did the job and decided there was no point even if he could get a new and secure number for them. Let the news run its course. White House involvement would be denied. They would suggest it was either a drive-by shooting or, if it was indeed intentional, that the object of the killing could easily be the work of an outraged patriot. Maybe one who served in the Korean War and who did not defect to the enemy? Such a patriotic mind, he thought, could easily be outraged by the celebrity status of Jack Fischer, the defector and his protector, possibly a spy herself, the good looking Babe Mattioli.

He was pleased with his spin and shared it with the vice president, who liked it as well. Just before quitting time and before shutting the television off, something caught his eye. A Chinese anchorwoman named Joy Jaing in San Francisco was telling the viewing audience that she was about to announce a break in the Mattioli killing. He pulled his chair up and turned up the volume.

Joy began.

"Before we start, I want to play you a recording of a conversation between Greig Rivers and the two killers who murdered Ron Goldman and Claudette Mattioli. This recording was made quite by accident by a detective working for the Lipset Detective Agency. He was on Broadway—just a half a block from the murder scene. The detective did not witness the crime, but his frequency scanner picked up the telephone conversation between the two killers and a man named Greig Rivers, who may work at the White House in Washington, D.C. We know that, because the scanner also picked up the actual dialing tones."

The tape ran for less than two minutes. Greig was frozen in his chair. His world dissolved from under him. He would have to go into hiding. He knew he was screwed. Someone else was going to have to figure this out. He called the vice president.

"Well, Greig, it looks like a proper cock-up. What the fuck did you think you were doing?" The vice president was practically screaming. He paused to collect himself and then continued in a colder and colder void. "We can't distance ourselves from you because you work here; you were the one who received that phone call. So we're all stuck in your boat and will have to figure something out. Don't go home or anywhere near a place that the press might find you. Call me when you find someplace to stay."

"Okay. It must have been a cock-up. Those Russians called me, but I had nothing to do with it. Anyway, I'll call."

Greig called just after seven o'clock to inform the vice president that he was staying in a small hotel across from Gramercy Park.

"Stay there; we will send a limo for you. Give me the address. By the way, do you have a current passport?"

"Yes, I do," Greig replied. "I guess I'll be using it."

The limousine driver picked Greig up an hour later; it made a U-turn from the hotel to Gramercy Park and stopped at the curb.

"What are we stopping for?" Greig asked.

The driver put his arm up on the backrest, turned to look at Rivers and casually replied. "We're picking up a lawyer and a publicity guy. They are going to meet us here."

A limousine pulled up. Two men got out and approached Greig's limo. They looked through the windows and talked to Greig like they knew him.

"Can we talk privately? Without your driver?" they asked.

"Where do you suggest?" Greig replied feeling a little nervous.

"Either in our car or we can sit on one of those benches over there," one of the men said.

Not wanting to ride in a stranger's car, Greig opted for a bench seat in the park. It felt safer. Across the street someone watched.

***

The next morning the headlines read "RIVERS SUICIDE." The president received a call from his vice president.

"Joel, it's me Al. Rivers took a dive. Killed himself."

"Jesus, this really is going to make us look bad."

"I don't think so, Joel. We can ensure that people realize that a live Rivers testimony would have cleared us. That tape specifically mentioned Russia and the truth is we had nothing to do with it."

"Look, Al, this POW thing is going to wreck us. We can do the discrediting job, but with that botched affair in San Francisco we won't be believed. Any thoughts?"

"Well, before Greig left us—if you know what I mean—he suggested a good strategy to deflect the damage on the hit. His idea was to blame it on a deranged Korean War ex-serviceman whose patriotism got the best of him, and who hates defectors and the women who supported them."

"Sounds like a long shot," the president responded, and paused for a moment. "Al, I hope you have nothing to do with this thing, if I thought..."

"Hey! Lee Harvey Oswald still gets the blame for the Texas hit. Let the conspiracy buffs have at it. Most importantly, I think that the story line will get us off of the front pages, for a while at least."

The president thought about the idea and agreed, but added, "if that woman and the escaped prisoner—what's his name? Fischer something—ever get together? The press will turn us into hamburger. Any ideas?"

Allen thought a moment.

"If that woman, Babe Mattioli, can be made to believe we had nothing to do with her daughter's death, maybe we can still patch it. I'd like to think a joint press conference with her would be a top priority."

"Maybe we should let the Russians do it?" Conklin replied sarcastically.

"That's not funny. I swear I had nothing to do with it."

"I've got calls into Moscow to verify if they are involved and if so to demand they call off the dogs immediately. How's the campaign going, Al?"

"I'm glad you asked, and yes, I could use your help."

"Ask away."

"I can't afford this POW issue to dominate my campaign. It gives too much leverage to McBain with his war record. I would like you to help us change the subject."

"You mean, like telling the senior citizens that the Republicans are going to steal their Social Security?" Conklin volunteered.

"Yeah! That and you could drag out that herring about school lunches about to be stolen," the vice president cracked.

"Okay, I get the picture, Al. Why don't I get the First Lady to campaign with you down there? She's dynamite with her down-home Betty Crocker look. It should play well with the Bible bashers."

"I'm glad you mentioned the Bible thing. Remember how we came out as strong advocates of the pro-choice position. Hell, I made speeches supporting *Roe v. Wade*, and the soccer mom's bought it. Now it's different. I'm campaigning right in the middle of the Bible belt and I think that son-of-a-bitch McBain is giving me shit about him being pro-life. He's starting to make me look bad on that issue."

"Al, listen. You are too close to it to be objective. Truth is, the fucking public doesn't remember what you said in the last election. Trust me on this. Come out as being pro-life while you're in those Bible states. Later, you can qualify what you meant and if that dog don't hunt, we'll find a pro-life vice president to balance your ticket. Maybe even a Republican. Wouldn't that be a hoot?"

"That's great, Joel. You certainly didn't get to be president by being a dumb shit. Anyway, let's get this stuff up and running. Time is of the essence. And don't worry about the Fischer bullshit. I'll take care of it."

"Thanks. Give some thought to an immediate press conference welcoming Private Fischer whenever he appears." Conklin hung up and walked back into the Oval Office where his wife was waiting.

***

Greig Rivers was left-handed. The gun had been fired into his right temple. He had no powder burns on either hand and left no suicide note. He was already dead when he reached the sidewalk. The men carried him into the park and laid him on his back. Naturally Greig's shoe bottoms had no grass on them. Everyone in Washington knew it was murder, but officially the Park Police called it a suicide: No one bothered about the details. The Justice Department showed no interest.

***

The Greig Rivers story was pushed off the front page by photos of the two killers that had been taken from the lobby security camera at the Mattioli residence. Television news replayed the video with the sound tape to a mesmerized audience. People saw an actual murder take place and they listened to the killers talk about it. Senator McBain and Babe Mattioli were in front of every news camera and were hosted on every radio and television talk show. McBain's polls jumped fifteen percentage points overnight.

The video clips of the assassination of Ron Goldberg and Claudette Mattioli brought new urgency to the matter of Jack Fischer and Babe Mattioli, because without those two, the story would peter out. Or so they thought in D.C.

Chapter Fifty Nine

Jack Be Quick

AS Jack watched Babe on television in the train's cocktail lounge, his emotions veered between fear and an almost unbearable sense of joy. She had waited for him all of these years. She had married another man, yes, but he had remained in her heart. He had a sense of not belonging to this strange world where people talked into tiny telephones and sat hunched over black boxes pecking out messages. Jack looked through the train window and was oblivious to the trees, hills and towns rushing backward in flashes of green and brown. Fifty years of prison life had taught him the bitter lesson that moments of happiness and hope were easily dashed. Better not to hope for too much. But thinking of and seeing Babe gave him ease and comfort in his strange surroundings.

Babe looked good on television, an older woman, but still gorgeous in his eyes. He was not surprised that she had missed him by only two days in Siberia. It seemed that his life had been a series of near misses. He wanted to plant his lips against the television screen and tell her that this time it would be different and that he would finally make it all the way back and into her arms. Jack was thrilled that his son was in America and wondered how Babe had managed the miracle of finding him and how she had even known of his existence. He thought briefly of Ati and a wave of sadness welled in him. If he had met her first he would have loved her because he knew that was his nature, but Babe had come first. Babe would always be first.

Returning from the dining car, the young man sitting next to him typed noiselessly into a small flat box on his lap. Sometimes he would laugh or smile; other times he frowned and shook his head.

"Excuse me for interrupting," Jack said, "but what is that?"

The young man turned and stared at him. "What is what?"

"That machine. I know it's not a typewriter."

The young man looked at his lap and then back at Jack, his eyebrow raised, a puzzled smile formed on his lips. "Are you putting me on?"

Putting me on? "I'm sorry. I don't understand."

"Haven't you ever seen a computer before?"

A computer, so that's what it was. Alex had told him about computers.

"I've been away," Jack said. "For quite some time."

"You must've been an awful long ways away not to have heard of computers. Like on another planet."

Jack smiled. "Very much like another planet."

The young man punched a key and the screen gave a musical beep and went dark. He closed the lid.

"This is a really weird conversation," he said. "I mean, who hasn't heard of computers?"

"I've lived in—well, I guess you might call it a kind of retreat, for many, many years. I just recently returned and a lot of things are new to me."

The young man smiled. "Hey, that's really cool. You're, like, a Luddite. Anti-machine age. I studied about them in college."

Jack's gaze returned to the computer. "Does it work like a typewriter?"

"Well, it's got a keyboard and you can type and print out hard copy, but I use it like a telephone. It has a built-in modem, see, and I can send and receive e-mails constantly and use the buddy system for multiple conversations—like, you know, cyberspace conferencing. In my business—I sell funeral supplies—I have to be in touch."

Modem, cyberspace, conferencing. What is this guy talking about? Jack thought as he listened. "How do you stay in touch?"

"I can either talk into my computer or type a message. Pretty simple really."

Jack nodded and pretended to understand, but was more than ever convinced that he had lost far too many years to ever fit comfortably into this new and peculiar world.

"Would you like a quick lesson in computers?" the young man asked.

"That would be great, if you have the time," Jack said.

He was a quick study, but fundamentals of the computers would have to wait for another day.

"I'm going to buy one of these," Jack said. "I have a few things I plan to write."

The young man left the train in Chicago and Jack returned to the club car. The track ran parallel to a highway for fifty or so miles—a much wider highway than he had ever seen, with four lanes rather than the two he had always known—and he watched the cars without recognizing a single model. There was no barbed wire on the houses the train passed; no border checkpoints with armed guards. He sat back in his lounge chair and fiddled with the knobs on the armrest; as in the airplane, he heard music coming from a headset. He picked it up and began listening and turned the knob a bit more. He heard a voice chanting nonsense in rhymes accompanied by a hard, jarring beat. *Is this music? Do people listen to this?* He quickly turned the knob to another station. He remembered songs like Vaughn Monroe's *Ballerina*, Frankie Lane's *Riders in the Sky*, and Nat King Cole's *Nature Boy. Do they make songs like those anymore? Are any of those singers still alive?* There was so little he knew, so much he was going to have to learn. He sipped his vodka, and dozed off listening to a series of old recordings by the Boston Pops orchestra.

The news came on again and Jack awoke with a start. He had heard Babe's name. There was a special report on the murder of her daughter Claudette and of an elderly neighbor. According to the report, it could be a case of mistaken identity, but the evidence pointed to a planned execution. *Is someone trying to kill us? Were those guns meant for us?* He drained his vodka and listened, barely breathing, as more news followed. He heard the audiotapes with Greig Rivers talking to an unidentified source about the murders. He saw the killers' faces and the actual act of murder played out on television. He had seen so much violence and death in his life, but this was gut wrenching in a new way. This was not a prison camp in Siberia. This was America. Such brutal acts were not supposed to happen here. He also realized that he was lucky. If he had found Babe's telephone number through information and called her from New York, the call could have been traced. *It might have been us. They were after us.*

He forced himself to examine the facts. He had to consider the possibility that the Feds were working with the Russians to prevent him from appearing on television as a live POW, especially with thousands of other live prisoners still being held in Russia. By now they must know that he had landed in New York as Ivan Guk and they would be looking for him under that name. He lay in his berth that night examining his options. He had used a false name when he had booked a first-class sleeper on this train, paying in cash, but his appearance could easily give him away. Twelve hours west of Chicago he considered getting off the train, somewhere before reaching his destination at the Martinez terminal in California. But, he thought, that might point suspicion at him. *What can I do? What can I do to help Babe?*

It seemed to Jack that all of America was now looking for him. The incessant chanting 'Go, Jack, Go' shocked him. *'Go, Jack, Go. Go, Jack, Go.'* He found it hard to believe that he was Jack. How could it be? The rallies and demonstrations he was seeing on television demanding the removal of President Conklin only added to his discomfort. Those scenes were everywhere. Turn the TV knob, and, bingo; there were the crowds and banners. DOWN WITH CONKLIN! UP WITH MCBAIN! Jack understood that, under attack, the Administration would be even more desperate to find him. He thought of all the men left behind in the Russian camps and prayed that the POWs would not be murdered to cover up the scandal.

Jack watched television news all the following day. Most of the fresh information, he realized, was not coming from New York or Washington, D.C. but from a Joy Jaing affiliated with a San Francisco television station. She seemed to be acting as a spokesperson for Babe. *Joy Jaing—Jin Jaing, his old friend. Could there possibly be a connection?* A plan took shape in his mind. But first he had to get to Oakland. Timing would be all-important.

The train moved through a valley and arrived at the East Bay Martinez station an hour ahead of schedule. Jack detrained through the economy class compartment, not wishing to be noticed, and he looked closely to see if anyone paid unusual attention to the passengers. Everything appeared to be normal. He had an hour to kill before boarding a bus for Oakland, so he crossed the street to a men's clothier. He outfitted himself in Nike running shoes, jeans, a T-shirt and an Oakland Athletics baseball cap. He had seen so many people dressed that way, even elderly men, he thought he would easily blend in. He packed his business suit into his luggage, picked up a newspaper and boarded the bus for Oakland. The headlines exclaimed: MYSTERY SHIP. The article described a vessel, the USS Montana, which resembled a troop ship. There were hints that it might have been involved in a firefight with a Russian submarine and might have been damaged, and that the American Navy was escorting it into San Francisco. It was due to arrive in a week's time.

Jack folded the newspaper neatly on his lap and closed his eyes.

Am I finally free? Will I ever be free?

Chapter Sixty

Leroy

LEROY Robinson avidly followed the Jack Fischer story on television. When the government began to hint that Fischer was a traitor, defector or possibly even a murderer, his mood turned dark. He was sickened by the lie. He felt guilty for not having come forward years ago with his own firsthand knowledge of live POWs held in Russia and China. He could have made a difference, but instead had stood by and done nothing. Robinson knew the two men who were denouncing Fischer: Corporal Zanier and Private Joel Gardner. Both had defected to the Russians at the same time, been through the same reeducation process together, and had graduated from the same spy school. Babe Mattioli's story, describing her pursuit of Jack for nearly half a century, resonated deeply with the former Army sergeant, and the pressure to do something to right this intolerable wrong kept him awake at night. He couldn't talk to his wife about it because she wouldn't understand, and even if he convinced her that he had to act, that he could no longer remain silent, she was bound to give him nothing but grief.

I'm three years older than Fischer. At the age of 75, I'm not likely to lose my pension. Even if they tried to take it away from me, it would take years to get in front of a judge, and I'd likely be dead by then. Arrested for treason? That's unlikely. The White House doesn't want any more POW bullshit in the newspapers than they already have. What could they do to me if I did come forward? He thought about that for a few minutes and speculated. *They might try to frame me for the Goldberg-Mattioli murders, but that won't fly. Those boys are white. Their faces are all over television.*

Robinson concluded that coming forward would result in a lot of negative publicity about him. His neighbors might not want to know him anymore and his wife would surely be humiliated. *But*, he thought, *I owe it to Fischer. I can't sit here and do nothing while they bring him down.*

Joy Jaing's producer received a telephone call from him that morning. She listened to the melodious southern accent, a fine blend of gentleness and politeness, and almost certainly a black voice. She was ready to treat it as just another crank call. Robinson, sensing her unwillingness to take him seriously, became a little more candid.

"Lady, I'm telling you that I was a sergeant in the Army. I was captured in Korea and later I defected. I've already explained that to you."

"We can't put you on the air with that story without proof," she replied.

With growing desperation, he decided to reveal even more. "I went to the same spy school as Zanier and Gardner. We graduated together. I have a picture of the three of us. I never knew what happened to those guys, but they—you know—the Russians, they sent me here to stir up some racial turmoil in the sixties."

"Mr. Robinson, if you have that graduation photo, or Soviet awards of merit, please come to the studio at two o'clock and we'll discuss taping an interview with you."

"I don't have any awards, but I might still have something showing me as an officer in the GRU. Would that help?"

"You're very convincing, Mr. Robinson. We'll see you at two o'clock."

Sergeant Leroy Robinson began to feel a reawakening of patriotic pride. For the first time in more than forty years, he felt like he counted for something, that he was important, and that maybe his story, once he told it, would help heal the country. *I was just a kid back then. What did I know about the Cold War? Looking back at it, hell, I was just a victim; a lot of the boys were getting their asses shot off. They did the same as me.* He knew he was rationalizing years of treason, but even so, he felt comforted and at peace with himself. He was finally willing to take action, positive action.

Joy came in to tape the story and decided not to wait until the six o'clock news to release it. Instead, she and her producer prepared to broadcast the story as a news special to take advantage of the European time zone. They hoped to maximize the global effect, and they wanted to do it before the White House released its own Zanier and Gardner story, complete with spin-doctors.

The story aired at four o'clock:

"According to my guest who is here with me in the studio, Jack Fischer was not a defector, contrary to allegations being made by the White House. Leroy Robinson is a former U.S. Army sergeant who served during the Korean War. He was imprisoned by the Russians and was coerced into becoming a spy for them," Joy announced.

Robinson sat erect and looked the camera straight in the eye as Joy Jaing introduced him. He hoped the camera would help make the statement that he had nothing to hide.

"You admit that you were a spy, Mr. Robinson. Why should we believe you now?"

"Miss Jaing, I'm not proud of what I did back then. The Lord knows I'm putting myself in a lot of trouble by coming forward now. I may even end up in jail. Maybe lose my pension. But what the government is doing to Jack Fischer is just plain wrong, and they know it."

"What made you decide to come forward now?" Joy asked.

"When those two people were murdered—it seems like they were mistaken for Fischer and his girlfriend—well, I just couldn't sit on the sidelines. That's not right. And those two guys—the defectors, the guys the White House has been talking to…"

"You mean Andrew Zanier and Joel Gardner?"

"Yes. I know them. We went to the same spy school together in Leningrad."

"Do you have proof of that, Mr. Robinson?" Joy asked.

"Yes. I brought a picture with me."

"May I hold it up to the camera?"

Robinson smiled briefly. "You can show the world, Miss Jaing."

The camera closed up on the photo. Television audiences could clearly see the younger Zanier and Gardner with Robinson, dressed in Russian-style quilt uniforms.

"We were young and naïve," Robinson said. "Although, I suppose that ain't no excuse. We had seen the evils of power and big money and felt that America was just out to lord it over the rest of the world."

"Why did you feel that way, too?"

"In my case, I grew up with discrimination. Lived in a small town called Roseboro in North Carolina in the thirties and forties. The public fountains had signs; white water and black water, back then. My lips were never supposed to touch that white water, and when I was maybe ten, I snuck myself a sip when nobody was watching. It tasted just the same."

"Is there anything you would like to add, Mr. Robinson?"

Robinson looked directly into the camera's eye, his gaze steady and unblinking. "We may have been wrong, but Zanier and Gardner and I, we only set out to make a better world. We were idealists; I guess you could say, who thought we could make a difference. There are bigger crimes than that."

"Mr. Robinson, I want to thank you for coming and granting this interview. You have given the viewing public much to think about."

Off camera, Joy said, "you were very moving, Mr. Robinson."

"Thank you. Only telling it like I see it."

"Can we offer you a ride back home?"

"No, the train is fine, thank you."

"Our security people think it might be a good idea if one of them drove you home. We're prepared to have a guard with you twenty-four hours a day—at least for the next few days." She cleared her throat nervously. "Some people are going to consider you a traitor, and I know there's no statute of limitations on that, even after fifty years."

Robinson smiled. "I can live with that. But I'm not sure the government wants to jail this grizzled old man."

Robinson left the studio at five o'clock. Two hours later, the fire department was called to put out a fire at the base of Mount Diablo. They found Leroy Robinson tied to a barbed wire cattle fence. His body was still smoking when they got there. The television crew that arrived at the scene minutes later elected not to show Robinson's charred remains, and instead speculated on what the motive might have been.

Chapter Sixty One

Before the Storm

LEAVING the bus, Jack checked into a hotel at Jack London Square in Oakland. He decided to have a drink at the bar before eating dinner and sat watching the passerbys through the plate glass window. It filled him with wonder to see well-dressed, contented, prosperous people promenading along the main street. Did they have any idea how incredibly free they were? Walking without fear of arrest, buying whatever they could afford and eating good food in clean places that offered a variety of choices? They were Americans at the top of the human heap, Jack thought, and they should get down on their hands and knees and bless each day they were alive.

Jack sipped his vodka, trying to relax, hoping that he wouldn't be noticed. He glanced up at a television set high on the wall above the bar, the audio turned down to a faint murmur. He leaned forward straining to hear. Something about the man being interviewed struck him as vaguely familiar. As he watched and listened to Sergeant Leroy Robinson, he drained his vodka and ordered a double. The interview was a replay from an earlier broadcast that day. Following it was the news of Robinson's murder. When the report switched to sports, Jack stared at the set intently, hoping it might tell him something he needed to know. Jack had faint memory of Robinson, much of it disturbing. Yet, the man had come forward to help him and was dead two hours later. He tried not to think of why, but in his heart, he knew, and it frightened him. *Are we gonna make it, Babe?*

Jack placed money on the bar and walked one block to another hotel and checked in, again using a false name. After informing the desk he would be expecting a telephone call, he returned to his first hotel on Jack London Square and used a pay phone to call Joy Jaing at the television studio.

Joy was still at the station at eight o'clock when a production assistant placed a note in front of her. Without glancing at the note, she said, "I'm up to my ears, Sarah. Would you hold my calls? This Robinson thing, it's taking on a life of its own. I'm on live in an hour by remote for an interview with his wife."

"Can't hold this one, Joy. This is *the* one you've been waiting for."

She snatched up the note and scanned it quickly. "My God—Sarah, quick—put him through." Sarah handed her the cordless phone. Joy held a breath, and said, "this is Joy Jaing."

"Jack Fischer," Jack replied softly, not wishing to attract attention.

"Are you here?" she said, trying to contain her excitement. "Are you in California?"

"Yes."

"Where are you?" she gasped nervously. "The world wants to know."

"If you don't mind, I'd rather not say just yet. I don't feel secure."

"Do you know who I am, Mr. Fischer?"

"I know you're a news woman. And your name is familiar."

Do you remember a man named Jin Jaing who escaped from China?"

Jack gripped the phone so hard his knuckles turned white. "How do you know about that?"

"Jin Jaing has a twin brother, Qi Jaing. He's my father. I know Babe Mattioli, or should I say Babe Barsi and King Poo Koo personally. We've all been on a worldwide quest to find you and bring you home."

Jack could not speak for a moment. Finally he said, "I'm so glad Jin is still alive." He could hear his own voice tremble. "There's just so much to take in. That fellow Leroy Robinson—I remember him from prison camp, and now he's dead."

"It's terrible," Joy said.

"I don't know what to do right now," Jack said. "I'm bad luck for anyone involved with me."

"It's going to be okay," Joy said.

"I'm not so sure."

"Can we meet?"

"Not yet. I need time. I have to think things out."

He gave Joy the telephone number at the hotel down the street, and told her he would call there every hour for messages.

"I can't wait to meet you, Mr. Fischer. Bye for now."

Jack was quivering emotionally when he returned to the bar and ordered vodka. He picked at a crab cocktail, had a bowl of clam chowder, put some crackers in his pocket, and went upstairs to his room, where he hoped he could catch a little sleep. But the anticipation of being reunited with Babe kept him awake most of the night. He called the other hotel for messages every hour, and at two o'clock in the morning he fell into a fitful doze.

Chapter Sixty Two

Ivanov's Ark

BABE was ready to act on Ivanov's faxed message, which had been hand delivered to her before she left Siberia:

After you read this I want you to be ready to announce to your press that the USS Montana will be arriving in San Francisco. It is a Latvian troop transport, originally the Azov, camouflaged as an American Navy transport. On board are King and 2,100 American and Allied POWs that I have freed from Russia. Releasing all of their names along with photos and other information about them onto the Internet through the Drudge Report website is King's responsibility. Whether the USS Montana arrives or not, Drudge will publish those names.

Jin Jaing is leading the escape of an additional 600 POWs who will arrive in Japan before the Montana arrives in San Francisco. Jin will not permit the Japanese government to disclose their presence until the USS Montana docks. It is important that the maximum press coverage be available to assure their collective safety. If only one escape is successful, it would be proof to the world that there are still live POWs in Russia and China.

Both escapes are scheduled for March. I felt a mass escape would also assure that prisoners' lives in the rest of Russia will be spared, because we have a record of them and can testify accordingly. Jack's escape from Mongolia will give our POWs escape a much higher profile. (Yes! We heard about it and all of Russia is praying for him.)

The Kremlin will attempt to crush everything we have done in Khabarovsk. Knowing this, and having long prepared for the certainty that either the Kremlin or their gangster associates will be coming here to take over, I decided to strike first.

We have shut down the power grids and sabotaged military and civilian computers. We also opened dams to create floods. I expect to be the Governor of Khabarovsk and I will announce my takeover to Moscow the minute the USS Montana arrives there. I need your help to publicize that event to the maximum—not just the POW escape, but also my story, as best you know it. People everywhere must know who I am, and without international opinion fanning the flames for the changes we are making, we could fail.

If we fail, give my love to Jack. I will never forget him. I send my love to you and John. If I succeed, we will someday talk again.

Until we meet again, my thoughts are with you.

Alex

***

Babe could not imagine Alex taking on mighty Russia and hoping to win.

"He could have just left the country and lived out his life anywhere he wished," she told John. "Saving the lives of the prisoners? Risking his life? What's gotten into him?"

"He's a decent man, Mom. He was very good to me."

"Yes, but I never thought of him as brave."

"Alex is an old man now," John said. "Maybe courage comes easily when you've lived a full life."

Babe telephoned Joy with Ivanov's news.

"I know it's practically dawn for you and you're probably still asleep," she said, "but I have to share something with you." Babe read her Ivanov's message.

"Fantastic!" Joy said. "That means the USS Montana will be docking in a few days. Probably near the Ferry Building. I'll orchestrate the international press, Babe, but I'm going to rely on you to organize a homecoming party for the ship. Let's try to get everyone there. There's still time to reach the Navy and Marine headquarters, several veterans' associations, school bands, security people, and so on. Set up a command post somewhere on the Embarcadero, near the Ferry Building. If possible get the mayor, Senator McBain and any other politician you can think of."

"That's a lot to pull together on the spur of the moment."

"If anyone can do it, Babe, you can."

"John knows someone who has a huge warehouse space at

Pier Five," Babe said. "We'll have mobile phones installed there. I'll handle the politicians and John can track down the marching bands. What about sound trucks?"

"I can take care of that," Joy said. "We'd better get started, Babe. We don't have much time."

Babe hesitated. "I keep worrying about Jack. What if something has happened to him?"

"Wherever he is," Joy said, "he'll feel safe knowing there are a couple thousand more POWs just like him arriving in San Francisco. My guess is he'll surface about the same time."

"I hope so."

Joy wanted to tell Babe that she had heard from Jack, that he was near, but she sensed that she should hold back that news. Babe needed to keep her focus; there was so much that had to be done in the next few hours. The most beautiful moment for them to come together would be during the parade itself, caught in the world's camera eye. Joy realized that she was rationalizing, perhaps she was even being self-serving, but this was a once-in-a-lifetime story and she not only wanted to draw from it every last drop of drama, she wanted Jack Fischer to be safe. And being safe meant his appearing the same time as two thousand other POWs.

"Just concentrate on what we need to do now," Joy said. "The rest is out of our hands."

Babe replied to Ivanov via fax a:

Alex,
A large gathering of television cameras and news people will be greeting the USS Montana at the Ferry Building in San Francisco. I will have the exact date and time soon. We will march the escaped POWs off the ship and up Market Street in front of a huge crowd. If publicity is what you wanted, you will have it. We also believe and pray that Jack will surface by then. You will need luck. Jack needs luck. We all need luck. We are with you, Alex.
Love and Godspeed.
Babe

Chapter Sixty Three

Ivanov the Terrible

"**P**LEASE tell President Vladimir Kruchlov that the new governor of the state of Khabarovsk wishes to speak to him urgently."

The call was put on hold while Vasili Mitrokin interrupted Kruchlov's breakfast, both to give him the news and to provide guidance, if needed. He was concerned about his leader's hair-trigger temper and his seriously elevated blood pressure. Also in recent weeks the president had increased his already prodigious consumption of vodka.

"Is this some kind of a joke, Vasili?"

"I think you had better take this call, Mr. President."

Kruchlov disliked interruptions, and it was too early in the morning to begin drinking. It was only Tuesday and the week was already a disaster. A group of dissidents in the Parliament House had been trying to unseat him with a highly decorated army general who had gone public about the corruption and criminal gangs in Russia. One of the cars in the general's entourage was bombed the day before, but unfortunately had missed the general. Kruchlov was forced to show his outrage, which meant appearing at the crime scene to console the relatives of those that died. He would have sent Mitrokin, but that would not have looked good. His nerves jangling, Kruchlov took the call.

"This is Alexander Ivanov from Khabarovsk, Mr. President. I have just been named the state governor."

Kruchlov felt a wave of heat pass across his forehead. "Named? Named by whom?"

"Myself."

"I know you, Ivanov. You're just a camp commander. You never amounted to anything. My father knew your father-in-law well.

He was a man of substance. I have one piece of advice for you. You're as good as dead."

When Ivanov laughed, Kruchlov reached for a paper cutter and rammed it repeatedly into his desk.

"Vladimir Kruchlov—today is not going to be a very good day for you. I suggest you exhibit a little patience and listen to what I have to tell you."

There was a brief pause on the line. Kruchlov had been surrounded by sycophants his entire career and Ivanov's forcefulness unsettled him. He pressed a button activating the speakerphone so that Mitrokin could hear Ivanov's end of the conversation.

"All right," he said through gritted teeth, "you have five minutes. That is, if you stay on the line that long. We will have your number and location in less than a minute."

"My line is secure," Ivanov said.

"Get on with it, for Christ's sake," Kruchlov said, his voice rising. He jammed the paper cutter deeper into the wood.

"As I told you, I have taken over the state of Khabarovsk as its new governor. The command structure for all military units here and the surrounding areas is under my control, with the exception of two air wings in Primorsky. I mention that because you'll find it out for yourself. Now take a minute and direct your flunkies to call all the commanders in these areas to verify what I'm telling you. I'll hold."

Kruchlov came back on the line, and Ivanov continued.

"I have all of the regions' mobile missile launchers with nuclear warheads at my personal disposal. You won't have any for your use from Irkutsk to Vladivostok. Don't bother to call and verify—just take my word for it. We have them well hidden, and targeted to take out most of the cities you hold dear in Mother Russia."

Vasili Mitrokin watched in alarm as the president's face drained of color. He had let the paper cutter slip from his hand.

"How many do you have?"

"You'll find that out as well, so I'll tell you. We started with twenty-three, and then we picked up another eighteen around Vladivostok and another twenty-two from the Chita-Irkutsk area. One of your generals sold nineteen to the Iranians, before moving to South America, and we intercepted those as well. You still have plenty in Novosibirsk and Omsk, but for the fun of it we decided to attempt stealing the warheads. And do you know something, Mr. President? It was surprisingly easy. All we needed was to issue the proper order and your fellows accommodated us."

"How long do you think you can stay alive in your precious little state, Ivanov? You can't hide forever."

"This is not a problem. I walk freely in the streets and will do the same in Moscow if you decide to invite me."

Kruchlov pounded a fist on the table. "I wouldn't let you take out my garbage."

"Let me warn you," Ivanov said. "Don't even consider trying to eliminate me. If I come to any harm, Moscow will be incinerated. I promise you that. You, of course, would be a special target."

"I don't believe you."

"You had better start believing."

"We can incinerate *you* anytime we want," Kruchlov shouted.

"I doubt it. But even if you were to succeed, you would separate your part of Russia from the east, and that would include your only warm water port of Vladivostok. You would be unable to reunite Siberia with your own forces because the Chinese Army will have driven across an undefended border, preventing you from doing that."

"Bullshit!" Kruchlov was breathing heavily and his brow had broken out in a fine sheen of sweat.

"I don't think so. This is exactly why the Chinese are supporting me for governor. In their minds they have two options. If I get defeated they will move into a weakened Siberia, and if I win with their support, they've extended their influence into our region *because we like them better than we like you.*"

Mitrokin whispered in the president's ear, "ask him if he has other support."

"Tell me, Ivanov, do you have other support?"

"I wasn't going to tell you this right away, but why not? At the moment we have three thousand Chechen volunteer fighters here. You remember them, don't you? We also have volunteers and political ties with Turkmenistan, Uzbekistan and Kazakhstan. Does that answer your question?"

"Go on," Kruchlov said, reaching again for the paper cutter.

"You, Mr. President, have two regiments of commandos in Irkutsk that you would normally send to kill us. The trouble is they received orders yesterday to come to Khabarovsk for a little reorganization. They will arrive in about an hour and our officers will take over and arrest your commanders. That is also true of three airborne units headquartered in Krasnoyarsk. If you think you have time to order these units back, don't bother. None of your communications can get through to them since they've acquired the new equipment we arranged for them."

"You seem to have thought of everything," Kruchlov said, staring blindly at Mitrokin. "Is there anything else I should know?"

"Yes. Shortly the international press will feature me as the new President Lincoln. You know the nineteenth-century American leader who freed the black slaves? Well, I have freed thousands of live allied and American POWs from their Siberian camps. One group will arrive in a country that I won't name just yet and a larger group will soon be docking in San Francisco. There will be a great deal of publicity. By the way, in case you don't already know, it was my ship that damaged your submarine out there. My ship was also damaged; it's limping along and the U.S. Navy is now escorting it. You were close, but no cigar."

"But why would you do something stupid like that?" the president asked, almost plaintively. "Freeing the prisoners is simply insane."

"I'm afraid you're wrong again," Ivanov said. "Communism is dead, and in a democracy slaves are unnecessary. Officially, that's my line. But realistically, their release automatically assures me the moral high ground in Russian politics and with the world's press. If you give our hero, Jack Fischer, the spiritual force behind the escape, any difficulty, you'll pay a high political price. Not only that, but your trading status will be affected by those who don't appreciate you keeping their soldiers for slave labor."

Kruchlov frowned at Mitrokin, breathing heavily. His assistant simply shrugged.

"You are a clever little rat aren't you, camp commander?"

"It's mainly hard work," Ivanov said. "Hard work and careful planning and I have an eye for detail."

"Well, we still have plenty of POWs and can live without a

few, so go fuck yourself, Mr. Lincoln," Kruchlov shouted.

"Our intelligence network covers all of Russia," Ivanov continued. "Over the past twenty years we've accumulated thousands of POW names, the location of camps, and in many cases, photo IDs. I guess what I'm telling you is you're going to have to become a hero just like me. It will definitely be in your best interest to release all of your prisoners in a grand speech before an awed press. This will help you with that general who wants to remove you from office. And yes, I know about him. He and I have mutual interests. You're going to claim you represent a new Russia, Mr. President, and that your discovery of the POW camps horrified you. Shutting them down will close the last chapter on the old Soviet's Gulag history."

Kruchlov stared at Mitrokin, who slowly nodded his head.

"That's not bad, Ivanov," the president said after a pause. "I'm going to think about it, but don't overestimate your hero status. This Jack Fischer business may end up backfiring on you."

"I'll take my chances," Ivanov said, "and you should, too."

"We'll see."

"Regarding Jack Fischer. If harm comes to him, Mr. President, even if it's not your fault, we have arranged a small retaliatory present for you." Pausing for affect, he continued, saying, "there are six suitcase-sized nuclear bombs placed inside Moscow. They can be triggered by radio from here. If Mr. Fischer is hurt or killed, you and your family will not live an hour afterward. I'll leave it to your imagination whether to believe we possess such weapons."

Kruchlov raised the paper cutter high above his head, preparing for a savage assault on his desk, and then thought better of it. He dropped it in a drawer.

"Are you declaring war along with your independence from Russia?"

"No. I have no interest in breaking up the country unless it's absolutely necessary. We will govern ourselves, pay you an agreed-upon tax and look after our own trade. We will be completely free of your Cleptocrats, your criminals and your secret police. We're trying to create a free society, which in the long run will out produce all of western Russia."

"We can't keep the criminals out of Russia," Kruchlov said. "I don't see how you think it will be different where you are."

"We've been arming and training the peasants for a number of years now," Ivanov replied, "and during the next year, it is our intent to guarantee every citizen unrestricted access to rifles and handguns. No criminal organization in Russia can overcome that. Think about it. The Russian Mafia barely exists here, in spite of their many and aggressive attempts to establish themselves. In case you haven't noticed, they're mostly all dead here in the east."

"You trust those fool peasants with guns?"

"I can only govern with their consent. Coercion won't work. Their consent is linked to my earning it, not demanding it, and if I get out of hand, they'll know they have the means to fight me. Just like I have the means to fight you."

Kruchlov sighed. He could hardly wait to end this interminable call, close the door and attack a bottle of vodka.

"I think we have a deal, Ivanov," he said. "I will hold a press conference on the POW matter shortly after your own."

A sweating Alexander Ivanov hung up. His astonished officer corps had heard his conversation on the speakerphone and a deafening applause went up.

"We did it! The gamble paid off! Ivanov—you were just great!" Someone started chanting, "Long live Ivanov the Great—Long live Ivanov the Great!" The colonel smiled. He was happy. He held a vodka glass in the air.

"Gentlemen, let us drink a toast to Private Jack Fischer, whose existence started us on this long journey. Long live Siberia!—Long live Siberia Jack!"

Chapter Sixty Four

Them or Us

"AL, what's the story on Leroy Robinson?" Conklin asked the vice president.

"It could have been the Russians," Hurst replied easily. "Maybe Greig had something to do with it. He sought to gain something out of everything he did."

"Gain?" President Conklin wrinkled his forehead in puzzlement. "Gain in what respect?"

Allen Hurst pulled a chair up to Conklin's desk and straddled it backwards. He looked hard into the president's eyes.

"Greig may have thought he was trying to do the right thing by getting rid of Jack and Babe without anyone being able to trace who had done it. If he had succeeded, he'd have become a star performer. But you and I know he fucked up."

Conklin closed his eyes. "I don't want to hear about it, Allen. I'm sick of all the intrigue, all the deception. Don't include me. I knew nothing about it."

"He could have brought us down, Joel. You see that, don't you? Greig did his best, but he bungled it. This could have been a fucking disaster for our administration and my election."

"Let's just do what needs to be done. Keep me out of it."

Hurst quickly changed the subject. "There's a ship called the USS Montana heading for San Francisco. The Navy is escorting it in. They say it doesn't match the Navy's description of it. There's been a firefight between it and a Russian sub. One of our aircraft has pictures of the submarine heading east trying to contain a fire in the hold. Satellite photos show it was near the Montana."

"Sounds strange," Conklin said, looking up from his desk. "Do you know anymore?"

"The Drudge Report," Hurst said.

Conklin heaved a deep sigh. "That fucking Drudge. The First Amendment should be suspended just to shut him up."

"One of our people says the Internet is flooded with thousands of names of live POWs who escaped Russia and are heading for San Francisco. Drudge is on the case."

"Shit! That's it." Conklin rose and paced the room, his head bowed, his hands clasped behind his back. "Are you thinking what I'm thinking?"

"POWs," Hurst said. "The Montana is carrying them."

"That's my guess. The Russians are doing this deliberately to make me look bad. They let those POWs escape. It'll give them clean hands and screws up our election."

Hurst nodded and said, "I'm not so sure. We've done secret deals with Kruchlov in the past year. How does he profit by releasing POWs? It's a sure way to lose us as his golden tit. I don't see it, Joel."

"Kruchlov is a pussy," Conklin said. "He has no guts."

"True. But he's good at protecting his own interests."

"All I know is, if that ship docks in San Francisco and there are escaped POWs on board, you can kiss the election goodbye."

"I'm aware of that," Hurst said. "I've already got people in place that can cause a diversion. Maybe get the POW story demoted to the back pages."

Conklin raised a hand as though stopping traffic. "You know the drill, Allen. Whatever is done, keep me out of it. There is simply no need for me to know."

"Understood."

Conklin sank into his chair. For a moment he stared out the window, seeing nothing, then turned to the vice president.

"What has happened to us, Allen? When I left law practice to enter politics I was an idealist. My goal was to be a public servant. Hell, I didn't need the money, I was making it hand over fist and had plenty to begin with. My mission was to make a difference. Now, fifteen years later, it's come down to cover-ups, shady dealings with the Russians and the Saudis, and all the rest of the world's scum. Jesus, Allen, what went wrong?"

"The real world is a hard place," Hurst said gently.

"I was a lawyer. I've been down in the pits."

"Yes, but politics is a whole lot rougher. Wouldn't you agree?"

Conklin nodded. "I never dreamed how rough."

"You have to pick and choose your spots," Hurst said. "We inherited a lot of bad stuff from previous administrations on this POW thing, and we have to live with it."

Conklin regarded the vice president quizzically. "You're a lot younger than I am, Allen. This is your world. I must confess I'm having a difficult time staying in step."

"The last thing you want is this POW mess damaging your image and legacy. Right?"

Conklin slumped back in his chair. "Do what you have to do, but exercise caution."

"You can count on me," Hurst said.

When the vice president left, Conklin asked his secretary to put him through to President Kruchlov in Moscow. He had to find out which side of the game the old drunk was playing on.

"Vladimir, I have to make this quick. Affairs of state, meeting after meeting, I'm sure you understand."

"Of course, Joel. What can I do for you?"

"Are you behind this POW escape and this ship that's arriving in San Francisco full of escapees?"

"Not exactly," Kruchlov said, and Conklin noted the trombone slide of evasiveness in the old man's voice. He was up to something. Conklin listened to the story of how Alexander Ivanov had become governor of a key Siberian state and was responsible for freeing more than 2,000 POWs.

"The East is turbulent these days," Kruchlov said. "All hell is breaking loose."

"There's no way to stop this fellow?"

"I'm afraid not." Kruchlov hesitated. "This business has blown up all out of proportion, Joel. I'm going to have to take immediate action myself."

"What do you have in mind, Vladimir?"

"World opinion is going to count heavily in this matter. Any taint of Stalinism in our current climate will not go unpunished. Russia lost more than twenty million soldiers and civilians during World

War II, but who remembers? Who will excuse us for imprisoning our adversaries for two generations? The world has a short memory, Joel. Stalin felt justified in calling you Americans imperialist aggressors. He was fond of saying that your country supplied the planes and we supplied the fighters. America lost four hundred thousand men in the war—a hideous inequity in Stalin's view."

Conklin drummed his fingers on the desk. *I don't need a history lesson, you old drunk. Cut to the chase.*

"What are you trying to tell me, Vladimir?"

"I'm going to free the rest of the POWs in Russia, and I'm going to put the best spin on it I possibly can. We can't undo the past, but to some extent we can revise it. I can hardly stay up with the shift of events anymore."

"You're freeing the POWs?" Conklin said, stunned.

"Every last one, Joel. And I suggest you get in front of the POW issue as well. Go meet the ship. Pretend it was your idea. Who are people going to believe—you or that blowhard incompetent George McBain? It really doesn't matter, because you will have created enough confusion to introduce doubt. After that you can spin in your usual way."

"I'm between a rock and a hard place in this thing," Conklin said.

"You hold the office. That weighs the odds heavily in your favor. Do a press conference, pose with a bunch of veterans—you know the drill. I'm here if you need me." Kruchlov hung up.

Chapter Sixty Five

Joy to the World

JACK responded to Joy's many messages at eight o'clock the following morning.

"I'm ready to go," he said. "But, I have to tell you, Joy, I'm scared, really scared deep down inside."

"Safety is an issue," she said. "We'll have security guards surrounding you and Babe, but we've had no time to work on crowd control."

"It's not that," he said. "I've lived in tight corners most of my life. My concern is Babe—finally seeing her, being with her at last. You have to understand I've dreamed of this moment every day for the past fifty years. Dreamed of it till the dream became reality. I would look at the sky at noon—we had promised that to each other—and I would focus on her features and listen to the sound of her voice. Now that the moment is almost here, I…" He tried to laugh. "Frankly, Joy, I'm terrified."

As Joy listened, she fought back tears. "Jack—may I call you Jack?"

"Of course."

"Babe loves you and you love her. That's all that matters. It's as simple and beautiful as that. You have nothing to worry about."

"I hope you're right."

"Let me bring you up to date on things," she said, and told him about the USS Montana and its political ramifications. Babe told Joy that King was in charge of a ship, soon to dock in San Francisco and that Jin had already transported a boatload of POWs to Japan. He was shocked and thrilled to learn that Alex has assumed control of Khabarovsk. *Four old men still in the middle of things and acting like age has no meaning,* he thought.

"My main concern is for the safety of you and Babe," she said. "The situation is so unstable. Whoever was responsible for killing Leroy Robinson—and everything points to the White House—they may come after you. The Russians and the Chinese may also play a role; they could try to destroy the USS Montana. It's even possible that the Administration could flip their strategy and show up at the Ferry Building claiming they and in particular the vice president, helped with the escape. Although, if I were them, I'd send a flunky to meet the ship—too big a risk of confrontation to do anything else, but we'll see. Vladimir Kruchlov might also be seeking the high political ground. He wouldn't want Ivanov to take the credit if public opinion were to shift entirely to the POWs."

"Life was simpler in prison."

"I'm sure you'll have many adjustments to make," Joy said. "But you have good friends to help you."

"Where are Babe and John now?" he asked.

"They should have arrived at Pier Five by now. And believe me, they're surrounded by security."

"I'll take a cab down there. I can't wait any longer."

"No, Jack, too risky. People may be looking for you. I may have a better idea."

Jack shook his head at the telephone. "I've taken a lot of risks in my life and a cab ride to the pier doesn't rank all that high."

"Please, you have to trust me on this. I want you to take a cab to Paoli's restaurant on Montgomery Street in San Francisco. Joe Paoli is a very close friend of Babe's and mine. He has a basement apartment there. Few people know about it. I'll call ahead and he'll hide you. My father has volunteered six of his security people and they'll arrive there before noon."

"That sounds pretty elaborate," Jack said. "Is it necessary? Life has made me a fatalist. If my number's up, it's up."

"The public didn't see the pictures of Leroy Robinson's body. I saw a video of it. He was chopped up with an axe before being tied to that fence. They poured gasoline on him. His body was still smoking when the camera crews arrived. If you think going to Pier Five isn't an obvious destination to your enemies, then let me tell you what Leroy's last words were when we offered him security."

"I'm sorry to be difficult," Jack said. "It's just, well—you know—it's been almost fifty years. Fifty years! Can you understand that?"

"I'm not sure I can. Do you want to hear my idea?"

"Go ahead."

"Babe is organizing a parade from the Ferry Building down Market Street to City Hall. As the POWs come off the USS Montana, the Marine Commander of the 12th Naval District will greet them. Cameras will never leave the faces of Babe, John and the off-loading ceremonies. I've been in touch with King Poo Koo on the ship and have instructed him not to let the POWs surrender to President Conklin, or his representatives, if they make an appearance. King will make exactly that announcement on his public address system when the ship docks."

"Will the Administration stand for that? It would embarrass the president."

"That's the idea," she said. "We believe they'll try to steal the POW show to save his political hide. King's refusal to turn the POWs over to the president's people implies they have good reason to be afraid."

"King has the courage of a lion, I can tell you that. But, won't he risk jail time for not accepting an order from the president or someone from his administration?"

"He's a non-citizen," Joy said. "Arresting him might be a problem. The POWs also present a problem. The president would have to order the ship to be taken by force, and he can't do that without risking a gunfight on the dock between the POWs and a sympathetic Marine Corps commander. Even the suggestion that the president or his flunky would board the ship and be rebuffed would underscore what the American people already think — the POWs are afraid of him."

"What do you think he'll do?" Jack asked. "Will the vice president show up at all?"

"I think it's a safe bet he'll be at the dock. At the very least, Allen Hurst will put in an appearance. They really can't afford not to have a presence here. The alternative would be some sort of diversion to get the POW story sidetracked. Say, arrest you and Babe, which at this point would be a public relations disaster. Or they might try to reverse their fortunes by grandstanding at the dock. We have one big ace up our sleeves, Jack. Neither Conklin or Russia's president knows about the six hundred POWs that are now in Japan just waiting for the Montana to dock."

"They might decide to kill Babe and me," Jack said.

"That's a possibility," Joy said grimly. "I've heard stories. People involved in the POW issue have been silenced, some, like Robinson, have died prematurely."

"I can't believe the Marine Commander won't obey the Administration's orders."

"The Administration is being extremely careful, Jack. If they order the Marine Commander to board the ship by force, they run the risk of his refusing. And if he does obey and a blood bath follows, leaving a lot of POWs and Marines dead—well, you get the picture."

"You remind me of your uncle. The same practical, strategic mind."

She smiled. "Just plain common sense. In front of a camera, politicians are predictable."

"Tell me what to expect," Jack said. "I don't want any surprises I can avoid."

"After the ship arrives, I estimate it will take a couple of hours for the men to disembark and organize for a march down Market Street. My bet is that the president will attempt to be in front of that march, but that's okay. We'll handle that later. The parade will hit the financial district just as offices are closing, there will be a massive traffic jam, confetti and lots of band music. Most importantly, my camera-guys will focus on Babe and the POWs—not the president or any representative of his."

"The public won't support the president being snubbed if he shows up."

"You've heard the chant '*Go, Jack, Go.*' It's been on radio and television all over the world. In fact, it's your story of trying to reunite with Babe that has electrified the world, not the docking of the USS Montana."

"I've heard it a lot in the last few days. Frankly, I'm amazed. It's hard to believe that the world would be willing to march behind me. It must be the instinct to be on the side of the underdog."

"It's more than that, much more. You've become a symbol for all that's unjust, not only in Russia, but everywhere in the world.

You've lived most of your life in jail and it's time for deliverance. Time to have what's rightfully yours. The public wants to see you and Babe reunited. They feel it in their hearts, and rationally they're demanding it. Anyone interfering with you two being reunited would run a terrible risk. I really believe the American subconscious was struck by the murder of Leroy Robinson. Our station is getting hundreds of calls. The people know, deep inside, that the Administration was behind it. You can sense the political ground shifting beneath everyone's feet. The public has heard the growl of a beast in the jungle and has collectively turned to meet it. Very eerie."

"I remember Robinson," Jack said. "He strutted like a peacock. He was going to make us all perfect little Communists. Very scary guy."

"He must have changed," Joy said. "I never met a sweeter or more mellow man."

"I guess life can do that for you if you're lucky." Jack shook his head, held captive suddenly by memories of detraining somewhere in the wilderness of Siberia. There was the line of emaciated black soldiers on their way to certain death in the mines and in the frozen fields of Chita. There was the strutting, shouting camp indoctrinator, Sergeant Leroy Robinson, preaching the gospel of a brave new world under Joseph Stalin. There, under the dark and roiling Siberian sky, was the certain smell and taste of doom. It was a past he would never forget.

"We'll have a secret camera team at Paoli's Restaurant," he heard Joy saying. "Our security men will be wearing uniforms, and together with them, you'll begin a march from California Street down Montgomery Street. The march will be timed to converge with the POW march at the intersection of Montgomery and Market. I've arranged for the transfer of six sound trucks from McBain's campaign to blare out the message throughout the financial district that we've found Private Jack Fischer, that you're marching on those streets and that you'll meet Babe at that intersection. From our studio on live TV, and from the trucks' loudspeakers, we'll call for the crowd to help escort you safely to your meeting with Babe. You'll be on the street, in the open, for the entire world to see. The chant '*Go, Jack, Go*' will sweep you forward. Our cameras will never leave your face, and using a split-screen, we'll also show Babe marching toward you up Market

Street in front of the POW column. That's our little surprise."

"Won't the crowd stampede us?" Jack asked.

"The Mayor arranged for the San Francisco Police Department to provide motorcycle escorts for your group of marchers and for Babe's. The Mayor has also agreed to keep this escort secret in exchange for his being part of your marching group. McBain's volunteers will be passing out thousands of little American flags, and at the right moment they'll raise banners saying 'Impeach Conklin.'"

"That will make them even angrier," Jack commented.

"His people have no idea we have you and that there's a second march. He won't know about it until the POW march is already under way. The last thing anyone expects is to see Senator George McBain standing at that intersection of Montgomery and Market Streets holding a sign saying 'Impeach Conklin,' with '*Go, Jack, Go*' chanting in the background. The Senator will be on the air explaining to the public his role in bringing you two together. If the administration attempts to upstage the event, Babe and King have instructed the marchers to bypass them, and instead, to come right up to you and for you to say to the cameras, 'Thank you, Senator McBain, for your efforts on behalf of the POWs.' You and Babe will embrace him. If someone from the Administration attempts to shake your hand, ignore it."

Jack sighed. "I don't recognize this America," he said. "It's as though I've come back to a foreign land."

"Fifty years," Joy said. "It's inevitable."

"It sounds like there's a great push to make McBain the next president of the United States."

"The country needs an honest government," Joy replied.

"If America has stonewalled on the POW issue," Jack said, "how many other things have they hidden from us?"

"That's a good question, Jack. I wish I had the answer for you."

***

Babe was standing at Pier Five discussing crowd control with a number of security guards when her cell phone beeped. She moved a few steps away before she answered.

"Babe," King said.

"King! Where are you? Are you all right?"

"We'll shortly be at the Golden Gate Bridge," he said. "Just as soon as we pass under it, I've made arrangements for three fireboats to pump water into the air announcing our arrival. A band will play on the forward section of the ship, and all the men are dressed in the uniforms of their respective services. Tell me what to expect when we dock."

Babe told him about the parade, the presence of the world press and the many politicians and celebrities who were expected.

"Joel Newman, Barbara Streisand, Tom Hanks, Edward Asner—that's just a few of the big names," she said. "You're going to be welcomed by the Commander of the Marine's 12th Naval District. John will call Alex and inform him of your safe arrival."

"Babe, if the president tries to upstage this event, we will refuse to leave the ship. It must be made clear that the United States did not arrange this rescue operation."

"Agreed," Babe said.

"Alex, you, Jin and I have risked everything to free these men," King said. "I want Alex to get the credit. He planned it. He deserves it and needs it for his plan to hold onto the Governor's seat. But, even more importantly, we are certain the administration was behind the murder of your daughter—at least indirectly. We heard all about it at sea. My heart aches for you."

"Thank you, King."

"I don't know how you're bearing it."

"It isn't easy, but I will soon see Jack. We have to keep going."

"Yes, because we can't stop now," King said. "And trying to stop could prove fatal. Any news of Jack?"

"He's close by. I can feel it. I just can't bear the waiting."

"I know how hard it is, but we'll all be together soon. We will plan a celebration at Alfred's when this is over. Is that an okay?" King still stumbled over the English idiom.

"That's a definite okay," Babe said, smiling.

"We plan to come down the ship's ramps with music playing," King said. "The men insist on holding onto their weapons until they're sure no harm will come to them."

"Why the concern, King?"

"They're aware that the government knew they were still alive and knew where the POW camps were located. The men also have been following Jack's escape. They know about Claudette's murder and the killing of Leroy Robinson. So, let's say they are very nervous. I'll explain all of that to the Marine Commander. Can you get in touch with Joy and tell her we want a couple of helicopter news crews over the ship?"

"Believe me King, you will be plastered with publicity. In fact, she has a camera crew on a speedboat hoping to board your ship. You know our Joy—first with the big scoop."

"Tell her to call me on this number. We'll lower a boat, maybe they can board that way. I think a camera crew on board ship will put the men at ease."

Babe wrote his telephone number down and promised to call Jin Jaing in Japan to coordinate the publicity there.

"I feel like this is the most important day of my life," she said. "The best, the most awful—I don't know—the most everything. I just lost Claudette, I'm completely beaten up inside, but I'm going to have Jack. He's finally coming back to me."

"Just a little more time," King said. "I know you can hang on, for you'll soon by with the person you've been looking for—for half a century."

Chapter Sixty Six

Market Street

JACK took a cab from Jack London Square in Oakland to San Francisco. Breaking a long silence, the driver said, "your first time in San Francisco?"

"Not exactly. But it's been a long time. I used to live in North Beach."

"A lot's changed in the old neighborhood," the driver said.

"Is Paoli's Restaurant close to North Beach?" Jack asked.

"Yeah. We gotta take the Broadway exit from the bridge anyway. You want I take you around for a quick spin?"

"Sure," Jack said after a moment's hesitation. His prisoner's instincts told him the man could be trusted. He was fat, jovial and well into his fifties. "Maybe a twenty-minute detour."

Leaving Broadway they turned right toward Fisherman's Wharf on Columbus Avenue, and the first thing Jack noticed was that Chinatown no longer ended at Grant Avenue and Broadway. He asked about it.

"The Chinese are all over North Beach. The Italians moved out and they moved in. They brought new life to the place. Mostly Italians on this street, though. I'm Italian myself, but I love that Chinese food."

"Is the Palace Theater still around?" Jack asked.

"Oh, you bet. We'll be passing it in a minute. You used to go there?"

"When I was a kid, a lot," Jack said.

He was surprised to see that Bimbo's 365 and the Italian Village nightclubs were still doing business. The Fior d'Italia restaurant was now located where the Bal Taberin nightclub used to be. He remembered the Bal Taberin because his father Bruno had played violin there twice. Luca's restaurant was gone. Coit Cleaners at Columbus and Union Street had also disappeared. The old Barbary Coast on Pacific Avenue had morphed into designer studios and offices. Hogan's Soda Fountain had vanished. Still standing, however, was the Fischer house on Union Street. Smaller, shabbier, but still recognizable, even though the beautiful elm tree on the sidewalk was gone. Not even the stump remained as a kind of epitaph. The sight of the house brought with it a flood of memories—friends he hadn't thought of for years. Bubby Black and his leather World War I cap and goggles; Lance Hightower, the neighborhood marble champion. He saw forgotten toys from childhood, a blue baseball bat he had always kept beside his bed. The sudden nostalgia tightened his chest. He had had such a short life, barely 18 years of it; all of the rest was survival and waiting and hoping and scheming—waking up each day bent on staying alive. How could he ever make up for all that lost time?

As the cab headed for Montgomery Street, they passed the old street clock, which still stood in front of the pawn shop where he had once tried to buy a secondhand microscope. He remembered the flashy, expensive pen he had found in the street and how it had made him feel like a young man of importance. He was smiling as the cab pulled in front of Paoli's.

He thanked the driver and tipped him five dollars. Joe Paoli was waiting for Jack at the door.

"At long last we meet," Joe said, grasping his hand. "I've heard so much about you, I feel like you and I, we're friends already."

"I want to thank you for letting me stay here."

"Thank Joy Jaing. Who can ever say no to that beauty? I'm eighty-two, but she could talk me into anything. I still love the beautiful women."

"Good for you," Jack said. "It sounds like you're living the good life."

The old man continued to hold his hand. "A prisoner of war? What is it? Fifty years they tell me? How did you manage it?"

Jack smiled as he slowly withdrew his hand. "I guess it's simple. Stubbornness. I just decided to keep on breathing. Didn't like the alternative."

Joe nodded. "At my age I have that feeling every day." He put a hand on Jack's shoulders. "So let's go downstairs and get ready for the big day."

He ushered Jack through the restaurant and down a flight of stairs into a small apartment.

"Throw your stuff in the closet and relax. TV's over there. The security guys should be here before lunch."

"Thanks, Joe. I know it's early but I could use a glass of vodka. In Russia we drank it instead of water. It's better for you."

Joe grinned and said, "coming right up."

Jack sat glued to the television while waiting for the guards.

Just before noon, Joy entered the restaurant breathlessly. She raced downstairs and into Jack's arms. They held each other for a moment without speaking. She then pulled back and looked into his eyes.

"I've waited for this day a long, long time, Jack."

He smiled, "not as long as I have, Joy."

"In a few minutes you'll be with Babe and your son."

"Time has stopped for me," he said. "This day already seems like a year out of my life."

"You look puzzled, Jack. Ease up, this is going to be a big event."

Jack asked Joy to sit down; he was pensive and determined.

"Joy, I've been thinking. Everything points to the president being behind all that's happened, but this is not Russia where such things like this are expected. I guess what I'm saying is that I'm not thinking that the president wants to hurt Babe or me and that maybe we should telephone his people. Maybe have someone from the Administration at the ship when it comes in."

"That could be risky, but okay let me get on it." Joy said hesitantly, "Meanwhile the Mayor's office has arranged for a motorcycle escort. We've got a sound truck here and it will follow us. It will only take me five minutes to cut an audio tape for our station to announce that you are in San Francisco. It'll be repeated every few minutes. If I'm right, we can fill the streets with people who can't wait to see you and Babe come together. I'm reluctant to notify some of the other news stations, but what the hell."

"Thanks Joy. I'll have vodka while you're getting things organized."

***

Jack watched the television roll out the news of his being in San Francisco.

"And you who are lucky enough to be here or watching on television will momentarily see him escorted down Market Street toward the Ferry Building. Reports are that his love, Babe Mattioli, has no idea that Private Jack Fischer is heading her way." He spun the television dial; every station carried the same message. Cameras were recording large crowds rushing toward Market Street. Newscasters spoke breathlessly about this being the most historic moment in living memory. The telephone rang and Jack answered.

"This is the office of the president, Private Fischer. I am afraid the president is not available to take your call, but I am certain that he is eager to talk with you. He's been following the breaking news about your being in San Francisco. Are you going to be at this number for say an hour?" a secretarial voice asked.

"No, I'm afraid not. I'd like to be, but you see, I've waited all that I can wait and I'm leaving now to find my Babe. Tell the president I will try calling him again." Jack hung up. He was not the least bit impressed that he had been talking to the most powerful office in the world.

"Let's go, Joy, let's go!" Jack said as he reached the top of the stairs and pulled on her arm to escort her out of the door.

She looked at him and her eyes asked the question. He answered.

"No, I didn't get through. He's expecting my call later. Now let's go."

A Mercedes convertible limousine sat at the curb. Jack and Joy rushed to it through a blizzard of cameras and climbed inside.

"How the hell did they get here so fast?" Jack asked as the door shut.

"I made a few phone calls to certain people who then made calls and so on."

"It looks like the motorcycle police are arriving—looks like six—no, there are nine! Unbelievable."

Joy nodded to the driver to begin as she said, "go slow, this is important. We want the world to see, and it's only a few blocks."

The driver saluted with a smile and pulled out onto Montgomery Street. He slowed to let the motorcycle escort catch up and surround the limousine and then two of the policemen let their sirens wail.

Montgomery Street was a madhouse, people rushed toward the car to get a look at Jack, others smiled or cried. 'Go Jack, Go' could be heard in waves and as they began their right turn onto Market Street. Both Jack and Joy were stunned. A solid formation of people greeted them, and for an instant the driver thought of putting the car into reverse. Jack rose from his seat; he smiled at the huge crowd and began a swimming motion with his arms. People grinned and the crowd parted to let them through. Overhead a television news crew in a helicopter caught the moment on camera. On television sets all over the world, reporters' words rang out.

"It's incredible, there must be over a hundred thousand people down there. They are stopped—no, no, Jack Fischer is standing up in the limousine—the crowd is parting. From here they look like an island all by themselves."

**

The USS Montana—dubbed the mystery ship by reporters—also dominated the news. Movie stars were arriving at the Ferry Building plaza, and reporters were holding forth, filling empty airtime. Slowly, mysteriously, a huge sea creature surfaced from beneath the Golden Gate Bridge—a ship, the USS Montana—surrounded by fireboats spraying fountains of water was approaching land, its foghorn blowing non-stop. The Coast Guard crew wore dress blues. There were so many small craft on the bay a viewer might think the Queen of England was arriving for a state visit. The Drudge report, with all of its details on POWs, was being quoted by every news organization.

Alexander Ivanov appeared on Chinese television where he described the escape. He announced being the new Governor of Khabarovsk and that it was his mission to introduce true democracy.

"A fresh, cleansing wind is blowing through our land," he said, in closing.

"A land within which all citizens will have a say in their own fate. We, in Khabarovsk, no longer have need for the Gulag, for prisoners of war, for secret prisons, for the punitive measures of the past. We promise our citizens a new beginning."

Joy turned her attention to the television in the limousine. Her crew was at the boarding plank of the USS Montana. A high level administration flunky from the State Department, oddly named John

Hazard, attempted to board the ship, but King refused to lower the ramp. "This is King Poo Koo, I am in command of this ship and no one is welcome aboard. I demand that you stand down," he shouted from a loudspeaker. "These POWs are afraid for their safety and are prepared to die if that becomes necessary."

John Hazard huddled with his advisors before approaching a series of microphones, his back militarily erect.

"To all of you aboard the USS Montana," he began. "I have come to welcome you back to America, after what must have been a terrible and prolonged ordeal for you. Our president informs me that he has been in touch with Russian President Vladimir Kruchlov, who joins him in saluting your safe return. President Kruchlov and the Administration worked together for your release. It took months of planning and secrecy. But it was worth the effort. You are here! You are back on American soil!" Hazard's voice vibrated with false emotion. "Believe me when I say that each one of you is a hero. Each one of you protected this country and helped make it safe for our children and our children's children. Bravery and loyalty are precious commodities in this world, and you men have exhibited both to the utmost. You are the best examples of what it means to be an American."

"I don't know you, *mister*," King replied, his voice booming over the ships loudspeaker system. "But two days ago a Russian submarine attempted to board or sink this ship. Our men drove them off. It was quite a fight. We narrowly avoided being sunk. And since you lay claim to working with the Russians on our escape, we feel that you have some involvement in our danger. There is also the feeling among us that your administration played a role in the murders of Leroy Robinson, Claudette Mattioli and Ronald Goldberg."

Again Hazard conferred with his advisors, who had rushed to his side and urged him to act compassionately but with authority. When he spoke again, his smile was fixed and he seemed to stretch himself taller and straighter.

"I'm sure that there was some kind of misunderstanding," Hazard replied, with quiet authority. "After all, you were on a ship— to quote the press, 'a mystery ship.' Accidents can happen under such circumstances. I also know how emotionally charged everyone is about those unfortunate murders. The Administration, and I myself, feel the grief for the victims and their families. But I can promise you this…"

His voice grew stern, paternal and responsible. "Every effort is being made to bring the perpetrators of these heinous crimes to justice."

King answered. "If both governments participated in this escape, then perhaps you can clear up these questions. How could you not have known that our ship was formally a Latvian vessel renamed the USS Montana? Why do I have an intercepted copy of President Kruchlov's order to its submarine commander to either board or sink our ship? Lastly, do you know there is another group of escapees? Six hundred of them landed in another country. They were part of our escape plan. Perhaps you would care to name that country."

The smile still stuck to Hazard's features as though glued, but his shoulders shifted slightly forward, the gravity of deceit settling in. He felt a sinking sensation, a collapsing into himself. He raised a hand with a kind of fluttering, pacifying gesture. Before he could form an answer an aide stepped up to the microphone, partially shielding Hazard from view.

"Mr. Poo Koo, this is vice president Allen Hurst's personal assistant speaking. First, let me commend you for bringing these men safely home. That is an act both of compassion and heroism." He paused, waiting for King to reply. When King remained silent, he continued. "I think the questions you've raised can best be answered in a face-to-face meeting. There are obviously areas of vast miscommunication. Let me suggest that you tell us your terms for coming ashore. After all, you did not come all this way for no reason."

Hazard glanced at the aide, nodding slightly, approving, relieved.

"There are no terms," King answered. "We are not open to conditions or compromises. Our men will come ashore in uniforms representing the services they belong to. Our band will escort them off. They will be fully armed. We intend to parade up Market Street to let the world see that there are live POWs here, in spite of your and previous administrations' denials and obstructions. When we arrive at City Hall, the men will speak for themselves. You have a Marine Corps Commander dockside. Have him, and only him, come aboard."

"That will be agreeable," the aide said calmly, as though he had won a debating point. "I'm certainly looking forward to meeting you and the other brave men in your group. I would like to take this opportunity to vigorously express our administrations heartfelt thoughts, that each and every one of these men is a hero, and we owe each and every one the greatest debt of gratitude."

A gangplank was lowered. The Marine Commander was piped aboard the USS Montana and the ship's band played the Marine Corps anthem.

Babe was standing just outside the perimeter of Hazard's security while he spoke to King. He was aware that she was there. When Hazard finished speaking, he approached her with both arms outstretched. He knew they were on camera and he had to make the most of this opportunity. Perception was everything; experience had taught him that it trumped truth every time.

"Mrs. Mattioli, I want you to know how deeply sorry I am for your loss. Words cannot begin to express the sorrow of losing a child." He was about to embrace her when she recoiled, and in a whisper, but a whisper with the lethal edge of a razor, and a whisper loud enough to be heard on a close microphone, said, "I hold your administration responsible for my daughter's murder. The buck stops with you. It's as though you pulled the trigger."

Hazard's fingers flew to his face as he took a step backward. Men in dark suits, with blank expressions closed in, forming a protective shield around him. He spun in the direction of the cameras, still smiling his best bureaucratic smile.

"Well, to say this is an emotional day for all of us would be an understatement. I am sure our administration will be looking forward to a lengthy discussion at the White House with Mrs. Mattioli and all the men on board the USS Montana."

Security men ushered the aide into a waiting limousine to a chanting crowd.

"Down with Conklin!" rang in his ears.

***

Joy turned away from the television and said to Jack, "We've got them on the run."

"Babe is still so beautiful," Jack said in awe, seeing her on the limousine screen. He sighed. "I have to confess something to you, Joy. I'm tired. I've been struggling for too many years just to stay alive. It's time to rest, time to stop fighting."

Joy touched him lightly on the shoulder.

"Others will do the fighting for you now, Jack."

He studied her seriously.

"You know," he said. "King just put his ass on the line for those guys on that ship. The Administration is never going to forgive him. It could be dangerous."

"He sees it as something he's doing for you, not just for those men. In his mind, it's all related. It was what King hoped for and he put the plan in action. And that's just what's about to happen. I don't know how many times he said to me or my father that he'd find you and bring you out of Russia."

Jack nodded. "King is probably the best friend I have in the world."

"He feels the same about you," Joy said firmly, feeling tears in her eyes

Chapter Sixty Seven

Visitors

IN a limousine a mile from the scene, and listening to the broadcast of the Azov docking, the president turned to Allen Hurst.

"This reminds me of the anti-war demonstration days, only now *we're* the bad guys." He shook his head; his left eye drooped with fear and exhaustion. "This is a fucking fiasco, Allen."

"Forget about that for a moment," Hurst said. "They're hurting us, but they haven't killed us. We can't show any cracks."

"I'm trying." The president sighed. "I remember how much I used to hate authority. Always on the side of right. The spear-carriers for justice. Jesus, Allen, I miss those days."

"Ancient history." Hurst's tone was brusque. "I'd better get on the horn to Kruchlov's people and find out about that second group of POWs."

"Good idea," Conklin said. "That submarine thing was a bad scene. Hazard nearly fainted. I hope you've got something that'll take this shit off of the front pages long enough for us to get on top of it."

"Playing it by ear," Hurst said.

Given the traffic congestion, security had decided to take Mission, instead of Market Street, to City Hall. They made their turn, passing just two blocks from McBain's flagged intersection.

"City Hall is coming up in a few minutes," Hurst said. "The Mayor should give us a good reception. We can weave a little spin on the front steps. That should help."

"What else have you got?"

"We've rounded up a couple of veterans' groups and put in a last minute request for them to participate in the ceremony. If we're lucky, we'll get maybe a hundred fifty and bring them to City Hall."

"That's a nice touch, using vets. Everybody has a soft spot for vets. I'd like to be filmed with them."

"Of course."

"You're going to make a good president, Al," Conklin said, suggesting his vice president was a shoo-in to be the next president.

"Thanks, but right now let's concentrate on the spin. These guys can't be POWs. We have to keep this firmly in mind and have to stress this at every opportunity. Why can't they be POWs? Because after each war, captured soldiers were returned to their various countries." Hurst grinned. "And how do we know that? Simple. Every administration since Truman's has proclaimed it thus. It's all in the records. They were returned. Clean slate, case closed. Don't you see, Paul? We're in the clear on this one because there's precedent. The story has just been handed down and down—and that's the way we spin it. So who are these guys? If not POWs, *who are they*? Put the seed of doubt in the public's mind about all this POW hero crap. Aren't they, in fact, just a whole bunch of Leroy Robinsons? Once we establish that doubt, we can arrest them and hold some military trials."

"Sounds right on target, I think my appetite is coming back."

Hurst's cell phone rang. He answered, listened, and frowned.

"Is there any way to abort that enterprise?" he asked the caller. As he continued to listen, his frown deepened. "Okay, Okay. It's in our court now."

Hurst whispered to Conklin, "That was a contact of Greig Rivers' on the East Coast. Says he's got an associate in San Francisco perched somewhere in a window on Market Street. Says he's enjoying the view."

Hurst regarded the president, enjoying the horror flooding his eyes. *No guts.*

"I don't want to hear about this," Conklin said. He knew there was a shooter out there, but he tried to keep that information locked in a separate compartment of his mind. Greig had had dealings with the New Jersey Mafia; he was aware of that. But as his mind engaged that reality, and dipped briefly into the consequences, his hands began to tremble. If someone were out there, honoring the deal that had been made, then Babe Mattioli and Jack Fischer, if he appears, would soon be dead. That could not be allowed to happen—not now. He would be blamed; he would be brought down, disgraced.

"Too late to abort," Hurst continued in a whisper. "Let's pray he doesn't get a shot."

"Christ," Conklin said. "People are going to speculate that we're behind it."

"It's that goddamn Rivers," Hurst said, honing the fine edge of his own spin. "He took matters into his own hands. Wanted to prove he had brass balls." He stared at Conklin.

"That asshole did it all for you, Joel. He loved you and thought he was doing you a favor. Some fucking favor," Hurst said uneasily, hoping to deflect blame from himself.

Disgusted, the president looked away.

"We've got to stop this," he said. "We've just got to."

Chapter Sixty Eight

The Parade

THE men formed lines five abreast with loaded rifles pointed skyward as they came down the ship's ramp. Behind was their own marching band; following them were the families. No one expected to see women and children and the sight created quite a stir with the press, who tried unsuccessfully to obtain interviews with them. The Marine Commander, Babe, King and ex-Republican Congressman Bob Dornan formed the front of the line with the men's officers. Just before the march began, Republican Senator Bob Smith ran forward, catching up.

John Fischer had called Dornan and Smith the night before. He thought it would be important for them to be part of the event. They had never stopped demanding uncensored POW documents from the administration. They were constantly outraged at the government's stonewalling and were often laughed at for advancing the notion that POWs could possibly be in slave camps in China and Russia, and that they might be still alive. This day would be their vindication. Both had dropped what they were doing and hopped red-eye flights to San Francisco.

There were two bands, one college and one high school, uniformed and carrying 'Go, Jack, Go' banners to celebrate the event. Camera crews flanked the march as it rolled down Market Street. Confetti floated down everywhere, a paper blizzard from office windows, while police motorcycle sirens blared, and the USS Montana blew its fog horn ceaselessly. The sidewalks were jammed, twenty people deep, trying to sing "God Bless America" over the noise of the marching bands. The cacophony seemed to create more happiness than confusion; tense and driven urban faces were suddenly transformed into hundreds of smiles. The mood was clearly festive.

Peter Mattioli, feeling self-conscious, did not march at the very front of the parade. He was keenly aware that this was not his show. He decided, as the former State's lieutenant governor, that marching along with police officers was a more appropriate slot for him. Three blocks up Market Street where McBain was barricaded, the crowd noise increased. Mattioli could hear the chant '*Go, Jack, Go.*' As he drew closer, the sound was deafening.

"Private Jack Fischer is here," the speaker proclaimed from a sound truck. "He's marching down Montgomery Street to meet his long lost love Babe Barsi. Let's join the march!" Mattioli's lips twisted with repressed anger, and when he caught sight of Senator McBain at the intersection surrounded by sandbags he understood, or at least he thought he understood, what was happening. He raced back to the marching column, ignoring everyone else at the front. He ran up to Babe, his arms flung wide open in a charade of happiness.

"Babe—Jack Fischer is here! Just two blocks up, marching in front of a huge crowd. The two of you are going to meet on Market Street." Mattioli began pulling her away from the march in the direction of McBain's bunker, hoping that once Jack and Babe were together the shooter could isolate them in the swirling crowd. They had to die. Mattioli had promised his New Jersey associates that this plan would go down without a hitch. He owed them a lot of favors. His dealings were with them; theirs were with contacts at the White House, of which Mattioli knew nothing.

***

The view from the Phelan Building was clear. The shooter could see a man who resembled Jack Fischer run directly toward Babe Mattioli. Her face lit up, she smiled, they embraced, and he took her hand, pulling her toward him, and away from the crowd. Both looked happy. The assassin raised his rifle. He squeezed the trigger and Peter Mattioli staggered a step forward and then fell into Babe, taking her down with him. Blood spattered her. Before the shooter could move away from the window, several POWs fired at the office window. Glass flew, shards of silver spiraled to the ground. It never occurred to the shooter, as he lay dying, that the marchers would have live ammunition. *Soldiers on parade? No way in hell.*

The POWs instantly formed a defensive perimeter with their guns aimed at every window. The music stopped and the crowd was stunned into silence. The officers, King and the Marine Commander ran over to Babe and someone called for an ambulance. The press was having a field day. Cameras zoomed in from everywhere. Chaos cut through the crowd and the strict rank-and-file grid was splintered into pieces. Groups broke off, weaving, twisting in snakelike lines.

Joy and Jack had seen the melee on a media truck's television and began running down Montgomery Street. McBain was at the intersection, and when Joy and Jack and the forward contingent of their march came around the corner, he joined them. As they rushed down Market Street, fighting their way through the confusion. Unseen hands suddenly lifted Jack up, propelling him through the throngs. At that height he could see a cluster of people and a body on the pavement a hundred yards ahead. He saw Babe, streaming with blood and trying to rise from the street with the help of a soldier. Jack wrestled free, dropped to the ground and raced toward her. Adrenaline crazed, he lifted her up in one swoop, screaming.

"Babe! Babe! *My God*! Are you all right? Are you hurt?" He was near hysteria, his voice cracked like a boy's.

When Babe put her arm around his neck and pulled him to her, her dark eyes swallowed him. He was in her heart, in her blood stream, in her mind.

"Jack—Jack—My Jack. You're really here? You came back to me. I'm fine. I'm not hurt. Jack, is it you? Let me see you." She kissed him lightly on the lips. "Is this a dream? I don't want to wake up. I never want to wake up again. Are you here, my darling? You're really here, aren't you?"

She cried, she laughed and she touched his flesh tentatively, caressing it like a precious object. They were oblivious to the crowd that surrounded them, but the cameras saw it all, recorded it all.

"I'm here, Babe. I'll never leave you again."

"That better be a real honest-to-God promise." She crushed her wet eyes against his shoulder.

John Fischer stood watching Babe and his father. Finally, he approached Jack and touched his arm.

"Dad?" he said.

Turning to the tall auburn-haired-man, Jack said, "are you little John?"

John smiled. "No more. But you can call me little John."

"I've missed you so much," Jack said, fighting back tears. "So goddamn much."

The two men embraced.

There were so many things he wanted to say to his son, so many thoughts whirled through his head: Siberia, entrusting little John's safekeeping to Alex, saying a sad farewell to Ati, and then the years without them, the long, lonely years. It all rushed back, overwhelming him. "The news said you were Babe's son. They called you John. I was afraid to believe that such a miracle was possible—that you could be my John."

"Well, I'm here, Dad," John said. "You look wonderful."

Jack tried to smile. "I look awful. I'm not used to crowds and noise, and I'm very old."

Security guards began moving Babe, John and Jack away from the center of the street, and for the first time they saw Peter Mattioli's crumpled body. Babe hadn't fully realized what had happened. All she could remember was Peter running toward her and yelling that Jack was on his way. Then a kind of mist descended until Jack stood over her. Drenched in her ex-husband's blood, she began to shake uncontrollably and tears again overwhelmed her.

The police carried Mattioli's body to the sidewalk and placed him in an ambulance, which had just arrived. Senator McBain stood in the back of a flatbed truck, and was joined by Congressman Bob Dornan and Senator Bob Smith. Cameras zoomed in on them and McBain held his arms wide to quiet the milling crowd. A battery-powered loud speaker was tossed to him, and he addressed the throng of emotionally charged people.

"Our president's administration has denied live prisoners of war were ever held in slave labor camps in Russia and China." Then pausing for effect, he pounded the side panel of the truck and screamed out, "yet here they stand before you as proof of the Administration's lies and cover-ups!" The POWs let out a roar of approval and the multitude joined in.

"The dead man who was lying here looked like Private Jack Fischer to the shooter—*and he is dead*!" The crowd murmured. "Babe Mattioli's daughter Claudette resembled her mother and their neighbor Ron Goldberg also resembled Jack Fischer." With a preacher's accelerating passion he roared. *"They too are dead!"*

Moving from side to side, as if agitated, the southern Baptist McBain again roared. "Sergeant Leroy Robinson went on television to defend the character of Private Jack Fischer—*and now he is dead! Is that a coincidence?*" The crowd roared in response: *"No—no—no—no."*

Focusing on Babe, he pointed at her. "Babe Mattioli stands here before you. *Covered in blood*!" He stopped a second for effect, and declaimed, *"is this America? Is this the kind of country we pledged allegiance to as little children?"* A wail went up and voices roared, *"No!"*

McBain gestured to Jack and Babe as they clung to each other and he screamed at the crowd.

"A miracle has brought these two lovers together after almost fifty years. Does anyone believe Jack and Babe should be prevented from being together?" The crowd roared. *"No! No!"*

Jack took Babe's hand and stared into her eyes. Yes, she was older, her hair was gray, her features were wrinkled, and yet her beauty was exactly as he remembered it. The puckish curve of the lips, the large dark eyes drawing the world into them—her skin still white and smooth. They could not stop touching each other. Each had to know that the other was actually, concretely there, there in the flesh, and not just one more heartbreaking, anguished dream.

Bob Dornan motioned to Jack and Babe to come forward and mount the truck. McBain then drew them both close and asked the crowd.

"Do you think that fifty years of separation for this couple is long enough?" Again the roar came forward, this time with a resounding *"YES!"*

"Do you think that these two people love each other?"

"Yes! Yes!"

"Can anyone think of a single reason why this Administration should be allowed to commit murder to keep this couple apart?" In true call-and-response style, the crowd roared, *"Noooooo."*

"All of you who believe that President Conklin deserves to be impeached and removed from office follow me to City Hall. Let us march together. For Justice. For Life. For Humanity!"

McBain jumped from the truck and asked Senator Smith and Bob Dornan if they would lead the parade to City Hall. "You two have been at the forefront of this live POW issue for years without a breakthrough," he said. "This is your moment in the sun. Go to City Hall. Stand on those steps and shout the truth to the world. Only you two guys can do it, and you deserve to do it!"

"Now you've got me all stirred up," Dornan said, grinning. "C'mon, Bob, let's go. The truth awaits America."

Dornan took the loud speaker and began the chant: "Down with Conklin! Down with Conklin!" He moved quickly to the head of a disorganized parade and boldly began the march. The bands played, the chanting continued, and Jack and Babe held hands and looked at each other.

"I don't care about the president or City Hall," Jack said. "I've waited almost fifty years to be with you again. Let's slip away now. Let the others celebrate."

"I want to more than anything, but we can't walk away, Jack. This is for you. For both of us." She pointed across the street. "King is standing over there. Without him, this day would never have happened."

"God, how I've missed that man," Jack said, from deep in his throat.

They made their way across to the other side of Market Street where King was organizing the POW columns and Jack nearly knocked him over with his embrace. They held each other tight for a moment and choked back tears. Nothing was said. Nothing needed to be said. They were blood brothers. They had been through the worst together. This was their moment of triumph. This was the dream of promises made and kept. This was the meaning of true friendship. Love united them, and together with Babe and John they formed an island in the midst of the parade that flowed past them. Former POWs saluted them silently.

"That was one hell of a long train ride you took the last time I saw you," King said when he could speak. He could see the love in Jack's eyes as he spoke. He thrilled to it. *Blood brothers.*

"A very long train ride," Jack said.

King looked at Babe and back to Jack.

"Before you two slip away I want you to pass through the ranks. Salute those guys. They all know you and you know them. They prayed for your escape to be successful, and you know what else I think?"

"What do you think, King?"

"When news of your escape reached them they cheered and you became a symbol for what might be possible. The men on this ship volunteered to come here, you know. The others stayed behind."

"I want you to come with us, King."

"No, Jack. You and Babe need time alone. Besides, I've been with these guys all across the Pacific. I'll catch up with you later. Is that an okay?"

Jack smiled. "That's an okay, King."

"Call us tonight," Babe said. "We'll celebrate."

"I must get very, very drunk tonight," King said.

"We both must get very, very drunk," Jack said.

"You're not going to leave me out of this," Babe said.

Jack took Babe's hand and they trotted to the front of the first column. He recognized many men, some of them former patients of his. The younger ones he knew were Vietnam era POWs. They saluted the men as they marched past. There was recognition, there were tears. One Marine removed his dress blue jacket and gave it to Babe to wear. Many men were crying openly as they passed. This was their homecoming—theirs and Jack Fischer's.

Chapter Sixty Nine

End Game

THE Secret Service agent posted outside the presidential limousine parked in front of City Hall was listening intently to his earphone.

"Holy shit," he said to himself and motioned to the vice president to lower the window.

"What is it, Charles?" Hurst asked.

"You won't believe what I just heard. The parade that was headed this way? It's been rerouted. There's been an assassination attempt on Fischer and the woman. Don't know all the details."

President Joel Conklin overheard the agent's remarks and slumped in the backseat, covering his eyes with both hands.

"What the hell do I have to do to get this crap behind me?" he muttered into his hands.

"Keep me updated as the situation develops down there. See if you can find out if McBain is directly on the scene," Hurst said.

"Yes, sir," the agent said.

The vice president raised the window and he and the president stared at each other for a full minute before Hurst spoke.

"If the Mattioli woman and Fischer are dead, there won't be a single citizen in America that won't put the blame on us. Plus, McBain is right on location exhorting the crowd with 'Down with Conklin' chants. I think we're in deep yogurt this time, Joel."

"What can we do?"

"Are you a religious man?"

"You know better than that. A nominal Lutheran."

"Do Lutherans pray?"

"I imagine some of them do."

"Well, I'd advise you to give it a try. I'm thinking of trying it myself."

"Allen, you're not serious."

"Not entirely. But desperate times call for desperate measures."

They sat in glum silence until the Secret Service agent again tapped on the window. He informed Hurst and the president that Babe Mattioli and Jack Fischer were still alive, the parade was heading back up Market Street and that the assassination attempt killed Mattioli's ex-husband instead. Hurst nodded and turned a thoughtful glance on the president. For the first time he began to see a clear path to his own presidency.

"You know Joel, we could invite Private Fischer and Ms. Mattioli to the White House. Treat them like heroes—even hint that I would consider either of them as part of my new cabinet, maybe even as vice president. What do you think? There's precedent for it. Remember when Ross Perot dredged that old duffer up from the living dead for the VP slot?"

Conklin responded hesitatingly. "The idea has merit Al, but it's tricky. If we jump too soon to embrace those two characters, we risk either being upstaged by them, or of raising the POW issue to an even higher level. Beyond that, I don't want to piss off the Russians or Chinese by rubbing the issue in their faces."

"Kruchlov has already rubbed it in ours."

"That's true." Conklin pressed fingers gently against his aching eye sockets.

"You know?" he said after a pause. "The more I think about it, the more I like it. Put them in Lincoln's bedroom. No one can ever resist that. It always works." He managed a faint smile. "They say that power corrupts, Al."

"And absolute power corrupts absolutely," Hurst added.

"The lessons of history are never lost on you, Al."

Chapter Seventy

Alfred's Restaurant

JACK held Babe firmly by the hand as they ducked out of the parade near Powell Street. They climbed onto a cable car rotating on its turnstile and sat away from the congested area. They were desperate to be alone. Babe pulled the Marine Corps jacket around herself to hide the blood stains.

While waiting at the cable car's Market Street turn-around Jack pointed.

"Babe, look over there. See that flower stand across the street?"

Babe slipped on her glasses and peered ahead. She smiled. "Now I can see it."

"It's not the same one but it's in the same location. That's were I got the flowers for the corsage I made for you the night we went to the House of Blue Lights in the old Barbary Coast. Remember?"

"How could I ever forget?"

"I've often thought about that night. You looked so beautiful."

"That was the first corsage in my life. A milestone in the life of a girl." She pressed his hand. "I'll tell you a very mushy secret. For many years I kept it pressed between the pages of a world atlas, but it didn't last."

Jack jumped off the cable car, which he judged was not quite ready to begin the climb up the hill, and raced for the flower stand.

"Quick!" he yelled at the attendant. "Give me those gardenias and some fern!"

As Jack paid him, the cable car began its slow ascent. He ran behind it for nearly a block before jumping aboard to the applause of the passengers.

"Not bad for an old man," he said, breathing hard.

"You idiot. I almost lost you again."

He grinned.

"Damn it, Jack, you haven't really changed, have you? Still a boy. No common sense."

"Whatever you say, my dear." He handed her the flowers.

She held them to her face and breathed deeply. "Are you really here?" she said.

"I'm really here."

"And are you here to stay?"

"As long as God wills."

"No joining the Marine Reserves, old man?"

"Think I'll pass."

They got off the cable car on California Street and took a taxi from the Fairmont Hotel entrance to Babe's home on Broadway. When they arrived, Babe conscious of her bloody clothes, quickly jumped into the shower. When she came out nude, neither spoke much. They felt shy and excited, more like children than an elderly couple, uncertain, full of breathless anticipation. They stared unseeingly at the bay view. Their hands came together, and they laced fingers.

"Did you look up at the sky today?" she said softly.

"Yes," he said, "at noon. Did you?"

"Of course."

"I've done it my whole life."

"Me, too."

Gracefully and with tenderness, Jack picked Babe up into his arms and moved toward the bedroom. Fifty years of wanting would peel away very slowly. With eyes lidded and bodies arched, they held each other close. They slowly kissed. They touched. Time stopped. No more words were spoken; no more words were needed. Now, at long last was the time for yesterday's plans to begin.

**

John arrived at the Broadway flat at nine o'clock in the morning. He could smell bacon frying when he entered.

"Sorry I'm late," he said, "but I got caught up watching television. McBain and the POWs are on every channel. He's demanding that Congress grant promotions, back pay, pensions and medals. That McBain is a really cool guy, you know? He's urging the POWs not to have contact with either President Conklin or Vice President Hurst. He says they're responsible, along with Russia's President Kruchlov, for their captivity and should be treated with suspicion."

"I guess there are a few clean politicians left," Jack said. "I hope he can make a difference."

"I'm serving bacon and eggs with hash brown potatoes," Babe said. "Toast, jams, juice and fresh coffee. Your father hasn't eaten anything like this in over fifty years and you're not going to interrupt this feast until we're finished. You're joining us, of course?"

"I wouldn't pass it up for the world. It beats my usual bagel."

As they sat down to eat, Jack turned to Babe, his fork raised halfway to his mouth. "How did you know I was still alive?"

She began her story. She talked about the FBI harassing and threatening her and his mother in the early 1950s, about meeting Peter who looked remarkably like Jack. She described the failed marriage, her children, her fateful meeting with Joy in 1978, and how that led to the return of the four-leaf clover pendant Babe had given to Jack when he left for Korea. Jack's letter to her was proof that he was still alive. She described the meeting at Alfred's Restaurant with Jin, Qi, King and Joy and their plan to go to Siberia to find Jack.

While Babe talked, Jack watched her and took in every gesture, the twisty movements of her mouth, her flashing dark eyes and her girlish habit of throwing back her head to remove hair from her eyes. *This is the girl I left so many years ago, the same girl. Only now she's gray and wrinkled, but just as beautiful and so moving in her gentle grace. How could I be any luckier?*

Babe described the soup factory, the trading posts and the Siberia Jack contest. She told him that it was King's discovery of his $46,000 deposit in Vladivostok that led to Alexander Ivanov. Her time in Khabarovsk and setting up the business took nearly an hour in the telling. She then described the weekly television show, the discovery of Ivan Guk and how that led John to Jack's prison camp at Khilok two days after Jack escaped.

Jack sat on the edge of his chair, grasping a coffee cup as he listened. When he heard what had happened to Ati, he closed his eyes, held his breath, and waited for a wave of sadness to pass. Babe and John watched him with concern.

"You're fortunate, John," Jack said finally. "You have had two of the most wonderful mothers in the world." John smiled proudly.

He lapsed into silence again, listening to the rest of the story. She ended her tale with a description of the two mass POW escapes from Khabarovsk—one to Japan led by Jin Jaing and the USS Montana's journey led by King Poo Koo. He felt that his own life had been puny by comparison. He also questioned himself. *Could I have escaped sooner? Could I have done something different that would have protected Ati and John?* He even flirted with the thought that maybe he didn't deserve a woman like Babe. Maybe he had developed a prisoner's mentality through the years and had given up without knowing it. Freedom was a very dangerous place, with uncertain, constantly shifting boundaries. He wanted it at the same time he feared its power to confuse him.

When she had finished her story, John broke in, saying, "I love you two with all my heart and I feel privileged to be part of both of you. But right now I have to split. I'm supposed to meet with Senator McBain in an hour."

"Your father and I are thinking about flying down to San Diego to make up for lost time," Babe said.

"No can do just yet. A lot of things are happening right now. You really need to be around. I would suggest you two wait a month before taking any trips."

"What kind of things?" Jack said, trying to hide his apprehension.

John grinned as he placed his hand over his mother's. "Yesterday Senator McBain asked me to deliver a message to you, Mom. He wants you to consider being his running mate in the upcoming elections and he needs an answer right after Claudette's funeral."

Babe stared at her son. "He wants me? No. I'm no politician. The whole idea is ridiculous."

"Well, we can table that for now. *Sixty Minutes* wants to tape an unprecedented three-hour segment with you two. If you agree, they'll have a camera crew here this weekend. I personally think it's a great opportunity. Not only to tell your story, but also to tell about the POWs still held in China and Russia. The exposure could help them."

Jack slowly nodded his head. "I'll do anything I can to help the men still in captivity. Is *Sixty Minutes* a magazine?"

John smiled. "Well, Dad, it's a television news magazine. And it has a very high national rating."

"We owe the POWs that interview," Babe said.

"Also I just made dinner arrangements at Alfred's Restaurant for Thursday night. King has called Qi and Jin and they're on their way. Joy will be there. I invited my half-sister Jenna, and I guess she'll be there if she isn't busy marching for some cause. I also invited your buddy Tara Carr, and Mary Alioto, and of course the three of us, your brother Bob and sister Carla and Nick, you remember Nick the Great. It will be a grand affair. I promise the champagne will flow freely."

"I don't think I like champagne," Jack said, clinging to Babe's hand. "Make sure there's plenty of vodka."

John slung an arm around his father's shoulders and drew him close.

"Will a case be adequate?" he asked.

***

Alfred's private dining room was an enlarged version of its secluded booths. The entrance was heavily curtained, but instead of the bench-style seating featured in the other areas of the room, it had mahogany-colored, padded captain's chairs and a long table on a large oriental carpet. The walls evoked hundreds of years of Roman rule. Soft light glowed from wrought iron sconces affixed to the walls surrounding the long dining table, and thick short candles were placed in a row on white linen.

The photographer arrived at six-thirty. He had picked up the 1978 photos of the first meeting at Alfred's from John and was busy mounting them on one side of the private room's wall when the first taxi pulled to the curb. Joy Jaing had come early to place microphones on two separate booms hanging over the table. She knew that the words spoken tonight should be memorialized for posterity, and she intended that no one would leave without a tape recording.

Joy's father Qi arrived with his brother Jin in a shared taxi just minutes ahead of King. The photographer took pictures of everyone arriving. Jack, Babe and John were just minutes behind, pulling to the curb in John's BMW sedan. Jenna had hitched a ride in a friend's minibus. She wore a flower in her long blonde hair and trailed a tantalizing scent that John breathed in deeply and unconsciously held. Tara Carr was the last to arrive. She stepped out of the taxi looking like a Russian princess. She wore a flat fur hat, fur collar and cuff trims. Her dark, ankle-length coat had tapestry covered buttons its entire length. Always dressed for the occasion.

At seven o'clock in the evening they still had the restaurant to themselves, and they reveled in hugging and kissing one another, jabbering away in excited conversations, drinking vodka, wine and beer, doing a collective dance of joy that featured much swirling of hands and arms. King stood with his glass raised and proposed a toast to Jack and Babe.

"The good grace of God," he said, "has brought them together"—he grinned impishly—"with a little help from us. This night belongs to them. We are here to help them celebrate it. I have lived a very long life, full of the good things and the bad things, but speaking for myself, this night ranks at the very top of nights. I salute you, my good friends Jack and Babe. May the rest of your days be cloudless." Everyone cheered and touched glasses. Plates of hors d'oeuvres arrived, and while the guests picked away, King asked Jack if he would mind telling his story.

"Start at the beginning, Jack. Tell us something of your childhood, how you met Babe, the war and so on. I know you're the world's most accomplished con-artist. I would not be here tonight if you hadn't talked me out of jail back in Manchuria."

Everyone laughed. Jack remained seated, sipping his vodka. Slowly he began to speak. "My story is hardly inspirational. I didn't have many friends growing up. I stayed pretty much to myself. I did poorly in school. Dreamed a lot. I looked out of windows. A pretty average kid, you might say. Nothing to distinguish me, except maybe my ability to draw. And then one lucky day I met Babe Barsi." He covered her hand with his. "That changed everything. At the age of seventeen I found something—someone—to live for beyond myself."

Jack sketched in his combat days in Korea. Speaking flatly and without emotion, he described the bloody battle that led to his capture. He told about his meeting the two pretenders, King and Jin, and how Jin, posing as King, had plotted to kill King, posing as an evil officer who had once tried to have Jin put to death. This anecdote drew smiles and laughter. But when he told about having to leave King at the train station to begin his long years in Siberia, Joy, Babe, all the women and some of the men, began to sob. Softly he recited the murderous camp regime and the horrendous death tolls.

"Luckily I had the chance to become a healer," he said. "That kept me sane and alive. They needed me. With all the death around me, I managed to save a few lives. I'll always be grateful that God gave me that chance." Alexander Ivanov's story was narrated with great affection, as was the description of how love transformed both the prison commander and the camp itself into an economic powerhouse. "If only Alex were here to share this evening with us," Jack said. "He's the one important missing person. He became my brother—like you, King. And you, Jin."

Jack told them about Ati, trying to hold in the emotion, about John's birth and the Vladivostok tale that ended drastically as Jack was shipped to Khilok. Lost to the world for another twenty five years. He told about his growing powers as a healer and hypnotist, and touched lightly on his despair during those many years with little hope to cling to. He turned and looked down at Babe. He touched her shoulder.

"Each day I stared up at the sky. Somewhere up there was the possibility of hope and eventual delivery. I never gave up hoping. I came close sometimes, but the sky always gave me just a little bit more hope. Enough to get by. Somewhere I knew that Babe was looking up, too, and that thought helped me through the very worst times."

He ended with his escape plan and the role Yuri Senya had played in it. From there it was Mongolia, Sweden, New York and finally home to San Francisco. He spoke for nearly an hour.

Each in turn told his or her story, and during dinner the stories continued. The proprietor, a close friend of Babe and Tara's, had made an all out effort for the reunion. He began with platters of Italian olives, feta cheese, marinated mushrooms and artichoke hearts. There were plates of prosciutto ham wrapped around fresh melon slices. There were bowls of giant fresh-peeled shrimp with a Fisherman's Wharf red sauce. The dinner began with a Caesar salad prepared at the table, which was followed by Nicolai Carlotti's own special Zuppa Di Cipolle. The pasta was his version of Spaghetti Alla Carbonara, featuring hot chili peppers. Roast chicken, grilled rabbit and pan-fried sand dabs, followed that course. Dessert featured Nick's signature creation: solid vanilla ice cream balls wrapped in white dough and deep-fried at the table. The dough, swelling to double the size of the ice cream ball, was garnished with fresh strawberries and chocolate sauce. Jack thought looking at it was about all he could do. *All this food!*

By two o'clock in the morning, Jack and Babe were exhausted. Jack stood, holding his ever-present glass of vodka.

"I don't know about the rest of you, but I'm feeling very much like a senior citizen. Isn't that the new term for old farts? It's time for us to go home. Thank you all for sharing this night with Babe and me. It has been the very best night of my life." He smiled wryly. "Fifty years, and I can tell you it was worth the wait."

Chapter Seventy One

Goodbye To All That

FUNERAL ceremonies for Claudette, her father Peter Mattioli and Ronald Goldberg were held together at the Grace Cathedral church on California Street. In spite of a heavy afternoon rain, nearly 10,000 people gathered, overflowing the church and lining the surrounding streets, hoping for a glimpse of Jack and Babe. Their celebrity, coupled with the political circumstances surrounding the murders, guaranteed that the ruling elite also would arrive in force.

A convoy of black limousines pulled up to the curb, disgorging the Mayor of San Francisco, the Police Chief, the Board of Supervisors, two state senators and the Mayor's Chief of Protocol, Miss Chong. Uniforms bristled, the air crackled with the snap of cameras and the entourage swept up the church steps and was ushered into the front pews. The White House had pleaded through its California senators and congressmen to be permitted to say a few words at the ceremony, but Jack and Babe adamantly refused. Instead, they asked presidential candidate Senator George McBain to speak.

There was a procession of memorial statements and they began to blur in Babe's mind. She felt weary and found it hard to concentrate on the words. She realized that she was no longer emotionally there. Even when McBain filled the church with fire and brimstone directed at the crimes of the Administration, she found herself curiously uninvolved. Yes, she wept for her daughter. Yes, she felt hatred, remorse and other confused, conflicting emotions for Peter, but it all seemed to be receding into the past. She felt a disconnect from all that had come before, and when she looked at Jack she could see that he too was weary and far away, even disinterested.

Afterward at their Broadway flat, Jack took John aside.

"Your mother and I are very possessive of our time right now.

How many good years we have left is anyone's guess. It's taken all of our strength to survive. Seeing everyone at Alfred's the other night made us realize just how lucky we all are, and we want that to be the framework for our retirement from active life. We need to spend time appreciating our good fortune."

"What are you getting at, Dad?"

"Your mother and I were separated fifty years ago. The last time we saw each other was in San Diego before I was shipped to Korea. We stayed in a little hotel near a beach there and we've decided to go back to San Diego and revisit our youth. It might take a week, maybe a month, maybe longer. However long it takes we will stay, until…well, until…" Jack shrugged. "I have no idea how long. We just need to be together without the pressures of fame, business or political opportunity. We think that tomorrow is your job now and San Diego is our job. Maybe we'll even visit Alex in Siberia. Who knows?"

"When are you leaving?" John asked.

"We have obligations to the men who have escaped and to those still trapped in Russia and China. We plan to make a lot of public appearances during the next few weeks, maybe even in Washington D.C. After that we're gone."

***

And that was what happened. Instead of letting his parents fly to San Diego, however, John chartered a 95-foot motor sailboat to take them there. He saw them off and watched them sail under the Golden Gate Bridge. He was crying as he repeated his mother's departing words. *"Son, love and friendship are everything. There is nothing else of true value in this world. When I found your father, I regained the world I had lost so many years ago."*

When the yacht was lost from view, he slowly waved a hand in salute, and then turned away.

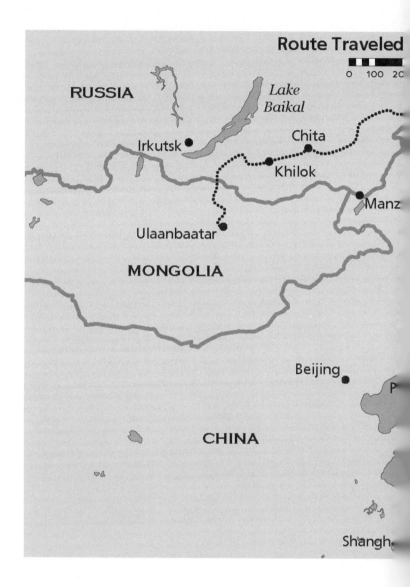

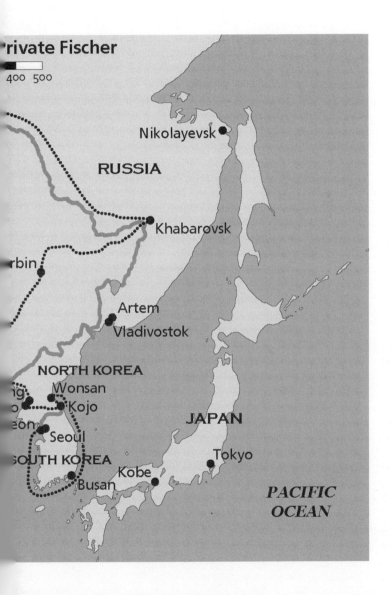

San Francisco, 1950
Robert Fischer, John Maldonado, Jack Fischer, friend.